Apocalypsia

Jerry J.C. Veit

BLUEWOLF
PUBLISHING
Waukesha, WI 53186

The Complete **Jerry J.C. Veit** Collection:

Apocalypsia
Into the Night
The Glass Demon
Capricorn
Days Gone By
Utopia
The Form

Library of Congress Control Number: 2022919602
ISBN 979-8-9871666-0-4

Contents

1
Welcome to Apocalypsia

The greatest threat to civilization is civilization itself. History taught us the key to survival was to band together and work toward common goals. However, when survival is challenged, and goods become scarce this once cooperative community declares war on one another. Survival is then based on either unwavering leadership or brute force. Despite the phenomenal leaps in evolution of the human mind and all the advances in health, science, and technology, one thing remains constant—war.

Three years ago, a global war broke out. Not between governments and nations or borders and resources, but between man and demon. Soldiers and citizens rallied together to fight hordes of goblins and imps while others found the transpiring events opportunity to loot.

No one knew how it happened, but our way of life would be forever changed. Morning commuters became tanks and convoys, malls and restaurants became bunkers, and neighborhoods and communities became their own towns. Everyone pretty much became a soldier overnight. Makeshift forts and towers were constructed, and neighborhoods became enclosed by barriers and walls. Guards would stand watch both day and night to eliminate creatures or people who may threaten their security. We become a medieval civilization in the middle of a modern metropolis.

Organizations were formed to research new ways to combat these monsters and demons. One such organization was named after an old military code name, Operation Demon Eradication, better known as, O.D.E. An O.D.E. lab was soon found in every country as scientists and the military worked side-by-side without rest.

O.D.E scientists studied DNA under microscopes and mixed liquid concoctions in flasks. With limited trading and the need for fast development, every lab was built in preexisting commercial offices or other buildings. The escalating threat of Hell on Earth united all the peoples of the world to share their findings and aid each other, but this alliance was only meant to be temporary. The large groups of people who once fought together dwindle down to only a few, while the demon numbers continued to grow. Those who once shared a common goal start fighting each other or going out on their own with little concern for others.

Unfortunately, in the third year of The Demon Wars, the worst thing that could happen did—we lost.

Our race is once again divided, and our cities are broken and lying in ruins. The few buildings that are left standing become prime shelters and people are willing to kill for them. We fight each other now as well as the demons infesting our world. There once was a camaraderie between strangers, but now we view everyone as potential enemies, not allies. This is not the same world we were born into—

Welcome to Apocalypsia.

Copper Bay was once a quiet suburb with diligently manicured lawns, blooming flower beds and pristine homes. It's now overgrown with weeds and littered with broken streets and crumbling homes. On the outskirts of this abandoned town is a small industrial block with factories and inoperative vehicles. One of the rundown warehouses still has a little electricity flowing to its flickering security lights and lampposts. Most of its truck loading bays are closed, except for one which is severely damaged and hanging off its hinges, but another one is completely open.

The first sign of life, in this desolate land, is a man named Ardian. He's been wearing the same outfit for as far back as he can remember; a torn pair of jeans and a button-down shirt with a mace and short sword stored in his belt. At this late evening hour, he searches around this weathered warehouse with its lights casting a yellow glow around the area. With night fast approaching, he needs to cut this exploration short and start thinking about returning to his shelter. He's a typical scavenger who seeks useful tools and anything edible. While he prefers to avoid confrontations, he's also one of the few who still believes helping others is important. He's been surviving alone for the last two years, but as soon as he got used to his new life, everything about it is about to change.

Ardian looks up at the setting sun to gage how much light he has left; the colors on the horizon suggest an hour at most. All is quiet except for the wind flicking the dangling chains against the aluminum dock door, but soon another sound puts Ardian on alert—the heavy footfalls of boots on pavement. He continues to listen and picks up on several bone-chilling snarls. He draws his mace in one hand and the sword in his other when his assessment proves these sounds are coming towards him. He bends his knees and takes his stance until he spots the outline of a person sprinting around the side of the warehouse. This individual leaps over debris and then off an elevated landing. Closing behind the fleeing person are two mangy wolves, that no doubt possesses more stamina than their prey. One misstep sends the stranger hurling to the ground with no time to regain their lead. Ardian decides to intervene.

He steps in front of the fallen body and waits for the wolves to come to him. The first wolf has a marginal lead on the other and it is the one that gets its face smashed in by Ardian's mace. The force kills it instantly, but the other one sinks its teeth into Ardian's arm. Hindered by the attack he relies on his sword to push it through the wolf's eye. It whimpers for a moment before falling over dead. Ardian can now turn his attention to the person he just rescued and discovers it's a girl, who's clothed in charcoal-colored pants and a black long-sleeve shirt.

To come across another person is rare, to come across one who is trustworthy is rarer, but to come across one who you used to know challenges the meaning of impossible. None-the-less, that is what happens here. At their first glance the mind identifies a familiar face, but how and where is always delayed. She is the first to make the complete connection.

"Ardian?" Her voice triggers his memory now. She was a ramp agent who worked with him at the airport over twenty years ago, but that was when they were both still in their late teens.

"Nydia," Ardian confirms. The relief of seeing a familiar face, who doesn't need to have his motives questioned, puts her at ease.

"Oh-my-God. It's been such a long time," she says while giving him a hug.

"Are you okay?" Ardian asks.

"I'm fine." Nydia notices his bleeding arm and gently feels around the wound.

"I'm okay," Ardian says before she can comment on his injury, but she has a different opinion.

"Don't play this down, Ardian. This could get infected. Who knows what kind of bacteria or parasite have infected these animals?"

"I have some meds and supplies in my shelter, but we need to hurry. It's too dangerous to be out here at night."

His explanation is accepted by Nydia and the two make the fifteen-minute hike through the debris field of this concrete and steel wilderness. Several heaps of junk piles occupy the wide-open vastness and downed live power lines demand a degree of caution to traverse. Ardian knows the area well and Nydia trusts him enough to walk close by. Rubble from collapsed walls are always sliding down the hills of rock, support beams and rebar. Nydia tenses up at every sound and looks around to identify the cause. Ardian assures her that the combination of neglect, weathering and gravity creates an ever-changing landscape that continues daily.

A broken-down, long-distance semi cab sits abandoned in the middle of a pothole littered road. It's fully intact except all four tires are missing and every window is taped up from the inside with duct tape. Ardian climbs up and then offers his hand to Nydia to lift her up. He closes the door and locks it after a quick scan of the nearby terrain.

Blankets are draped on the backs of the seats and piled on the bed in the back while bags of food and supplies are stored inside the open dresser drawers below the mattress. Ardian turns on a flashlight and leads Nydia behind the seats. He finds a travel-sized first-aid kit in one of the drawers and then hands it to Nydia.

"Will this do?" She digs through the items and nods.

"I think so." Ardian sits down on the side of the bed next to Nydia. "Lift your arm," she instructs. She pours a small bottle of antibacterial liquid over his bite mark and then dabs the wound with a cotton swab. She repeats the process until the foaming action lessens. She unravels a cloth band-aid and then wraps his arm and ties it up to secure it.

"You are good at this," Ardian observes. Nydia glances up and smiles.

"A few years ago, I went back to school for an emergency medical technician degree. Little did I know the world was going to end a year after I graduated."

"A time ended, not the world," Ardian points out. She smirks but doesn't respond. "I have some granola bars in that drawer if you're hungry."

"Thank you, I'm starving." Nydia rummages through the bags and picks out two bars. "Where did you find granola bars?"

"The factories around here actually have a lot of vending machines. I ate all the chocolate ones though." Nydia giggles.

"I'm not going to complain at this point, but just so you know; I do like chocolate." Ardian lets her eat her dinner before continuing the conversation.

"Are you by yourself too?" Nydia slowly nods.

"I was with my sister for a little while, but then we got separated. I haven't seen her since." Her voice exposes her sorrow and worry despite how hard she tries to look strong.

"I'm sorry, we can look for her together if you want." Nydia gives him a weak smile.

"Thanks, but there's no place left to look. She was always stronger than me. If anyone can survive out there it would be her." Ardian kicks off his shoes and then lies straight on the bed. He folds his hands on his stomach while Nydia finds her spot next to him. "How about you? Do you have anyone left?" Ardian shakes his head.

"No, they all died during The Demon Wars."

"I'm sorry," she says sympathetically.

"It's okay. They were the lucky ones."

"There was a time when I wanted to believe that too." Nydia wraps herself in a blanket and the two drift off to sleep moments later.

The next morning, Ardian is practicing jabs and swings with his weapons when Nydia steps down from the cab. She watches him amusingly, but also a little envious. She's been surviving by hiding and running and never learned how to fight or hold a weapon.

"You're good with those," she says. Ardian rests his arms at his side and smiles. "Can you teach me?" Nydia continues.

"Of course," he replies. Ardian holds the blade of his sword, so the handle is ready for Nydia to take. "It will be my pleasure." Nydia takes the sword eagerly and Ardian welcomes the chance for a sparring partner.

Another day of scavenging, another day of surviving. Somewhere a battle is fought, somewhere someone wins, and somewhere else, someone loses. This is the way the world operates. The day is now almost over, and time is up for one man who failed to reach his shelter.

Beyond the industrial block is a wild field that was never zoned for construction and beyond that is the edge of the forest. The only thing that occupies this land is a lone cabin that was erected during the war. It's home to a sole survivor who doesn't feel like sharing her shelter to a strange man who just happened to come across it on his travels.

He goes by the name of Kito and is dressed in a black trench coat with a red trim around the sleeves and collar. He looks tired, but Amiku isn't about to underestimate anyone she doesn't know. She stands guard in front of her door with folded arms and a standoffish stance. She has yet to determine how this stranger needs to be dealt with, but for now only observes as he advances closer.

"Who are you and what do you seek?" She barks.

"I was betting on a safe place to stay for the night. That is all."

"You just lost that bet. This place is mine. I suggest you keep looking."

"I am not here to claim your shelter or steal from you. In the morning I will be on my way."

"You do not listen. I said keep looking." Amiku is driven by a take-no-shit attitude and isn't in the business of handing out charity. Kito is argumentative, bull-headed, and always has something to prove. This confrontation has no chance of ending peacefully.

"But there aren't any other shelters around here and there's only minutes of sunlight left."

"Then you'd better hurry," Amiku replies.

"Why are you being so stubborn. I am not your enemy."

"Everyone is an enemy nowadays. Your hidden agendas will not be executed. You just messed with the wrong girl." Amiku unfolds her arms and pulls her shirt back before drawing a katana. "Leave here at once—or not at all. It's your choice."

"I never think far enough ahead to have an agenda," Kito responds. "But I guess this is unavoidable." Kito pulls back his trench coat and takes out a wide blade long sword.

"Very well. This will be the last mistake you will make in this lifetime."

Amiku attempts to slash across his chest, but Kito's blade stops her katana before it can make contact.

"Was that practice?" Kito's arrogance is apparent, and he never hesitates to patronize or antagonize others, but at the moment, he just wants to instigate his opponent. It works, and Amiku returns with fast combo attacks from different angles and directions as she spins her sword around her body or over her head. Many would have fallen to this skilled fighter, but Kito has deflected every one of her moves without breaking a sweat. This is made possible due to a hidden ability to slow down movements through intense concentration. Though Amiku's attacks are actually quite fast, and very accurate, they appear to be in slow-motion to Kito. He just moves his sword into position and then waits for the hit to come. He could have struck back with a deadly blow several times but has decided only to play defense for the moment. Amiku doesn't know about his ability but knows by now that she isn't fighting a common foe.

"Your long swings are easy to avoid. Why don't you try shorter attacks?" Kito suggests.

"I don't need your advice!" Amiku yells in annoyance.

Several drops of blood escape from underneath Kito's sleeve to stain the grass below. The wound was from a previous altercation which Kito was trying to hide, but Amiku notices it.

"You're bleeding, but it's not from my blade." Kito looks down at his blood-soaked sleeve. Amiku eases up on her fighting stance, but Kito attacks with his sights on her waist. Her reflexes kick into gear to place her katana in the path of the oncoming blade and then jumps back in case he tries to attack twice.

"You let your guard down. Do you think an injury makes me less of a threat?" Kito says.

"I can see you have a death wish. Lucky for you I'm willing to appease it," Amiku replies.

Kito goes in for another attack, but Amiku back-flips while swinging her leg around to kick Kito hard in his side.

"You like pointing out mistakes, do you?" Amiku begins. "Well then, allow me to return the favor. You can defend well enough, but your attacks seem more like a guess than actually planned. I don't think you know how to fight."

"You think you've got me figured out, huh?" Kito steps forward to pierce Amiku's stomach, but she plants her sword into the ground beside her, and then lifts her body up and over it. This avoids Kito's attack, but now she turns her defense into an attack. She swings her leg around to kick Kito in his ribs as soon as she lands on the ground. She then combos this move into another one by spinning in the opposite direction to kick him on his other side with her opposite foot. Kito falls to his knees with a grunt after the double blow. This technique wasn't what he was expecting and never saw it coming. Adding her acrobatics to the fight has changed the style of fighting Kito is used to.

"Just as I thought. I can defeat you without my sword," Amiku jokes. "Why don't you give up?" Kito pushes himself back up with the help of his sword while huffing.

"I'm not dead yet."

"I think you have stubbornness confused with courage. There's a thin line between bravery and stupidity and for you to continue this fight is closer to the later."

Kito lunges toward her with a final wild swing just to be difficult. Amiku squats down and blindly thrusts her sword upwards in defense. Neither could've predicted the outcome of this action as the katana unintentionally pierces deep into Kito's lower stomach. A weak laugh exits his lips when he pulls himself off her blade.

"Good job. I did not expect that." Amiku regrettably looks at the blood gushing from Kito's wound.

"Why the fuck did you do that!?" They may have started this fight as enemies, but during the course of the scuffle, each had developed admiration for the other's fighting abilities. It almost became a game between two rivals than a struggle for survival.

Kito's sword slides from his hand and his view shifts from the horizon to the sky when his back and head meet the ground. He realizes he has fallen, but never felt it as it was happening. The last thing to enter his vision is Amiku's face with her jet-black hair falling over her shoulders.

Amiku has finished what she had originally set out to accomplish—to eliminate a stranger's threat to her safety. Why then would she decide to drag him inside her cabin? Maybe she doesn't feel an unconsciousness man with a hole in his stomach poses a threat. Maybe she has a sudden change of heart and regrets nearly killing him; or maybe she just doesn't know.

The one room wooden cabin has several lit lanterns hanging throughout the space and the only window is boarded up with planks of wood. Near the wall facing the outside door is a worktable with jars and flasks filled with different colored liquids. Pushed up against the right wall is a small twin-sized bed, and a flat screen monitor security system is on the left. Kito is lying on a mattress that had been laid on the floor with a blanket over him. Cloths and bandages, along with scissors and a bowl of bloody water are resting at his side. Amiku is resting on her bed with her back leaning against the cabin wall. She's tired but doesn't want to make herself vulnerable by lying down and falling into a deep sleep with Kito there. She still doesn't know him or what he would try to do to women. She continues awaking throughout the night; only to return to her nap when she confirms Kito has not moved. There are no further incidents for the remainder of the night.

The morning sun is peeking over the trees when Amiku opens the cabin door. She keeps one hand on the handle of her sword that is strapped at her side and a keen eye on everything that's nearby or may have been recently. The day looks calm, and the surrounding area is void of any movement other than the wind. She knows her plot and she knows when it's been disturbed. The grass is pressed down from something lying on top and dirt had been flung around as if something was digging. She squats down to inspect the ground for clues. A dried blood spot from Kito on the long blades may be what attracted some creature to roam where they had not been before. She rises again to scan the open field, but whatever was here during the night has left for now.

Kito finally awakes just as Amiku enters the cabin again. The sunlight rushing in disorients him and he squints to see Amiku's silhouette in the doorway. The room becomes dim again when she shuts the door allowing Kito to focus.

"Where am I?" He asks. Amiku stands in front of him with her arms folded.

"Where do you think you are? Don't you remember asking me to stay?"

"Yeah, and then you stabbed me."

"You brought that upon yourself. I actually already came to the decision to let you stay before you came at me that last time."

"Why?" Amiku kneels down and pulls the blanket down to inspect the bandages on his arm and stomach.

"When you fight someone in a real battle you find out what kind of person they are. I can tell if they are skilled, or reckless, fair, or dishonest. Anyone can say anything, but when a sword is held at their neck, they return to who they really are."

"So, you were testing me?"

"No, I never felt threatened by you." Kito is usually quick with his comebacks, but Amiku somehow has the upper hand in word battles too. Amiku leaves Kito's side with the bowl of bloody water and places it on her workbench. She will have to discard it someplace else now that she knows something may be lurking nearby. "You lost a lot of blood, but I guess you are too stubborn to die too." Kito tosses the blanket off his legs and rolls off the mattress. "What are you doing?" Amiku asks sternly.

"I'm leaving." Kito struggles to stand on his feet as he takes a moment to rest on his knees. He's slow but manages to weakly push his hand off his knee to make it the rest of the way up. "Thanks for your help, I guess." He ignores his vertigo and looks around for his sword.

"You don't have the strength to survive one minute out there." Amiku begins, "And what's up with that weak ass apology? Thanks for your help, I guess!? You look at me right now and you say thank you!" Amiku demands assertively and in a huff.

"Well, it's morning, so I'll be on my way—as promised." Kito locates his sword leaning in a corner and approaches it as Amiku follows behind him.

"You are rude, ungrateful, incapable of listening, and I'm amazed that you've survived this long!" Kito picks up his sword and then heads toward the door.

"Lucky for you the chances of meeting again are slim." Kito was able to find a way to piss Amiku off so much that she became unable to form words. Amiku clamps her hand on the back of his neck to freeze him in place instantly; a moment later he collapses to the floor unconscious. Amiku is not only skilled in gymnastics and parkour, but also trained in karate and perfected the sleep hold.

"Great, now I have to drag you back. You're starting to annoy me," she says out loud and with a sigh. A part of her would normally just let him go and his fate would be none of her concern, but if there's one thing she hates, it's wasting time and resources, and she's already spent both on Kito.

She concludes that she can't stand Kito or his inconsiderate attitude, but she also can't help but feel somewhat responsible for his condition. Then again, it was his foolishness that led to this turn of events, and that's all the thought she's willing to put into that.

Meanwhile, Ardian and Nydia return to the warehouse in hopes to explore it more in depth. A small cache of stored goods would be a great find or even a break room with vending machines could replenish some of their food supplies. At first glance the interior loading dock zone is completely bare except for several empty boxes that are tipped over. The structure of the building itself is another concern. The stone walls are cracked with large chunks missing and the many puddles indicate a poor roof that could cave in at any moment.

"This appears to be a dead end, Ardian," Nydia observes.

"We just got here. There might be more stuff further in." Nydia was afraid he would indicate exploring deeper. She can't put her finger on it, but everything about this place makes her feel uneasy. Ardian reaches into his pocket and takes out a flashlight and then turns it on. He shakes the flashlight as if showing off his resourcefulness to Nydia.

"Ooo, a little beam of light. I feel so much safer now," she says sarcastically.

"Don't worry, Nydia. This place is completely abandoned." Nydia doubts his assumption is correct but reluctantly follows him with only a warning.

"If you get me killed, I will never forgive you."

There's plenty of broken glass, planks of wood and sawdust littering the floor, but so far not a glimmer of hope that this place will yield anything useful. The poor condition of the concrete wall causes another chunk to give way and shatter when it hits the floor. The sudden crash startles Nydia and she lets out a soft yelp. Ardian shines his light on the rubble but doesn't see any cause for concern.

"It's okay, Nydia. It was just part of the wall falling down."

"That absolutely doesn't make me feel any better," she says in her most relaxed tone.

The warehouse appears to have been cleared out long before Ardian had arrived to this area, which means it had to occur before The Demon Wars were lost. The reason for this reveals itself as what was once the foreman's office. Ardian and Nydia creep inside to investigate the repurposed room.

It appears to have been an O.D.E lab that consists of two aluminum tables. It also seems to have been cleared out in a hurry or ransacked a long time ago. It's littered with glass, papers, and journals that are submerged in puddles of water. Cabinet doors hang off their hinges or lie detached on the floor. The office door is all but missing and the big observing window, separating the office from the rest of the warehouse, is cracked throughout the entire pane.

"I don't like how this looks, Ardie," Nydia says with a nervous demeanor. Ardian becomes more fascinated by a strange vine-like plant climbing up the walls. The flower heads are yellow on top that gradients to orange on the bottom and the vine itself is a strange variation of blue. Ardian studies the plant with an intriguing curiosity due to its unusual appearance.

"What kind of plant is this? I've never seen anything like it before. It almost looks alien." He picks one of the flowers from the vine and puts it to his nose to smell it, but Nydia quickly slaps it away.

"Don't just grab something you've never seen before and

inhale it. This could be poisonous." Ardian looks down where the flower fell and notices one of the notebooks hidden underneath a fallen chair. He bends over and picks it up and then shines his flashlight on it as he starts flipping through the pages. Nydia leans over his arm to look at the book with him.

"What is it?" She asks.

"Looks like notes from some O.D.E. scientist." The page shows a colored illustration that resembles the plant that's growing on the nearby walls. He doesn't know why, but he feels this plant is important for some unknown reason. Nydia walks out of the room and gives the darkened warehouse a worrisome scan. With her back towards him, Ardian grabs the vine and pulls it away from the wall. Part of the vine breaks away along with three flowers. He puts the plant in the notebook and then closes it before Nydia glances back.

"Okay, I think it's time to get out of here," she begins. "I just got a horrible feeling that we aren't alone all of a sudden."

"I'm sure there's nothing to worry about, Nydia." He places the notebook in his belt and, despite his thoughts, agrees to submit to Nydia's wish to head back to where they had entered.

Unbeknownst to them are two small red eyes piercing through the darkness near the rear of the warehouse. Nydia's senses have developed into an advanced warning system that she isn't fully aware of yet, but in the future, it will be wise to take her advice into consideration.

The natural world has been disrupted. The environment, the wildlife and all the rules that demand two worlds that should never meet have changed. Why then, would people think they are exempt from this abnormality? It surrounds them, they breathe it in, they walk through it, and it enters into their bloodstream; all without hinting at a clue that it has happened. It cannot be predicted how this energy will affect those who encounter it. Some will merge with it and use it as a power, others will be overtaken by it and become a host down to their bitter end. Another variable is how strong this power can become. Abilities are not always realized right away and after they are, it takes time to hone them. These magical qualities will change the human DNA forever, both for the better and for the worst.

The end of civilization was just the beginning of a new era.

2

An Escalating Danger

Food and supplies are found in forgotten spaces or taken from newly discovered places, but after one spot has nothing left to take, another must be located. These are the times when groups of survivors venture somewhere they have never been before, but that does not mean they are the first to find it or the only ones looking. It is true that the most dangerous time is during the night, but the highest risk comes from exploring for resources. This is when people meet—and that doesn't always end well.

Amiku is very orderly and only scavenged for what she absolutely considered to be a necessity. She leads a minimalistic life with an organized and clutter-free shelter. Everything has a place and if something is moved from it, she makes sure to return it to its original position. The only thing that's different now is Kito's presence and the space he's taking up. She's inventorying her supply of flasks at her workbench when Kito inquires about their uses.

"What are these?" He asks. Amiku glances up before pointing to one of the flasks that has a red liquid inside.

"This one I used on you. It speeds up the body's natural healing capability. It's called Plasma rejuvenation." She then points to another flask storing a green liquid. "This one is highly toxic and can be used to coat the blade of your weapon. It basically melts your insides when used in this way. I call it, green death."

"How do you know how to make this stuff?" Kito questions.

"My father," Amiku sighs and then continues. "He was an O.D.E. scientist. He showed me how to make everything on this table." Amiku's past isn't something she feels like discussing with Kito, and doesn't elaborate any further about her father or his job at O.D.E. She decides to change the subject instead. "I suppose you will be on your way now that you are better."

"Yes, I stayed much longer than I said I would." Kito has an inclination to say his thanks but cannot muster the words to do so. "It's a good thing you had an extra mattress," he continues. Amiku gives him a serious look.

"It wasn't extra, it was mine. I had two. For three days I had to be uncomfortable because of your dumbass. Now, I don't even know if I want it back."

"You could always check the town to the south. I doubt you will find a mattress there though." Amiku seems intrigued from this information and takes a step towards Kito.

"What town?"

"I don't know the name, it's about three miles from here. That's where I was coming from before ending up here."

Kito spaces off while thinking about the events that took place on that day. Not so much what transpired between him and Amiku, but what happened in that town and who he encountered. Amiku suspects he's hiding something but the need for food and medical supplies make a new area very attractive.

"Since I had to waste most of my stockpile on you, I think showing me where this town is will make us even," she says.

"Very well, I was meaning to head back there anyway."

Kito is reacquainted with his sword and waits for Amiku to join him outside. Amiku exits the cabin with her katana strapped to her side and a compass which she puts in her pocket. She then takes out a small remote fob and clicks the button. Large metal panelings rise from where the cabin meets the ground and stack up the siding and over the roof to completely shield the shelter. This shield is another development from O.D.E. and her father helped design it. Known to be impenetrable by any man or beast, ensures anyone inside will always be protected. Kito remains glued to the shielded cabin with a look of surprise and confusion.

"How—?" Kito begins. Amiku waits a moment before saying as much as she's going to on this matter.

"It's a long story. Can we go now?"

"I thought I was rather set with a sleeping bag and a tent. But here you are with a damn fortress," Kito admits. Amiku smirks as the two begin their hike toward the nearby town.

The small town resembles a historical boom town that was lost in time. Through the center of town is the main and only road, which is littered with potholes, blowing papers and is almost fully overgrown with weeds and small trees. A clothing store, grocery store, and other shops line both side of the street, but there's no indication of any residential homes.

Amiku's first step lands on a grime-covered metal sign that's lying face-down where the broken road meets the grassy field. She squats down and flips it over and reads what it says.

O.D.E Townships & Housing Development
Taking care of our own, so we can save others.

"This was an O.D.E. township," Amiku says.

"What does that mean?" Amiku stands up to explain.

"It was kinda like a company store for O.D.E. employees and their families. They made us believe that they cared about keeping us fed and clothed, but all they really did was take everything away from public stores. They wanted exclusive rights and control over all the remaining resources and the general public never found out."

"That explains why all the shelves were shown empty on the news."

"My father was considered pretty high up, but some of the lower ranked workers never received paychecks. They spent everything they made before the end of the week."

"How?"

"Profit margins. My father knew it. Toward the end he said

O.D.E. will do nothing good for humanity—then they killed him." Kito gives Amiku a stunned look.

"What?" She catches her slip up and shakes her head with aggravation.

"Never mind. Let's just see what's left over in this place."

Kito doesn't press it. He agreed to come back to this town for his own reasons, which he never divulged to Amiku.

Amiku believes that the grocery store is the most important place to visit and decides to head there first. She also expects Kito would be thinking the same thing, but when they near the storefront he continues past it without signaling the cause for his detour.

"Where are you going?" she hollers after him, but he doesn't respond or turn around. "Hey!" She follows up, but he continues around the corner of the store and out of sight. Amiku feels like ignoring him and just fending for herself, but she also feels Kito may be heading into trouble. She, of course, owes him nothing, and whatever befalls upon him is his own doing, but some deep-seeded feeling pulls her after him.

She discovers three dead goblins on the sidewalk with blood splatter on the brick wall of the store. The goblins have gray skin, tiny red eyes, and two rows of sharp teeth. Kito is standing just past the slain group of goblins but seems to be preoccupied with scanning the town and then across the countryside.

"Was this your fight?" Amiku asks.

"It wasn't my fight—but it became it." This could explain his injury when he first appeared outside her cabin, but she doesn't want to waste time talking. Amiku has two key rules for survival. The first is to get as much as you need as fast as you can, and the second is never venture far from your shelter unless in need of stocking up.

"Let's see if we can find anything of value in these stores and then get out of here," she explains.

The grocery store shows evidence that it had been previously rummaged through, but several useful things are still left on the shelves. Amiku takes several plastic bags from the checkout counter and then heads to the first aisle. She tosses in the few cans of fruit that are remaining, and then the last two cans of soup.

Kito looks around the front endcaps and bags a few lighters and pocketknives lying across the shelf. The next aisle he visits is completely bare. He looks up at the sign that reads: *Beer, wine, and spirits*. He lets out a disappointing sigh and walks down it with a lowered head. Near the end, he spots the bottom portion of a travel bottle that's partially hidden under the bottom shelf. A glimmer of hope comes over him as he goes to pick it up with anticipation and excitement. To his amazement he finds a full bottle of infused vodka. He is about to put it in his bag, but then takes a quick glance around him. He doesn't want to risk sharing his find and quickly uncaps the small bottle and downs the entire shot. He shakes his head while blowing a breath out and then tosses the empty bottle to the side.

Meanwhile, Amiku is celebrating from just finding band-aids, peroxide, gauze, slings, and a large medical kit. By the time she meets back up with Kito she has three full bags of food and supplies to his one bag that isn't even filled halfway. She gives him an exhausted look but didn't expect very much from him to begin with.

"Is that all you have?" she asks.

"I think my side was more cleaned out than yours," he replies. Amiku just shakes her head.

"How did you survive this long?" She hands him her bags. "Carry these."

"Why."

"Because you aren't using your arms for anything else."

Kito and Amiku walk across the street to the tailor shop next. Amiku steps up onto the display platform that's littered with broken glass from the smashed display window and disassembled manikins. Kito remains standing outside still pondering how he became stuck carrying her bags. Amiku checks the racks for something that might fit her as Kito becomes increasingly more impatient and shouts into the building.

"Are you done looking at the same thing multiple times yet?"

"Don't act like you weren't in here too," Amiku shouts back.

"What makes you think that?" Amiku strolls out of the shop and stands with her hands on her hips while glaring at Kito.

"Because I found your coat." She' wearing a trench coat that's almost identical to Kito's except this one is medium purple in color with a gold trim around the end of the sleeves and collar. She jumps down and takes one of the bags from Kito. "We can go now," she says. For the second time Kito has nothing to say back.

Kito finds himself walking back to Amiku's cabin instead of his own shelter. He doesn't care where he ends up and wouldn't ask to stay, but he cannot deny his chances with Amiku are somewhat better.

It's only noon when the dark clouds roll across the sky and the wind picks up to suggest a storm is fast approaching. Kito remains fixated on the sky until Amiku's hand swings into his stomach to stop his pace. Kito doesn't understand the reason until he notices movement in the bush just ahead of them. She gently lowers her bag and then draws her katana. Kito follows her silent hint that danger is near. A gray goblin steps out from behind the bush while letting out a gurgling snarl.

"I can take care of this," Kito chuckles. Before Amiku has a chance to respond another goblin steps out from the other side of the bush, and then two more until they find themselves facing six goblins. Amiku shoots Kito a glance.

"You were saying?" Kito lowers his eyes in defeat. "You block and I'll attack," she continues.

"Why?"

"Because we need to use our strengths here." Kito takes a deep breath and holds it before letting it out.

The duo stands facing the group of goblins before both sides charge into battle.

Amiku leaps up to kick one of the goblins in their face. Kito sees the goblin flying backwards and Amiku's coat fanning out, as she soars through the air, in slow-motion. He deflects a goblin trying to scratch him with his sword while Amiku slashes the attacking goblin across its mid-back. She quickly turns around and slashes another one while Kito pushes away claws and teeth into the path of her swinging blade.

Their coats flap in the wind and flow with ease around their body as they continue their fight like a perfectly rehearsed dance. Kito uses his wide blade for crushing and when it's forced against a goblin's mouth its teeth fly out in a stream of blood just before Amiku's katana lobs off its head. The last goblin attempts to retreat, but it's not faster than Amiku who catches up in three strides. Her blade splits the back of its skull with so much force that she must pull it out of its shoulder. Kito's adrenaline lessens, and his vision returns to normal.

This was the first time either had fought with an ally, and

it has created a bond the two was not expecting to experience. Amiku had said, you never truly know anyone until you fight them, but the same can be said about fighting with them. Kito meets Amiku standing over the last goblin she slaughtered. She glances at him and smiles.

"I'm sorry."

"For what?" Amiku returns her sword to her side and then points to Kito's arm.

"I didn't even feel that happen," he admits as he inspects the large bleeding gash through his coat sleeve.

"It looks manageable. I'll tend to it when we get back."

Luckily the two reach the cabin just as the first few raindrops begin to fall and a flash of lighting splits the sky in the distance. Amiku reactivates her shield as soon as she and Kito make it back inside. The storm has shortened the day into a lingering night, but both feel safe from the dangers that may be lurking outside, and more at ease with each other inhabiting the same space. They drape their coats off the back of their chairs while sitting at a table with a lantern in the center. Amiku uses the soft flickering light to finish wrapping another cloth gauss around Kito's arm. She also feels it's a good time to question Kito on his last experience in that town.

"What had you so distracted back in town?" Kito is silent for a moment before he agrees to talk about it.

"I was in that same grocery store last time I was there. It wasn't until after I started walking away that I saw them."

"Those goblins?" Amiku asks. Kito shakes his head.

"No, it was two guys." Amiku looks at him surprised he ran into other people. "They ran out of some building with those goblins right behind them. They ran right past me. Never stopped. Goblins attack whoever is closer, you see. I didn't have a choice, I had to drop my bags to defend myself. I was still fighting when they came back to take my bags. They saluted me and then ran off. I was hoping to run into them today and separate those hands from their arms, but I guess they just get away with it."

"They always get away with it," Amiku begins. "My father was involved in the research that developed this shield, among other things. It was near the end of the war when I watched three of his colleagues murder him in cold blood."

"I'm sorry," Kito says showing his more sensitive side. Amiku doesn't want to think about her father's murder and risk losing her composure in front of Kito. She changes the subject again.

"Where did you learn to fight?"

"I think over time I just got better at it," he says. "Sometimes I can even see things slowed down. But that wasn't until—" Kito stops his explanation and falls into a distant thought, but quickly tries to play it off. "I don't really remember how that happened, actually." Amiku ignores his hesitation. They both have their secrets but aren't ready to fully trust the other with them just yet.

"I used to be in gymnastics and also practiced parkour," she begins. "So, I incorporate a lot of those techniques into my fighting style." They take a moment to look at each other as the lantern light casts dancing shadows across their faces.

"If you want. I will help you with your battles," Kito suggests. Amiku smirks. She is apprehensive about relying on someone else, and still questions if Kito will remain a gentleman while they share the close quarters night after night. The earlier battle today proved the benefit of having another person by her side. If he's indeed trustworthy then they could have a strong team. There are no doors to lock inside the cabin or rooms in which to divide them, so she keeps a degree of caution until she feels she knows Kito better, but for now she agrees.

"Thank you, and I will help you with yours too."

For the next several weeks the two teams have been sticking to their own usual hunting grounds without stepping out of their unspoken territory boundaries. Ardian and Nydia have found the industrial block lucrative, while Kito and Amiku have relied mostly on the ruined town for supplies. Unfortunately, when one taps into a single resource over and over, that resource eventually becomes exhausted, and vending machines do not replenish themselves. The many employee lounges and break rooms of the production plants have little left to offer and Ardian and Nydia both agree the warehouse isn't worth the trip.

The semi-cab remains their base, but they must now venture farther in hopes to find a new source for food and supplies. If they fail to discover something close, they risk having to migrate to a new location, and that will carry its own set of risks. To their relief they find an abandoned town that appears to have a possibility of providing them with food, clothes, and tools. Neither team is aware of the other's presence and have yet to discover evidence of each other's visitations; however, repetition and probability now make a meeting almost imminent.

Ardian and Nydia scavenge through the grocery store while keeping a vigilant eye around their surroundings. Nydia packs a few bottles of water, from an opened case, into her plastic bag. Ardian finds the display box of lighters and tests several of them until finding one with a steady flame. He also grabs two pocketknives after sliding them open and close to ensure they operate smoothly. He pockets the lighter and knives and then looks up to see if he can see Nydia.

The sunlight darkens and a shadow of a person appears on the floor beside Ardian. The figure doesn't linger long and continues past the entrance of the store. Ardian puts his hand on his sword and whirls around, but he's only met with the bright sun in his eyes. The cause of the body, that blocked the door, is no longer there, but he's already on alert and is prepared to investigate this further.

He cautiously steps out of the store and concentrates down both sides of the cracked and uplifted road. He keeps his hand on the handle of his sword as he advances to the corner of the store but stops before looking around the building. He concludes there's no one here after all and turns back around to head back inside. If he had taken that last single step, he would've known his assumption was incorrect. On his walk back he hears a sword being withdrawn and instinctively draws both his weapons and turns to face his attacker.

Kito doesn't know anything about him but has an automatic and natural dislike for other people. His assumption is that every single survivor is guilty of some heinous crime, and no proof is needed to convince him otherwise.

"Well, well, well. Looks like I found a rat," Kito taunts.

"I do not wish to quarrel sir, but I did not come here for nothing."

"Then this is about to get interesting."

Kito performs a horizontal slice aiming for Ardian's waist, but he evades the attack and then counters with his mace, which Kito blocks.

"I wish you no harm," Ardian says trying to prevent further fighting, but Kito is not ready to give up.

"Then throw down your weapons and die."

Kito pushes Ardian's mace back with his wide blade forcing Ardian to swing his short sword forward. Kito deflects it and then moves in to stab Ardian, but he sidesteps while bringing his mace down to hit Kito's sword into the concrete. He takes advantage of Kito's slow reaction time to get a lucky slice just inside his coat flap with the sword.

"You dual wielding bastard!" Kito yells as he checks his wound. He spots a small amount of blood on his fingertips, but it's nothing more than a scratch.

"I would have wished that it did not come to this. Will you lower your weapon now?" Ardian begs. Before Kito can respond, Nydia hurries out of the store with a bag and walking stick in hand while shouting Ardian's name in concern. She doesn't know what triggered this fight but worries it will end unfavorably for one party.

"Stay there, Nydia," Ardian orders while keeping his focus on Kito.

"Don't just stand there—" Kito begins as he swings his sword up. "—Do something." Kito's quick attack catches Ardian by surprise and leaves a long slice up his ribs. It fails to be a deep cut but succeeds in tearing his shirt almost in two.

Nydia ignores his advice and hurries to his aid. She swings the walking stick at Kito, but he ducks, and it sails over his head. Amiku runs over from across the street and arrives just in time to cut Nydia's stick in half with her katana.

"I can't leave you alone, can I," Amiku says.

"I was just minding my own business..."

"That's bullshit! You came at me first," Ardian interrupts.

Nydia rolls her foot on top of the second half of the walking stick to bring it closer to her before picking it up. She then holds them in each hand like batons while Ardian holds both his weapons at arm's length. Facing them is Kito and Amiku holding their swords in preparation to block or attack.

"Now we have to face two dual wielding bastards," Kito says.

The four stand in their defensive poses while waiting for someone to make the first move.

"Is that one of them?" Amiku asks referring to one of the men who Kito had encounter earlier.

"No," he admits.

"One of who?" Ardian inquires.

"None of your concern," Kito snaps back.

"We didn't do anything to you," Nydia says.

There are many confrontations in Apocalypsia. Some fights are necessary, and some enemies are deserving of the title, but sometimes two groups who should not be at war end up on opposite sides. Many factors can contribute to the development of this predicament, but at its core is the clash of beliefs between those who consider all to be enemies and those who hold onto the hope that camaraderie isn't dead.

If not for a single maniacal goblin this interaction could have ended very differently, and the future would have had a completely different turnout. The goblin becomes interested in this stalemated group but advances slowly due to being outnumbered. Kito smiles and sheaths his sword before walking away.

"Have fun with that," he says with Amiku following his lead.

"Are you kidding me?" Ardian says, taken back by the lack of concern someone can have towards others, but to Kito this somehow counts as revenge. The fact that Ardian and Nydia are innocent of such cruel acts doesn't protect them against others who have been wronged.

Kito faces forward with his arms at his side as Amiku leans her back against his left side with her arms folded across her chest.

"We are not your allies. This is survival. Adapt or die," he says before saluting them with a sly smile. He and Amiku then depart to leave Ardian and Nydia to an unknown fate.

The goblin is now surer of its odds and sprints toward Ardian and Nydia. It leaps up to attack Ardian's chest, but a quick thrust of his sword rips through the goblin's torso with little effort. Ardian cringes and grasps his side after feeling the sharp sting from the open wound caused by overstretching his reach. With the goblin threat removed, Nydia inspects his injury.

"I don't think this requires stitches, so you're lucky there," she says.

Ardian and Nydia make the slow trek back to their shelter. Once inside she begins to gather the remaining medical supplies to mend Ardian's cut. She pours a little of the water she found in the store into a bowl and then dips a cloth inside. She then sits on the bed beside Ardian and washes the dried blood away before wrapping a cloth bandage around his ribs.

"You are starting to look like a mummy," she jokes as the two share a laugh. They gaze at each other admirably for a moment before Nydia shyly turns away.

Later that night, while Nydia is sleeping, Ardian is busy working under a dim flashlight. He has taken the two halves of her walking stick and duct taped dressing knives to both ends of each stick. This will become Nydia's new weapon. Now they are ready for anything—or anyone.

It is the last day of September when the wind is still warm, but the nights are a little cooler. For the past week there's been an uncanny peacefulness in the surrounding area. No further meetings between the two rivals, no goblins to kill, no signs of creatures roaming the night. It's easy to pretend that danger is always someplace far away; to assume times are safer and guards can be lowered, but this is never true. It is wise to judge the silence harshly and keep a note that most storms follow a calm.

Kito peers through a pair of binoculars while surveying across the open field near Amiku's cabin.

"Anything new?" she asks as she approaches. Kito lowers the binoculars with a sigh.

"No, still nothing. It's been too quiet around here." Amiku takes the binoculars from him and then scans the surroundings herself.

"Quiet is good. You should appreciate it."

"But I grow restless. I just need a small goblin to chase down."

"Why, so you can get cut up again?

"Well as long as you have that plasma rejuju—or whatever it's called, I should be fine, right?" Amiku lowers the binoculars and gives Kito a look one normally does after hearing something dumb.

"Plasma rejuvenation—and it's not like I have an unlimited supply of it either."

"How do you get more?"

"You can't. The main ingredient is from a plant called Adonia.

"It was genetically created and grown by O.D.E., so you can't just find it anywhere. Unless you happen to know where one of their labs are?"

"Can't say I do. Where would one be?"

"Most likely in Copper Bay, but I'm not going back there."

"There's nothing there now but zombies and demons," Kito replies.

"You were in Copper Bay?" Amiku asks with interest.

"Yes, but that was a long time ago." Kito keeps his experience there a secret, but a slight look of dismay escapes from his furrowed brow.

It's been a long time since anyone lived in Copper Bay. It was once a population of thirty-three thousand, but now it's a hunting ground for the damned and home to the restless spirits who will never find peace or closure.

"Me too," Amiku nods in agreement. Kito breaks the brief silence by coaxing Amiku on another topic.

"Can we explore something?" Amiku smirks and then sighs.

"All right, Kito. North to the woods, or east to the coast?"

"I've always liked the coast."

"East it is."

"Good, maybe we can find a goblin to kill."

"Your eagerness for battle concerns me," Amiku says with a degree of seriousness.

Kito and Amiku are not the only ones who are traversing the nearby landscape. Ardian remembered spotting a lighthouse to the north, but never had the chance to visit it. Now with a full day's light ahead of him, and a partner to watch his back, he feels confident to venture towards it. Little does he and Nydia know that Kito and Amiku will reach it first. Another chance meeting awaits these two groups, but this one may come to a very different resolution.

The white and blue striped lighthouse sits at the edge of a rocky cliff overlooking the ocean. The steep vertical drop-off would be a fatal fall, but the spray from the waves crashing against the cliff face still manage to soak the rock piles surrounding the building. Kito and Amiku carefully observe the lighthouse from a distance until the moment Amiku lowers her binoculars.

"It may be someone's shelter, but I don't see any movement."

"Then let's get a closer look." Amiku grabs Kito's collar to stop him from advancing further.

"Don't rush into unfamiliar territory. It could be dangerous."

"I'm touched that you care about my safety and wellbeing," he replies with a coy smile.

"That's not it at all," Amiku snaps back. "I just don't want you to drag me into it."

The soft, muddy ground has claimed most of the stone walkway that once led to the attached lighthouse cabin. What's remaining now are broken and partially submerged remnants of its former glory. To the vigilant, this is a clue of the ominous nature that awaits any who dare to approach. To the wise, it demands a hasty detour. But to many, knowledge is gained through experience, not assumption.

The cabin's exterior door has been completely torn off its hinges and splintered wood and glass litter the nearby ground from the smashed windows and their frames.

Kito and Amiku stand outside while inspecting the damage with silent reveries of what violence or creature could have produced this much devastation, and what were the reasons behind it?

"I guess you were right," Kito says reluctantly, but Amiku doesn't even feel a response is necessary.

The interior living quarters paints a gruesome picture and indicates a desperate struggle. The walls have huge holes punched into them and deep scratches are embedding in the hardwood floor. The dresser, tables, and chairs are all smashed to almost unrecognizable furniture pieces. The bed sheets are shredded, and the mattress is leaning halfway off the bed with deep slashes on top of it. Every footfall crunches the pieces of drywall, glass, or wood shavings. The door, that leads into the lighthouse tower, is lying on the floor in a pool of blood and the walls and floor are covered with bloody handprints and streaks.

"This doesn't look good," Kito observes further.

Kito and Amiku draw their swords and then slowly peek around the corner to glance through the doorway of the tower. The blood streaks continue up the spiraling metal staircase before disappearing from their view. Kito grips his sword and holds it close to his chest before taking the first step onto the staircase.

"Be careful," Amiku whispers behind him. Amiku follows close behind as they make their way up and around to the top of the tower. At the uppermost platform of the inner circle is the rotating light, that has long since been inactive, along with a badly mangled body lying face down. Kito and Amiku exchange a questionable look before he flips the man over onto his back.

His entire stomach cavity has been completely hollowed out and his face is frozen in a silent scream. But there is another reason for Kito to become interested in this man.

"That's him," he says.

"Who?"

"The bastard that stole my food and left me for dead."

"I guess he got his after all," Amiku adds.

"Yeah, but where's his buddy?"

On the other side of the glass enclosure is the widow's walk. It's the only barricade between Kito, Amiku, and the dark hulking beast that's peering through the glass. Something triggers inside Amiku to turn around, an unsettling notion that they are being watched. Overcome with horror and in disbelief, she is unable to find the words fast enough to warn Kito, who remains unaware of the creature behind him. This beast stands like a man, and even holds a sword in its strong grip, but its skin resembles a rough scaly tan hide. It has a disfigured face with enlarged eyes and a wide mouth with large extending canines.

The beast bends its knees and leans back before propelling itself forward through the glass window while letting out a deafening roar.

"Kito!" Amiku finally shouts.

The window explodes sending sharp shards in all directions. She puts her arm in front of her face to protect it from the flying glass. Kito turns around just in time to block the beast's sword that slams against his. The force throws him back into the rickety railing that gives way and snaps from the bolts that held it in place. Amiku fails to reach him in time and watches him fall backwards off the platform along with the railing section.

"Kito!" she cries out.

The beast now turns its attention to Amiku, but with a quick glance down she leaps to the nearest landing and narrowly escapes the swinging blade. She leans over the railing to spot Kito holding onto the broken railing with one hand.

"Hold on, Kito!"

The brute begins to descend the steps after Amiku. Its heavy steps shake the weakened railings and staircase as fasteners and brackets become loose and fall. She knows this monster cannot be fought here. Retreat is the only option for now. She stores her katana and then shakes her wrists in the air while opening and closing her fists. She will need to rely on her balance and agility to make her intended escape route viable.

Amiku grabs the top of the railing and leaps off the staircase but catches the spindles just below to slow her fall before her feet land on the lower railing. Amiku lets go of the next set of spindles and swings her body around to land on the next flat surface. She immediately pounces off the step and pulls the railing outward as she leaps over it. She suspected it would break apart, but this time it's part of her plan.

The last anchor point from Kito's railing snaps and he begins to fall. Amiku swings her feet out and around to slide her legs in between the higher spindles of Kito's railing and guide it closer to the staircase where he's able to reach for the stable platform. Kito takes the last few steps with ease, but Amiku's action has put too much stress on the base of the staircase. The entire contraption leans to the side and begins to break apart. The brute lets out a roar as it plunges past Amiku with the top platform right above it. All she has to do is stay ahead of the falling spindles, and the other metal pieces, while making sure there is something below her to grab. She makes the rest of the way down by letting herself fall from each set of spindles until the very end when she dives under the last opening of the railing and then leaps off the step. She lands on her feet just as the entire staircase collapses into a heap of twisted metal behind her.

Amiku tosses her hair back and straightens her body back up from her crouched landing. She finds Kito staring intensely at her with a shocked expression.

"Are you alright?" she asks. Kito tries to formulate words but can only utter incoherent groups of sounds. He finally gives up speaking and just nods. If there was ever any clue that he was in total awe and completely smitten by a dame, it would have been right here at this very moment. Unfortunately, their moment is interrupted by a growl coming from under the downed staircase. What was thought to be a fatal fall for anyone was only a temporary cage for a demon.

Kito and Amiku dash back into the cabin just before the beast bursts up through the debris pile. It hurls several large, heavy sections away from it with powerful throws until it can advance unhindered.

"There's no way it could have survived that," Kito says

astonished. The brute then chucks a spindle toward Kito and Amiku, who luckily dodge the fast-spinning spear-like projectile as it slices the air in between them. Amiku grabs Kito's sleeve and pulls him alongside her.

"We need to get out of here." The monster pursues them with its sword in hand.

Kito and Amiku stand outside side by side as the beast meets them. It roars while glaring at them as if silently choosing its first target. It advances with a long gait towards Kito before swinging a forceful blow. Kito's wide blade blocks the attack, but he feels the force travel throughout his entire body. Amiku doesn't waste time and hurries behind it to slash a deep wound into its side and lower back. They need to take this demon down as fast as they can, or they risk growing tired and weak long before their opponent will.

The brute turns to focus its next attack on Amiku. She avoids every attempt the monster makes while preforming a set of sidesteps spins and flips. Kito intercepts to taunt the demon back on him. The speed of this creature is surprisingly fast, but Kito can predict its movements due to his ability to see its actions slowed down. Just as before, Kito and Amiku have developed an unspoken fighting strategy; he defends, and she attacks. Kito continues to distract the demon and block its attacks while Amiku draws blood. Their tactics are almost flawless, but their mistake was assuming demons are incapable of learning.

The beast allows Amiku to come in close, it waits for her sword to dig into its flesh before unleashing a surprise turn. This one was too fast for even Kito to predict. Amiku receives the palm of its hand into the center of her chest. This blow delivers an instant blackout and sends her soaring backwards and rolling across the ground.

"Amiku!" Kito cries out, but she remains motionless.

Her sword remains embedded in the beast's torso, but it does little to slow it down. Kito must resist the demon's relentless onslaught alone, but it's his sword that eventually fails him. After the countless barrage of slams and impacts the next one shatters the metal blade. The demon's sword travels past the broken blade to pierce Kito's abdomen. This moment is frozen in time for Kito. He glances down at his injury but cannot feel it. His useless sword falls from his grip as he directs his head up to look into the demon's eyes. If it could smile, it would have grinned victoriously.

The demon draws its sword out of Kito as blood flows freely from the wound that is no longer blocked. All his warmth dissipates, and a full-body numbing robs his balance. Kito falls to his knees and awaits the oncoming deathblow, but something else happens instead—

Elsewhere, Ardian and Nydia are navigating the vast grassy fields. Nydia glances behind them periodically throughout the journey. Her frequent inspections finally catch the attention of Ardian.

"What is it, Nydia?"

"I feel like we are being followed." Ardian stops to look behind them and inspects the ground they had just covered as far as his eyes can see.

"I don't see anything."

"Neither do I, but that doesn't mean it's nothing." Ardian and Nydia resume their excursion as she explains her gift further. "I've always had unexplainable visions and feelings. It begins with a slight touch or a glance, and I would see a picture. Whoever they are, whether I knew them or not, it didn't matter. I would see them in some accident or get a hint of some emotion they feel. Sometimes it's in a dream, other times it's just anywhere. It doesn't always happen, but when it does, it's never wrong. But no one ever believed me."

"I believe you," Ardian says without hesitating.

"You do? Why?"

"Because I believe some people have special abilities, and I think now, more than ever, those abilities should be embraced, not dismissed. I wish I had an ability."

"But you do, Ardian." Nydia takes his hand in hers and holds it with both of hers. "There's a peacefulness that I've never felt until now, when I'm around you, a calm, and that's because of something that's inside of you, your aura, the kind of person you are." Ardian smiles.

"Is that what you see in me?"

"I can pick up on energy. You have a still mind. Completely unshakable."

"Then I have you fooled." Ardian says with a shy smile. He places his other hand on top of hers and leans in closer to her. Nydia lifts her chin to line her lips up to his. They draw closer with anticipating heartbeats and a desire to rekindle a lost friendship into something more. Staying out of touch after the airline fell under was a regret, that they both shared, but now a second chance to cherish their time together arises. They each feel the warm breath of the other entering into their parted lips, but a distraction interrupts their moment. Desire must take second place to survival.

An unnerving roar echoes from someplace nearby. Ardian's and Nydia's eyes open and they look ahead with concern.

"What was that?" Nydia asks.

"I don't know." The two march up the grassy knoll until they can spy on the valley below. They have reached the lighthouse and have also chanced upon Kito and Amiku in a heated battle with the beast.

"Are those the same two people we met before?" Ardian asks after recognizing them from his vantage point.

"Yeah, but what the hell are they fighting?" Nydia confirms after observing the scuffle for a moment.

Not many has seen a demon like the one yet. It occurs when demon blood enters the bloodstream of a human. The person then goes through two main stages of transformation. The first is demonized, this will affect appearance, adoption of abilities and change aggression level, but they still know who they are and others around them. The last stage is demonoid, at this stage all memory of their former selves has been taken over by an instinct to only kill and feed. The time in between stages, final appearance, and their ability or power, varies greatly from person to person, with no possible way to predict the outcome. A person can fully merge with the demon DNA and keep all their memories as well; however, this is rare.

The creature that's warring with Kito and Amiku has reached its final stage and is most likely the partner of the dead man. It's almost never known what causes a person to change. It can be a scratch, a bite, some other form of physical injury or nothing more than ingesting contaminated food and drink. At any rate this is no longer a man, but a fully formed and seasoned demonoid.

"I never saw anything like that," Ardian admits as he and Nydia continue watching Kito successfully block all the beast's blazing fast and powerful attacks, while Amiku inflects a multitude of agile and precise wounds.

"They are good though," Nydia admits. Ardian is also

amazed at their fighting style and teamwork. Despite viewing them as enemies he still finds himself admiring Kito's skill.

"How is he able to deflect those attacks? I can't even spot an opening," he questions.

After witnessing Amiku being knocked backwards Nydia takes out her doubled bladed sticks from their holster positioned on her back.

"We can't just watch this."

"You do realize they wouldn't help us if this situation was flipped around."

"I don't care; if I can't sleep at night, I don't want this to be the reason."

"You have a good heart, Nydia. Let's hope they don't try to stab it."

Kito has just been slashed across his chest and falls to his knees. Unexpected are the unlikely rescuers who have arrived just in time.

Ardian intercepts the beast before it can deal the final blow to Kito. He knocks its sword away with his mace and then attacks with his sword. Nydia runs behind the beast and slashes its side and back while rotating her bladed sticks to utilize all four sides. Ardian smashes his mace into the beast's cheek that knocks its jaw offline. He then swipes his sword and slices its neck. The beast snarls and growls as blood squirts from its wounds. It makes one last attempt to get a strike in by raising its sword, but Nydia jabs one end of her weapon completely through the beast's bicep to stop the attack. Ardian brings down his mace near the same spot to sever the limb from the rest of the body. Nydia pulls out Amiku's sword that was still inside the demon's stomach before forcing it through its heart with the last of her strength. The demonoid finally succumbs to its injuries and falls.

Ardian discovers Kito has passed out during the fight, while Nydia aids a dazed and disoriented Amiku to her feet. Amiku gives Ardian and Nydia a surprised glance but becomes more concerned when she notices Kito lying on his back.

"Kito—" she mummers and then rushes to his side. She reaches into her coat pocket to take out a bottle of plasma rejuvenation and lets several drops fall along his cut and then gently rubs the liquid across the entire length of his wound with her fingertips.

"Wake up, Kito," she whispers.

Ardian and Nydia watches sympathetically. They aren't sure if they can trust either of them, but they can tell they care for one another. Any sign of compassion in this dead world shows a glimmer of hope for humanity. If this reveals anything to Ardian and Nydia, it's that maybe these two are not as cruel as they first made themselves appear.

The moment for reintroductions will have to wait; however, as Nydia's feeling that something was following them proves to be correct. It makes itself known by letting out a horrifying screech followed by a roar. Disbelief is quickly replaced with fear at the sight of the sleek, stream-lined, red, and orange body with a long snout jam-packed with serrated teeth. Stalking them with a lowered head is an adolescent raptor.

Amiku leaves Kito's side to retrieve her katana left in the heart of the beast. She then joins Ardian and Nydia to help them with this new threat.

The raptor charges toward Ardian with its mouth open and its neck arched back. He holds his sword out horizontally and the reptile bites down hard on the blade and almost yanks it out of his grip. Amiku and Nydia begin attacking the raptor's belly but a whip from its tail sends Nydia to the ground. It then jerks its neck viciously swinging Ardian to the side as he tries to hold on to his sword still clamped inside the raptor's jaws.

Another sword joins the fray and slices a deep gash on top of its neck. The raptor lets out a loud bloodcurdling screech and releases its hold on Ardian's blade. He takes this moment to slash the bottom of its neck, just below the jawline. The two neck wounds bleed profusely, but Amiku adds another gash along its ribs just to be sure it does not have any surprise energy to leap onto someone. With its powerful jaws and sharp talons, even an injured or dieing raptor can produce a fatal attack.

Weakened, the raptor falls on its side, but fails at trying to lift itself back onto its feet. Ardian's mace smashing into its skull finally finishes it off.

The mysterious sword that helped with the kill was the gatekeeper belonging to the demonoid and wielding it is Kito. He doesn't look like he's completely aware of his surroundings and may have been solely fueled by an instinct to recognize a threat. Once the threat has been resolved Kito drops the sword and collapses with only a tiny groan exiting his lips.

Amiku rushes back to Kito's side to inspect his rapidly bleeding wound.

"He's losing too much blood," she says worried. She holds up the nearly empty bottle of plasma rejuvenation in her hand just to be even more disheartened. "I don't have enough to save him."

"What is that?" Ardian asks.

"It's called plasma rejuvenation. It allows the body to heal faster by speeding up the making of new blood cells, but I'm all out."

"Can I see him? I have EMT training." Amiku looks up and finally nods. Nydia kneels down on Kito's opposite side to look over his injury. She peels back the layers of clothing to get a clearer view of his stomach and chest. "All things considered he's actually quite lucky," she begins. "No organs have been hit, or major blood vessels, but he will need stitches or there is a risk of him bleeding out. Unfortunately, we can't replace the blood he's already lost. We just don't have the capability for that here."

"A little Adonia would help with that," Amiku says.

"Adonia?" Ardian questions the unfamiliar name. Amiku shakes her head thinking its futile trying to explain it.

"It's a plant that O.D.E. used to grow in their labs."

"A plant—in a lab?" Ardian reaches into his belt and takes out the notebook with the odd-looking plant still inside. "Something like this?"

"Where did you find that?" Amiku responds with both surprise and excitement.

"I can explain, but we shouldn't stay here any longer. The smell of blood will attract who knows what else to this spot." Amiku agrees with Ardian from recalling her last experience with just a dab of Kito's blood outside her cabin. Where they are now is a slaughterhouse compared to that.

"I will take you to our shelter; it's not far. Can you carry him?"

"Yes." Ardian picks up an unconscious Kito while Nydia retrieves the gatekeeper sword.

"Is your shelter safe?" Nydia asks inquisitively.

"Yes, I assure you, it's very safe."

3

The Calm Before the Storm

Amiku's cabin was perfect for one but becomes a bit cramped when four seek refuge through a long night.

Nydia begins lighting the lanterns with a lighter as Amiku crushes the Adonia into the nearly empty flask of plasma rejuvenation. She then swirls the liquid around until a vibrant red color appears.

Ardian becomes fascinated with the flat screen monitor attached to the wall and a keyboard under it. The screen shows a short perimeter around the cabin in the night vision green hue.

"What's this?" he asks. Amiku glances up before responding.

"It's called an AI-Eye. Artificial Intelligence Eye. It's my security system."

"How does it get power?" Ardian continues.

"There's a small solar powered panel on the roof. It's not enough to power anything else except for that unit."

Amiku holds a candle flame to the bottom of the flask until

tiny bubbles can be seen rising to the surface. This completes the last step in the crafting of this potion. "There, it's ready." Amiku kneels beside Kito on the floor mattress, and then pours some of the red liquid down the length of his wound

"I can help with the bandaging if you would like?" Nydia asks. Amiku responds with a weak smile and a nod. She and Nydia begin wrapping the bandaging cloth around Kito as Ardian holds him up. Nydia observes his current wound, but also scars from previous injuries.

"Why do you guys always get yourselves so beat up? He's worse than you." Nydia says while glancing up at Ardian.

"Are you hurt?" Amiku inquires. Neither Ardian nor Nydia had to offer their help to her or Kito, especially after their first meeting, but the fact that they have, and are still, suggests they may be worthy allies.

"I'm okay." Ardian shows her the bandage around his ribs. "Except this nice gash from your friend here."

"It seems both of you left your mark on the other," Amiku says.

"Yes, but was there a reason for it?" Ardian asks.

"There's always a reason for these things," Amiku replies softly.

"What was it." Nydia chimes in.

"After we get Kito stabilized we have a lot to talk about," Amiku answers.

Amiku has decided to look at Ardian and Nydia in a new light. They have proven to be good people and she knows those are far and few in between. Her survival strategy included avoiding others, but now with the evidence of an increasingly hostile world making demons evolve and bringing back prehistoric predators, the need for a team is more necessary than before. How will Kito react to her choice can only be imagined, but there's a strong chance he won't be easy to convince.

By the time morning arrives the three survivors have been talking throughout the night. They've shared their experiences and survival techniques and now feel more relaxed being in each other's company. The monitor screen of the AI-Eye security system now shows the natural colors of the cabin's surroundings due to the deactivation of the night vision.

People turning into demons and raptors coming back from

extinction defy the laws of nature, time and what's possible. The world is becoming more dangerous day by day with threats becoming larger in size and increasing in numbers. There is more to surviving now than just scavenging for food and water and then finding a safe place to lie low until morning. Nydia is first to suggest that fighting amongst themselves is not a viable solution.

"We will have a better chance of surviving if we work together," she begins. "I think that's something everyone must have forgotten."

"A good start would be showing me where that O.D.E. lab is," Amiku begs.

"We can show you exactly where it is," Ardian responds, but Nydia's apprehensive expression reveals her feelings about returning to the warehouse.

For Amiku it's a chance not only to stock up on Adonia, but also search for a clue that led to O.D.E.'s sudden downfall and uncover their mysterious intentions during the latter part of The Demon Wars. Not fully knowing the details that surrounded her father's murder has left an open wound in her heart. How can she avenge his death if everyone responsible is long gone? The best she can do is know why he was targeted.

The springs of Kito's mattress squeak and crackle. There is an uneasy and extended stare-down as everyone looks at Kito sitting up.

"What are they doing here?" He finally says.

"They saved our lives," Amiku responds calmly

"They are plotting against us." Kito continues.

"You're delusional and need to rest," Amiku strikes back in a more aggravated tone. "It took a long time to patch you up, so just stay there and don't get up."

"How can I rest with our enemies here?" Amiku stands up and walks toward Kito. She pinches a spot on the back of his neck and holds it until he falls back to the mattress.

"What did you do?" Nydia asks.

"It's amazing what a little pressure on the right nerve can do."

Ardian leaves the journal he had found with Amiku before he and Nydia depart back to their own shelter. They draw her a map of how to find them and then decide a good time for them to visit. Amiku passes the time by reading the journal from the unknown O.D.E. scientist. It speaks in depth about plant species, breed of demons, company inventions, locations, and departments within O.D.E. According to the text Adonia grows fast and is easy to transplant. Amiku thinks it would be useful to have this plant growing a little closer to home, especially with Kito's recklessness. Another species mentioned is the fungus known as, Blood Fire Mushrooms. They're small red cap mushrooms and the main component in Green Death, but there is no guide of growing or finding it. Amiku has one flask of it, but so far has not been in a situation where she needed it. Despite this, she carries it with her just in case. She keeps the journal close to her to reference it when she feels it may be beneficial.

She wonders what she might find in the lab Ardian and Nydia discovered. She never found one since the war ended, but will take every opportunity to explore anything related to O.D.E. Most of the times this leaves her with more questions than answers, but her current problem is trying to convince Kito to accompany them.

"Despite our first encounter they still decided to help us?" She points out.

"I am under no obligation to get along with them."

"You're just looking for someone to hate more than you hate yourself." Sometimes she thinks she's being too harsh with him, but then again, he never makes anything easy.

"What do you want to do? Bake them a casserole? Invite them to the neighborhood?" Kito pesters. Amiku takes a deep breath and holds it, but it does little to calm her down.

"You said you would help me, so fuckin' help me! Put your damn hang-ups behind you," she snaps. Kito remembers his promise, and this seems important to her. His cooperation is only to aid her and putting up with Ardian and Nydia is just an unfortunate part of it. He agrees to go with Amiku to the warehouse, but nothing about this deal signifies he has to be friendly to their guides.

Ardian and Nydia return to the abandoned town on their way back to their truck cab shelter. Besides restocking their food supplies, they also visited the same clothing store Kito and Amiku had. They shed their old clothes, that resemble two exiled pariahs, and adopt a new look of two battle-ready soldiers of a new world. Just because one war is lost doesn't mean you stop fighting. Another one is always on the horizon. Ardian picks a pair of brown cargo pants and a deep forest green vest with a black shirt under it while Nydia chooses black pants and a gray long-sleeved shirt with a dark blue mesh shawl.

Later that day, Amiku, Ardian and Nydia walk in a tight cluster while talking as if they were long-time friends, but Kito trails behind at a distance. He doesn't want to make new friends or pretend to be social. Ethics and etiquette have been dead for a long time and there's no need to bring either back. A handshake isn't going to patch civilization back together and neither will kind words. Amiku somehow became the exception to Kito's reclusive lifestyle, but he's not making any more compromises. He's perfectly comfortable accepting the title of outcast.

The warehouse is in the same dilapidated shape as it was when Ardian and Nydia first visited it.

"Are you still getting that uncomfortable feeling, Nydia?" Ardian asks. She looks at him with a stern brow.

"Yes, there's something in there. I can't see it or hear it, but I can feel it." Amiku reaches into her coat pocket and takes out the flask of the green death toxin.

"Don't worry, I brought a little backup with us. It doesn't matter how big or strong anything is; once this enters their bloodstream they are as good as dead."

"I just don't believe in tempting luck twice," Nydia admits.

The ray of light, from the girls' flashlights, illuminate just enough of the dark warehouse to surround the group and their direction of travel; all else is shrouded in complete darkness. Nydia occasionally darts her light to her sides or up towards the ceiling. Drips of water falling into puddles or pings from the tiny pebbles and rocks coming loose from the deteriorating walls are the only sounds echoing throughout the damp, forgotten building.

Nydia's beam of light finally finds the large, cracked window of the lab. With their destination reached, Nydia hopes Amiku is quick with her assessment of the lab so they can head back, but she does not voice this concern. Amiku spots the Adonia vine almost immediately and slices a decent length of it with her katana. Kito rummages through some of the cabinets, but there seems to be nothing of any value left at this location. Amiku checks some drawers and under tables or on top of the countertops. The broken glass shards and the damaged beakers, tubes and flasks offer zero clues of what they once held or were meant to. There are also no labels or signs to suggest what this particular lab was used for. It could have been solely used for growing plants, but that's unlikely due to being a waste of space, talent, and resources. The reason for this lab's existence is now a mystery and all who would know are missing or dead.

A sudden flapping just over Kito's head causes him to duck and step back. His sword is now the gatekeeper recovered from the demon at the lighthouse. He draws it and slices the air above him and two halves of a tiny bat fall to the floor. The sighs of relief are short-lived when a vibration travels through the floor and up everyone's legs at this very moment.

"Did you guys feel that?" Nydia asks concerned, but before anyone can confirm they had, a stronger vibration is felt. The next one after that begins with a thump before the vibrations rattle the window and make the glass tubes roll off the counter and shatter on the floor.

"Something's here," Amiku says softly. The thumps become louder as whatever is causing it is clearly advancing closer to the group. Kito steps out of the lab and peers through the darkness toward the back wall of the warehouse.

"Someone shine a light over there?" Kito asks. Amiku and Nydia step up on either side of him and slowly lift their flashlights ahead of them. Encased in the circle of light is a large bat standing at least ten feet tall. It uses its folded wings to walk forward and its piercing red eyes glare at the group. It opens its mouth to reveal two long fangs before letting out a high-pitched screech. This finally shatters the cracked lab window completely. The bat spreads its wings out and then lunges forward. It doesn't have any intention of letting the team escape without a fight.

"Hello, bad feeling," Nydia says before drawing her weapon. Ardian and Kito also have their weapons ready near her, but Amiku is studying her surroundings intensely. She observes the windowsill of the lab and the nearby support beam. Her gaze then goes from the beam to the wall of the warehouse and then to a broken suspended walkway, which the bat is standing directly underneath.

"Everyone, stay here," Amiku says. She pours a little of the green death on her sword and lets it run down to the point. She holds the sword out at her side and then jumps onto the windowsill before leaping up to push off the support beam and then vaults off the wall, into a flip, before landing on top of the broken walkway. She then back-flips off the walkway and brings the blade down over the bat's head, but a swarm of smaller bats sacrifice themselves by intercepting her sword. She loses the grip on her sword but manages to land on her hands and feet in a squatted position.

"The smaller bats are protecting the big one," Nydia points out.

"At least it looked cool," Kito adds.

Amiku looks up just as the giant bat slowly raises one of its wings and then brings it down over her. Ardian collides into her and the two roll out of the way just before the wing slams down where she was standing. Kito notices the katana on the floor near the large bat with traces of the green poison still on the blade. He just needs to get to it before the bat has time to react. The bat's focus appears to be on Ardian and Amiku and this gives Kito confidence to dash for the sword.

"Don't rush in, Kito," Nydia hollers after him.

Ardian darts back to the bat from its side while Kito charges head on. The bat expands one of its wings again and knocks Ardian back several feet. Kito slides across the floor to grab Amiku's sword, but the bat slams its clawed foot down just in front of it. A horde of the smaller bats fly down from the rafters in a congregation of screeching.

Ardian holds the handle of his sword towards Amiku.

"Take it." She smiles and thanks him.

Ardian's mace crushes the bats that are swarming around him while Amiku helps by slicing through the same swarm. Nydia twirls her bladed sticks around her body to annihilate another swarm that has formed around her. She tries to keep her eyes on Kito, who is still trying to make it to Amiku's sword but remains on defense as the large bat continues to step on him or squash him with its wing tips.

A third swarm of tiny bats begin to hover over Kito, but Nydia hurls one of her bladed sticks toward them. The stick spins through the air and then through the group of bats without losing speed or direction. It may not have been planned, but her aim was perfect. It clears the group of bats and pierces into the giant bat's chest. The bat lets out a loud screech and rears up to snap the walkway from the wall and send it crashing to the ground.

Kito is now able to reach Amiku's katana and wastes little time to thrust it into the bat's lower stomach. The toxin causes the fur of the bat to catch on fire and the skin starts to melt away leaving a widening hole in the bat's body. Engulfed in flames, the bat falls on its back while flapping its wings against the floor until it finally stops thrashing. The body of the giant bat is now nothing more than a smoldering burnt heap of bones and ash. The remaining smaller bats retreat further into the darkness of the warehouse, and all is silent once again.

"You didn't say anything about this potion making things catch on fire," Kito says as he returns the katana back to Amiku.

"I never actually saw it used before, but from what I read it wasn't supposed to do that," Amiku admits.

"Must be some chemical reaction," Ardian adds.

"I hate to interrupt, but can we leave now," Nydia says. For once, even Kito is in agreement; no one wants to remain in this building a second longer.

Amiku came for what she was initially after, but the hope to discover something new or uncover more information about O.D.E. only lead to an attack by a giant bat. Perhaps there could be a connection between the two, but for now leaving the entire experience behind her is all too desirable.

The two teams split up once again to carry out their individual tasks and daily routines. Kito and Amiku return to her cabin where she begins to plant the Adonia into a recovered flowerpot while Kito watches.

"Nothing explains it," he says after a long silence.

"What?"

"There must be some explanation how a bat could grow to that size. Some cause, a reason, something."

"You don't need to try to explain it, Kito. Evil has no limits; it doesn't have a scientific explanation. There is no evolution to consider. These monsters are born from hell and then unleashed into our world; and two worlds that never should meet, collide into one another. Finding out how to kill them is good enough."

Kito understands now what Amiku had said the first time they met. *You don't truly know anyone until you fight them*, or in this case fight with them. Kito wanted to hate Ardian and Nydia but cannot deny they held their own very well. He will base his final thought on Amiku's opinion.

"Do you really like those two people?" He asks. Amiku sighs and looks up from her planting.

"It's rare to find good people these days and I think Ardian and Nydia are trustworthy. They're also decent fighters. I think we would make a good team, but will you give them that chance?"

"I never trusted anyone. Never wanted help from anyone. Never felt I needed it. But for you I can at least try." Amiku smirks.

"I suppose that's good enough."

Meanwhile, Ardian and Nydia return to the industrial block and begin inspecting a large pile of discarded manufactured parts and machines. Ardian pulls out a generator, but it doesn't seem to be anywhere close to operational, and even if it was in good shape there isn't any fuel nearby to make it run. This is probably a gold mine to someone who is mechanically inclined, but neither Ardian nor Nydia know how to fabricate any of these metal components together to create something useful.

Several yards ahead a group of ten snarling goblins scatter around a similar pile of debris as they advance into the open. Ardian and Nydia quietly duck behind a tipped over commercial freezer and then slowly peek over the top. So far, their presence has gone unnoticed. This would be a hard battle to win considering their opponent's numbers and the fact that Nydia is now down to only one bladed stick.

The goblins stomp the ground or dig in the dirt while others smell the air. Suddenly, they huddle together as if they've been alerted by some scent on the wind. Their quest for food seems to be halted as they nervously glance around in every direction. Ardian and Nydia remain hiding as they observe the strange behavior. They were worried that it was their scent that may have been picked up, but it looks more like the goblins are actually afraid.

The subject of their dismay reveals itself as a demonoid sprints out of a demolished factory with a roar. It claws and shreds the goblins to bits with its teeth. The goblins organize an attack, but it proves to be futile against the larger, faster, and stronger enemy. The commonality between this monster and the one at the lighthouse does not escape Ardian and Nydia. This creature was once a person, but now lacks every feature of his former self. This demonoid has subtle differences from the first one, such as tiny spines and spikes on its limbs and its skin is green with black blotches.

The demonoid only sustained a few scratches before it dissembles the last goblin. The ground is covered in severed goblin body parts and pools of blood as the creature picks up what it wants to feast on and then leaves the rest for the scavengers that roam the night. It has been confirmed that demons hunt each other, but why wouldn't they? They are predators surviving in an untamed post apocalyptical wild.

After having its fill, the demonoid sluggishly creeps back into the ruins. Ardian and Nydia decide it's also a good time for them to head back to their shelter and call it a day. The increasing activity of dangerous monsters and demons are starting to get closer to where they live and scavenge. As they settle in for the evening, they hope tomorrow will be less eventful. Little do they know the time of running into a lone goblin here and there is no longer the case. Unknown enemies are plotting, unseen demons are spreading out and a new war is on the horizon. There won't be peace or rest for a long time. This is only the calm before the storm.

Beyond Amiku's meadow is a deciduous forest that used to be the training grounds for green soldiers entering into the army. It's also rumored to be where O.D.E tested their weapon prototypes or other developments. With the assumption of finding abandoned gear, weapons, or supplies, from either O.D.E. or the army, Kito and Amiku agree to set forth to explore the wooded area. Even if nothing is discovered the trek will still give them a better idea of their surroundings. This is a journey of curiosity, discovery, and hopeful recovery, fueled by passion, necessity, and a hint of boredom. Unbeknownst to them is how much will change after this mid-afternoon jaunt.

The once green, dense canopy is now an array of colors that allows a greater amount of light to pour in from some of the bare branches. The forest floor is moist and covered with the fallen and dried leaves that make a silent hike all but impossible. Navigating through this first part of the forest eventually leads to a rocky clearing with patches of grass and low-growing shrubs. The forest continues ahead, but to the left is the cliff-side. The faint sound of the surf crashing into the rocks below indicates this landmass is much higher than where the lighthouse is. The strong wind bombards Kito and Amiku while making their trench coats flap behind them. A quick glance below reveals the steep drop into the ocean below, but it's an island in the distance that catches Amiku's attention. She raises her binoculars to spy on the piece of land. The remains of a dock barely connects to the beach with most of its wooden construction washed away to parts unknown. The trees on this plot of land are coniferous and seem to make up the entire middle of the island. She is about to lower her binoculars, but movement on the beach catches her interest. She zooms in and focuses her lens on three raptors running along the shore. These look to be fully grown adults and are soon accompanied by two more that sprint out from the trees.

"Well, that stirs up more questions," Amiku says before handing the binoculars to Kito. The raptors appear to be testing the waters as they take turns swimming out into the waves before heading back toward the shore.

"I think they are trying to find a way across," Kito observes.

"Let's hope they don't. We can't fight against a pack of adults, let alone one of them."

"Maybe they will just stay by Ardian and Nydia," Kito chuckles, but Amiku isn't amused.

"That's not funny," she says with a frown while snapping her binoculars back.

They continue into the next section of the forest more aware of the changing times and the greater chance to meet a hostile encounter. It's not long before this fact is proven, and a new foe is discovered. Amiku spots it first resting on a thick branch about twelve feet up. Momentarily, this large demon appears to be sleeping due to its head being tucked down against its chest and its massive wings folded up against its sides. The body is covered with black and gray randomly shaped markings and two spiraled horns sprout from the top of its head.

Amiku puts her finger to her lips to warn Kito to be quiet as they try to tip-toe around the monstrosity. The task is an impossible one as there is nowhere to place a step that is not on a leaf or twig. A soft snap under Kito's foot is all it takes for the demon to lift its head and open its black eyes. The demon roars and fully extends its wingspan before diving down towards them.

"Get down!" Amiku shouts while throwing herself into Kito. They both hit the ground just as the demon flies over them. It then soars up into the canopy while weaving through the branches and foliage before disappearing in the treetops. Leaves and branches fall around Kito and Amiku as they pick themselves up and then draw their swords while looking up into the trees.

"Where did it go?" Kito asks.

"I don't know." They turn in circles while keeping their focus above them, but the demon doesn't return.

"Maybe it flew away."

"I don't think so." Amiku's assumption is correct and the winged beast bursts back down through the trees with incredible speed. Kito sidesteps out of its path and swings his sword but fails to make contact. The demon now sets its sights on Amiku. She blocks the demon's talons with her katana when it collides into her. She is sent sailing backwards and hits the ground on her back with her sword falling out of her reach. Her ability to recover is slower than the demon's speed as it glides with great agility around the tree trunks before circling back around and landing directly in front of Amiku. She kicks the ground and uses her hands to move back as the demon slowly advances, but Kito is quick to intercept. He stands in front of her while holding his sword outstretched with both hands and the sword tip to the demon's throat. It recoils and roars to show four rows of fang-like teeth, but Kito is not deterred, he stares the beast down with a focused glare and a determined expression.

"Fight me, demon! For as long as I stand you will never get close to her." Amiku is a little surprised to see this side of Kito. She doesn't know where this sudden urge to be protective came from but, she can't help but feel admiration toward him.

The beast spreads out its wings and darts forward with its mouth open wide, just as the sound of a gunshot rings out from somewhere nearby. A small trickle of blood escapes from the wound in the demon's side. It turns to take note of it but seems unfazed as it turns back to Kito. Without warning the entry point from the gunshot explodes so violently that the demon is torn in half. Kito and Amiku shield themselves with their arms as flesh, guts, blood, and body segments are blown in all directions. After the raining down of the demon's innards cease, it's discovered that its torso and head occupy one area of the nearby forest while the legs and its wing are in another. The fact that Kito's and Amiku's coats are drenched in all the foulness of this creature is a small price to pay.

"What the hell just happened?" Kito asks.

"I don't know," Amiku answers softly. "Is someone out here?" she calls out louder.

Whoever fired the shot may be contemplating if their identity should be revealed, but after a moment a man steps out from behind a tree while holstering his pistol.

"I do apologize for your current state. There wasn't enough time to warn you," The man confirms.

"You saved our lives; you do not need to apologize. Besides I would rather be covered with demon innards than being inside of them." Amiku answers.

Kito brushes pieces of demon guts from his shoulders with a disgusted look. "I'm a bit less gracious, Amiku."

She is about to scold him, but this stranger's look of interest after hearing her name makes her hold off.

"Your name is Amiku?"

"That's right," she answers puzzled why someone she doesn't know has taken interest in who she is. The man smiles and chuckles.

"I see, it looks like the world got smaller after all. My name is Anyo; I used to work with your father." Now it's Amiku who's intrigued. This may be the moment she's been waiting for—to finally be able to talk to someone from O.D.E. and find out what really led to her father's murder.

Anyo suggests it's best to talk in a safer place since the conversation will be a lengthy one and Amiku will no doubt have a lot of questions. He assures his shelter is nearby and leads the two for a short walk deeper into the woods. Kito has his suspicions, but it would be nothing new to Amiku if he voiced them. He keeps his feelings to himself but remains vigilant during the hike.

Anyo clears an area of leaves and branches until a metal disc comes into view. He pulls up the hidden handle and then turns it. The clicking and grinding of sliding bolts are heard before the trapdoor creaks open. He then leads Kito and Amiku down a few steps into a moderate sized room with lit floor lamps. Wall cupboards line the left side of the room with a counter and drawers below them. A bed and reading chair are against the opposite wall and the floor is covered with a plush carpet.

Connected to this room is also a kitchen with apparently working appliances and running water from a hand pump hanging over the sink. It could pass for an underground hotel suite since no one has had comforts like these since the end of civilization. Anyo pulls the hatch door down and locks it into place before rejoining two people who are completely in awe.

"How do you have electricity?" Amiku asks as she continues admiring Anyo's shelter.

"First things first," Anyo says while lifting a slab section of the counter. "Toss your coats in here." Stored under the counter is a small modular washing machine. Kito and Amiku gladly take off their soiled coats and drop them in. Anyo taps a button, and the washer begins as soon as the counter is lowered back down. Both Kito and Amiku are beside themselves with how advanced and efficient this shelter is despite it being less than 450 sq. ft., yet it's roomy enough to still feel comfortable.

"Everything in here is powered by hydro fuel cells located behind the walls," Anyo begins. "The process involves a generator that forces water to move through the fuel cells. The separation of the hydrogen and oxygen from the water creates energy and generates an unlimited supply of power, since the fuel cells also charges the generator."

"This place is like state of the art," Kito admits.

"O.D.E. never spared any expense. They researched, developed, and manufactured this shelter, and then had its livability tested by housing two scientists here for a month. From what I heard they didn't want to leave after their term ended," Anyo chuckles as Kito and Amiku nod their heads.

"I can see why," Amiku adds.

Anyo leads the two on a short tour of the O.D.E hatch shelter. The first room doubles as the bedroom and living room with an under the counter washer and dryer. The open concept room leads seamlessly into the kitchen where an electric stove, mini fridge and table and chairs fill the room nicely. A sliding room divider on the far wall of the kitchen reveals a tiny bathroom complete with a shower stall and toilet. The toilet sits on top of a seven-inch drilled hole that appears to go quite deep. A plastic container nearby reads:

Waste Dissolver Crystals with Ocean Breeze Scent.

This is scooped and poured into the hole to prevent a buildup of excrement and odor.

"I have to admit this is a very fascinating place," Amiku says. Anyo smiles and takes them back into the living quarters.

"Every O.D.E. department had their own motto. The Shelters division's motto was, all the comforts of home, only fortified."

"My father worked in the chemicals and chemistry division," Amiku begins. "He said their motto was, using science to reinvent science. Speaking of my father, you said you knew him?"

"Please have a seat and I shall explain." Anyo places an ottoman in front of Kito and Amiku before sitting down in his chair.

"I used to be an O.D.E. scientist, your father was my friend and colleague. I mourned for Charles when I heard what had happened. I thought they may have assumed that you were injected also, but I'm glad you got away."

"What do you mean—injected?" Amiku asks baffled.

"Didn't Charles tell you? The event that was directly responsible for O.D.E.'s final destruction—and possibly the reason why we lost the war?" Amiku slowly shakes her head eager to learn more.

"No, I've been trying to find some clue or explanation, but never had any luck with it."

"I see. Well then, I shall start at the beginning—"

Anyo and the other scientists are dressed in their O.D.E. lab coats while placing tubes of blood into a centrifuge. Along the wall on one side of the room are cages with goblins inside. On the opposite wall are cages holding sedated chimpanzees. Anyo steps to the front of the lab to address his colleagues.

"Today, we start testing demon to human blood manipulation and transfer. O.D.E.'s goal here is to discover if demon blood has the capabilities to give people additional abilities. We have chosen chimps because their mental aptitude is similar to our own. Does anyone have any questions before we begin?" Charles steps out from the crowd with his pointer finger in the air.

"Up until now we've been trying to prevent people from being infected by demons, now we are actively doing the complete opposite. I've seen enough zombie movies to know how this will end."

"Thank you, Charles for your insight. Lucky for us you're

a scientist and not a screenwriter." Some of the other workers chuckle and giggle at Anyo's snarky response, but no one defends Charles' comment.

The scientists move ahead with their job assignment and take blood samples from the goblins and then inject the needles into the chimps. Within the next few days animal trainers test the chimps with a series of puzzles and tasks inside an enclosed facility. Several scientists peer through the large observing window and jot down their notes in their journals.

The chimps have developed better eyesight and better hearing, as well as, greater strength and speed, one man records.

As the tests carry on into the next week the chimps become more aggravated, and their facial features transform with deformities—the demonized monkeys soon begin attacking and killing the trainers. Soldiers equipped with assault rifles are forced to rush in and slaughter the rampaging chimps.

Scientists return to their research and modify their calculation to develop a second batch with great promise. Ignoring Charles' advice for the second time the department conducts their testing on a new group of chimps. Just as before a small gathering of scientists observe the chimps inside a caged playground while taking notes. This batch of primates display greater agility and strength as they move through an obstacle course.

For two months our subjects have been displaying all the positive qualities we want to see with none of the negative. I think we have it perfected.

O.D.E. is happy with the reports from the animal tests and have agreed to start human experimentations. Six volunteers agree to act as test subjects and for two weeks follow the procedure by living in a comfortable, brightly colored room. With twenty-four-seven surveillance there is never a moment when they are not being observed. They mostly pass the time by playing cards or watching TV, while O.D.E. executives and military personal watch the volunteers from an observation room day after day and monitor their progress.

Unfortunately, before the second week can end, four of the volunteers become demonized and attack the other two who haven't turned yet. Blood and gore paint the walls of the room and the floor becomes covered with detached limbs and human organs. A demonized man pounds on the glass with his fists while glaring at the shocked observers. His skin is peeling away from his face and his fang-like teeth are covered with blood. His eyes are also colorless with very small pupils and the low-pitched growl it utters is unnerving to even the most seasoned army generals. Soldiers have no choice but to assassinate the damned group of volunteers.

This incident should have halted all future testing indefinitely. Under normal circumstances an investigation would have been carried out that would have shut O.D.E. down and sentence those responsible, but a wartimes mandate state as follows:

O.D.E. cannot be challenged nor be required to explain actions or relinquish information at any time. Any person, group, or organization disobeying this edict will be charged and punished with the maximum penalty the crime of treason allows.

For some reason elected officials thought that it was a good idea to give O.D.E absolute power, and so the tests continued. A letter from some unnamed prestigious intellect suggests yet another method that may offer favorable results.

I believe if the blood from the monkeys were added to the serum it would be enough to prevent the demonfication and those injected would not become demonoids. I'm basing this hypothesis on the notion that the demon blood is too concentrated and needs to be diluted.

Update: No demonfication after four months.

A conference room is filled with top-ranking army personal and O.D.E executives. They are watching a recording of several people moving or lifting heavy objects with ease and without the help of equipment. A stopwatch also clocks a man who just finished his 100-meter dash in 4.29 seconds. Someone pauses the tape and waits until he gets a nod from a man who has more medals pinned on his chest than there is space for.

It was announced to the masses as a vaccine against demonic infection with a latent benefit to increase stamina and agility. Everyone thought they needed it. Everyone was told they should get it. Some wanted it, while others resisted, but those were shamed and ostracized until they conceded. Clinics are crowded with citizens, soldiers and scientists as doctors inject their patients with the new serum labeled, F6VI. However, after eight months the demonfication begins. Citizens became demonized at home and attack their families, or on the streets attacking their neighbors. The soldiers transform on the battlefields and attack their own men. In the O.D.E. labs the infected scientists are killing others who are still human. O.D.E. finally loses their authority, but with no one able to restore order, every infrastructure crumbles and dissolves.

Anyo finishes explaining his experience in O.D.E and their last assignment as Kito and Amiku try to take it all in. How could O.D.E. become so corrupted and irresponsible with the public's safety? Amiku doesn't have any reason not to trust Anyo's story, but something must be missing that he didn't share, or maybe doesn't even know himself. There could be another player involved who has yet to be named, or a hidden agenda that hasn't been fully flushed out. Her thoughts are interrupted when Kito asks his question.

"So, O.D.E. is responsible for demonoids?

"Not exactly," Anyo replies. "O.D.E tried to manipulate demon DNA into something beneficial; very much like the concept behind flu shots and anti-venom. They just failed at it."

"We fought one of those demon things before," Kito continues.

"That's quite possible. But any transfer of demon blood into the bloodstream will infect that person." Kito places his hand on his stomach and lowers his gaze.

"You mean—it's unavoidable?" Kito asks softly.

"I'm afraid so," Anyo confirms. "The time frame can vary from days to months, but there's no stopping it. Anyone who has demon blood in them is doomed." Amiku picks up on Kito's look of dismay as he appears to be lost in a distant thought or worried by some mysterious cause. She can see him touching his lower abdomen as if he's in pain and had noticed an older scar in that vicinity while she was patching him up prior. Kito is clearly hiding something from her, but this is neither the time nor the place to interrogate him. Kito notices Amiku's glare and snaps out of his thoughts. He pulls his hand away from his belly and acts like nothing was bothering him. Anyo continues with explaining the rest of his answer in greater detail.

"However, the final outcome is impossible to predict. Some become mindless monsters while others show intelligence and can even communicate and plan. Hell, I've even heard some people are able to freely change from their demon form back into human. Sometimes transformation can lie dormant for a time too. This means physical changes do not occur, but some abilities might."

"So O.D.E. went rogue," Amiku says aggravatingly. "They were established to help people and fight demons, not create them or use people as fucking lab rats!"

"Hence the name, Operation Demon Eradication," Kito adds. "When did it become, Operation Demonize Everyone?"

"I can't lie. We tried to play God and ended up finding the devil," Anyo admits. "F6VI was an acronym that meant, *For those 6 Volunteers Injected*. However, with closer inspection we made a terrifying discovery. F is the sixth letter of our alphabet and VI is the roman numeral six. The serum we injected everyone was 666."

"How could you inject innocent people with that serum and put them and their families through that?" Amiku barks.

"I only worked with creating the serum not administrating it," Anyo pauses, and his voice becomes monotone. "After the distribution, O.D.E. tried an emergency damage control by seeking out anyone known to receive the serum. They were marked for elimination. This may not be easy for you Amiku, but your father was one of them." Amiku stands up trying to fight back her tears.

"You knew about this! You continued making that serum with full knowledge that more people were going to be injected with it?"

"We are all slaves to the decisions of others," Anyo says while lowering his head.

"I can't believe this. I won't believe it. My father would never have taken that shot. He wasn't hunted, he was silenced!" Anyo is stumped with a response after Amiku's outburst. It is the first time he has slipped up and hints at a clue he hasn't been completely forthcoming with the entire story.

"I understand your feelings. I lost many close acquaintances at the hands of O.D.E." Anyo says sincerely. "Seems like in the end O.D.E. made more problems than came up with solutions." Amiku sighs and sits back down after recomposing herself.

"That's what my father said. He said he didn't know whose side he was on anymore," Amiku recalls.

"I liked Charles, he was a good man."

"Did you come across any other groups around here?" Kito asks wondering how sparse other bases and shelters might be. Anyo begins by shaking his head.

"Not since everyone left the army camp up ahead."

"There's an army camp nearby?" Amiku asks.

"Yes, but there's not much left now. Everyone from the fort picked it clean."

"What fort?" Kito asks intrigued. Anyo looks as if he had just said something he shouldn't have and forces a recovery statement.

"Well, there are a few scattered forts to the west. That is, if you want to travel for a whole day."

"Speaking of a full day. We should be getting back before it gets dark," Amiku suggests.

"Actually, you might want to hold off. The forest becomes active right about now. I would feel better if the two of you stayed here for the night. I can escort you back to your shelter tomorrow."

Neither Kito nor Amiku took his response as a comforting gesture, but at the same time they cannot deny the dangers of navigating the forest, cliffs, or fields at night. Amiku gives Kito a glance and then turns back to Anyo.

"We would really hate to impose." Anyo flicks his hand through the air.

"Don't worry about it." Anyo removes the pistol from his holster and then places it into the drawer of the nightstand but doesn't shut it all the way. Kito and Amiku look at the gun and then each other as if thinking the same thing about Anyo's intention.

"You can get some rest, Amiku. I'm not that tired," Kito says.

"You don't trust people, do you?" Anyo questions as he squirms in his chair looking for a comfortable spot.

"Not trusting people has kept me alive." Anyo smiles and leans back in the chair.

"I can't argue with that logic."

Anyo appears to have fallen asleep almost right away, but neither Kito nor Amiku are planning on sleeping much this night. Anyo had given Amiku more information about O.D.E and her father than she would have been able to find any place else, but she must question the authenticity of his story. How much of it is true? How much of it has been embellished or changed? Maybe she's overthinking it. It's easy to assume everything means something, when in fact it means nothing at all.

4

Kito's Past

The morning begins overcast with a cool wind and the promise of rain soon to arrive. Anyo makes good on his word and prepares to accompany Kito and Amiku to their shelter. Neither feels this act of neighborly kindness is necessary, but perhaps it's wise not to burn any bridges unless absolutely certain they will not be needed.

The voyage is a pleasant one as Anyo enjoys talking and sharing his knowledge about O.D.E. related topics. He explains the bullet he used on the watcher the day before was developed by the weapons and warfare department. They're called exploding bullets and are on a timer as soon as they leave the barrel of the gun. Within moments of entering the victim's body they detonate. Curious about the island off the coast, Amiku asks about that as well. Anyo is aware of it and calls it, Raptor Island. It was another failed O.D.E. experiment called, Guard Dog in which they bred raptors to hunt the demon population; however, the trainers became first to be on the menu.

Amiku decides not to mention Ardian or Nydia to Anyo when he inquires about other people in the area. She doesn't want to bring them into a situation if she realizes Anyo cannot be trusted. She always tries to have a backup plan or an exit strategy, the more knowledge she has, the less power her enemies have.

When the group arrives, they discover a single goblin digging in the ground near Amiku's shielded cabin. Kito reaches behind him and draws his sword. The goblin looks up and lets out a yelp before running in the opposite direction.

"Don't let it get away, Kito or you will have an entire clan here by nightfall," Anyo advises. Kito and Amiku exchange looks, but the threat of more goblins showing up is a plausible one.

"Alright, I'll be back in a few minutes," Kito says.

"Be careful!" Amiku yells after him as he jogs away.

"Don't worry, he'll be fine," Anyo says.

Amiku doesn't care for him making light of this incident. One goblin may not be a huge threat, but what if there are more nearby, or something else? They are a team, and no one lets a teammate fight a battle on their own. Amiku hopes this is not a moment she will regret later.

She deactivates the shield and then leads Anyo into the cabin. She sets her katana on the workbench before walking over to the monitor and taps a key several times. The image of the cabin and its surroundings fade into view.

"This is my security system," she begins. "It also controls the indestructible shield that was just over my cabin," Amiku explains.

"Fascinating, I heard about this project before it went into development. How did Charles know about it?"

"My father helped design it. He used to be in technology and programming before being moved to chemicals and chemistry."

"Charles never told me he was in technology. He was holding out on me," Anyo chuckles. "I started out in weapons and warfare and then was placed in shelters before finally becoming part of chemistry. Do you mind if I take a look into the user settings? My hatch has all the necessary hardware and I want to see if there is a way to copy this program."

"Sure, I guess."

"Thank you. It would be nice to have a pair of eyes on the

outside before I open the door, you know?" Amiku smiles.

"Makes sense. I didn't even know it had user settings."

Anyo smiles and approaches the monitor as Amiku watches.

"It's a computer program with files, folders, data, metadata, and coding. All the things software needs to do what we design it to do."

Anyo holds down several keys and then types keyboard commands. For someone who never worked on this project he apparently has knowledge of this program and how to hack into it. A black screen appears with lines of white text and abbreviations.

"Ah, here it is." Anyo continues typing in developer commands with an acute understanding of its inner workings and coding language. Maybe he's just savvy with technology, or maybe he knows more than he's sharing. "Hmm, interesting."

"What?"

"It seems this program wasn't fully activated. It's only operating at eighty percent."

"But the shield and the cameras work fine."

"Yes, those have been activated, but there is more to this program than just that."

Anyo continues typing on the keyboard while inputting symbols and letters which appear to be random and without meaning. The screen turns blue and then black.

"It's just restarting," he assures Amiku before she has a chance to question his actions.

The O.D.E logo appears followed by a status bar slowly loading. Within a few moments the screen fades to a white background and a computerized male voice is heard from a hidden speaker somewhere on the ceiling.

"A.I dash Eye, property of O.D.E., advanced security system, activated and functional. Please standby, searching for geographical location."

Amiku looks up trying to find the source of the voice. "I never knew this was possible," Amiku says with astonishment.

"Yes, artificial intelligence has come a long way. This program can see, hear, and communicate as well as make cognitive decisions. It's just like a real person and is capable of learning as well as teaching. From what I saw in its files it also has a sensitivity to human emotions which was impossible until a few years ago."

"The current time is 1:46PM, it will be dark in 6.3 hours, please plan accordantly. The temperature is 72°F. Good afternoon, Anyo."

"How does it know your name?" Amiku asks confused.

"While I was setting it up, I indicated my name, and it stored that information. There is one last thing I should tell you about this program. It registers its owner's fingerprints during setup and will only obey them," Anyo laughs. "Which means, I no longer need you."

"What?" Amiku's fears are starting to become a reality.

"I control this system now. Ever since I heard about this project, I've tried to get close to it. If I had known Charles helped design it, I would have tried to get him on my side. His secrets were his downfall."

"What aren't you telling me about my father?!"

Amiku puts her hand to her side to grab her katana but forgot she had removed it. She turns to the workbench, but it's no longer there.

"Did you lose something little one? You know you shouldn't leave things just lying around." Anyo reaches behind his back and takes out her katana. "Anyone can just pick it up."

"Bastard, I should have known you were up to something."

"Such hush words, very unladylike. Didn't your father teach you any manners? Speaking of your father, I'm about to reunite you with him, you should be thanking me."

"You were planning this ever since you learned who I was?"

"Stupid girl. I already knew who you were. I was waiting for my moment to come here and earn your trust, but you came to me instead."

"Why?"

"It's nothing personal. We just can't have any loose ends."

"You're still working for O.D.E.?"

"No, there is no more O.D.E. But your existence still threatens our goals; you should have been killed with your father."

Amiku jumps up and spins a kick into Anyo's ribs to send him into the wall. He pushes himself away and regains his posture.

"That's right, Charles told me you were good in gymnastics and that you also studied parkour after high school. Fascinating sport, but it won't help you here."

Amiku attempts a high kick to Anyo's chest, but he blocks it with his forearm and then strikes with the katana. Amiku backflips and lands upside-down on her hands before pushing off and continuing the flip to land on her feet. She squats down in pain to notice her leg was slightly cut in the process.

"Very impressive, you do have a talent for that. But you have no chance of winning against me. I told you that some of the scientists took the demon DNA serum. What I didn't tell you is that I was one of them." Anyo paces in front of Amiku. "I was unique, I didn't become a slave to the blood, but merged with it. I've been hiding it, but my increased strength and speed will be too much for you to outmaneuver, especially now with a wounded leg." Anyo reaches into his pocket to take out a small flask and then places it on top of the workbench.

"I will give you a choice. Stand up and drink the serum or stay hunched over and die by your own blade."

"You like making deals, don't you? Then I have a deal for you. Give me my sword and I'll only stab you once with it." Anyo smirks.

"You are your father's daughter. He didn't take the serum either. He said it wasn't worth the risk of losing one's own humanity. I think if something has a chance of making you stronger it's always worth the risk. But a missing bottle had to be accounted for. I had no choice, really. In order to avoid prosecution, I had to give a name to O.D.E. Conveniently, Charles had already left." Amiku's eyes swell up with tears, but her mouth remains in a tightly clamped frown. "I gave them your name as well, but somehow fate kept you away." Amiku responds in a calm, determined tone.

"I will destroy every fiber of your essence so you cannot even exist on a subatomic level."

Anyo raises the katana and brings it down over Amiku, but she rolls out of the way. He turns around and swings at Amiku's neck faster than she can react.

"Amiku!" Kito shouts. His sword clings against the katana's

blade with a successful block. Amiku is safe behind Kito who has returned just in time.

"I don't know how you blocked that," Anyo says surprised. A normal human wouldn't be able to block Anyo's demonic speed, but Kito's secret ability to slow down movements while speeding up his defensive reaction times was something Anyo did not expect. He now knows there is something special about Kito. But before the battle can continue another unexpected event unfolds.

"Default settings overwritten," the computerized voice begins.

"What the hell?" Anyo utters.

"Previous settings deleted, please stand by for reboot."

Kito looks around with a baffled expression.
"Amiku—?"
"I'll explain later, Kito."

"All settings activated, loading new A.I," a new soft, female voice takes over. *"My name is Ania, your personalized security system. I am now fully operational. Hello Amiku. Welcome home."*

Amiku's tears stream down her cheeks after hearing the voice of her dearly departed mother.
"Damn it!" Anyo yells. "Charles must have reprogrammed this unit with the likeness of his late wife."

"It seems you have an unwelcomed guest in your midst. Would you like me to kick him out, Amiku?

"Yes," she answers calmly, but sternly.
A blue lightning bolt shoots out of the wall and explodes into Anyo's back as he attempts to escape through the door. Amiku picks up her katana after Anyo dropped it during the attack. She advances outside toward him just as he rolls over onto his back and looks up at Amiku. She points the tip of her sword over his heart, but Anyo only laughs.

"You don't have it in you."

"I'm afraid you are mistaken," she replies calmly. "I most definitely have it in me."

She pushes the blade deep into Anyo's chest—he gurgles and gasps as blood oozes out from the side of his mouth. As soon as his eyes close and his head falls to the side she withdraws her sword from the lifeless body and then limps back to Kito.

"I'm sorry, Amiku. I shouldn't have left." She shakes her head as tears run down her cheeks. She now knows her father was betrayed, and supposedly by a friend. Kito softly puts his hand on her forearm; she falls into him and embraces him while burying her face in his chest. She allows this moment of grief to consume her. She trusts Kito will be her strength until she recovers from this sudden crippling weakness she feels. He keeps his arms around her until she begins wiping her tears away.

"Thank you, Kito." She pulls away from him and heads back into the cabin with him following.

Kito notices the flask that Anyo had sat down and picks it up. Amiku glances back to see him admiring it in his hands.

"Put that down, Kito." He stares at the swirling liquid inside. As if it has a mind of its own and is trying to hypnotize him.

"Is this the serum he was talking about?" he asks. Amiku stands in front of him with an open hand.

"Please hand that to me now," she demands, but Kito ignores her command.

"Can this tiny bit really give you power?" Kito continues appearing to be in a trance. Amiku fears he's contemplating about taking the serum and needs to snap him away from the temptation. "I feel drawn to this. Like it's a drug," he admits. The blood swirls different shades of red and becomes more active while in his grasp—something about Kito is making it react.

"Kito!" Amiku says louder.

"I could use this to fight people like him. I won't become him."

"It will be out of your control. It's not worth it. Kito, this is the last time I will ask for it!" Amiku keeps a firm grip on her katana as she watches Kito intensely. His heart beats faster and the blood begins to bubble. Amiku places her other hand over Kito's hand that's holding the flask. He finally lets out his breath and loosens his hold on the serum. Amiku quickly closes her fingers around it and takes it away. The liquid stops all forms of activity and returns to a single shade of red as soon as she snatches it. She immediately takes it outside and drops it on the ground before cracking it into pieces under her foot. She then turns around to see Kito watching her action.

"I know something is eating away at you," Amiku says. "You don't have to tell me, but I want you to know that I think you are better than it." Kito doesn't respond, but it also doesn't escape Amiku's attention that for once he has shown vulnerability. Kito can't quite think of a way to tell Amiku how he felt like someone else while holding that flask. It was a strange energy, his body, but not his mind.

Back inside the cabin, Amiku is elevating her leg on top of the table while Kito wraps a cloth around her cut.

"I hope you aren't planning on keeping this a routine," he says attempting to lighten the mood.

"No Kito, from now on I'll let you get all cut up," she jokes. "How did it go with that goblin?" she continues.

"I guess it didn't like me chasing it. At some point it stopped and then tried attacking me."

"What happened?" Kito smirks.

"It was too slow." Amiku giggles.

"Dead goblins tell no tales," she says.

The mid-autumn thunderstorm arrives just as expected and the two remain indoors for the remainder of the day. Ania activates the cabin's shield through Amiku's voice and even though it isn't really her, Amiku is comforted knowing her mother is watching over her once again.

The next morning, Anyo's body is discovered to have mysteriously vanished from the spot where he had died. The reason is simply agreed to be the result of nightly hunters. Demonoids, goblins, raptors; some creature or thing sought out a free meal and left zero trace of it behind. The truth may never be known, but at least for now this explanation satisfies Kito's and Amiku's curiosities. After all, it's not completely out of the realm of believability.

Anyo's demise does present a potential benefit to the four survivors of Copper Bay with a new place to live. Amiku leads her new friends to Anyo's hatch as she and Kito fill them in on the events from the previous day. Anyo's betrayal may have been a blessing in disguise as winter is fast approaching and the hatch offers a far better shelter than a truck cab or a log cabin with no fireplace.

The hatch was designed to house two comfortably, but four can still be acceptable with a little rearranging of the living room area. The new shelter offers the team the ability to store more food, cook, keep up on hygiene, and stay warm; all of which are essential during the brutal and unpredictable winter months.

Amiku gives Ardian and Nydia the full tour as Kito discovers a monitor and keyboard behind one of the cabinet doors. He turns on the screen to the message, *No Program Loaded.* Anyo mentioned that it may be possible to load Amiku's security system at the hatch as well. If that's true, this move almost has no downside unless you factor in Kito's likelihood of being civilized with his roommates for an extended time period.

Each group returns to their own shelters to make the necessary preparations and gather supplies. The voyage on foot makes it impossible to take anything large or heavy, but Amiku packs her potions and potted Adonia plant. Kito has nothing of value that belongs to him so he works on loading Ania onto an external hard drive so the program can be installed at the hatch.

Meanwhile, Ardian and Nydia are gathering their food and medical supplies at their shelter. Ardian stands outside giving the cab a long heartfelt stare. It was his home for so long it's almost hard for him to say goodbye to it. Nydia smiles and gently rubs his back.

"This is the last time we will be back here," Ardian says.

"Maybe it is, and maybe that's okay," Nydia says supportively.

Ardian and Nydia meet up with Kito and Amiku at the cabin and the group makes their final voyage to the hatch. Just like Ardian felt about his truck cab is how Amiku feels about her cabin. Her things, her space, her father's last gift to her. She's leaving it all behind. The hatch doesn't have a need for the Tintuntanium metal shield as it is completely underground, but she will miss that security feature too. Everyone can agree the hatch is the better shelter, but it's never easy to leave something behind that's familiar.

Today, two teams of two become one team of four—this will be their future. They have a long road ahead of them and leaving this valley is only the beginning. Nothing beyond this moment will be easy and the days will be far from unpredictable. Man, and demon will clash in furious conflicts, and when the dust settles no one will be quite the same. Survival is defined as merely being alive, but living is thriving. Earth is a demonic inhabited wasteland, thriving here means only one thing—preparing for war.

The team spends the next several hours rearranging furniture and working out sleeping arrangements. Kito finds the reading chair and ottoman to his liking while Amiku and Nydia decide to occupy the queen-sized bed. Ardian lucks out with finding extra blankets, pillows, and cushions in one of the drawers to make a worthy daybed fit for a stately manner.

Kito connects the hard drive to the all-in-one computer and monitor system and begins the installation process. A loading bar slowly starts creeping across the bottom of the screen along with a countdown timer, 6:24:59.

"This will take over six hours," Kito says impatiently.

"What do we do for six hours?" Ardian asks.

"Anyo said there was an army camp not far from here. We could check that out," Amiku suggests.

"Yea, but do you trust anything he said," Kito questions.

"Not everything, but I still think it's worth familiarizing ourselves with our new surroundings," Amiku points out. It's a valid reason to motivate the team into their first exploratory mission around their new home. Either they find an army camp, or they don't, but then at least they would have mapped one location of the area.

A twenty-minute walk brings them to a clearing with dirt roads and pebble walkways. Anyo seemed to have been right about an old camp being here after all. The army base consists of six buildings. On one side of the clearing is a clinic, identified by the red cross above its doorway. Occupying the opposite side is a large shed, with a shield logo to indicate it's an armory. The white building, in the center of the base, is the largest building and shows an emblem of crossed utensils, hinting that it was once the cafeteria. Lastly, there are three long barracks at the far end of the clearing with a bed icon above their doors. It can be assumed that this locale housed about sixty soldiers, but whether this was used as a training ground, or a checkpoint remains shrouded in secrecy.

"This place has been vacant for a long time," Amiku begins.

"Who knows what may be lurking in these buildings."

"Okay, so where do we go first?" Ardian asks. Kito begins walking toward the armory without uttering a word or giving a clue that he's interested heading in that direction. Searching for food and water from the cafeteria would have been Amiku's first choice, but there's no point of making a suggestion now or trying to call Kito back. He didn't want to debate it; he was going to do what he wanted and cared not about the feelings of his teammates. Amiku lets out an annoyed sigh.

"I guess we are going that way."

The armory door breaks loose from its hinges and falls to the floor sending a cloud of dust into the air. Swords, knives, and guns are sprawled across the tables or still hanging on the wall racks. These guns have no clips or spare bullets that match the caliber required to make them operable. The clips that are found also clearly go to guns that are not among the ones stored here. It would have been nice to get a hold of better firepower, but everything here is missing a vital component to make it viable. Ardian picks up a sword and lightly taps the blade on the edge of the table. The blade breaks loose from the hilt and clings to the floor. He lets the useless hilt and guard drop nearby while making an expression that proves his low expectations about finding something here were correct.

"This looks to be a bust. Everything in here is crap," Ardian says.

Nydia finds an intact compound bow on another table and begins inspecting it. She pulls back the bowstring and then the cams, limb, and sight. It glides easily and seems to be in great shape.

"This bow looks almost brand new," she says.

"Yeah, but how's your aim? Kito asks in a snarky tone. Nydia keeps her focus on him for a moment before taking an arrow out of the nearby quiver and then heads back outside. Everyone follows her to see what she's planning to do.

She loads the arrow and then raises the bow into firing position. She takes aim at the center of the red cross, above the clinic's door, more than twenty-five yards away. She takes a long breath in and then holds it before firing the arrow. The team watches with anticipation until the arrow successfully hits dead center of the red cross. Nydia looks back at Kito and smirks.

"How's that?" Amiku and Ardian giggle, but Kito just slowly shakes his head with a bewildered look.

"All you had to say was you knew how to shoot—showoff."

"That's Kito's way of saying good job," Amiku jokes.

The carefree moment soon becomes more serious when a loud explosion of splintering wood rings out from the other side of the camp. A large hole is now in the side of one of the barracks and stepping through it is a demonoid wearing plated armor and wielding a sword. Two men seem to have stumbled upon it while they were scavenging and are now in a heated battle. The demonoid's swinging arm knocks one of the men flying backwards as it lifts its sword over the second man. Suddenly, Nydia's arrow sores into the beast's temple. A small stream of blood runs down its cheek, but it fails to stop the monstrosity.

Ardian is quick to smash his mace into the demonoid's chest as Kito slashes the demonoid behind its knees. This forces the monster to lose its balance just long enough for Amiku to pierce her katana through its neck. The well-orchestrated attack by this team finally brings the beast down.

"Wow, you killed it," one of the men says surprised and relieved at the same time.

"We've dealt with these before," Amiku says modestly.

"You guys aren't from the fort, are you?" the second man asks when he joins them.

"We did hear a rumor about a fort being a day's journey from here," Kito reiterates.

"A day? That must be a different one. Ours is only half an hour away," the man confirms.

"Maybe an hour tops with supplies and gear, but no more than that," the second man adds. Kito and Amiku figured Anyo was flat out fibbing about some things and telling half-truths about everything else.

"Our commander will be very interested in meeting all of you. Good fighters are scarce in times like these."

The group had wanted to continue exploring the camp for more food and supplies but figured they could always do that on their return trip. Normally they wouldn't follow two strangers to an unknown location, especially now that they have a hatch waiting for them and software that still needs to finish being installed. But the concept of a fort being this close with a population, and the fact that Anyo did not want them to find it, has stirred everyone's curiosity. Even Kito agrees that finding out what this place is all about is worth changing their initial plans for.

The two men lead the group out of the forest and into a large pasture facing the distant sandstone and granite cliffs. The remainder of the forest borders the upper and lower portions of this vast open area. A short trek across the field ultimately brings everyone to their destination.

The stone fort is a five-story construction that's built into the mountainous granite cliffs behind it and consists of cutout portions for open windows and archways that lead onto small lookout balconies. It's a marvel to behold and looks to be well maintained and very secure. Guards and militiamen stand guard on the balconies with ready crossbows or on the ground near the entrance with long swords hanging from their belts. The group continues through the large archway entrance with its raised metal gate.

The watchful guards glare at the new faces suspiciously and a tiny crowd of people gather nearby while whispering amongst themselves who the newcomers may be. The two men ask their guests to wait just inside the entrance while they set out to locate and notify their commander to meet them. The foursome has little choice but to wait for the leader of this fort to arrive, but they also get the feeling their presence is not wanted.

A tall, skinny man named, Lazul pushes his way through the crowd disrespectfully and glares at the strangers intensely before speaking in a deep, raspy tone.

"Well, well, well, it seems we are running short on everything except fools. I don't know what you hope to accomplish here, but the inn is full, and we don't give charity." Amiku is first to respond to this man's rudeness.

"You sound like you have a lot of personal problems. You should go deal with them." Lazul scowls and snaps his head to face her directly.

"Besides fools, I hate whores more."

Amiku immediately brings her katana to Lazul's neck as Kito backs her up by positioning his sword at Lazul's chest. The guards become alert of the hostility and draw their swords toward Kito and Amiku. Ardian takes out his sword and Nydia pulls her loaded bow back as both defend Kito and Amiku from the guards. The tension doesn't let up as Lazul continues his taunting.

"Do you see everyone? These strangers, under the guise of lost sheep, actually mean us harm." Lazul's ploy works, and the surrounding citizens begin to shout and holler their demands.

"Kill them!"

"Protect the fort!"

Lazul doesn't care about the safety of the guards or the general public who resides in the fort. He only cares about riling up others in his favor or increasing his status and power over them. He is the quintessential vile mastermind who knows how to use the emotions of others against them or to his benefit. He's a plotter, a conspirator, and a saboteur who's hell-bent on usurping the fort from its current leaderships. Lazul isn't yet content and feels one more jab will be enough to trigger a deadly fight. He leans in close to Amiku with a heinous smile to antagonize her further.

"I will slit your throat and pass your corpse from demon to demon so they may defile you even in death."

"I will lob off your head before your next breath!" Kito shouts.

"I dare you to make good on your threats and meet your end as well!" Lazul snaps back.

The onlookers continue yelling and waving their fists in the air as the arguing proves to soon be the spark that ignites the use of weapons. More guards have descended the stairs from the higher levels and now surround the warring parties. Bloodshed is deadly close to being unavoidable, but a booming voice soon echoes throughout the fort.

"Enough!!" The crowd falls to a deathly silence almost instantaneously while parting to give the man an easy path to the front.

His name is Anthulios but goes by Lio for short. He' the commander of the fort and is strong both mentally and physically. The people hold him in high regard and consider him to be a fair and just leader, along with his captains. Anthulios will offer aid and support to where, and who needs it, but he demands respect and his rules obeyed in exchange. Order and laws must be upheld, and deviants must be prosecuted accordantly, yet he's not without compassion.

"I've kept the peace in this place for far too long to have it disrupted now over some petty quarrel! No human blood shall be shed on these stones as long as I'm commander here! Now, lower your weapons!"

Weapons remain raised with no one willing to back down. Anthulios' gaze falls upon Kito and his expression changes to shock.

"Kito—?"

"Lio," he confirms.

"Please Kito, lower your weapon." Anthulios calmly says in hopes that talking to a long-lost friend might help to diffuse the boiling situation.

"This creature insulted my friend," Kito nudges his chin towards Lazul who can be seen grinding his teeth.

"I will deal with him," Anthulios says.

Out of respect for a past friend, and their experiences together, Kito reluctantly lowers his sword. His action also signals his teammates to follow suit. The guards then relax their weapons, and an unnecessary battle is avoided. Anthulios then turns to Lazul.

"Do you always have to be an instigator? Go back to your work." Lazul glares at Kito one last time before walking away. "Break it up everyone. Go back to your posts and assigned duties," Anthulios says as he swings his arms in a sweeping motion to disburse the crowd and guards. Now with the area cleared Anthulios can turn his attention back to Kito and the others. "You have to excuse the behavior of my men and our citizens. Everyone is a little on edge these days."

"Who was that walking dead talking shit?" Kito asks.

Lazul is in the company of several men who are still glaring at him in the background. The men pass a bottle amongst themselves while laughing and patting Lazul on the back. Even when Lazul is chugging down the bottle he remains focused on Kito with a threatening stare. These men admire Lazul and look up to him for some unknown reason. Perhaps they are all rabble-rousers, who like to congratulate one another for committing mischievous acts and creating unrest. Anthulios explains his feelings as he makes eye contact with everyone in Kito's party.

"His name is Lazul. I've kept an eye on him ever since his arrival. He's always involved in almost every brawl in one way or another and his hatred for others run deeper than I care to explore. Unfortunately, he has sway over some of the population and I can't take action against him without a riot breaking out. Personally, I don't consider him a moral person and I don't condone your actions against him." Anthulios looks back at Kito. "You know what happened last time the peace was broken, Kito. I won't make the same mistake twice. I'm responsible for too many lives here. Outside these walls, I care not of his fate." Anthulios motions the group to follow him further into the fort. "Follow me, I can set you up with a room for the night."

"That may not be needed," Amiku says fearing another encounter like Anyo's, but she's a little more at ease here knowing that Kito and Lio seem to have a history. Regardless, the team follows Anthulios up a flight of stairs and then down a narrow hallway.

"Is your base nearby?" Lio asks.

"South of the camp," Kito replies.

"South? Towards Copper Bay?"

"That's right," Amiku confirms.

"You have guts leaving so close to that city. I have reports that it was overrun by goblins and demons."

"The countryside wasn't too bad at first, but I will admit encounters are becoming more frequent," Ardian says.

"Something is happening," Nydia adds.

"Yes, we can feel it too," Anthulios agrees. He opens one of the doors on their right and leads everyone into the medium sized room with a table and chairs near the right wall, two twin beds in the middle and two recliners on the left side. The floor is covered with several area rugs and the cut-out window overlooks the meadow and part of a swamp to the left. "I hope this will suffice; we are a little short on space." This room has stolen the thunder away from the cramped living quarters of the hatch, and on the very first day of their move too. But no one is planning on making this fort their new home and will be returning to their own shelter in the morning. "I will also get someone to bring you dinner. I would let you go yourselves, but I don't think the general population will be happy if I let strangers roam freely."

"We understand, thank you for your hospitality, Ardian says. Anthulios gently lays his hand on Kito's shoulder and smiles. "I'm glad you survived; we have to catch up some time, but please rest for now." Kito smiles and nods before Anthulios departs.

Several minutes later a teenage boy carries in a platter of bread, carrots, and fish and sits it on the table. A teenage girl accompanies him with a pitcher of water and four plastic cups. She fills the glasses on the table and then places the pitcher on the platter. The teenagers smile at Amiku and Nydia who thanks them very politely while Ardian and Kito start eating.

"This actually doesn't look bad at all," Ardian observes. The girls join them and the four begin eating and drinking their fill.

Kito is oblivious to the fact that everyone is looking at him until he glances up from his meal. His team is eager to know the details surrounding his and Lio's past.

"So, Lio, that's his name, right?" Nydia begins. Kito nods but doesn't get the hint. "The two of you seem to have some history," she continues. Kito nods again, but again fails to understand she's prying for a little more information. Amiku is more direct.

"How do the two of you know each other?"

"That's kinda a long story," Kito says.

"It looks like we are here for the night, so it appears there's plenty of time," Amiku responds. Kito hesitates at first.

"Yeah, what are the mysteries that surround the man known as Kito," Ardian joins in. Kito takes a sip of water and then offers up a few pieces from his past.

"Not much to say, really. Five-minutes after I was born, I died." Kito observes everyone is listening to him now with their undivided attention after his chosen opening. "My lungs hadn't fully developed, and I needed to live on some machine for the first year of my life. My mother told me the last thing my father said, before he walked out, was that he didn't want a weak son. I never knew who he was and that was the longest conversation I had with her.

She was never home for long or sometimes never came home at all. She liked her cocktails and she liked whoever bought them for her more. She must have found some fun place to stay because she disappeared sometime when I was fifteen. Never found out what happened. She either decided to run away with someone, or her lifestyle caught up to her. I didn't really care; she stopped being a mother as soon as I learned to walk. My family became a group of people who liked the night life and knew how to make fast cash. By the time I was in my twenties, most of that crew was in prison or on the run. I didn't find my place in this world until after it ended—"

Demon sightings are just beginning to appear in Copper Bay with amateur videos going viral and the evening news entertaining the fascination about strange reports and spine-chilling creatures that haunt the imagination. This soon develops into more cautionary broadcast warnings, rules, and survival tips. It isn't long before civilization is in disarray and order can no longer be upheld. Neighborhoods deal with this by becoming their own villages and adopting their own set of rules.

Kito is wandering around concrete roadblocks which had been placed on alternating sides of a quiet residential street. He appears to be on an aimless hike with no destination in sight and, without a weapon or supplies of any kind, he's surely ill-equipped for the times. Anthulios is standing guard ahead of him near a pair of roadblocks blocking the gate to a fenced in neighborhood.

"Hey, where do you think you are? Sunday afternoon at the beach? Where's your weapon? Anthulios calls out as Kito walks past.

"I don't have one," he admits. Kito can see watch towers rising above the fence posts and hear sawing and hammering of some construction project taking place from within. "What's going on in there?" he asks.

"We're fortifying homes and strengthening our defenses," Anthulios replies. "Where are you heading?"

"I don't really know yet." Anthulios picks up a sword that's leaning against a pile of wooden planks and then hands it to him.

"Here, you should have a means to defend yourself." Kito takes the sword from him as he continues. "Have you used a sword before?"

"No," Kito admits. Anthulios shakes his head slowly.

"Not sure how well you're going to do on your own, kid, but we could use the help if you want to stay with us."

Kito attempts to come across as someone who will be fine on their own, but he eventually takes Lio's offer and for the first time, in a long time, has a home and a place to belong. He also proves to be a fast learner with the blade under Lio's tutelage as they spar with one another in the cooler evening hours. Kito is finally ready to take his place in the militia and becomes a soldier and defender.

He and Anthulios, along with some other men dispatch a small group of goblins that managed to scale the village walls. One of the men is scratched by the last goblin, but it's such a minor wound that no one thinks anymore of it. This event is celebrated as a victorious battle where every threat was annihilated, and no human life was lost. What reason did anyone have to make a fuss about a scratch? A scratch that ended up not only damning the one who was inflicted but also the entire society.

It took a week for the man to change. He was once a good friend, a trusted soldier, and a loving husband, but he's now strapped down to a cot as a growling monster; infected by a poison that kills the heart, but not the brain.

"We are all at risk and he's unfortunately past the point of our help," Anthulios says during a town meeting. "It's with a heavy heart that I suggest we put him to rest." Those who attended this meeting bow their heads and understand the difficult decision that had to be made. Those who decided not to take part never had a chance to voice their rejection.

That night, Anthulios enters the man's quarters to find him wide awake and still snarling. He draws a pistol and points it at the man's head. "I do apologize for this. You were a good man and I hope you can understand and forgive my decision." The demonized man growls and tries to free himself to attack Anthulios. The pull of his trigger silences the man, but the sound of the gunshot does nothing to restore the peace.

The man's wife is past reasoning with; she wants revenge, and the population is split. Some side with her while others stand by Anthulios' choice. The debate eventually turns violent, and weapons are turned on each other. While everyone is fighting amongst themselves no one is watching the gates as imps and demons ransack through the neighborhood.

Kito is on top of one of the watch towers when he finds a man who is no longer loyal to Anthulios. When he refuses to betray him, the man puts a dagger in Kito's side and then pushes him off the ledge. He falls into a patch of evergreen bushes and nothing more from that event can he recall. The bushes may have saved him from sustaining a life-threatening injury, but he is still sore when he regains conscience.

The scene is that of a battlefield. Maimed bodies lie in the street or lawns and puddles of blood pool like the aftermath of a heavy rain. Slain people and imps share their final resting place together and homes are battered and burning. Nothing is salvageable; this safe haven is lost. He searches for any sign of someone that may still be alive but all who had survived left a long time ago; all that remains now is carnage. He is somewhat glad not to find Lio's body, but that also means he was left behind. Kito is once again on his own, but what happens soon after this, will haunt him fiercely.

"That was about a year ago now." Kito finishes his story and has given his teammates some insight into his past.

"That's about the same time I got separated from my sister too," Nydia recalls.

"Yeah, everyone seemed to have disappeared at the same time," Kito replies.

The cool night breeze suggests it's a good time to get under their blankets or covers and try to sleep. The girls take the beds and Ardian and Kito claim their recliners. After the wholesome meal, and their adventurous day, the four drift to sleep in no time.

The sunrise awakes Nydia from sleep as she observes that even now there's still such a thing as a beautiful morning. The warm sun and the trees in full color make a picturesque scene. A smile comes over her as she admires the quietness of dawn and the gorgeous landscape—like a princess from her castle tower. Eventually, Amiku and Ardian awake to find her gazing out the window, but Amiku soon discovers that Kito isn't among them.

"Where's Kito?" She asks. Nydia turns around to see only an unfolded blanket on the recliner where he had slept.

"I didn't even look over when I woke up," she says feeling guilty.

Kito woke up long before dawn and had snuck out of the room. His thoughts kept him up most of the night and his memories continue to wake him. His companions set out to look for him as they follow the stairs down to the first floor. They stop in the stairwell when they hear Kito and Anthulios talking around the corner.

"Have you been back to Copper Bay?" Anthulios asks.

"No, too many ghosts."

"I did look for you that day. I just couldn't find you."

"You wouldn't have found me."

"What happened?"

"Some guy I never met decided he didn't like me. When I finally came to everything was gone."

"I should've stayed by you," Lio says while shaking his head.

"How were we to know what was going to happen?"

"It was still my fault."

"I don't think anything would have mattered. Sometimes the only choice we get is to surrender or die."

Amiku and the others step around the corner to reveal their presence. Kito glances at them before turning back to Anthulios. "I think we'll get an early start today." Lio looks up at the sun and nods his head.

"It's a good time to do so." He places a hand on Kito's bicep and shakes his hand with the other. "Take care, Kito and stop by again sometime." Kito nods and smiles as Ardian and Nydia thanks Lio for the room and last night's dinner. The three began walking outside through the archway while Amiku also gives her gratitude to Lio.

"Thank you again for the hospitality," she repeats.

"It was no problem at all," Lio replies. Amiku begins to follow her friends when Lio grabs her attention again. "Amiku, take care of him for me. He has a good heart; he just doesn't know it yet." She glances at Kito who's walking away.

"I'll keep an eye on him," she promises.

After a final wave the foursome retraces their steps back towards the army camp to hopefully finish what they set out to do the day before. Along the route Amiku ponders why Anthulios told her to watch Kito for him. Does he suspect something will happen to him, or that he's troubled in some way, or is it just something one person says to another before leaving? Another question on her mind is why he chose her? Maybe he assumes they are more than just acquaintances, or that he thinks she is more capable of keeping him in line. Amiku knows Kito is hiding something and maybe Lio picked up on it too. In the end Kito is only good at lying to himself.

They reach the army camp in a little over thirty-minutes and begin looking for food in the cafeteria. Ardian finds a box of MREs and picks it up. These meals are a far cry from the one they had last night, but when starvation kicks in this will taste like a steak dinner. With nothing further to claim from the cafeteria, the group makes their way to the clinic next. There isn't much here except for a few boxes of band-aids carelessly thrown on the floor.

"No medical supplies should ever be left behind," Nydia explains and retrieves the ignored boxes.

Once outside the group contemplates if it's worth checking out the barracks. They already claimed what they could from everywhere else, but a steady rumbling underground halts the discussion. It sounds like thunder, but feels like a slight earthquake, yet neither time nor place meets the conditions for either. The rumbling gets louder and the ground shakes more violently as everyone remains motionless while listening.

"What is that?" Amiku asks, but no one can answer this mysterious event. The ground suddenly explodes upwards underneath Kito's feet. He is tossed into the air and falls on a steep hill that leads to an abrupt drop-off to the ocean below. Kito frantically tries to grab onto roots or bushes as he slides helplessly down the hill. Ardian dives after him in a rescue attempt as Kito spirals closer to the edge and certain death. His feet slide over the edge of the cliff just as a hand grabs his arm. Ardian is holding his sword, with its blade forced into the ground, as he pulls Kito up with his other. Kito is now able to find his footing and pulls himself the rest of the way onto land.

Meanwhile, Amiku and Nydia look up at the cause of the disturbance. If they thought a giant bat was the most unnatural sight one could behold, then this monstrous pit viper towering over them will make them reconsider that claim. Nydia takes aim and shoots an arrow at the giant's head, but its thick scales prevent the arrow from reaching its flesh. Amiku draws her sword and begins running around to the snake's rear. She isn't trying to strike this time but acts as a distraction so Nydia can get another shot in. The plan seems to be working as the snake lowers its head to follow behind Amiku. Nydia carefully aims her bow again and releases the arrow directly into the snake's eye. The agitated snake shakes its head violently while squirming and hissing. Amiku now takes offence and slices the serpent's soft underbody just as Kito and Ardian join her.

The snake opens its mouth and then strikes at Amiku. She flips onto her hands and carries it through until she's back on her feet to escape the attack. Kito gets an easy opening and takes it by slashing the snake under its jaw. It recoils and hisses again to expose its fangs. Nydia fires an arrow into the roof of the snake's mouth and then quickly takes a second shot to send another arrow through its forked tongue. Ardian, Kito and Amiku hurry to the snake's raised underbody and jab their swords in as far as they can push them. When they pull their swords back out blood gushes out like water from a damaged dam. The viper lets out one last hiss as its body curls before collapsing to the ground with a thud.

The vanquishing of the leviathan was the primary concern for the team, but now with that complete a discussion begins about another matter. Everyone knows if it hadn't been for Ardian, Kito would have fallen to his doom. The fact that Kito refuses to accept this fact, irks Amiku to a whole new level.

"You think you don't need anyone's help, do you?" She begins. "Well, I have news for you. You can't fight everything by yourself!"

Amiku's phrase triggers the memory Kito had been trying to suppress and it resurfaces with a vengeance. He can't hide or run from it this time and it becomes an unbearable burden on him as it shreds his insides. His defenses are down, his heart is heavy, his mind is filled with blame. Kito remembers the day his destiny changed—

It was several weeks since the fall of Anthulios' neighborhood and Kito had been on his own ever since, but he's now facing a new foe. It's the first time he encountered a person that resembled closer to a demon rather than a man. This man is demonized and still has enough of his own thoughts to talk, rationalize, and fight with his spear; however, his increased strength and speed is something Kito is not yet familiar with.

"You look determined to kill me, but all I smell is fear and doubt," the man says with delight.

"You are restricted with your spear, but I'm not that limited," Kito replies smugly.

"I will feast upon your roasted flesh when I skew you," the man responds.

Kito thinks he has the upper hand and dives in with a slicing motion. The man darts to his side and then thrusts his spear towards Kito. The quick action prevents Kito from reacting in time to defend himself or escape the oncoming spearhead. Another person intercepts with their sword colliding into the shaft of the spear to direct it upwards. This buys Kito the seconds he needs to reset himself and take his stance. Standing next to him is now a girl with red hair.

"Don't underestimate this creature, friend. It has abilities that make it tough to fight alone."

"I don't need any help," Kito replies.

"You can't fight everything by yourself," she says.

Kito ignores her and takes another swing at the demonized man. He deflects the sword away with his spear, and then slaps the pole against Kito's ribs. The sudden jolt drops him to his knees and his sword slides out of reach. Luckily, the girl rushes in to chop the spear in half with her sword. Kito grabs the front half of the spear and thrusts it through the back of the demon's neck while he's distracted blocking the girl's next attack. The demon frantically tries to remove the spearhead, but the girl runs her blade into his chest to finish it off.

"You see? Teamwork is how we fight these things. This isn't a game of egos," she says.

"I didn't want to involve you in my fight."

"Don't turn someone down who wants to help. It may not happen that often." Kito smirks, but the girl is suddenly forced into his arms and a sharp pain is felt in his lower stomach. She is frozen in place; her eyes are wide open, and her lips are slightly parted. Kito can see the demonized man kneeling behind her with the front half of the spear he had pulled out of his neck through her back. Blood gushes from the man's neck before he finally succumbs to the blood loose, but his last action was not in vain.

She gently pushes herself away from Kito to notice the bloody spear tip protruding out of her shirt. The spear had completely pierced through her body and partially into Kito's stomach. He catches her in his arms when her legs give out and eases her to the ground. Kito ignores his wound and regrettably holds her in his arms.

"I'm sorry, tell me what I can do." Her voice is weak, but clear.

"Nothing."

"There must be something," Kito's voice cracks and his eyes tear up. The girl smiles and strokes his cheek with her bloody hand.

"It's too late for me," she whispers. "And you will never be the same."

"What do you mean?"

"Blood ties—Blood that takes and blood that gives. You will never be the same." Kito doesn't understand her words but assumes it's because she's getting weaker. Her body becomes cold, and her breathing becomes softer.

"I cannot let you come to this fate, not through my action," he says sorrowfully.

"Do not be burdened with regret. What is your name, friend?"

"Kito."

"Kito, I will remember your name, and you will remember mine—"

The memory floods his senses once again. He can still feel her in his arms and hear her last dying breath. Her death has forever stained his hands with innocent blood. He becomes ostracized and unforgivable. His heart is heavy with sorrow, regret, blame, and anger. These self-loathing emotions merge with his ever-present fear of being weak to give him an unstable mentality. He finds himself whispering her name again, a name he had buried, but never forgotten.

"Sonya."

Nydia keeps a focused and piercing glare at Kito.

"What did you just say?" Kito glances up as she walks toward him with the same intense stare. "Did you say Sonya? Did you meet someone with that name?" Kito dreads the moment to follow. He asks a question but doesn't want to hear the answer.

"Do you know someone with that name?"

"Yes, she's my sister. Did she have red hair? Where was she? Is she okay? I've been trying to find her."

This cruel moment cannot be real. Of all the siblings Sonya could have had, why did Nydia have to be one of them. Kito's peace is forsaken; every moment is meant to torment him further. Kito doesn't respond, he can't answer, but this only agitates Nydia further. "Tell me, Kito!" He keeps his eyes low and refuses to look up. Nydia has reached her limit of patience with Kito while also being overwhelmed with worry for Sonya. Why isn't he answering her; she can't take his silence any longer. "Tell me!" Tears swell up in her eyes as she swings her arm out in front of her. This action immediately sends Kito soaring backwards and rolling across the ground. Everyone, including Nydia is taken by surprise.

"How did you do that?" Amiku asks in shock.

"I—I don't know. I was just mad," she admits. Nydia's heightened emotional state has allowed her to tap into a dormant telekinetic ability she always had. Now that it has been awakened, she will be able to use it as she sees fit, but first she will need to hone it with practice and concentration; only then will she master this power to its full potential.

Kito's guilt escapes in a fury of anger and sorrow as he slowly picks himself up.

"It's always in my head; it never goes away! It doesn't let me sleep; it's a thorn in everything I am! It was my fault." The others continue watching him in silence. They can guess where his explanation may be going and how it's affecting him, but they allow him to continue without interruption. "I wish I could go back to change it. It was my fight. Some demonized man. We thought he was dead—we were wrong." Kito lifts his shirt to show the scar left by the spear. "The reason why I can slow movements down is because I have demon blood in me; given to me by a spear, that demon pulled out of his neck, and after it went through Sonya." The group stares at him in disbelief. "I'm sorry, Nydia. It should have been me. She saved my life." Kito falls to his knees and pounds the ground with both fists. "She died in my arms!" Kito can't hold back his tears any longer and cries.

Nydia's worst fears have come true. Ardian wraps his arms around her as she weeps in his shoulder. Amiku kneels in front of Kito and tries to make eye contact with his lowered head.

"You've been keeping this bottled up inside of you all this time?"

"I'm not a person anymore, I'm cursed." Amiku lifts his head up from under his chin.

"Sometimes the biggest risk one has to make is to put their trust in someone else."

Nydia is still teary-eyed from learning the news of her sister's death, but Kito has given her the closure she needed.

"Sonya died fighting a beast, not saving one." Nydia's message hits Kito hard. He believes he deserves to be hated, instead he is shown compassion. "Honor her sacrifice by never giving up," she continues.

"We are a team of four and that will never change," Amiku adds.

Kito has been able to keep the demon blood in check and not fall victim to it. Either he's stronger than he realizes, or it has yet to fully test his resolve.

5

Lazul's War

Apocalypsia during the winter months resembles the surface of a frozen moon where the bitter cold wind turns the world into a solid hunk of an endless desolate tundra. No one ventures out of their shelters now unless they are scavenging for food, but well-planned groups have a cornucopia of food and supplies to limit their need to trek across the deep snow. The demons during the winter are just as fierce and agile as they are during the summer, but the intense cold and long, dark days put people at a disadvantage. Hibernation almost becomes necessary for survival and the longer one can stay hidden, the better their chances will be.

Anthulios' fort has a good stockpile of supplies and their guards have fixed thick, clear acrylic sheets over the windows to let in the light but limit the cold drafts. They have also erected a firepit in the large open entrance area to produce as much heat as they can.

With Ania successfully installed and in operation, the group of the underground hatch can spy on the outside without putting themselves in danger. Tracks in the snow show some creature was roaming nearby not too long ago. They also had planned accordingly and remain hunkered down in the warmth and security their shelter provides without sacrificing anything that's vital.

Nydia also takes this time to practice her newly discovered ability by concentrating on moving objects abound the hatch. At first, these are small items, such as a cup or pillow, but eventually advances to chairs and even lifting the bed two inches off the floor. There doesn't seem to be a limit to her power, as long as she continues using it. Day by day her control gets smoother and the time she needs to concentrate before an action begins lessens. She reaches the point where she can now use her ability on command and at will, without preparation. Soon she won't even need her hands to guide objects but will be able to do so by thought alone.

Six months of winter has come and gone, and spring returns to the world. The snow has melted away and the grass, flowers and trees are beginning to grow and blossom. But this gives a false impression of rebirth; the truth is a new storm is brewing and beginning to show itself on the horizon. Just because demons won the first war doesn't mean they won't declare another. They are no longer satisfied with the mere defeat of society and civilization, but now aim to annihilate life.

Anthulios and his captains, Rona, and Brax, oversee and order the civilians and guards who reside within the walls of the fort. Rona boasts an Eastern European accent and values physical fitness and hard work. Laziness and slacking off among her ranks are simply not allowed and are dealt with harshly. She's in charge of assigning duties to the guards, organizing training exercises, and checking the fort's defenses.

Brax keeps track of all food and supplies levels and their daily distribution to everyone, or when requested. He's a heavy-set man, but his excess weight doesn't slow him down or shorten his stamina. He's strong, muscular, and can outlast men half his size on the battlefield. He's also known to be laid back and easy going, but if provoked he can hold his own in a fight. He wields a battle axe with unyielding ferocity and prefers close combat with his enemies. He's also completely smitten by Rona and makes his feelings towards her very obvious, even though he may not always notice it. Unfortunately, Rona doesn't share the same admiration towards him and is no way shy when it comes to showing her annoyance or voicing her blatant opinions.

Today looks like a typical spring morning, but Rona gets a hint of a pungent odor in the air. She doesn't know what it is or where it's coming from, but she has a good inclination that it smells like trouble. She glances up to observe the sky and catches a glimpse of two guards on one of the balconies. They have their full attention on a cute woman carrying a basket of bread and rolls, while forsaking their assigned watch duties. Rona isn't happy seeing this behavior from her guards. They lack discipline if a flirty little tease can completely capture their attention.

These guards need to take their responsibilities more serious; she thinks to herself. *If there's an attack and no one is paying attention, we lose the best chance to repeal it.* The seclusion during winter and now the warmth and greenery of spring has made everyone forget the world they occupy. This is still a dangerous time, but everyone's defenses have suddenly come down. Rona decides to put the guards to work with some training exercises since it's obvious they do not have enough to do. She glares at the two soldiers still engrossed with the pretty woman and knows the first ones she will be sending to the yard.

The guards continue gossiping with the girl and do not notice Rona approaching.

"I always sleep naked," the girl teases.

"If you ever get cold, I'll be glad to keep you warm," one of the guards responds.

"I don't think your wife will be happy about that," the second chimes in.

"Bring her along," the woman entices the two guards as they laugh and cheer.

Rona puts her hand on the woman's shoulder and gently moves her aside to reveal her presence. The men immediately stand up straight and turn back to face the horizon.

"Am I to believe you only start working when you see me?" Rona says. She then turns to the girl while glancing at the basket of bread. "Unless all of those are for you, I'm assuming you have some place to be." The woman departs with a smile but no response.

"Sorry ma'am. It won't happen again," one of the guards answers.

"Bullshit! Both of you head to the training grounds immediately."

"Training? We've already passed all our training," the second guard boldly snaps back. Rona grabs the brave man by his collar and pulls him toward her.

"Are you arguing with me?! Maybe you want to challenge me right now and test your skills?" The man has a look of pure shock and fear. "Go ahead, say something else and your ass will be sailing over this railing," Rona continues.

The man rapidly shakes his head. "N—no, I apologize. We are heading there now." Rona continues making her rounds to gather more of her men she feels could benefit from further lessons in obedience.

Meanwhile, Anthulios meets up with Brax who's eating an apple while overseeing several citizens separating baskets of fruits and vegetables from edible to spoiled.

"How's our food supply?" Lio asks.

"Not too bad; could be better. The fishing team left this morning but hasn't returned yet. The fruit trees are doing well, but our vegetables are rotting on the vines. It's almost as if the soil itself is tainted. Most of our vegetable harvest from last year needs to be discarded." Brax takes another bite of his apple.

"This is concerning news. If we run out of food this safe haven well become useless."

"I don't think we are at that point just yet. Hopefully the fishing team has some luck today."

"How much do we have in our stores?"

"About a month or two."

"We used to have four," Lio says with a sigh.

"That was before winter. We'll get back up there." Brax decides to change the subject to stop Anthulios from worrying. His humorous persona is known to lighten the strenuous of situations. "Rona seems to be in a bad mood today." His observation has gotten a laugh out of Anthulios.

"She's always in a bad mood. She hates to see people who aren't working. So, I advise you not to get caught stuffing your face."

"I don't mind when she yells at me. Besides, we're the same rank."

"When has that ever stopped her?"

Lazul crosses the far end of the room along with another man following closely behind him.

"What's he up too now, I wonder?" Lio says after observing them.

"I don't know what he does around here, but his very presence makes me nervous," Brax admits.

The training grounds are positioned to the left-rear of the fort and hold several rows of targets and dummies for the guards to practice either their melee or range skills. Rona is standing with her arms folded while observing the guards practicing their swordplay on the dummies or with each other. Lazul and his companion stealthy approach her from behind.

"Glorious day for some spring training, don't you think?" Lazul says. Rona glances behind her but then turns back to face her men without a response. She too doesn't care for or trust him and tries to limit her interaction with him as much as time will permit. "Your men seem to be out of practice," Lazul continues to coax.

"Would you care to fight one of them and see for yourself? She answers without making eye contact.

"I must admit I'm not a fighter, at least not anymore. But I'm willing to make a wager. One of mine, against any of yours." Rona turns to face Lazul.

"One of yours? What do you mean by that?" Rona observes the man standing next to Lazul. "This man is a citizen—guards do not train with citizens."

"He was a citizen. I have trained him myself with my experience as an ex-drill sergeant."

"You seem to be full of secrets; I never knew you were in the army. However, that doesn't matter since you are not authorized to train anyone here and your so-called soldier will not be recognized as part of this force.

"My soldier can defeat every man here easily. Would you like to prove me wrong?" Rona is notorious for having a short fuse and Lazul has pushed her to her limit.

"You conniving bastard!" The guards stop their drills to observe the confrontation. "This is not up for negotiation, and you should mind your place. What rank you held in the past does not apply here. You are unranked among us, so don't you dare address me as your equal. Anthulios will hear of your secret training of unauthorized citizens, and you will be dealt with accordingly! If it was up to me, I would have you banished." Lazul's temptation has failed, and he uncharacteristically accepts his defeat calmly.

"Very well, sorry for interrupting you. I meant no disrespect. Let's leave the captain to her work, Reginald."

Rona watches the two men exit her field, but his retreat does not put her at ease. Lazul gave up too quickly and without bickering. Taunting Rona was only a ruse, his true motive must lie elsewhere. Rona turns back towards her guards who remain standing in place while staring at her. "Why do I not hear fighting?!" The guards immediately return to their drills without a word.

Elsewhere, the two anglers, Brax were referring to, are still fishing off the shoreline of a small lake framed by shrubs and patches of coniferous saplings. Pacing back and forth behind them are two guards that are tasked with protecting them. A bucket shows a small bounty of small fish that may not even fill the men who caught them, let alone an entire fort. The foliage begins to rustle followed by slow footsteps navigating through the patch of bushes. The guards draw their swords and wait beside the fishermen unaware of what is approaching. A fawn soon leaps into view and curiously scans the banks. The men laugh and smile relieved it was something so innocent and harmless. They relax and gleefully observe the small deer lick up the water.

It never fails that wherever there's prey, there's also a predator lurking nearby. A beast with the body of a bear, but the head of a boar, bursts through another bush. The grizzly boar viciously attacks one of the guards who didn't even know he was in danger. The animal pounces to take him down and then sinks its teeth into his neck while shaking its head violently from side to side. Its enormous paws hold the lifeless body down as it swallows a few large chunks from the man. Blood, guts, bones, and maimed body parts lay sprawled around the spot where the man fell. The last guard holds his sword at the ready and takes his stance.

"Return to the fort," the last guard orders the men. The command doesn't need to be repeated as they abandon their poles and morning catch before bursting into a full sprint towards Lio's fort.

A blood chilling scream is heard from the guard behind them and then an eerie silence. A thunderous stampeding shakes the ground and echoes into the men's ears. One of the fleeing men looks back and is horrified to see the grizzly boar closing in.

"Oh-my-God! It's chasing us!" He slowly begins to fall behind from exhaustion while the other man is able to keep his lead. He hears his partner's desperate yells for help, but he neither looks back nor slows down. He closes his eyes and continues running as fast as he can. The last yell he hears is the worst one yet, it's from a man choking on his own blood. After a roar the beast begins feasting on its third victim.

The last survivor of the fishing team reaches the fort and screams out to get someone's attention. The two guards on duty at the front gate become alert. The running man falls from exhaustion and struggles to pick himself back up. The commotion also brings Anthulios and Brax running to join the two guards already hurrying to the fallen man. He weakly looks up at the four men by his side as he tries to regain enough of his breath to talk.

"Beast—attacked us at the lake—dead—I think everyone is dead." The uproar has attracted several more guards to the man's aid, and civilians pour out of the fort into the field to observe the unsettling event.

"Get this man inside and give him some water," Anthulios orders two of the guards, he then looks at the five remaining guards. "Come with me; there's been an attack." Lastly, he turns to Brax. "Find Rona and then meet us at the lake." Brax nods and hurries back to the fort as Anthulios leads his selected men to the lake.

The first spot Anthulios and his men reach is where the other fisherman was attacked. The ground is soaked with blood and shredded intestines, but there is no sign of a body. Could this monster be capable of devouring an entire person? The men continue their quickened pursuit of this unknown behemoth until they reach the lake where the initial attack took place. The grassy shore and shrubs are painted in blood, but only some leftover innards are all that remain here as well. No bodies, or severed limbs, not even a finger can be located; but the lake is not deserted. Standing on the blood-soaked earth is Lazul's companion that he was toting around at the fort earlier. He remains fixed in place with a focused glare, but no expression or hint of a feeling or emotion. Any friend of Lazul is guilty by association and Lio brashly engages him.

"What is your business here?" The man doesn't respond or moves from his place. Lio isn't in the mood for games and draws his weapon as the others follow his lead. "Where's the creature that is responsible for this slaughter?" Lio continues. The man remains steadfast and silent with an eerie look that's now unnerving the other men with Anthulios, but someone else answers Lio's question instead.

"It's not here—anymore." Lazul gruffly announces as he strolls out from the patch of coniferous saplings to join his lackey. "It must have had its fill for now." Anthulios alternates his gaze from Lazul to his companion and then back to Lazul. Their presence here is not a coincidence and he's going to uncover their purpose and plot once and for all.

"What mischief are you up to now, Lazul?" Lio demands.

"Mischief? Very well, since you asked so nicely, I will enlighten you. I want to see you die and claim your people as my slaves." Anthulios takes a moment to make sure he just heard what he thought.

"You have been able to weasel your way out of too much. Now you shall pay for your villainous deeds." Lazul lets out a deep rumbling laugh at Lio's sincerity to bring him harm.

"You've been waiting for this day for a long time, but then again, so have I." Lazul slaps his companion on the back. "Show them what you've learned, Reginold."

The man shows the first sign of an emotion in the form of a sinister grin. He opens his mouth and roars as fangs sprout from his gums. Horns extend from his head and above his eyes and then his skin turns a reddish hue and his pupils and irises merge into a solid black abyss. Next, his fingernails grow into long claws and his feet become larger and morph into hooves. He draws his sword and holds it ready to strike.

Anthulios and his men stand awestruck at the transformation that just took place in front of them.

"I'm sure you are all familiar with O.D.E.'s demon serum by now," Lazul begins. "But this is my own creation. Can you guess how many of them I have hiding among your own citizens, Lio?

You should have acted on your suspicion about me long ago. Your inability to do so has allowed me time to build an army of demons."

"I will not allow you to escape punishment for your heinous crimes," Lio says trying to hide his fury with a calm request. "Subdue him." The men approach Lazul eager to restrain him and hope Anthulios will just decide to kill him right here. Suddenly five tentacles shoot out from Lazul's back and pierces through each of the men's hearts. He retracts the appendages and let the men fall to the ground dead. Anthulios is left to face Lazul and his companion alone with little chance of reaching a favorable ending.

"Fuck you, demon!" Lio bolts towards Lazul and then slices his sword through the air at his neck. Reginald intercepts Lio's attack and the two blades collide furiously.

"Your fort is your ship and it's sinking. The captain should join it, kill him." Lazul watches Lio and Reginald fight with amusement. Their blades continue to deflect one another during the heated battle with neither opponent able to draw blood on the other. Reginald finally adopts a new method and kicks Anthulios hard in the stomach to knock him back. He then brings his sword down over him, but someone else has just entered the fray. His sword takes the full impact of the demon's blade followed by a mace tearing flesh from the monster's cheek and jaw. A katana slices the demon's throat and then an arrow rushes into his temple just in case the first several attacks were not enough to stop it. Lazul's creation falls to the ground and expires from the multitude of injuries he sustained.

Kito rests his hands on his sword with the point buried in the ground as Amiku folds her arms across her chest while leaning against Kito's left side, and Ardian and Nydia are standing next to them.

"It looks like you are in need of some assistance," Kito says smugly. Anthulios smiles at his rescuers just as Brax, Rona, and eight other men reach the area after a long jog.

"What happened, Lio?" Rona asks after noticing the dead men.

"Lazul is responsible for this carnage. It appears he's a demon after all." Anthulios looks at Lazul sternly and points his sword toward him. "You will not live past today."

Brax brings his battle axe close to his chest and Rona takes out a pair of batons from either side of her belt while the soldiers draw their swords.

"Nice sticks, but wouldn't a sword be a better choice in this particular situation?" Kito says almost trying to poke fun at Rona.

"Silly boy, always putting your trust into something that's sharp." Rona responds.

However, Lazul doesn't seem to be nervous about facing his opponents.

"You think you've won, but like I said before, I've been building an army for a long time." Lazul holds his arms out and curls his long slender fingers. "Rise."

The ground begins to breathe, it rises and then falls and rises again. The grass begins to part and the soil shifts. A bloody hand spirals up from the disturbed earth followed by a long arm that leads to a skull rising out of the dirt. It has one eye intact and the other is a hallow void, it has its mouth gums and teeth, but no lips and the flesh is peeling from its cheek bones. It lifts itself out of the hole and rises to its feet as several more hands and skulls begin to escape from their underground prisons. The last three to rise from the ground are the dismembered bodies of two guards and the fisherman just killed by the grizzly boar. A mixed army of twenty undead and demons now surround the team.

"Now is the time of your final demise," Lazul roars.

Rona flicks her batons downward to make them extend another two feet and picks out first few targets. The mob of undead and demonized people close around the group and then attack as one. Rona's fast swings create resonating thuds when they slam into her victims' skulls. When two demons rush towards her from each side she connects the bottom ends of her batons together and then turns them into grooves to make one long stick. She helicopters the stick around her body to knock her foes backwards before jabbing it into the ground and then launching herself forward into a flying kick. She then turns the batons out of their grooves to give her two weapons again. She switches between these two fighting styles as she desires. Kito has been watching Rona's technique and admits that she possesses some skill with her chosen weapon after all.

Amiku barrel rolls in the air while cutting a demon's head off in the process. She then quickly slices the neck of a skeletal reanimated individual in front of her. As soon as it falls to its knees, she pushes her foot off its shoulder and sores over to stab another one that was behind it.

Ardian blocks with his sword and then attacks with his mace to smash faces in with one powerful hit.

Brax swings his heavy axe with ease to decapitate and dismantle arms and legs from their victims' bodies. Despite wielding such a heavy weapon his attacks are fast and he's able to swiftly turn directions to face his next foes.

Anthulios stabs and slices the monsters in his way trying to push through towards Lazul, but he's unable to ever get close to have the opportunity. He doesn't want to waste his time with his minions, he wants Lazul's head for himself, unfortunately his foe has a solid defense.

Nydia's arrows hit temples or foreheads of her enemies without missing any of her targets. Her accuracy is flawless and her reload time is almost instant.

The guards fight as well as they can, but most have already been overwhelmed and defeated. Rona tried to train them to be great warriors and teach them better swordplay. But while she was outside in the snow with her batons, they were inside by the firepit eating and drinking. Perhaps now they understand why she was strict. Maybe now they are reconsidering their assumptions or regretting their choices. Some things are just realized too late.

Kito cuts the hands and arms off four undead creatures surrounding him, while Amiku's katana slices down the middle of their soft skulls. Amiku's twirls around in the air like a graceful ballerina, only this one has a katana blade whipping around her body. The spinning attack decapitates the last three demonized individuals, who were standing in a triangular formation. Three heads hit the ground simultaneously followed by their bodies. Lazul appears to be somewhat shocked his entire army was defeated, but he remains calm. This group have just shown him that being outnumbered doesn't mean a damn thing.

"You are beginning to frustrate me," Lazul growls. "But I do have one final surprise for you."

The rustling of the nearby evergreens redirects everyone's attention to someone making their way toward the clearing. Kito and Amiku are stunned to see Anyo standing before them with a conniving smile. How this became possible is another matter—

Sometime during the night Anyo awakes outside Amiku's cabin. He sits up and looks where he was stabbed to find it has completely healed over. His shirt is still torn and bloody, but not even the slightest hint of a scar is observable on him. Anyo gets to his feet before noticing Lazul is standing in the field ahead of him. He advances toward him knowing he will not be in a pleasant mood.

"You have failed me," Lazul says in an angry, but calm tone.

"I'm sorry, my liege."

"These two will be a problem for me. I can sense it."

"How can I rectify this?" Lazul loses his calm demeanor and grabs Anyo's throat.

"I told you to try to win them over, but I didn't care if a watcher tore them to shreds instead! Do I have to explain everything to you?!" Lazul releases him as Anyo begins rubbing his sore neck. "If they find the fort, I'll have to try to get them to draw their weapons," Lazul continues. "Maybe the guards will kill them." Anyo then tells Lazul something he finds intriguing.

"Kito has demon blood in his veins."

"Does he? That's interesting. He may be of some use to me."

"He's afraid of it. He can't be valuable to us."

"His fear makes him more valuable to us. Don't forget you were nothing more than a petty thief until I got you inside O.D.E. Your demon rejuvenation doesn't make you immortal. Fail me again and it will prove to be useless."

"I'm sorry. What are my new orders?"

"Just remain out of sight for now; you are supposed to be dead after all. Soon, I will have a large enough army to kill Anthulios and all who are loyal to him. Then I will stand unopposed—"

Amiku doesn't care about explanations surrounding a mystery or any of its details. She tightens her grip around her sword and takes a step toward Anyo.

"It looks like I have to kill you again."

Kito advances to stand beside her, but she gently pushes him back. "I got this, Kito," she says sternly.

"Don't be so confident," Anyo says with delight. "I held back the first time in hopes that you would join us, but now I can unleash my full strength."

Two bumps begin to get larger on Anyo's back before two long spines tear through his shirt and continue to grow into two giant wings. His hands become larger, and his fingers extend into sharp points. His legs transform into the hind legs of a wolf and become covered in thick black fur. His feet burst through his shoes into large paws and his teeth become serrated. He lets out low-pitched growl before speaking.

"Witness my resurrection! This is what a full merging of human and demon DNA looks like."

"Do you want my help now," Kito whispers to Amiku.

"No, he still has a neck," she replies.

Lazul raises his hand, and several cracking sounds follow from the nearby trees. A moment later a decent sized blue spruce rushes out through the other trees. Nydia raises her hands in front of her to make the tree stop in midair before anyone can be impacted by it. The tree follows her gesture when she jolts her hands to the side, and it comes to rest on the ground away from everyone in the group.

"My, my, you have a little witch with you," Lazul says.

"I'm not a witch," Nydia snaps back defensively.

"Oh, no? It seems very coincidental that you arrived here when Anthulios was in peril," Lazul continued.

"I have vivid dreams," she replies.

"No matter, you will all be dead soon. This has dragged on long enough."

Lazul holds his hands upwards and arches his fingers; his eyes turn red as he starts to mumble something in Latin. The sky turns dark and low black clouds form as the wind picks up. Ardian holds his hand in front of his face while squinting his eyes from the pounding wind.

"What the hell is this?

"I don't know, but I'm going to stop it," Kito says before running against the blinding wind toward Lazul with his sword ready.

"Fool!" Lazul roars when Kito gets close enough to swing his sword. Lazul loses his concentration on his spell to dodge Kito's blade. The wind begins swirling above them while getting stronger and uprooting the trees. Anyo flaps his wings and flies towards Kito, but Amiku and Ardian intercept. They try to shield their eyes as they attack Anyo flying above them, but he is just out of their reach. Lazul coils one of his tentacles around Kito's arm and then wraps another one around his waist. Nydia is unable to aim her arrows in this fierce wind, but neither side appears to have an advantage any longer.

A lightning bolt strikes Kito's raised sword and then explodes. Everyone is blasted to the ground as the bolt travels through Kito and Lazul. Kito lands on the ground unconscious while Lazul is blasted backwards into the lake. A funnel cloud descends upon the group before touching down as a tornado. Everyone is helpless as they are pulled up from the safety of the ground. Anyo cannot resist the spiraling wind and is drawn higher into the sky and away from the others.

"Stay together!" Anthulios says over the roar of the tornado. Everyone tries to grab onto each other and hold on as they carried up. Amiku wraps her arms around the still unconscious Kito and Rona grabs Amiku's coat. The last two surviving guards lose their grip on Lio and Brax and get sucked up into the tornado's funnel never to be seen from again.

Ardian catches Kito's sword while holding on to Nydia and Anthulios and Brax finish the connection by taking Nydia's and Rona's hands. After several intense, and anxiety filled moments, the tornado begins to rope out and everyone drops through the trees somewhere in the forest.

Everyone attempts to grab a branch to stop their fall and then begin to climb down at their own pace. Amiku loses her grip on Kito when she collides into one of the branches. He continues falling toward the ground with no ability to stop himself. Amiku lets out a panicked cry as she watches him free-fall. Nydia holds her hand over Kito's falling body while squeezing her eyes shut. Her hand begins to shake with all her fingers spread as far apart as possible. Kito finally stops about two feet above the ground before she lowers him gently down. As soon as Amiku's feet touch the underbrush she runs to his side.

"Kito? Kito, wake up." She caresses his chest and then gently shakes his shoulders as tears stream down her face. Rona rushes over to them while everyone else is still working their way out of the trees.

"Let me in there, dear." Amiku moves aside as Rona places two fingers on his neck. "He doesn't have a pulse." Rona compresses his chest three times and then tilts his head back and breathes air into his mouth. She checks his pulse again before continuing with CPR. Anthulios joins Amiku's side; she looks at him with a worried expression.

"It's been too long." Anthulios puts his arm around her shoulders.

"No, it hasn't." Rona repeats the CPR again, but Kito isn't showing any signs of being revitalized.

Kito sees himself back in Copper Bay looking down at the demon that he and Sonya had fought. His peripheral vision catches movement and causes him to turn his head; walking towards him is Sonya.

"Sonya? I'm sorry—" She puts her hand on his cheek.

"Shhh, I know what's in your heart, but there will come a day when the blood of the beast will take over. That's when you need to decide who you really are, Kito."

"What do you mean?"

"Now is not the time, Kito. You have to go back." Sonya jabs her palm into Kito's chest just over his heart.

Kito sits up with a jolt while gasping and coughing. He looks around to notice everyone is standing around him. An overjoyed Amiku hugs him and then scolds him.

"You idiot. What the hell were you thinking?" Kito notices her tears.

"Amiku, were you concerned about me?"

"Shut up."

"Rest there for a few minutes, Kito. A lot of volts just surged through your body. You don't want to put your heart under any further stress," Rona warns him. Kito puts his hand on his knee as he begins to lift himself up.

"I think I'll be okay." Amiku pushes on his shoulder to make him fall back down. He observes her stern expression with her arms folded. She doesn't need to say a word to keep him seated. "I suppose I can sit here for a little while," he agrees.

Ardian looks concerned and points to Nydia's bleeding nose. She raises her finger to wipe it away while shaking her head.

"I'm fine."

Kito thinks back about his recent experience with Sonya. He isn't sure if it was a vision or a dream. He will never speak of it to anyone, but he finds himself wondering what message Sonya is trying to give him. She will find a time to talk to him again.

She's always attached to him from her blood that's been flowing through his. She may have died, but she's not done with Kito just yet.

Back at the lake, the sky is once again blue and sunny with no clouds in sight. The tornado carried away the living, as well as the bodies of the slain, only some blood spots remain on the grass, otherwise any sign of a great battle taking place here is lost. Lazul swims to shore and is helped onto land by Anyo.

"Where are they?" Lazul asks.

"I don't know, the tornado took them."

"Good, maybe they fell to their deaths, but if not, they won't be back anytime soon." Lazul motions for Anyo to follow him back to the fort. "It's time to carry out the next step in my plan, and this time there won't be any interruptions."

Meanwhile, in the surrounding forest, Amiku, Kito, Anthulios and Nydia are sitting while Brax, Ardian and Rona are standing nearby.

"I didn't know you had telekinetic abilities; you seem to be well advanced in it too," Anthulios says to Nydia.

"Thank you, but I'm still learning to control it," she admits. Brax extends his hand to Ardian and shakes it rapidly with an iron-grip squeeze.

"The name's Brax, I'm one of Lio's guard captains." He then points to Rona as she's making a fire pit. "And that sweet flower over there is Rona. She's also one of Lio's captains."

After introductions everyone is sitting around Rona's roaring fire with a small collection of mushrooms, moss, and berries from Brax's extensive knowledge for foraging edible food in the wild. A pile of extra firewood is also nearby since the group will have to spend the night in the woods and a blazing fire will be essential to their survival. Brax, Rona and Lio will sleep in shifts so someone will always be on guard and be able to feed the fire when needed.

Nothing is darker than a post-apocalyptic night after it blankets the great outdoors. The only light is from the campfire as it snaps and crackles with everyone huddled around it. The others can tell Anthulios is afflicted by the latest turn of events. He sits with his arms resting on his knees and keeps his eyes on the ground. Though he and Lazul had plenty of contentions he never thought Lazul was scheming behind his back; however, in retrospect he can't understand how he had missed it.

For two years he kept the fort standing; everyone was safe, and everything was organized. Then little by little things started to become less secure and more hectic. Problems arose and solutions came up short. Lazul knew the perfect time to strike, and nothing was in place to prevent or counter it. His captains said if it wasn't for Lio that fort wouldn't have lasted a day. He succeeded in building a civilization in a war-torn world where disorder ran rampant and peace was nothing more than a fleeting memory. Under his astounding leadership Brax and Rona saw a beckon of hope and have sworn to uphold his rules and follow him into any situation. Even in his darkest hour they aren't about to abandon him. This isn't over, not by a long shot.

"I'm going after Lazul tomorrow," Lio says in a serious, but gentle tone. Kito makes eye contact with him after a short moment.

"I stood beside you once, I'll do it again," he says. Ardian, Amiku and Nydia exchange looks and then nods in agreement.

"Looks like Lazul messed with the wrong group," Adrian replies.

"Let's make him regret it," Nydia adds.

"That's right; we are all in this together," Amiku concludes. Lio smiles and then glances at Rona.

"Oh, you should already know by now that we're coming," she announces.

"Yeah, you don't even have to ask, Lio," Brax chimes in.

"Thank you," Lio says warmly. "Then we should get some rest. Who knows what tribulations await us tomorrow."

Rona stands up to take first watch as the others lie down and try to fall asleep. Every member of this group has agreed to side with Lio and fight against Lazul and his ilk. They unknowingly leave their home and familiar surroundings for the last time. They are no longer survivors of a dying world, but soldiers of a forgotten one, protectors of an uncertain one, and heroes of a new one.

6

The Awakening

Dense morning fog covers the ground and conceals everything farther than an arm's length away. Nydia can't remember how she got separated from everyone else, but she's now alone in the forest with no idea where she's heading. She finally spots a figure ahead of her and is relieved to find it's Kito. She calls out to him, but he remains standing motionless with his back towards her and his head down. She can sense something is wrong with him and that he's not himself. She gets a little closer and calls out to him again in a worried whisper, but he doesn't acknowledge her.

She walks slowly around to face him just as he lifts his head to reveal his blackened eyes. Nydia gasps and takes a step back. The fog begins to drift up Kito's legs and then begins to swirl as it fades to black smoke that spirals up and around his body. The smoke takes the shape of a serpent as it rises above him before forming into the head. Nydia watches helplessly and frozen in place as the snake constricts Kito tighter and tighter. It sways its head from side to side while hissing and glaring at Nydia. Kito loses the ability to take in air and begins to suffocate, but Nydia can't act. The snake opens its mouth and lunges toward her with its fangs bared. All she can do is let out a loud drawn-out scream.

She wakes herself up and everyone else sleeping around her. They jolt to their feet and draw their weapons while trying to discover the cause of Nydia's distress. She retreats her head into her shoulders in embarrassment for causing this mass panic.

"I'm sorry, I had a bad dream."

The group sighs in relief and relaxes their weapons.

"It's alright, Nydia," Anthulios says. "We should be heading out soon anyway." The last dying embers of the campfire are hastened when Lio kicks dirt into the circle. The early morning sun through the canopy signifies a bright, clear day, unlike the overcast, foggy morning in Nydia's dream. Ardian knows her dreams always come with a meaning and leans in close to ask in a whisper.

"What did you see?"

"Kito, he's in danger," she replies in a hushed tone.

The group reaches the rocky cliffs, to the west, by late morning and then travels alongside the bluffs toward the south. This will allow them to reach the fort from behind where a narrow tunnel can be used to sneak inside. It was designed to be an escape route in case the fort was ever breached, but that secret is only known to Lio and his captains. However, before reaching the fort they must traverse through Forlorn Swamp. Brax calls it the most unholy and evil place imaginable, but the citizens of the fort have another nickname for it; they call it, the Swamp of Death.

During The Demon Wars, this area fell victim to deforestation and the extraction of the rocks and stone, from the nearby cliffs, were used to build, not only Anthulios' fort, but were also hauled away to build other fortifications. The changed landscape could no longer absorb the rainfall and the overflowing lakes never receded. None has ever made it through Forlorn Swamp—at least not alive.

All who are unfortunate to perish in this cursed bog will return as zombies. Some were citizens from the fort or guards on patrol, but many date back to the war, when a fierce battle with the demons claimed countless lives. Some skeleton remains of these victims still occupy the marsh while other corpses rest more preserved under the muddy goo and still water. Corpses with rotting flesh, empty eye sockets, teeth, but no lips and long twisting fingers reach out of the swamp grass and ooze. It is a most unpleasant area expanding far beyond the lush forest that once boarded it. The foul stench of decomposition taints the air and patches of ground fog float above the peat. It is home to giant insects and bugs, reptiles, and amphibians; all of which will deliver an infectious bite or make one feel uneasy at their appearance alone.

The lush green forest gradually becomes deadwood and wetlands. The ground becomes a mixture of soft, muddy earth and murky water. The few patches of solid, grassy ground are scarce and sparsely separated in between the trees and aquatic plants sprouting up from the waterline; and the surrounding ground fog has a blue tint to it. The group slushes their way through the shallow water as they head to the next patch of solid land. Kito misplaces his footing and falls to his knees in the murky water.

"Shit," he exclaims. He's quick to stand back up and continues following the others a few paces behind.

"Everyone be careful. The sooner we get out of here the better," Lio suggests.

The group continues walking forward, but a tiny splash stops Kito. A second small splash puts the others on alert as well. Brax brings his axe close to his chest while looking around. A small frog hops in front of Amiku before diving underwater.

"It's just a little frog guys," Amiku says with a sigh. The sight of the frog being the only cause for their anxiety does little to ease anyone's nerves. This is no place for a stroll and there is no reason to lower one's guard here. That doesn't become more obvious until the moment when Kito's next step is in a deeper section. His foot fails to find the ground he was expecting to touchdown upon, and his balance becomes off kilter. He completely disappears under the water leaving behind only ripples. Amiku stops and looks back ready to deliver a sarcastic comment on his clumsiness when he resurfaces, except he never does.

"Kito? Kito!" Amiku rushes back to the spot where he went down as the others quickly retrace their steps toward her.

"What happened?" Lio asks worried.

"I don't know. He's not coming back up," Amiku answers in

a frenzy. Nydia points to a spot a few feet away where the water is a little clearer.

"Over there! I see him." A thick root can be seen coiled around Kito's waist. He attempts to free himself, but the large root keeps him submerged under the water.

"I'm going in after him," Amiku says. She takes off her trench coat and then dives underwater without hesitation. She tries to pry the root away from Kito, but also appears to have difficulty succeeding. Noticing their struggle, Brax is next to swim to Kito's aid while bringing his axe with him. He begins to chop at the root with long, time-consuming strokes as the water's resistance prevents the buildup of momentum. When Amiku comes up for air Nydia points back down towards Kito.

"He's drowning, Amiku!" Amiku takes a deep breath and then dives back underwater. She embraces Kito and connects her lips with his to transfer the air.

Nydia doesn't realize she's being hunted as she stays invested in Kito's condition. Behind her a zombie that's dressed in a poor farmer's attire slowly creeps closer. Ardian spots it just in time and draws his mace to tear half of its face off. Four more zombies rise out from under the water as three others slowly walk out from behind the waterlogged trees.

"This is what I was afraid of," Lio admits.

The zombies are clothed in either old and torn attire or uniformed as soldiers. They are clumsy, sluggish creatures, but determined to advance no matter the obstacle. Anthulios and Rona aid Ardian while Nydia shoots her bow to protect their blind spots, but somehow the zombies continually increase in numbers despite the many that are struck down.

Amiku and Brax swim up for air and Rona gives her order to them.

"The two of you help Kito. We'll take care of these."

What once were only a few have developed into a large horde and more zombies are still approaching in the distance.

"Damn it! Where are all these coming from?" Ardian says in frustration.

"Don't think about how many there are. Just keep killing 'em," Lio advices.

Brax is about halfway through the root as he continues chopping while Amiku breathes air into Kito.

Nydia lowers her bow and flicks her hand in front of her to toss a zombie to the ground. A moment later an arrow enters its forehead. Rona is using her batons as a staff and twirls it into fast jabs and swings. She then puts the staff perpendicular to the ground and uses it to propel herself forward. Her feet collide into the chest of a zombie to force it into the path of Anthulios' swinging blade. The blade severs the head and launches it upwards in a trail of blood. Nydia dispatches another zombie just as a new one rises behind her from the swamp water. It grabs her ankle and pulls her back as she lets out a scream. Ardian rushes to her rescue and amputates the zombie's arm with his sword before nailing his mace into its face to send it back into the water. He then helps Nydia back up as they exchange grins.

Everyone takes one of the last four zombies to finally annihilate the zombie onslaught.

"Goddamn zombies," Lio says.

Brax finally breaks through the root and Amiku pulls Kito free as the three swim to the surface. They gasp for air and cough when they resurface while the others hurry to help them onto solid earth. They lie on the ground and take deep breaths to regulate their heartbeats.

Kito struggles to find the right words to announce his feelings of gratitude, but Brax doesn't need to hear it and Amiku already knows.

"Is everyone alright?" Rona asks as she kneels beside the three to give them a quick medical assessment.

"I never saw a plant behave in such a way before," Nydia admits.

"It's called an anaconda root. It's a carnivorous plant that holds its victims underwater until they drown, and then it consumes them," Lio explains.

Nydia remembers the snake from her dream that was coiled around Kito. Her dreams are subjective and offer metaphors or little hints of things to look for, but it's up to Nydia to piece together the puzzle or decipher the riddle her dream suggests.

"Anaconda—Oh-my-God, I should have been more observant," she says feeling responsible for Kito's mishap due to her inability to see the clues given to her.

"What do you mean?" Rona asks confused why Nydia is taking the blame for the transpiring events.

"This morning, my dream, it was about Kito trapped by a snake. I was given the warnings and failed to act—" Kito can tell Nydia is obviously disturbed by what happened to him, but also feels some things are just plain unavoidable.

"Sometimes knowing something bad is going to happen to someone; still doesn't give you the power to stop it," he says. Nydia gives him a hug.

"I'm glad you're okay."

"Thank you, Nydia," he responds with a smile.

The team continues sloshing through the sludge before the top of the fort becomes visible above the grotesque dead trees with twisted branches. Amiku begins with a slight cough that gradually becomes more frequent until it develops into a deep raspy fit. She takes a deep breath and then falls to her knees.

"Are you okay, Amiku?" Kito asks concerned.

"Don't worry about me, Kito. I'm fine," she replies. Rona squats down and looks into her eyes and then places her hand on her forehead.

"You're burning up."

A sudden wave of nausea overcomes Kito unexpectedly. He turns away from the group before hunching over to vomit. Rona walks over to Kito after he recomposes himself and lays the back of her hand on his forehead.

"Damn it, you too. Who knows what kind of bacteria is swimming around in this godforsaken water?" Rona pinches Kito's wet coat and rubs the wet material in between her finger and thumb. "And your wet clothes aren't helping."

"We have antibiotics in the fort. We just need to get to them," Lio says.

"We need to hurry. Their fever will take them down fast," Rona continues.

"I hate to change the subject, but we got company," Ardian says while drawing his weapons again.

Ten zombies are closing in around the group and force them to huddle closer.

"We just can't get a break here, can we? Brax says.

Anthulios cuts an arm off one of the zombies before stabbing it through its chest while Brax cuts off a leg of another before embedding his axe in its skull. Nydia stays behind everyone else to ensure she has ample time and distance to make her bow a valuable asset. She knocks back a zombie with her hand motion and then fires an arrow into it to finish the job. Ardian continues to utilize both his weapons by stabbing with his sword and then crushing with the mace. This double attack method allows him to make quick work of a single threat or attack two targets at once. Rona's batons deliver catastrophic trauma to the head and temple area of her foes and her fast strokes send shockwaves throughout the zombies' brains that kills them instantly.

Kito's legs give out from underneath him and Amiku struggles with her movements with her weak limbs as well. Both are deteriorating fast from an unknown parasite or virus they swallowed from the swamp water. Neither can protect themselves or those near them. Dizziness and double vision throw off their aim and their bodies begin to shut down. Rona's hypothesis of their recovery time is not only unknown, but also uncertain. Of all the dangers this world can muster, it's the smallest particle in a short moment that poses the highest threat. The group finally dispatches the last zombie even though Kito and Amiku were unable to follow through with a single attack. Rona and Lio fear that the upcoming battle with Lazul and his minions, no matter how many they are, will be a demanding task in itself. Now with Kito and Amiku practically out of commission, they have lost two great allies, but even if that were not an issue the fact that they make easy targets are.

Concealed behind dense green hanging moss is the mouth of a dark and damp tunnel. Lio guides everyone through the short passage that echoes with dripping water and a hollow wind.

A lowered iron gate is the last thing that stands in their way. Anthulios and Brax jointly lift the gate that's on a pulley system and allows the others to walk underneath it. They then duck under the gate themselves and gently lower it back down. They are now standing in an empty stone room that's no bigger than a prison cell.

"All right everyone, be ready for anything. We don't know how many of our citizens have been infected," Lio warns. He carefully pulls the door open and exits with everyone following into one of the fort's corridors. When the door shuts again it blends into the stone blocks of the wall quite well. This is the reason why no one else knew about the tunnel or accidentally found it. For all the times this hallway was walked through no one realized one patch of the wall was fake. So far, the fort is quiet with no sign of citizens or patrolling guards. Each turn of a corner puts the group on alert as they expect to eventually run into someone, but every guard post is vacant, every balcony is empty, every room is abandoned and not a soul occupies any of these hallways. There's only one last place to look, everyone must be in the main hall. Assuming Lazul and Anyo will be guarding the main entrance hall everyone moves ahead steadily while trying to soften their footsteps.

As they draw closer to their destination the unnatural calm begins to worry them. No voices or noises are heard in an area that has never been silent. The most startling discovery they make is when they finally enter the vast open space of the main hall to find it's completely void of anyone. The area is clean except for the empty food baskets and plates on top of the wooden community table. Breadcrumbs and tiny amounts of unconsumed vegetables and other leftovers also litter the floor around the table.

"This entire place is deserted," Brax observes.

"There's no one left," Lio adds in disbelief.

"Lazul took every last one of them," Rona says mournfully. Brax inspects the baskets and discarded food.

"This was the daily ration for everyone in the fort," he says.

Kito advances around to the opposite side of the table. After a few steps the sound of broken glass under his foot redirects his attention to the floor. He lifts his foot and picks up the larger shards of glass that are loosely held in place by a sticky label. His expression indicates a terrifying discovery. Lio eventually can no longer stand the silence and questions his discovery.

"What's that, Kito?" Kito slowly closes his fist around his find and glances up.

"You don't need to see this," he replies.

"I'm not in the mood, Kito. Show me," Lio orders softly. Kito reluctantly opens his hand and sets the remains of a tiny flask on the table. The black text on the tiny white label clearly reads, F6VI.

"That's O.D.E.'s demon serum," Amiku says emotionally.

"Lazul must have poisoned the food with it," Ardian adds respectively.

"They are all dead then. We are too late," Anthulios says as he slumps down on the bench in defeat.

A feminine giggling resonates from somewhere above them. Squatting on one of the support beams about twenty feet above them is a Japanese woman. She has long platinum-blond hair, that descends to her mid-back, and she's dressed in a Chinese cheongsam. The dress is black except for the red floral pattern that runs diagonally from the top left of her shoulder to the bottom right end of the dress. She jumps down and lands unscathed on her hands and feet.

"Konichiwa. My, my—so many beautiful boys and girls in this group. Lazul told me to kill you if you should return, but I'm almost tempted to keep you as my pets."

"Who are you and what have you done with my citizens and guards?!" Anthulios says after standing back up. The girl giggles again.

"Such a booming manly voice you have. Forgive me for not introducing myself. My name is Alma," she bows and then continues. "As for everyone else—they are now under Lazul's command as demons. In fact, they probably already attacked the next fort in the mountain passageway." Alma puts her hand over her mouth. "Oops, I wasn't supposed to say that. I was always told I talked too much."

Nydia brings her bow up with a loaded arrow and shoots it toward Alma, but Alma lifts her hand and stops the arrow in midair.

"Now, that wasn't very nice, little girl." Alma closes her fist, and the arrow explodes into splinters where it was suspended. Though they possess the same power, Nydia's ability is still in its infancy while Alma has honed hers to almost perfection. Within only a few minutes Alma has picked up on what makes Kito and Nydia different than their comrades, but she keeps this information to herself. She's not here to oust Kito or show off to Nydia, she was tasked to kill them, but now would rather play cat and mouse with them instead.

Kito starts coughing as his illness continues to spread throughout his body. Alma looks at him with a concerned look that teases him.

"Awww, you seem to be ill. We need to get you out of those wet clothes and under my covers." Alma giggles as she brushes the back of her hand down Kito's cheek. Amiku immediately raises her katana to Alma's neck.

"Don't you dare touch him!" Alma snickers at her reaction.

"You have a very take-charge attitude, I like that, but you don't need to be jealous. I like girls too."

"I don't know what your angle is, but if you don't step aside then we'll be stepping over you." Amiku can't hold back and begins the same cough Kito has.

"You seem to be ill also," Alma continues. "You're lucky I can be very nurturing. As it stands no one here has the strength or the ability to fight me, and I really would hate to kill so many cute boys and girls. We could have so much fun together. Now kindly lower your weapon," she says to Amiku.

Kito brings his sword up and holds the point towards Alma, but she just smiles and sighs.

"You look like you are about to keel over, honey. You should let me nurse you back to health." She moves her hand towards Kito's face again, but Amiku lightly sets her blade on Alma's wrist before she can reach him.

"You must not want that hand anymore," Amiku says sternly.

"I was so hoping that we could come to an agreement, but it doesn't look like I'm dealing with the negotiating types," Alma responds.

"If you are with Lazul then you shall share the fate that awaits him," Rona claims.

"Very well, I guess I will have to follow my orders after all."

Alma darts her arms out in front of her to release a strong gust that throws everyone backwards. She then turns to Kito and pulls his sword from his grasp with the motion of her hand. "Sorry love—" With a flick of her wrist his suspended sword flips around and rushes into Kito's stomach. His already weakened body cannot withstand this ferocious attack and he drops to the ground and blacks out. Fueled with anger and worry gives Amiku a sudden burst of stamina to charge Alma with her katana ready to strike. Alma propels her hands forward to send Amiku diving into the stone wall which knocks her out on impact.

"Stop it, bitch!" Nydia pulls back her bow and releases an arrow that becomes a yellow energy bolt as soon as it leaves the bow. The bolt explodes into Alma's lower stomach and sends her sliding across the floor with a profusely bleeding wound.

"That is far too much power for you to have," Alma says in bewilderment. Even Nydia is surprised at what she had just done, but those in her company spot their opportunity. Brax and Lio stampede towards alma, but she vanishes before they get into range to use their melee weapons.

"Where did she go?" Brax asks confused about her sudden disappearance.

"She can teleport?" Nydia half answerers Brax's question while pondering the possibility of it herself.

"We need to find and kill her now that she's weak," Brax says as he heads for the main gate.

"Peace, Brax, let Alma go," Lio hollers.

"We may not get another chance like this," he fires back. Anthulios raises his voice to counter his argument.

"This is not up for debate! Taking care of our own is more important." Brax lowers his axe and feels ashamed for forgetting about Kito and Amiku's injuries.

"My apologies, Lio. That is the right choice."

Brax and Lio carry Kito and Amiku into the infirmary room that contains two beds and a medicine cart. Rona administers the antibiotics to them and then stitches Kito's severe stomach wound. She feels Amiku will naturally wake up in time, but she's less sure about Kito. She voices her concerns to everyone as they stand around their incapacitated teammates.

"He's lost a lot of blood." She drapes another blanket over him and continues. "His temperature is 97.9° and that's with the fever. I don't know what to do for him."

"There may be a solution," Nydia says.

Ardian and Nydia explain that Amiku has a plant in their shelter that is capable of healing Kito. Nydia remembers how to work with the Adonia to make plasma rejuvenation, but first they need to retrieve it. Brax agrees to accompany them and the three set out on the two-hour round-trip journey. They should be able to reach the hatch, pick up their supplies and then return to the fort before dark. Rona continues to look after Amiku and changing Kito's bandages while Lio keeps a lookout on one of the balconies.

Nydia is still thinking about her arrow turning into a yellow energy infused bolt. She doesn't know how that happened or if she would be able to repeat it. No one has addressed it and maybe they won't, but the more she uses her abilities the more magic-like they become. The best advice she ever received was from Ardian moments before they left.

"I think you have a lot of hidden power within you and it's only just starting to surface. It seems adrenaline, stress, and emotion tend to bring it out. I don't think you should fear it, or fear what others think of it. Try to understand everything that you are capable of, and then use it. You aren't a witch, you're a mage."

Later that evening, Lio observes the three returning and lets them back in before securing the fort for the night. They are toting the Adonia that Kito will need but have also brought back more medical supplies and food from their stash. This time they will be providing dinner for everyone. It may not be able to out due Lio's dinner to them, but as hunger sets in several hard rolls and MREs are just as good as a steak dinner.

Nydia and Rona return to mending Kito and notice a large improvement after receiving the plasma rejuvenation. His chances of pulling through have greatly increased now thanks to their efforts.

That evening Anthulios, Rona, and Brax talk amongst themselves about their next plan of action. The sanctity of the fort has been soiled. What once was a living, breathing society is now a forgotten catacomb. If nothing is done Lazul will continue to spread his vileness and others will experience what Lio just has. It would be irresponsible to ignore what has happened and what will or could happen in the future. Surviving is no longer good enough; the time has come to go to war. Maybe it's time people united once again.

"I think the world needs more heroes," Brax says.

"Or maybe just fewer villains," Rona adds.

"It's settled then. Our fate is sealed, but the others don't need to be dragged into this." Lio says thinking everyone was with Amiku and Kito on the floor above them.

"By others. Do you mean us?" Amiku says as she rounds the corner with Ardian and Nydia.

"Amiku? You should be resting," Rona says happy to see her awake and moving, but also knows she should be taking it easy.

"I'm glad to see you are better. And yes, I was referring to your group," Lio admits.

"I think we're past being tactful, so I'll just come out and say it. We're fuckin' coming along." Amiku's response gets a smile from everyone, and they know there's no way to convince her out of something after her mind is made up.

The sun is almost set in the horizon and Ardian, Amiku and Nydia are standing on the highest balcony while looking down at Forlorn Swamp. Nydia raises her bow and takes aim at a zombie that's roaming near the swamp's edge. Her arrow finds its mark in its forehead as Amiku and Ardian cheer.

"They don't seem so scary when we are up here," she says while smiling proudly. Behind them a familiar voice is heard.

"Nice shot."

"Look who it is. Lazarus, back from the dead," Ardian jokes when he sees Kito standing behind them.

"It looks like everything is changing for us again. But I hope something that won't ever change is the four of us standing together; just like we are right now, at whatever end," Nydia says in a heartfelt speech.

"We will be," Amiku says. "We will be."

Based on what Alma said, prior to her swift retreat, Lazul traveled through the mountain passageway. This is also the only way to reach the other side of the crags, which no one on this side has ever had a need to travel or investigate. This will be uncharted territory for everyone.

The following morning, Anthulios motivates his team with a speech before they venture into the unknown.

"One day people will rebuild their homes. Towns will become cities, and families will flourish. We will not disappear from the pages yet to be written. But in order for this to become a reality, we must first walk into unpredictability, where amity may be scarce and dangers many. Our fate is defined by our oath. Everyone has made a vow or a promise and that's what we need to remember."

The journey to stop Lazul and his demon army has begun.

7

Esperanza

The granite crags tower above the stony earth and boulder filled pass with several hardy shrubs peeking through. The gravel ground crunches underneath everyone's feet as the group navigates through the twists and tuns of the passage. As the voyage progresses ominous cloud cover squeezes the last hint of sunlight from the sky and flashes of sheet lightning jolt through the dark clouds followed by rolling thunder. The concern for the weather is soon forgotten when the group advances upon a debris field of splintered wooden beams and large sections of masonry walls. Slightly beyond the damaged construction materials is an area where a volley of arrows had fallen. Some of them are snug in the earth while many others lie broken from snapping on the stone-covered ground. More of a mystery is the fact that not one corpse can be seen among the arrows. Were people shooting at nothing, or did they miss their targets completely? Perhaps, whatever fell—rose again.

"Something happened here," Ardian observes. The group treads carefully ahead with their hands close to their weapons if they should need them in a hurry. Blocking their view ahead is a large stone structure that's broken in two pieces at a cutout that may have been a window. The massive obstruction blocks the entire passage save for a narrow slit in between the two halves. One-by-one each member squeezes through the opening to clear it. Only when they reach the opposite side do they discover the ruins of a fort that has been blown asunder by some violent explosion.

The surrounding area is littered with wood, stone, and the maimed bodies of the fort's previous inhabitants. It is a disgusting scene of blood-splattered mountain sides and limbs and organs sprawled across the pebbled earth. Nydia swiftly turns around with a hand over her mouth as she gags but refrains from vomiting.

"We have to kill this bastard," Brax says somberly. Anthulios takes the lead as the others follow him around the death and destruction. They clear the battle scene but find one last man lying ahead who has four deep slashes across his chest and stomach. He may have had been trying to escape when he was attacked. Lio and Rona inspect the body for clues, but unlike everyone else he is the only one who is somewhat still intact. Lio and Rona become startled when the man opens his eyes abruptly and takes in a deep breath.

"Shh, stay calm. We mean no harm," Rona says.

"An army of demons attacked us two nights ago," the man begins. Rona places a comforting hand on his shoulder as he continues. "We were unprepared, but our archers managed to get one round off before our dynamite storage blew up. Incapacitated, I watched the dead rise and the wounded turn into monsters. Everyone is dead, but that didn't stop most of them from walking away."

"We are going after them," Lio says. Lightning flashes and thunder explodes overhead.

"You will need help. Look for Esperanza—" The injured man takes his last breath before his head falls to the side and his eyes close for the final time.

The septet cannot linger in this location any longer and continue to follow the rocky passage until it meets a grassy knoll that connects to an open field that curves around a patch of trees.

A fort in the far west is barely visible as several lightning strokes flash near it. The wind picks up and the thunder and lightning become more frequent. The closer the storm draws nearer the more urgent it becomes for the team to seek shelter. The fort ahead is still quite a trek and crossing an open field with lightening flashing so regularly may not be the best option. Unfortunately, the luxury of having a choice is robbed from them once more.

Anyo swoops down from a ledge above them and wraps his arms around Nydia's neck. She struggles to free herself, but his grip is too tight.

"Let her go, demon," Ardian yells as everyone draws their weapons. Another surprise awaits them as Alma reveals her presence by advancing from behind a large rock formation protruding from the cliff-side. They have been here waiting to see if Lio and his allies would follow them. Now, they aim to finish what was already started. Alma's dress is torn and soaked with blood at the spot where she was injured, but her stomach wound is completely healed.

"Poor lost sheep; so far away from home," she says smiling.

"So, you did survive," Rona says.

"Of course, I have the fastest demon regeneration of anyone, even Lazul."

"Shut the hell up, Alma! You talk too damn much," Anyo barks.

"Speaking of which, you owe me a new dress, little girl," Alma says while looking at Nydia. Nydia squirms and pulls Anyo's arm away from her throat.

"Why, isn't this the longest you've had one on?" she fires back. Her team would expect such a response from Kito or Amiku, but not her. While they are taken back by her answer Alma laughs.

"Ooo, a spitfire. I would never have guessed," Alma says amusingly. She then rises her hand and curls her fingers before a yellow sphere of energy materializes and hovers above her palm. "I have the same power as you. The difference is I've perfected mine," Alma explains to Nydia. "I can summon it on command and without the help of objects, but to hold it suspended like this indicates you are at the height of your skill." She extends her arm out and fires the energy ball across the open field. With nothing to collide into, it slowly dissipates into thin air as it travels into the distance. Nydia has seen what her ability could become and now knows Alma shares her talent, but what chance does she have against someone who is far more advanced than she is?

"Is Lazul lurking in the shadows also?" Lio gruffly asks.

"No, we are more than capable of conquering your little resistance," Anyo replies. Alma sets her eyes on Kito and smiles as she advances while swaying her hips.

"I have to admit, I'm surprised to see you standing. Not many have survived after I leave my mark on them."

"I challenge you to try again," he replies with a calm sincerity. Alma chuckles.

"My, my, that was a perfect response."

Alma is more interested with playing mind games and satisfying her lustful word play with her enemies, but Anyo desires bloodshed and physical violence.

"I'm afraid your time is up. Your mission has failed," Anyo growls as a loud clap of thunder explodes and the torrential downpour begins.

Kito and Ardian attempt a joint attack on Anyo, but he throws Nydia into Ardian and then flies up to avoid Kito's sword. Brax and Anthulios attack Alma, but she jumps up and twirls in midair, which makes her cheongsam fan out. She then lands a flying kick into Brax's face that sends him rolling down the hill. Alma dodges Anthulios' sword and then returns with a fury of high kicks followed by a hard punch to the middle of his chest.

Amiku uses her parkour and kicks up the nearly straight rock-side before pushing off and landing a foot into Alma's chest; she then quickly jabs her katana forward, but Alma cartwheels backwards and escapes from the blade. Alma tosses a kick at Amiku's ribs, but she blocks it with her arm and then squats down as Rona rushes behind Alma. Rona jabs her stick into the ground and swings her body around it to land a double kick into Alma's back. She is thrown over Amiku, who flips her over her back and then slashes her sword across Alma's torso. Alma takes a moment to rest on one knee while inspecting the minor wound.

"I have underestimated your skills," Alma begins. "I admire your tenacity, but you will not succeed in landing another strike on me."

"Then you have still underestimated me," Amiku replies. Alma stands back up and cracks her knuckles.

"Do you think you're better than me? Discard your sword and fight me like a lady."

Alma's challenge begs Amiku to choose between her reliable weapon or proving herself in a fight that rides a thin line between pride and honor. She chooses the latter and tosses her katana to her side.

Meanwhile, Ardian has blocked Anyo's incoming claws with his sword, but never saw his kick aimed at his gut. The force of the impact knocks him backwards into the cliffs. Nydia raises her bow for a clear shot; however, Anyo's wingspan swats the bow from her grip before she can fire. He now turns his attention to Kito. He raises his foot to prepare a swift kick that had worked on Ardian, but Kito slices his ankle.

"You aren't fast enough for me," Kito taunts.

In the meantime, Alma rushes toward Amiku attempting a round kick to her ribs, but she blocks it with her forearm. Amiku counters with a punch to Alma's head, but she dodges it and then dives low to sweep her leg around to trip Amiku. Amiku recovers quickly by rolling backwards onto her shoulders and then pushing herself back to her feet. They are almost evenly matched as every attack is blocked and counter attacks are fast and accurate. Each ducks, dodges, or sidesteps from the incoming attacks and then throw a fury of punches or different style kicks. Alma attempts a high kick, but Amiku catches her leg and then twists it around her before slamming her to the ground. She is in the perfect position to thrust a downward elbow, but Alma suddenly teleports. If there were a judge, she would be guilty of cheating, but realizing Amiku is actually a formidable opponent, she decides to end the fight before she loses it.

She reappears behind Amiku with only one thing to say, "Lights out, darling," followed by her palm striking the middle of Amiku's forehead. Her concussed head is jolted back, and she drops to the ground unconscious. Kito shoots a concerned glance in Amiku's direction, giving Anyo a chance to land a well-placed punch into his ribs. Ardian smashes his mace into Anyo's thigh giving Nydia another chance to strike. This time her arrow finds the middle of his chest. Anyo slams his fist into Ardian's chin and darkness overcomes him after the flash of light fades. Anyo ignores his bleeding leg and snaps the arrow shaft off and then drops it to the ground as if it was nothing more than a splinter.

"Foolish bitch." Anyo slams his shoulder into Nydia to knock her off her feet with only a small yelp exiting her lips. Kito attempts to stab him from behind, but Anyo proves his speed. He whirls around and uppercuts Kito to make him drop his sword and then puts both his fists together to clobber Kito into the dirt. Kito has trouble recovering from the bash and remains in a dazed state. Anyo picks him up by his collar and lands a direct punch to the side of his head. Kito collapses into the rain and blood-soaked earth with his eyes barely open. Anyo picks up Kito's sword and holds the point just above his neck.

"Now, you are done," he says before lifting it higher in preparation to skew Kito's jugular. A sudden gunshot rings out and a bullet enters Anyo's arm to make him drop the sword. A group of people firing guns and riding on ATVs, and one motorcycle, are fast approaching from the field.

Alma cartwheels away from Rona with one foot coming up to smack her under her chin. Alma then spins a kick into Rona's ribs to finally take her out of commission. Alma peers at the approaching men just as a bullet ricochets off a rock near her shoulder making her jerk her head.

"How unfortunate. Everyone always wants to ruin my fun," Alma whines. Anyo retreats into the sky not wanting to mess with this new group, who seems to be well armed, while Alma advances to where Kito is lying half aware. He weakly lifts his head and looks up at her. "Still alive? Even after that beating, huh? You are an interesting individual." She squats down and embraces Kito just as Nydia peeks through her heavy eyelids. She sees Alma leaning over Kito and then both of them disappearing. Nydia passes out just as the ATVs and the single motorcycle reach the defeated group.

Together Anyo and Alma completely took out a very capable team of seven, even though no one was killed, it still should be noted that if these two were this challenging, imagine an entire army with their strengths and abilities. Unless others are willing to join them, Lazul will win his war.

A bald, muscular man named Thyst, and his captain, Nichi arrive, and begin assessing the fallen.

"It looks like their opponents got away, sir," Nichi says.

"Nothing we can do about that now. Get everyone back to the fort and start medical treatment immediately."

Some time later, Amiku, Ardian and Nydia are still being checked out by the fort's medical team, but Lio, Brax and Rona are well enough to be sent to the common area where they are given a fair portion of turkey meat and water. Thyst joins them after making his rounds around the fort.

"Good evening, strangers. Are you enjoying the turkey?" Everyone nods and replies with extreme gratitude. "Turkey and rabbit are about the only game that's not tainted around here." Thyst sits down and listens to his guests explain their last few days and the events that brought them to this moment.

"If you're looking for a secure place to hunker down, you've just found it," Thyst begins. "No demon horde has ever breached these walls and the last of the world's technology is found right here. Our roof contains gun turrets to fend off attackers and tower viewers to scout over three-hundred feet in every direction. We have rocket launchers, flame throwers, machine guns; my personal favorite is the AK47, we also have solar powered ATVs and motorcycles with machine guns mounted on them. Not to mention more than five hundred trained soldiers ready for battle, twenty-four-seven. All accumulated from lots of scavenger hunts and good old fashion human ingenuity. I admire your courage for fighting with your medieval weapons, but if you want to try something a little bit more modern, then you came to the right place. You're in Esperanza now."

Thyst decides to give the three an exclusive tour of Esperanza and its inner workings as he explains.

"We try to keep this place a democracy. Every department has its own administrator, who's responsible for any issues or decisions that affect that department. For an example, Nichi is the captain of the army and Lako is second in command. I play the role of commander in chief in times of high threat. The head of the council is, Aiza. The council is much like a courtroom. It is made up of fifteen people who decide rewards or punishments for all crimes or deeds carried out by our citizens, soldiers, or outsiders. Mika, who we are about to see, is the head of the medical department as well as our head doctor. And I, along with my wife, Aifina, oversee the entire operation of the fort and make sure everything is in pristine working order. That includes kicking a few butts from time to time."

Thyst leads everyone into a room with several hospital

machines and devices spread around the entire area. Humming and beeping sounds fill the air and flashing line graphs pulsate on the monitors. Several beds also stand side by side with small aisles in between them and the room is well lit.

"Wow, this looks like a real hospital," Brax says surprised at how well-equipped and operational this place seems to be. Mika pulls back a blue curtain to reveal her presence.

"That's because it is. Everything in here actually came from the hospital in Silver Rock City. We have several generators to power this room alone since it can be the difference between someone living or dying."

"How are they doing, Mika?" Thyst asks.

"I was just about to check on them. Please follow me."

Mika makes her way to the opposite side of the room and then pulls back a white curtain. In three of the four beds are Ardian, Nydia and Amiku sitting up and seemed to have recovered well.

"How is everyone," Lio asks like a concerned father.

"I think we just got the wind knocked out of us," Nydia replies.

Mika shines a flashlight into Amiku's eyes and then pushes lightly around her head. "Does this hurt?" Amiku shakes her head. Mika finally agrees that everyone is well enough to be released from her care. Amiku notices the empty bed next to hers and assumes Kito had already been released.

"Where's Kito?" she asks. Nydia takes a moment to think about how to explain what she saw to Amiku.

"He—was taken—by Alma—"

In an area where three terrains meet, the mountains, the woods, and the field, lies a stone cabin. It's a cozy, single room hideaway consisting of a shabby wooden table, sandstone hearth and modest bed. With no other amenities or stored supplies, it can be assumed this shelter was not a permanent residence. It was always known to be vacant by those in the area. Some believe its builder most likely met their end in an unknown confrontation, but ever since its abandonment this cottage has been a welcoming resting point for long distance travelers who happened upon it. Today, it became occupied by someone who desired a secluded place out of the rain.

The gentle patter of raindrops on the windowsill indicates the storm has died down and the raining will soon end. Alma stands at Kito's bedside while hovering over him. Her fascination has intensified, and she lets her hand caress his cheek. Kito slowly opens his eyes but jolts up when his gaze falls upon Alma. She pins his arms down and uses her bodyweight to keep him in bed.

"Stop struggling, I'm not a threat to you at this very moment," she says in a playful tone.

"Why should I believe that?"

"I'm not like Lazul or Anyo. I don't believe in fighting someone who is unable to defend themselves."

"So, you think I'm no longer a challenge?" Kito replies smugly, but Alma only smirks.

"Don't play the, tough guy card, with me Kito. Though it is slightly cute it is only a clever disguise. I like my fights to be a challenge to both me and my opponent."

"What do you know of honor?"

"More than you might think. I was born in Kyoto, that's in Japan in case you didn't know your geography. I bounced in and out of dojos all around Osaka ever since I was five. I've been fighting my entire life. I learned karate and judo at an early age and advanced in these arts as I grew older. I was born with my weapons already attached to me." Alma holds her hands out before squeezing them into fists. "It is for this reason that I will never fight with anything other than my own body. Amiku was the best I've fought in a long time." Alma pauses to recall the fight in full detail. "Her style was graceful, but lethal. I would love to fight her again." Alma turns away and then glances over her shoulder to give Kito a sly smile. "I can see now why you like her."

"What?" Kito responds ready to deny any accusation Alma might have about him and Amiku.

"Don't play coy with me. She's beautiful and she's someone who pushes you. You're a man who needs to be pushed, Kito, but that's not necessarily a bad thing."

"You do talk too much," Kito replies. Alma giggles and leans over to place her hands on either side of him. She presses her chest against his and rubs her breasts up to his chin and then back down.

"What are—" Kito begins, but Alma puts her finger on his lips to hush him.

"Shhh." She presses her lips to Kito's cheek and gently kisses him and then moves to his lips. Kito nudges her away, but she doesn't want to stop. She holds his wrists down and then forces her lips against his and kisses him continuously before letting up.

"You are like me, Kito. You belong with me; we've both been exiled into a lonely existence. Don't try to deny it." Kito finds it difficult to think outside of her words. Alma has a great talent for playing with emotions and he's starting to sense a kinship with her. She has also reversed his natural tendency to repel others and her advances are now beginning to be desired.

"What do you know about me?"

"I know you have demon blood in you. I can smell it." Alma climbs on top of the bed to straddle him. "I understand you, do your acquaintances? They will suppress you, cast you out, but I will take you in. Stay with me and I will empower you. Give yourself to me and we will rule this world together." Alma slowly slides her hand inside Kito's pants. "I like you Kito. I might even let you be on top, but not the first time." Kito is suddenly gripped by an overwhelming madness as his eyes transition to black. Torn between his quiet affection toward Amiku and Alma's tantalizing attention finally makes him snap.

"Don't fuck with my head!" He yells in a voice far deeper than his normal tone. Alma is taken back at first, but soon recovers from her shock.

"My, my, you do have a temper. Do your friends know you're a demon like me? If they saw you at your worst, would they still feel at ease in your presence?" Kito takes several deep breaths until he returns to normal after calming himself down. "Everything revolves around the ability to deceive. That's the way the world was, and that's the way it still is."

"Is that what you were doing to me this whole time, deceiving me?"

"No," she begins. "I do want to possess you, but I would have cared for you too." Alma looks away and becomes somber. Her demeanor has changed from the aggressor to someone who is mild. "I may have learned my fighting techniques, but my telekinesis I was born with." Alma focuses on a glass of water on the table. The glass slowly rises and floats toward Kito. "Drink, you are dehydrated."

He hesitates, but then takes the glass as Alma continues.

"I used to hide my abilities for fear of rejection, but that soon changed.

I was training late one evening in preparation for an upcoming tournament. I knew the older kids practiced at that time, but I never put much thought to it. I didn't know those three boys were attracted to sixteen-year-olds. I didn't know I was the only one there when they followed me into the locker room. They forced me over a bench and held me down. I don't remember if I said anything. I don't remember if I screamed or cried. But I do remember feeling each of them have their turn with me. I thought maybe it wouldn't last long. It was actually the longest night of my life. Then they just left me on that cold floor. Left me to pick up the pieces of my shattered world." Kito remains silent hearing her account. He doesn't know if she's still playing mind games but feels sorry for her none-the-less. "I saw them again a few days later. That's when I sent an energy bolt into each of their faces, in front of everyone. I just didn't care who was watching anymore. I think one of them survived, but no one will ever call him pretty again. From that day on people called me a witch. Before I knew it, I was alone. I never fit in anywhere, so I kept running away to places where no one knew me. All the time continuing my fighting in dojos and tournaments as I traveled. When I learned everything I could from one place, I moved on to another. Eventually my travels brought me here to America. I wanted to learn to fight naturally, maybe for a deep-rooted desire to be accepted.

Nydia has the same power as me. What a lucky girl she is to have friends who accept and support her; I'm a little jealous. If I had friends like her, my path could have been very different." Alma and Kito exchange a soulful glance.

"When I met Lazul he promised me I would have my revenge against everyone who showed me disdain. I accepted his proposal without knowing the type of man he was. Whatever I drank granted me a rejuvenation ability, but I've never tapped into my demon form. We were always demons, Kito. Demons with damaged souls and torn hearts; how can anyone truly know us? I thought compassion had all but died out, but when you looked at me, I didn't see hate. A desire to defend, yes, but not hate. I forgot there may still be good people caught in the aftermath. How ironic, I became what I wanted to destroy. I fear nothing more now than I fear myself. Evil isn't a choice, Kito, it takes over when you run out of options." Neither utters a word for a long moment until Alma's expression becomes a scowl. "Don't think this little talk of ours changes anything. When you are healed up you will once again be my enemy. So, get stronger Kito; because if you lower your guard next time we meet—I will teach you regret." She teleports away before Kito can respond.

Elsewhere, Lazul's army of enraged demonoids are slaughtering the straggling survivors of his recent invasion. Neither hiding nor retreating are successful for the previous occupants as they are sought out or chased down and then ruthlessly maimed or devoured.

The stone fort consists of a high watch tower that overlooks the surrounding hilly field with the silhouette of the mountains framing the horizon. This will become Lazul's permanent base where he will put his villainous plans into motion, as well as devise his future attack strategies.

Emulating a king on his throne, Lazul takes his seat in a high-back chair facing the entrance of the fort. He rests his feet on the hunched over corpse of the fort's previous commander lying in a pool of blood. This victim becomes his footstool, a trophy of his conquest. Anyo is of course standing next to him as his personal guard and advisor.

Sounds of screaming and demonic growling, along with the destruction of property, are still taking place in the adjacent rooms. The slain bodies of the former occupants line the walls and their blood coats the bricks and slabs. What was once hospitable now resembles a lair in the underworld, and Lazul, with his flailing tentacles behind him, is Satan incarnate.

Alma fazes into view and begins to slowly advance toward Lazul and Anyo. She tries not to notice too much around her as she hides her disgust.

"Where have you been?" Anyo immediately questions.

"I was playing," she replies in an innocent tone.

"Playing, huh? I bet you were. The last I saw you; you were leaning over one of the boys. I can only imagine what you were doing."

"I'm surprised you could see anything at all while running away."

"Shut that little cock warmer you call a mouth," Anyo growls, but it doesn't upset her.

"You sound jealous," she says grinning.

"That's quite enough," Lazul chimes in. "Did you at least find out anything that's useful?"

"They have sought shelter in Esperanza."

"I could have guessed as much," Lazul says a little disappointed. He turns to Anyo and waves him away. "Stop the rampage and bring me anyone who's somewhat still intact. We will need a bigger army to go up against Esperanza."

"Right away, sir." Anyo says with a nod. He gives Alma a mean look when he passes her, and she returns the glare while adding in a hiss.

"Grab your things and pick out a room. We'll be here for a while," Lazul orders.

"Thank you. I will." Alma says and bows. After taking only a few steps she stops and turns back around. "If you should happen to capture Kito alive. I would like it very much for him to be turned over to me. I care not about the others, but he interests me."

"Do you want to fuck him that bad?"

"It's not just that, I think I will have the most fun with him."

"Fine, win Kito over using whatever charm you desire. His abilities may be useful to our cause." Alma smiles and bows again.

"Arigato."

"I also suggest you follow orders a little more closely in the future. When I send you to kill someone that doesn't come with a caveat."

"I'm sorry. I admit I did act out of selfishness."

"You are dismissed."

Meanwhile, Amiku, Ardian, Nydia and Lio are conversing amongst themselves, but Amiku can't sit still and paces back and forth with quickened steps.

"I can't just sit here and do nothing. Not when Kito is out there; especially with that woman," she says almost grinding her teeth at the thought of Kito alone with Alma.

"I understand how you feel, but picking a direction and walking isn't a very good rescue plan," Lio adds.

"And staying here isn't a plan at all." Amiku stops pacing to think, but it's not long before she turns around to walk away. "I'm going after him."

"Amiku!" Lio glances at Ardian and Nydia. "I'm going to

need your help with her."

"I'm going with you," Ardian says without hesitation.

"Me too," Nydia agrees as they hurry to catch up to Amiku while leaving Anthulios standing alone.

"I meant in convincing her to stay," he says voicing his thoughts to himself.

Thyst and Aifina are talking near the entrance when Ardian, Nydia, and Amiku storm past them.

"Where are you guys going?" Thyst asks.

"To find Kito," Nydia answers.

Anthulios jog finally allows him to catch up to them.

"I tried stopping them," he tells Thyst.

"Okay, everyone stop! I know you are worried about your friend, but you don't know where he is and it will be night soon," Thyst reminds them.

"Exactly, we can't leave him out there at night by himself. He has no way to defend himself," Amiku snaps back. Thyst stares at Amiku for a moment and then sighs.

"All right, but I cannot allow this search party to go past two hours. After that amount of time, we are coming back no matter what." Aifina puts a concerned hand on Thyst's arm.

"Two hours? Isn't that cutting it close?" Thyst kisses her.

"We'll make it back," he assures her.

Moments later, Nichi, along with two other men, ride out two ATVs with attached machine guns and the same wide body chopper that Thyst rode on to rescue them from Anyo and Alma. Ardian hops on one of the ATVs and Nydia sits behind him. Amiku immediately singles out the chopper and throttles it a few times.

"Um, Amiku? The motorcycle is mine," Thyst says. She looks at him without a response before speeding away. Ardian quickly accelerates after her, leaving Thyst dumbfounded as he observes her driving away with his motorcycle.

"It looks like she has commandeered your chopper," Lio says. Thyst shoots him a retired look while shaking his head.

"What did I get myself into?" Thyst gets on the last ATV and races to catch up with the others. Anthulios smiles while talking under his breath.

"Just wait until you meet Kito."

Kito has left the cabin and is now nearing the patch of trees in the mid-section of the meadow. He remembers there was a fort behind them and hopes that's where everyone went. Alma teleported away with him before the rescue had happened, so he still doesn't know the true fate of his party. Kito's mind is crammed with worry for his teammates, but now also carries some concern for Alma.

I'm perplexed. Is she my enemy? Would she have been an ally if she never ran into Lazul? Would I be an enemy if I met her before Amiku? I know everything I'm not; what I don't know is who I am. She's like me, and now, I'm like her. I looked into the eyes of my foe, and, like a mirror, I saw my own reflection. Now, I have to pretend that never happened. I can fight the world, but when it comes to my own thoughts, I am defeated. The funny thing about hunting demons is after a while—you begin to see yourself in them.

Kito doesn't know how things would have played out in his series of alternate realities. He doesn't know what to think or what his feelings mean. Alma has instilled doubt in his mind. No one can understand his point of view. He will be looked at as a traitor and be thought of with the utmost of disgust. A betrayer, a double agent, a demon. He will be ostracized. He will await the hangman's noose and the only cheers he will receive is once his feet stop kicking. He's faced with a conundrum and his choice will not be favorable. This is how he thinks of himself.

Kito reaches the patch of trees and puts a hand on the trunk of one of the trees to rest. The fort is closer now, but still appears to be a very long walk. Deeper in the trees something observes Kito just outside the tree line. He glances up at the sun low on the horizon. The need to advance faster is strongly known, but exhaustion demands his body to stop. The creature inside the trees draws closer, but Kito doesn't acknowledge the impeding danger. He remains resting until snapping trigs followed by several growls echo out from within the trees. Kito peers into the darkness while slowly backing up. Six gnolls exit the trees while cackling; their appearance is that of a hyena walking upright. Kito instinctively reaches for his sword but lacks a weapon to grasp. Without it he has no chance to survive an attack by this group of predators. Kito continues to take slow, soft steps backwards as the gnolls advance and begin to surround him until he's completely enclosed. They prowl towards him to close the gap in between themselves and him. When they are close enough they will pounce as a group, Kito cannot escape.

The distant sound of humming motors distract the gnolls away from their hunt. They put their noses in the air to decipher the mysterious sound as it becomes louder. Amiku emerges from around the trees with her sword held out at her side. Kito dives to the ground as Amiku crashes into some of the gnolls while slicing those in the path of her katana. Thyst and Ardian fire their machine guns at the remaining gnolls. The bullets explode through their tiny bodies and blast off limbs as Kito remains in the fetal position with his hands over his head. When the shooting stops his rescuers stop their vehicles near him. He slowly peeks over his arms and then sits up. A gruesome scene of blood is splattered across the grass and trees and severed body parts surround the area.

"Kito, I presume," Thyst says with a smile.

"Get on," Amiku says with her hand outstretched toward him. Kito is still in awe and recovering from his speechlessness when she takes his hand to pull him up.

"Are you riding a motorcycle?" he asks.

"Yes," she replies. Kito is still dumbfounded but manages to nod his head. He then glances at Ardian and Nydia on the ATV and nods to them too.

"Guys."

"Kito," they reply. Kito still remains standing in place until Amiku makes a snarky comment.

"So, are we camping out here?"

"I would rather not," Kito replies.

"Good." She nudges her head behind her. "Then like I said, get on."

"Right," Kito responds and then sits down behind Amiku.

"Hold on Kito, this baby flies," she warns. Kito wraps his arms around her waist before she throttles the bike forward. The spinning rear tire kicks up the dirt, grass, and gnoll guts before roaring after the ATVs already heading back to Esperanza.

8

Silver Rock City

Esperanza is hugged by a field of puffy white flora from the many dandelions that have gone to seed. Amiku woke up early to practice her sword techniques, and art form during the calming moments of dawn. The countless swirling white dandelion seeds seem to dance around her as she spins and moves her blade around her body and above her head. Her hair waves in front of her face and sways in the wind with every perfect execution. Her arms, legs, and even the swing of her katana is that of a graceful dancer. Her actions send a swarm of puffy orbs into the air to ride the wind currents back to Esperanza and beyond.

Kito gazes up at the sight from just stepping out of the fort. He follows the wave of dandelions to discover Amiku in a glorious light. He becomes infatuated with her at this moment and cannot turn away. He feels as if this is the first time seeing her. She doesn't notice his gaze as she continues her tantalizing parade. Her playful motions slice the puffy clumps into smaller clusters. Her flowing hair hides most of her eyes but reveals them just long enough for Kito to catch a wink. Was it a blink, or a wink? He cannot tell, but there's an unexplainable magic aura around her this morning.

Later that morning, a meeting has been called in the main hall. Anthulios and Nichi stand on either side of Thyst, with Lieutenant Lako standing next to Nichi. A large gathering crowds the room with boisterous gossip and rumors being passed along by the attendees. Everyone knows something is going on, but nothing has been clarified or authenticated. To the general public the newcomers either bring bad news or are bad news, but they wait to see how Thyst deals with them first. They trust his judgment and have never felt he was unfair in any call he has made. Whenever he was unsure of something he put the subject to a vote. For this reason, the people of Esperanza feel they have a voice and are willing to support or enforce Thyst's decision, whatever it may be.

"Alright everyone, quiet down, Thyst begins. "I have been talking with our new visitors and learned a few things that we weren't aware of before. We can no longer just play defense but must also start planning a counterattack or we risk our enemies becoming too strong and too many. We must defeat this evil if we are to ever have a future for our children. We the people, declare war once again. It's time we teach demons fear!" The crowd cheers while waving their fists in the air. Thyst raises his hands to silence everyone down. "We have decided to try to start an alliance with the surrounding forts and assemblies of people. We will start with the nearest establishment located in our ruined neighbor, Silver Rock City. I will be taking our visitors with us and leaving the army here to protect the fort. Nichi and Lako will also remain here to organize the troops. And as always, in my absence, Aifina is in command. We leave in two hours."

The party members wait outside near the ATVs and chopper that had been brought out into the field. Many of the soldiers and citizens gather on the walkway waiting to send off those on this brave mission. Up until this moment people only left the fort to hunt and scavenge. The preparation for war and the joining of estranged factions hasn't taken place since the beginning of The Demon Wars. This is a turning point in the Apocalypsia age and of human history.

Kito and Amiku race towards the chopper, but Amiku proves

to be faster and shoos Kito toward the nearby ATV with a sly smile. Ardian claims the second ATV with Nydia sitting behind him and Rona accepts the last ATV. Before the team can question how the remaining members of their party will travel the ground begins to vibrate and a roaring rumble soon follows. Everyone except for Thyst appears to be baffled at the sound of some mysterious large heavy machine drawing closer. The cause of this commotion is discovered to be a M1A2 Abrams tank rolling around the fort and stopping in front of Thyst.

"You have a tank?" Anthulios says wide-eyed and with a dropped jaw. Thyst smiles the widest he has ever grinned.

"We have a tank."

"You can have the cycle, Amiku. I'm driving that," Kito says.

"Nobody's steering the tank except for me," Thyst replies after overhearing his comment. The top hatch opens and Lako climbs out and makes his way to the ground before reporting to Thyst.

"All the machine guns on the ATVs are loaded and ready. There are also a few AK47s and M4s, along with a few ammo boxes in each of the storage compartments. I also have the tank loaded, but you only have two HEAT rounds on-board."

"Thank you. Hopefully we won't have to use them," Thyst replies. A HEAT round stands for High-explosive anti-tank and is a warhead designed to penetrate heavy armor. While no one expects to encounter any enemy planes or tanks, this type of ammunition is useful to eliminate large single targets or a densely packed group of smaller foes.

Thyst gives a final wave to Aifina who kisses her hand and then blows him the kiss. He smiles and grabs it before placing his hand on his heart. He then turns to Lio and Brax. "You two are with me." The two excitedly follow Thyst up to the hatch while the others look on with envy. The soldiers salute the departing tank as the citizens wave and shout their best wishes.

The tank advances slowly behind the others who have the speed to scout ahead in the direction Thyst and Lio gave over the walkie. *"Come in Rona,"* Lio says over the walkie clipped to her collar. She tilts her head down and holds the button to respond.

"Go ahead."

"Silver Rock City is just ahead. Do not let anyone enter the city until we arrive."

"Copy that." Rona leads the others ahead to the outskirts of Silver Rock City and then stops before the city limits.

"Hold here, guys," she says.

Office buildings are crumbling or have already collapsed, and weeds have reclaimed the roads and sidewalks. Abandoned vehicles litter the sides of the street and forgotten trash and recyclables blow across the ground. Amiku shoots a mischievous smile in Kito's direction while revving her bike.

"Are you challenging me?" he questions.

"Are you going to back down?"

"I should warn you, back in the day I used to street race."

"You never raced against me." Kito is somewhat surprised Amiku was part of the car modification scene. He thought only rebels like him got caught up into stuff like that. There is more to this girl, and her history, than Kito ever imagined, and she becomes increasingly more interesting to him day after day.

"You raced? What did you drive?"

"Ninety-seven twin turbo Supra."

"You had a ninety-seven Supra?"

"Royal blue."

"How did you get that?"

"Don't worry about it," she responds with a smile.

Without notice Amiku accelerates onto the parkway with Kito in hot pursuit. Ardian follows them unwilling to miss out on the fun as Nydia grabs on tightly to his waist. Rona's cries are futile as they cannot be heard above the sound of the motors and the distance that's quickly being placed in between them and her.

Amiku weaves around debris and large slabs that had fallen from the weathered buildings while Kito relentlessly follows her. They drive aggressively and take calculated risks by swerving around broken-down cars occupying the middle of the street or driving on the sidewalks if the road becomes too gridlocked. They take a sharp turn and fly down another street toward a car that had been smashed from a large block of concrete. This produces a raised ledge and a tempting stunt for the adrenaline seeking daredevils. Amiku aims for the middle of the ramp and becomes airborne as she soars over the car and lands on the other side of it. Kito follows Amiku's lead and flies over the obstacle before landing back on the road as well. Nydia witnessed the feat but is less enthused about the thought and gives Ardian a warning.

"Don't even think about it, go around it!" Ardian ignores Nydia's advice and jumps the ramp. Nydia remains screaming throughout the entire time they are soaring through the air. When the tires return to the road she follows up with a slap to the back of his head. "What's your problem!? I almost fell off!"

"Sorry, Nydia. I didn't have enough time to avoid it," he lies. Amiku veers down another street with Kito close behind. They fail to notice Rona accelerating diagonally towards them as Kito and Amiku reach neck and neck. Rona suddenly hops the medium and comes to an abrupt stop to block their path just ahead. Kito and Amiku brake hard to leave skid marks on the street. Rona glares at them with an expression that demands obedience once they come to a stop.

"That's enough foolishness! What's wrong with you two? You have no idea where you are or what you are heading into. This is not a playground! We are in the lion's den, so I suggest you try to stay unnoticed." Rona leads the others back to Thyst, Anthulios and Brax who appear to be quite impatient while leaning against the tank. When everyone stops their vehicles Thyst approaches them.

"I hope you had fun because your driving privileges are hereby revoked."

They keep their focus low after the scolding and walk alongside the tank while Rona takes the chopper and Lio and Brax on the ATVs with the extra one being towed by Lio. Somewhere in the downtown district, Thyst finally stops the tank and climbs down with a crowbar in hand.

"I have an old war buddy who used to live in these sewers. Hopefully he still has his platoon with him." Thyst pries a sewer lid up and pushes it aside with Lio's help. He then looks at Amiku and the others. "You four stay here." Thyst begins to descend into the sewer but looks up one last time. "And no driving." Lio, Brax, and Rona follow him as the rest stand by the open sewer on guard duty.

A single row of flame-lit sconces marks a path through the grimy sewer corridors. Why anyone would pick this place for a home is beyond the logic of Lio and his captains, but Thyst understands a hidden shelter is far better than one out in the open.

When the group reaches the last sconce Thyst knows they

have reached their destination, but with no sign of a door it is easy to assume one is lost or have been misled. Thyst begins to study the large stone blocks of the wall in front of him. With the right amount of pressure, he pushes them in until they click into place.

Three blocks to the right from the last light, fifth one down, and then left by two. With the sequence complete, a section of the stone wall separates into two parts and then slides to the left and right sides. A large green metal door with no handle is revealed. Thyst pounds his fist on the door and can imagine those inside wondering who discovered their secret base and how they knew the code. Since it's only given to trusted acquaintances there should be no debate that a friend is on the other side, but a curiosity of who is another question entirely. A multitude of sliding bolts are heard until the heavy door groans open to reveal a man still in his U.S. army uniform.

"Sergeant Kaz, it's good to see you're still breathing," Thyst welcomes his old friend.

"Thyst? What brings you to my neck of the woods?" Kaz responds with both shock and excitement. Thyst's reply is short and directly to the point.

"War." Kaz steps aside and allows his guests to enter.

One would not know they were in a sewer by the fully LED lit room. On one side is a lounge area that's furnished with couches cots and tables, while the opposite side contains portable generators, shop lamps, workbenches and racks of machine guns and pistols hanging on the wall. A group of men are cleaning guns or assembling them after inspection, while another is fidgeting with disassembled walkie-talkies. The rest of the inhabitants watch their newly arrived guests with hostile glares but remain silent as the group converses with Kaz.

"Tell me old friend. What do you know that I do not," Kaz begins.

Meanwhile, above ground, Amiku, Nydia and Ardian continue to wait for the others to return but being idle for so long is starting to take its toll on the impatient group. Across the divided highway is a plaza that leads to the rotating glass doors that mark the entrance to a mall. Kito's restlessness sows a seed that sprouts into an idea. The longer he thinks about it the more powerful it becomes, and the harder it is to dismiss it, until it matures into a fully grown motive.

"Maybe we can get some scavenging in," he says. The others follow his gaze to the mall ahead of them.

"We were told to wait here," Nydia reminds him. Kito glances at her with a small smile.

"We were told not to drive. I didn't hear anything about taking a walk." Kito has an interesting way of finding an interpretation that also doubles as a loophole to fit his desires. Even if a meaning is obvious, he will spin it and then claim his innocence if he's caught. Kito takes his first few steps toward the mall as Amiku gives her reason to follow him.

"We should keep an eye on him. He needs constant supervision."

"That's an understatement," Ardian adds. Nydia loses the argument and is persuaded to accompany the others into the mall.

There's immediately something different about the interior of this mall. Instead of storefronts with wares, or at least the evidence of them, there are rooms that contain long aluminum tables, lab equipment and gear and complex machines and computers. Nothing appears to be operative, but notebooks and loose papers litter the main hallway. The entire mall had been converted into an O.D.E. lab and the many different departments within suggest this was a huge operation.

In place of the department store branding above the glass display windows are metal die-cut letters spelling out the sectors of O.D.E.

Bio Weapons Development

The tables inside are littered with telescopes and a large poster showing enlarged gnarly virus spores with protruding appendages. The headline on the poster reads:

It's easy to kill a group when you just have to target one.

This is where O.D.E. was developing a new virus that gives an impression of being very contagious and deadly. A more frightening thought is, were they referring to demons or humans?

Further down the hall is another room with floor to ceiling circular glass tubes filled with a yellowish liquid. This sign reads:

Animal Research

Inside one of the tubes is a pig with its head half melted away and long canine teeth that extend far below its jaw. It also has a distorted and elongated skull structure and is clearly demonized. Ardian looks repulsively at the experiment while Nydia thinks out loud.

"I thought O.D.E. was supposed to find better ways to fight demons and invent new technology to protect everyone. More and more it looks like O.D.E. became obsessed with ways to harvest or recreate demons instead." Amiku nods in agreement.

"O.D.E.'s intentions were questioned almost as soon as they were formed, but what do you expect from a completely unrestricted government agency?

"Only bad leadership prevails," Kito begins. "The good ones are oppressed and anyone who disagrees is ostracized. People have been failing people since the bronze age. Under the guise to save the world they finally defeated it. Why was anyone surprised?" Kito's activism surprises the members of his group. He deviated away from the structure of society and was labeled a rebel; he just never saw anything wrong with it.

The room across the hall proves to be yet another department:

Demon Captivity & Control

This one catches the group's attention as they enter. Spread out on one of the tables is a large hand drawn illustration of U.S. military helicopters dropping off goblins near soldiers. It depicts the goblins attacking some of the soldiers while others retreat in fright. The nearby notebook explains the department's mission statement and reinforces what the illustration is showing.

The entry is as follows:

Demon Captivity and Control's mission is to gain the ability to control or sedate and transport non-human or no longer human expendable soldiers to the battlefield. Fear will destroy enemy morale and their territories will become infested with a force difficult to completely annihilate. Future goals will be to amplify aggressiveness and overall efficiency to seek out and dispatch targets. We understand the likelihood that wounded enemy soldiers will turn on their own and with the absence to recover our deployments

*a residual effect may occur. This; however, will be ruled as
an interior issue that doesn't warrant our involvement.*

O.D.E.'s purpose went from destroying the demon threat into
adapting them into weapons. While O.D.E. was international,
each country's government regulated their own branch
independently. This meant departments that were formed and
operated in America may not have been in Germany or France
and vice versa.

The team continues to study the poster and read through
the notes from an unknown scientist. Behind the involved group,
a little girl drags her feet with her head lowered and her long
black hair concealing her face. She sluggishly advances out of a
darkened corner of the lab and advances toward the distracted
group. When she gets closer, she lifts her tiny hand and lets it drop
on the surface of the metal table. The sound redirects everyone's
attention to the child, but while the others suspect a lost girl Kito
notices her crippled fingers with mud and dried blood underneath
the nails.

"Are you okay?" Ardian says as he approaches the girl.

"Ardian, wait," Kito tries to warn him. Ardian squats down
in front of the unresponsive girl.

"Do you want to talk?" Ardian continues. The girl throws her
head back to reveal an extra wide dark void for a mouth and lets
out a high-pitched wail. Most of her skull is visible including her
abyss-like eye sockets while the rest of her skin is flaking off. She
swipes her unnaturally long fingernails at Ardian who manages
to marginally avoid them. Nydia forms an energy ball in her
hand and blasts the demon girl through the window of the room.
The limp body of the girl flops to the floor and slides down the
hallway before coming to a rest.

Nydia is progressing well with her abilities. She understands
that this energy force is produced inside her biology and then can
be unleashed by a sensation or thought. Nydia holds her palm up
and forms an energy ball, but it blasts up and explodes into the
ceiling. Everyone protects their heads with their arms as shattered
florescent lights and chunks of plaster rain down on the group.

"Oops, I was trying to hold my energy in place like Alma did,
but I guess I can't do it yet," She explains apologetically.

"Perhaps practicing that is best done outside," Kito says

sarcastically.

A sound that could be an explosion from miles away rattles the hanging light fixtures.

"What was that?" Nydia asks nervously.

The sound continues as evenly spaced and timed rhythmically, which only means one thing—they're footsteps, and they are getting closer. This is definitely not the footfall of a little girl; this is made from a large and powerful foe. The quartet cautiously steps out of the lab and venture back into the hallway. There is little need to be quiet as whatever is heading their way already knows of their presence. The footsteps stop to create an eerie moment of silence. It is in this interim that nerves and anxiety is at its highest as the anticipation of what will happen next pulsates through everyone's thought process. Whatever was approaching is now lying-in wait just around the corner; waiting for someone to foolishly investigate—none do, and the creature grows restless. The hulking monster shows itself as it stomps around the corner and its large, bulging red eyes become deadlocked on the group.

These manufactured monsters were the creation of O.D.E. and vary in appearance greatly; however, this one has two saber-tooth-like fangs and several rows of sharp teeth lining both the upper and lower portions of its mouth. Its head is riddled with large warts and its feet have three clawed toes. Around its wrists and ankles are broken steel cables attached to metal cuffs, indicating it was once restrained, but for how long will remain a mystery. Nicknamed as Destructors, for their innate ability to destroy everything in their path, there are few ways to take one down and this group doesn't possess any of them.

"Fight?" Kito says unsurely. The destructor roars and begins to paw the ground.

"Run," Amiku replies as a better alternative. There is no objection and the team sprints toward the rotating doors from whence they had entered. The destructor lunches forward and agrees to chase them. Windows rattle and the floor shatters where its foot crashes down from its wide stride. Support columns crack and chip and lights and chunks of the structure narrowly miss the retreating gang.

Thyst, Anthulios, Rona, and Brax exit the manhole and look around for the second half of their group, but they don't need to ponder their whereabouts for long.

In the distance, the behemoth smashes through the glass doors just as the four make it out. The beast tosses the mangled heap of bent metal framing and broken glass to the side and then continues its pursuit.

"I just knew we couldn't leave them alone," Rona says.

Thyst hurries to one of the ATVs and starts tossing machine guns to everyone as they catch them and then take aim at the beast.

"Everyone scatter!" Ardian yells. The team splits up into four different directions giving a small moment when the monster is alone. The chance cannot be wasted and Thyst takes the opening with a clear order.

"Fire!" A stream of bullets dart into the beast. It backsteps and roars while trying to swat at the bullets. The continuous fire from four machine guns explode into its hands, chest, and face. After several carefully aimed shots to the neck and head the beast drops onto its back and expires.

The group reunites at the corpse, happy no one was injured. Anthulios inspects the chain attached to one of the destructor's cuffs.

"These look like cable car cables. Very heavy-duty stuff." He then takes note of the mangled contraption that was the system of sliding doors and then the gaping hole in the building where it used to be. "If I didn't see it for myself, I may not have believed it."

"Send O.D.E. the bill," Kito jokes.

"What was this thing?" Brax questions.

"I don't know, but it reeks of O.D.E.," Amiku replies.

"Based on what we just found out, my guess is this was an experiment," Ardian adds.

"What did you guys find in there?" Thyst asks suspecting they may have valuable information.

"Just another one of O.D.E.'s dirty little secrets," Amiku answers.

"You can explain on our way to the airport," Rona says not wanting to waste any more time standing around.

"We're going to the airport?" Nydia says intrigued.

"Yes, according to Kaz, many will be reluctant to join forces and less are willing to fight, but some radios are still in operation, meaning the control tower will be the best chance to reach them.

He'll meet us along the way, but for now we'll take this road northwest," Thyst explains.

The group returns to their vehicles, but just as Kito and Amiku were hoping they may have been forgiven for their race earlier, Thyst points his finger at them and Ardian.

"You three are still passengers, I'm letting Nydia off the hook." She makes a fist and brings her arm towards her body in a celebratory motion.

"Yesss," she whispers and gives her friends a smile, but they don't share in her excitement.

The ride to the airport was surprisingly easy and uninterrupted. It may be a popular scavenging location for Kaz and his men, and they must have taken great care in keeping it accessible.

A 737 with no departure time is gated at Charlie 25, the codename for the terminal belonging to the C concourse. Beyond that are more corroded planes abandoned on the tarmac. The nose of a Boeing 757 has crashed into the ground with its front landing gear snapped off beside it and its windshield cracked. A little closer is a 70-seat regional jet with its stairs lowered, but this one is occupied by a pack of raptors. Their skin is rotting away to reveal red muscle tissue and white bone. Their skulls flash the exposed teeth through the missing lips and white or yellow eyes give a cold, menacing glare to any who see it. Raptors were already a concerning sight, but confronting demonized raptors is a very different disturbing and unnerving experience.

Advancing past this pack to reach the control tower is a risky move, but luckily, it's one the group doesn't need to take. Thyst is looking at the small screen on the tank's control panel with the hairpins positioned on the jet, while everyone outside remains huddled behind the tank. The large cannon groans into position and within a few short moments fires the projectile. The warhead whistles through the air before exploding into the fuselage causing the plane to be engulfed in a massive fireball. The blast radius shatters windows and loose bricks and siding from the terminal. The booming aftershock reaches the tank in a second and rattles the metal gate in front of them. The flaming plane is scattered across the tarmac along with raptor innards and the ground is scorched around the indentation the projectile left.

"That was the most satisfying experience in my life," Kito

admits as he steps around the tank to inspect the aftermath. Thyst climbs down from the tank with a wide grin.

"Our path has been made cleared," he says when he reaches the ground. Anthulios begins handing out the AK47s or M4s to everyone. "Now put those swords away ladies and gents. It's time to get introduced to the twenty-first century. I doubt you want to get up-close and personal with these bastards," Thyst continues. Nydia receives her M4 but looks at it with bewilderment.

"So—how does this work?" She asks. Thyst gives everyone a crash course in assault rifle training while demonstrating on his AK47.

"Alright everyone, gather 'round. Here's what you need to know. Hold the butt of the gun to your shoulder good and tight. Here's your safety; press down for single shots or forward for full auto. Bottom loaded, pull back on cocking handle and pull down the mag. To load, just slap the mag up, pull the cocking handle and boom, you're ready to go; same thing with the M4s. Any questions?"

Kito, Amiku and Nydia stare blankly at him with an expression that proves they were unable to follow along with the quick lesson.

"What?" Amiku answers for everyone.

"Just get mine ready so all I have to do is pull the trigger," Kito says while handing his AK47 to Thyst.

"Second," Amiku replies.

"Third," follows Nydia as she and Amiku hand their rifles back to Thyst.

"Alright, let's start with single shots for this situation," he says with a chuckle. "Just be cautious of the knockback. This may take some getting used to." Thyst sets each gun before handing it back to their owners. He then looks over at Ardian. "Do you need any help?" Ardian cocks the gun, checks his mag, slaps it back in place, cocks the gun again, and then sets it to single shots.

"Nope, I'm good." The group stares at him dumbfounded.

"Have you fired these before?" Lio asks surprised.

"Just in Call of Duty," he admits.

"And they say video games don't teach you anything," Brax jokes.

The tank drives through the chain-link fence and crushes over it beneath its tracks. The ATVs and chopper follow close behind with Kito and Amiku riding as passengers. Amiku glances at Rona riding the motorcycle and makes a long face while shaking her head. Anthulios is behind at the .50 caliber rifle, on top of the tank, but not even a minute can pass before he shouts a warning to the others.

"Raptor, twelve o'clock!" The convoy comes to a stop a few yards from another demonized raptor near a fuel truck. The demonized raptor discovers the advancing group and charges toward them with a lowered head and open mouth. The sound of pops and patters spray a barrage of bullets into the raptor until it collapses in a pool of blood. The secession gunfire must have alerted two other raptors and they make their presence known by leaping onto the roofs of the baggage carts.

"Raptors at three o'clock and nine!" Lio calls out. Everyone emulates seasoned soldiers despite half of them never picked up a gun before today. They continue to advance diligently while picking off the raptors trying to ambush them. Anthulios continues to operate the .50 caliber while everyone else fire their AK7s, M4s, or the machine guns on the ATVs. After each threat has been annihilated the group continues to advance steadily toward the control tower.

The tank carefully maneuvers around a collapsed jet bridge as the following vehicles move around to its side, but when it clears the buckled obstruction, it halts in front of a massive pack of demonized raptors. The raptors turn their heads, almost in unison, toward them. As soon as one of the raptors lets out a screech Anthulios yells his order.

"Full auto, everyone! Full auto." Thyst joins Anthulios on top of the tank with his AK47 as the others get on foot for maximum mobility.

The raptors begin their onslaught while eight fully automatic machine guns explode into the pack. A raptor leaps onto the downed jetway, but Kito and Amiku share the task to kill it. Two more dart around their six, but Ardian and Rona are there to take them out. Another one jumps onto the hood of a tug next to Ardian, but Nydia fires everything she has into its face. Lio and Thyst has a good vantage point to mow down the ones farther away. This allows those on the ground to eliminate the raptors without becoming overrun by their reinforcements. One last raptor gets past the defense and scales the tank to claw its way up behind Lio and Thyst. Brax catches sight of it and fires into its hind legs. It tumbles down the tank to the ground where Brax finishes it off at close range. He glances up with a smile and salutes the men with two fingers. They return the salute with a grateful grin for his vigilance.

The full extent of the battle shows by the puddles of blood and guts, along with the dissembled body parts covering the entire area. Ardian checks his magazine and then slaps it back into the gun before resting the rifle on top of his shoulder.

"Level complete."

The convoy finally stops at the control tower and the team assembles in front of the door.

"We're here," Lio says with a sigh of relief.

"It's days like these I wish I could soak in a nice long bubble bath," Rona adds. Brax turns to her and grins, but she cocks her gun before he can get a word in. He gets the hint and looks away.

No one has worked in the control room for a long time, but it's evident that some of the equipment was hijacked in the not-so-distant past. The remaining computers, radar and radios seem to be inoperative while others look to have been deliberately smashed. Electrical and server wires lie exposed from the ransacked consoles or dangle from the ceiling, along with some of the light fixtures.

Thyst thinks to himself why Kaz never mentioned raptors at the airport or the possible state of the control room. Could someone who was trained to gather intel and know their surroundings be so out of touch with a location that at least would have been scouted if not fully explored? Kaz had to have been here, and most likely more than once, which means he either based his advice on old reconnaissance or cruel intent. Thyst decides to give his old friend the benefit of the doubt, but there is mutual assumption that this task will fail to yield a successful result.

Anthulios sits in front of one of the last few transceivers and begins turning knobs before testing out the hand microphone.

"Hello, hello, is anyone reading me?" He releases the button, but the only audible sound coming through is static. Nearby is also a portable transceiver in its charger. Anthulios picks it up and turns it on as a faint red light illuminates. "Hello, is anyone picking this up?" Everyone remains still and silent, but there's no response.

"Try another channel," Nydia advises. Anthulios flips the switch from 5 to 6.

"If anyone can hear this, please respond." The waiting begins again, but just when any attempt to make contact seems futile, a faint voice comes through.

"Who's this?"

"Hello, my name is Lio. Are you reading me clearly?" Anthulios excitedly replies.

"We're reading you, buddy." The group cheers as Anthulios smiles and motions them to keep down with his hand.

"I'm coming to you guys from the Silver Rock City Airport. My group have journeyed here from Esperanza with hopes to reach all who are willing to stand together once more. We have discovered new information and a common enemy. Here is what we know so far—"

At another base the radio transmission is being picked up. The radio operator is joined by three others who listen to Lio's message through the receiver.

"The leader of a massive demon movement goes by the name of Lazul. He has created a serum that can change people into demons, and then add them to his army. We have personally come in contact with him, as well as his followers."

Another man soon approaches to listen to the broadcast. His name is Dixon and he's the leader of this fortification. He looks at one of the men and snaps his fingers.

"Authenticate this." The man puts on a pair of earphones and then begins looking at GPS and radar while turning nobs to home in on the exact location of the transmission.

"Lazul and his collaborators, Anyo and Alma, will stop at nothing less than the extinction of our race—" Lio continues.

A flashing blip appears on a satellite image of a map on the connected monitor. The radio operator takes off his headphones and then looks back at Dixon.

"It seems legit, sir."

"Has anyone heard of this, Esperanza?" Dixon asks.

"I know where it is," another man admits.

Meanwhile, at the control room, Anthulios is finishing his speech.

"Hiding is no longer an option. We must unite and show sympathy for our fellow man. Only then will we have a chance to finally end this opposition. All who are able, please find us at our fort, Esperanza located south of Silver Rock City."

Anthulios lifts his finger off the button and waits for a reply; however, the voice through the scanner comes in choppy and incoherent. The dim red light slowly begins blinking indicating the battery is dying. Anthulios attempts to make his closing statement.

"Please pass this message to everyone you are able to reach. I do not have the power to continue broadcasting." The light finally fades out. Lio sets the dead device down, but at least their message was able to get out to someone.

The sound of slow clapping draws everyone's attention behind them.

"Great speech—I was really moved by it. Truly spoken from the heart." Alma says in a condescending tone. "I don't know if I appreciate having my name blasted over the airwaves though."

"Alma—" Kito utters mostly as a whisper. Once he gets over the shock of seeing her, he develops a strong desire to avoid this encounter entirely. He doesn't want to be forced into making a regrettable action by choosing between his own team or her. He finds himself in a no-win situation where he can't help Alma but doesn't want to harm her either.

Alma puts a hand on her hip while giving Kito a wink and a tantalizing smile. "I love it when you say my name, Kito. Isn't it ironic how we keep running into each other like this?"

"Detain her before she teleports," Lio orders. Amiku and Rona grab each of Alma's arms as everyone else except for Kito, point their guns at her.

"Don't move, Alma!" Thyst commands.

"Don't worry, I like where this is going," Alma replies as she continues to play her games. Ardian notices Kito doesn't have his gun raised and whispers to him.

"Are you okay, Kito?"

"Yes, what's the matter, Kito?" Alma chimes in after

overhearing Ardian's question. "After all we've been through, I hope you aren't the type of guy to have his way with a sweet innocent girl and then ignore her phone calls." Amiku darts a stern look at Kito.

"What is she talking about, Kito?"

"You mean you didn't tell them what happened between us?" Alma continues. "With his head in betwixt my thighs he showed me how much he cared. He didn't resist when I held him down and beneath me, I took what he so willingly gave up."

"You sicken me, Kito," Amiku says unable to think of any other way to voice her disgust and shock.

"Don't listen to her, Amiku. There isn't any truth behind her words," Kito says trying to defend himself.

"So, you didn't let me kiss you?" Alma reminds him. Kito's silence is enough to prove his guilt. He didn't consent to her advances, but how does he explain it?

"I didn't kiss her," he begins, but then falls short with a followup.

"But you let her?" Amiku tries to confirm. Alma has outwitted Kito and used Amiku to land the final blow.

"Don't be jealous, Amiku," Alma says. "Kito said we can share him."

"That's not even true!" Kito shouts. Denials tend to become meaningless if repeated too many times, but Kito doesn't know what else to say. He's been setup, but to everyone else he's been compromised. Amiku loosens her grip on Alma and glares at Kito.

"I thought you had more willpower than that! But you don't, do you? You are just another degenerate lacking in morals! I no longer have any respect for you, Kito!"

Alma takes advantage of the distraction to body slam Rona off her feet. She then twists Amiku's arm and lifts her up onto her shoulders before flipping her over her back. Anthulios holds his rifle steady and begins to squeeze the trigger with a clear shot at Alma. Kito quickly jabs the butt of his gun under Lio's muzzle to force it up just as the bullet leaves the barrel. The bullet is sent into the ceiling as the gunshot echoes in the room.

"Why did you do that, Kito?" Nydia asks baffled.

"Isn't it obvious? He's protecting his mate," Alma continues her con.

"Shut up, Alma," Kito finally snaps.

The barrel of a Browning pistol appears behind Alma's ear just as someone cocks it. Alma didn't expect this and remains frozen in place.

"You so much as sneeze and I will blow your head off," Kaz warns. He then glances over at Thyst. "You got her?"

"I got her," Thyst replies while keeping his gun on Alma.

Kaz lowers his pistol to take out a coil of plastic cord and then ties Alma's hands behind her back.

"Are you alone?" Thyst asks.

"Yeah, my men will meet us at Esperanza tomorrow, but I decided to meet up with you today." When Kaz finishes his knot Rona reclaims her hold on Alma. "We can put her in the Humvee I brought," he suggests before looking up at Kito. "Is he with her?"

"No, he's with us," Lio says.

"Then why did he help her?" Kaz questions. Anthulios looks at Kito, but he refuses to return eye contact.

"We don't know yet," Thyst replies instead.

"We should arrest him too then," Kaz suggests.

"He's like a son to me. He wouldn't betray us," Lio says trying to defend him, but Kaz ignores his comment.

"Do you have any holding cells in Esperanza?" He says to Thyst.

"We do, but—"

"It will only be temporarily until we find out what's going on," Kaz assures him.

Kito has grown tired of Kaz and of his opinions. He turns to face him and in a threatening tone says, "I don't answer to you."

"You will explain your actions, or you will be detained," Kaz snaps back.

"Fuck you!" Kito points his gun at Kaz who raises his pistol in defense.

"Oh-my-God, stop it, Kito!" Nydia shouts fearing this altercation will soon get out of hand.

"Put your weapon down!" Kaz orders.

"Do you want to test me?" Kito shouts back. Kaz and Kito keep their weapons pointed at each other as Thyst attempts to diffuse the hostile situation.

"Calm down, Kito. This is only temporary."

"This is bullshit! It's this guy you hardly know!"

"Kaz and I knew each other way before I met you. But that's not the point. Stop resisting; it will be easier on all of us if, for now, you just cooperate," Thyst responds. Not wanting to see Kito harmed Lio lets out a sigh.

"Please hand me your gun, Kito," he says. Kito hides his disbelief at the request and becomes angrier.

"You have all turned against me so easily. Fine, then you'll have to kill me because I'm not giving up."

"Please stop this, Kito!" Nydia screams.

"Come to your senses. You can't win here." Ardian advises him. "Just back down for now." Kito keeps his AK47 pressed against his shoulder and brings his sights closer to the gun. He has no intention of lowering his weapon.

"I'm not giving you a choice," he says to Kaz. Amiku knows Kito can be irrational and stubborn, but she's now also worried for him.

"I will shoot you," Kaz says.

"Then you better make it count because I have more bullets than you."

"Then unfortunately you will not survive past this day."

Amiku hurries in between them and punches Kito in the face. It's the only thing she can think of that might knock him off guard and save him. Anthulios grabs Kito's gun as soon as he's thrown off balance while Thyst and Ardian wrestle him to the ground. Kaz holsters his gun and then rushes over to bind his hands.

"Get off of me!" Kito says while trying to squirm free.

"Shut up or I'll club you," Kaz barks.

"That won't be necessary. I'll take him," Lio calmly answers while lifting Kito to his feet after Kaz secures his hands. Everyone believes what they are doing is for Kito's own good, but to him it's an attack.

Anthulios guides Kito to the backseat of the Humvee while Rona directs Alma inside from the opposite side.

"Should we have them together like this?" she asks.

"Don't worry. She won't get away with anything while Kaz is inside," Thyst says. Kito feels his imprisonment beginning when the doors are shut.

"Wow, I was almost in the middle of a fire fight. My heart is still beating fast." Alma begins. "Just so you know, I was cheering for ya."

"Leave me alone—just—leave me alone," Kito says in a defeated tone.

The convoy rolls out of the airport on their way back to Esperanza. Alma may have succeeded in creating a rift in the group. Her prediction that Kito's company would turn on him, in a sense, has come true.

9

The Trial

The end of a busy day brings a calming night over Esperanza. No one expected a mission to reunite people would end with their own team separated and one of them in prison. Despite how much care and planning goes into advancement, society still manages to withdraw from achievement and revert backwards.

Thyst and a few of his men are standing guard on top of Esperanza's roof. It's a safe place to watch the surrounding countryside, but also provides Thyst a venue to get some fresh air and gather his thoughts. He was hoping to be left alone, but it isn't long before Kaz finds him and leads him out of earshot from his men.

"What are you going to do with Kito?" He asks.

"That depends on the verdict from the trial."

"What do you mean a trial?"

"That's how we operate here," Thyst explains. "We will find out why he did what he did and then take it from there."

"We all know what he did. He obviously has been manipulated by Alma. If he was in my custody I would have him executed." Thyst is shocked by Kaz's conclusion and his harsh sentence.

"Then it's a good thing he's in my custody and not yours," he replies.

Slightly below ground level is an area no larger than a typical two-car garage. It is here that two prison cells sit side by side with Kito in the first and Alma in the second. Each cell has a small bed and is completely enclosed by iron bars, save for the stone wall that doubles as the backside of the cells. Kito leans forward with his elbows resting on the horizontal bar and his arms dangling out through the metal columns.

"My shrink always said I would end up here," Kito reflects somberly. Alma grabs onto the bars that separate their quarters.

"Your parents made you seek help too?"

"No, my school did. My dad was gone as soon as I was born, and my mom spent every night with someone who offered her a bottle of anything." Alma legitimately seems sorry for him.

"Yeah, my folks gave up on me too." Alma lets a moment of silence pass before talking again. "Why do you care about saving the world? It didn't do shit for either of us." Kito turns to look at her.

"I'm not trying to do anything. I'm just surviving and killing your boss just happens to be part of that." Kito heads to the bed and lays down on his back. The mattress is too hard, and the pillow is too soft. There's no chance for a good night's sleep for him tonight, and if he does manage to acquire some, his aching back and neck the next morning will make him regret it.

"He's not my boss," Alma says as she lowers her head. "I was just a girl out on the streets, and he had a place to stay. Maybe I still feel like I owe him something." She looks back at Kito, but he remains staring at the ceiling. "No one has ever stood up for me, Kito and I gave you no reason to do so. I don't think it's fair your comrades banish you so hastily."

"Why don't you just teleport out of here?" Kito says in a monotoned reply.

"I can't teleport through iron. None of my abilities work when I'm around it. Something about its chemical makeup reflects my energy," she admits.

Footsteps can be heard coming down the stone steps. Alma looks to see who's approaching, but Kito could care less. Aiza steps through the archway and continues toward Kito's cell.

"Good evening, Kito. My name is Aiza, head of Esperanza's council. You have been accused of scheming with the enemies of Esperanza and putting innocent lives and a mission at risk. I'm here to get your side of the story before your trial."

Kito turns on his side to face away from Aiza without responding. This insulting action causes Aiza to respond in a less friendly tone.

"I will not talk to the back of your head. You are in no position to test your luck, so get up and face me." Kito continues to ignore her. "Stop sulking like a little boy. You are being very disrespectful. If you don't answer my questions, I will have to make my ruling based on speculation. If you are found guilty, you may be kicked out of Esperanza or thrown off a nearby cliff to your death. Personally, I feel neither should be your fate. So please stop this childish behavior and meet me halfway." Kito answers without making eye contact.

"Do whatever you want." Aiza is taken back by Kito's refusal to help himself. She had already discussed some of the details with Lio and the others and saw little reason to turn this into a big case. It's mostly just formalities, but Kito's attitude is turning this into something it doesn't need to be, where a punishment he doesn't deserve, may be the turn out. To Kito, however, everyone has betrayed him, and he refuses to cooperate.

"I will let you sleep on this. I hope you are smart enough to look me in the eyes tomorrow," she says before walking away.

"Why didn't you answer that woman's questions? It seemed like she was trying to help you," Alma asks after Aiza had been gone for a short time.

"I don't need anyone's help."

"That tough guy attitude you're fronting isn't fooling anyone except for yourself. Stop pouting and feeling sorry for yourself." Kito refuses to respond to Alma's lecture. "You're pissing me off, Kito! You have no idea what I would give to switch places with you!" Alma retreats to her bed and lies down, but neither discusses anything further.

The fort is quiet after everyone has retired to their rooms for the night, all except for Amiku who is sitting at a table in the common area. Anthulios also isn't sleeping and decides to join her.

"Not tired either, huh?" he says. Amiku slowly shakes her head while keeping her focus on her hands as she plays with her fingers. "What are you thinking about?"

"I don't know what to think anymore," Amiku begins. "I can't believe Kito would do anything against us, but after what Alma said. I just don't know."

"There are two kinds of truths, Amiku. The truth will always be the truth, but what makes them believable or not are the lies. It's the definition of anarchy." Amiku gives him a bewildered look.

"What do you mean?"

"Let's say I tell you a fact that you know to be true and then I tell you a lie that you could not be aware of. You are already considering it, playing with the probability of it. You may believe the lie without question since I initially proved myself to be reputable.

Now switch it around. I tell you several lies that you know are lies and then I throw in the truth. Since you know everything I said before is false you will tend to denounce the truth also.

Besides fear it's the best way to control others."

"How does that apply to right now?"

"You know Kito was alone with Alma, that's the truth. Alma spent a great deal of time explaining how she bedded him and then how she kissed him. Kito never denied the latter. So, the question you have to ask yourself is, who do you believe more?" Amiku thinks about it for a moment. She will always trust Kito over Alma. "You already know the answer, Amiku."

"Thank you, Lio," she says with a tiny grin.

"In a lot of ways, I think of Kito as my own; due to his own father's abandonment and the fact that I never had any children of my own. I try to look out for him while at the same time letting him fall." Lio stands up and then places a hand on Amiku's shoulder. "But he doesn't need a mentor anymore. He needs someone with a little more influence." Amiku tries to hide a smirk that escapes her lips as Lio returns to his room.

Later that night, Kito is lying in his prison bed half-awake when a familiar voice makes him open his eyes.

"You learn your lessons hard, Kito." He sits up to see Sonya in the cell with him.

"Sonya? Why do you haunt me?"

"Haunt you?" Sonya takes a few paces to reach the foot of his bed. "My blood courses through your veins, Kito. I'm a part of you." Kito gets out of bed and walks away from her.

"You aren't real."

"You've been running away from yourself your whole life. Stop for a moment and find out who you really are, or are you afraid what you might see?" Kito shakes his head.

"You're dead." Sonya advances behind him and puts her hands on top of each of his shoulders.

"I made a sacrifice for you, and you will make one for someone else." She leans in close to whisper in his ear. "You will save a life by forfeiting yours." Kito spins around but Sonya is gone. He can feel someone watching him and turns back around to see Alma standing at the bars separating their cells.

"Do you see spirits, Kito?"

"You wouldn't understand."

"You might be surprised," Alma replies. Kito returns to the bed and sits down as Alma continues. "I can't save your accomplices, but I do have some say in what happens to you. Come with me, Kito, please. I'm not all bad. We can save each other."

"In another life, Alma. In another life." Alma sighs and then returns to her bed. She talks to herself, but loud enough for Kito to hear.

"False prophets and smiling serpents. Their eyes speak of trust, but their hearts were made to deceive. We fall prey to their webs and believe we are safe. We sleep with our hearts open, but our minds closed. For the desire to be loved makes us ignore the smoldering jaws of our caretakers. We are made to suffer as they take from us what satisfies them and then leaves us to rot. Betrayed and deceived we are entwined in vines with thoughts of shame and self-inflicted doubt; for it was us who willingly walked into our fate. To live, is to feel pain, to die, is to feel sorrow, to roam in between both worlds, is to feel anger and hate. Our killers come wearing smiles and wrapped in blankets of friendship. For the lost it is trust that must be avoided, or we will be depleted of hope and defeated."

Morning arrives and Aiza returns as promised. She stands on the other side of the bars calling to wake Kito. She will give him one more chance to meet her halfway, but something tells her he will remain stubborn. Some people enjoy bringing themselves pain. Sometimes it's the only moment they get a chance to feel something. The self-loathing believe they deserve pain and sorrow, and their actions bring more of it, which only reiterates their assumptions. No amount of pleading from those who question the actions of those who act against themselves will ever make a difference. They've lived on the outside for so long they have stopped looking in.

Kito stirs to sit on the side of the bed after hearing Aiza call his name several times. "I'll make this easy on you and only ask you one question. Why did you save Alma?" Aiza asks. Kito stands up and walks toward her. He puts his hands on the bars and stares directly at her.

"You wouldn't understand my reason, so I'll make it easy on you and not give you my answer." Kito turns his back to Aiza and walks back to his bed. Once she has overcome the shock of his response, she gives him her reply.

"I hope you have a better reason than that for the council. I came to you as a favor for Thyst and this is how you repay his leniency. You just made this harder on yourself. If you had been cooperative, I would have been forgiving. Your trial is at noon." Aiza hurries off with heavy footsteps as Alma stares at Kito while shaking her head.

"Don't hang yourself on my account," she says.

Just before noon, Thyst, Rona and Anthulios arrive at the prison cells. Thyst opens Kito's cell first and leads Anthulios and Rona in.

"It's time, Kito," he says.

"I care not of your laws," Kito replies calmly.

"That's quite enough immaturity from you," Rona says and takes hold of him by the arm. Anthulios stands just inside the cell with a hardcover book in his hand. He opens the book to where he has his bookmark and begins reading, as if it was his last rights.

"Console me in my exile, and ease my sorrow, for all my longings are for Thee. And all the comfort the world can give only adds to my burden. I wish to lay hold of eternal goods, but temporal things and my unchecked passions keep me back; I am forced against my will to become a slave to them. Unhappy man that I am, in this way, I am at war with myself."

The passage was written by Thomas à Kempis sometime during the 1400's and speaks of a common theme that resonates to this day. The internal struggle, man verses himself. The desire to live in peace is challenged by another desire for power, fortune, or fame. The end result is anything but a calm and sound mind.

Anthulios and Rona chaperone Kito while Thyst escorts Alma, with her hands bound in iron handcuffs, into the courtroom. The walls are cream in color and several pews in the back offer seating for Kito's companions and other citizens. Kaz remains leaning just inside the doorway with his arms folded. His demeanor suggests he's hoping for a guilty verdict; however, no one understands why he wishes someone he doesn't know such an ill fate.

Kito and Alma are stopped in the middle of the room facing a long, wooden, ornate table with Aiza sitting in the middle and seven council members on either side of her. Thyst, Rona and Lio leave their prisoners at their podiums and return to the first pew where Brax, Amiku, Ardian and Nydia are sitting.

"It is now noon, and all council members are present and accounted for," Aiza begins. "The reason for this hearing is to discuss Kito's actions the day before. I will now bring everyone up to speed on the details. While on a mission to reach isolated people, in order to form an alliance, Kito directly interfered in the shooting and possible death of Alma, who was considered a high threat to the safety of all who were present at the time." Aiza continues while occasionally glancing down at her written notes. "The group consisted of Thyst, Rona, Brax, Anthulios, Ardian, Amiku, Nydia and Kito. All of whom are present here today. These strangers were taken in and cared for by Mika after being injured in a previous battle with Alma and another named, Anyo, who are known allies to Lazul.

After Kaz apprehended Alma, he inquired about Kito's actions. Kito responded by pointing his AK47 at Kaz in a threatening manner saying, and I quote, you'll have to kill me because I'm not giving up. Kito's own companions were required to use force to subdue him." Kito rolls his eyes and shakes his head while smiling as Aiza continues her introduction.

"Alma is also present; her crimes include, but are not limited to, an alliance with Lazul and Anyo and acting upon several murderous attempts on each of Kito's companions including Kito himself. She is also known to have been present and aided in the destruction of several forts and the deaths of their occupants including Anthulios' fort. She is known to have kidnapped Kito; however, the details of that time frame are yet unknown." Alma smiles at the thought of what others may be thinking.

"The events that occurred during Kito's kidnapping as well as his loyalty are being questioned. This court is now in session. It has been decided, prior to the start of this hearing, that Rona will help defend Kito at this trial." Aiza holds her hand out to motion Rona forward. "You may now approach and stand beside Kito, Rona."

Rona steps forward and announces her advice to Kito in a strict, reprimanding whisper.

"Keep your mouth shut." Kito only replies with a sly smile. Aiza takes a moment to read her notes and then faces Alma.

"My first question is for Alma. At the time when you took a clearly injured Kito into your possession, what were your intentions?"

"My intentions, you ask?" Alma smirks. "I was planning on nursing him back to health and then make ferocious love to him. Or was it the other way around? I forget now." The council members jot down their notes on the pad of paper in front of them. In the audience, Amiku makes a fist and holds it on top of her thigh, but Nydia gently puts her hand over hers as they exchange heartfelt looks.

"I see, your reputation precedes you, Alma," Aiza replies and then turns towards Kito. "Kito, what occurred between you and Alma during your capture?" Rona glances at Kito with a look that informs him to behave. He begins with a sigh.

"She told me her life story and then left." Thinking there is more to Kito's story, Aiza allows a moment of silence to pass.

"We are all familiar with Alma's persona. You expect us to believe nothing further took place than a backstory from a woman of her nature?"

"I'm sorry, I was under the false impression you were looking for the truth," Kito replies. He doesn't want to go into detail of his entire experience, and he doesn't feel it's any of their business. Anything he would admit to would just be blown out of proportion anyway.

The audience begins to whisper amongst themselves, and their opinions are not in Kito's favor.

"You are out of line, Kito. I did not ask you for your assumptions or give you permission to speak freely," Aiza says in a raised voice.

"What's the point of asking me anything if you aren't going to believe what I say?" Kito snaps back in an annoyed tone.

Rona forcefully grabs Kito's upper arm and leans in close to his face. "Remember who you are talking to, Kito. Your brash attitude will not be tolerated here!" The audience bursts into a deafening chatter that forces Aiza to talk even louder.

"You obviously have no concept of authority! If I were you, I would mind my tongue!"

"I bet you have other plans for my tongue!"

The courtroom, that was just in an uproar, falls deathly silent almost instantly. Nydia gasps and puts her hand to cover her dropped jaw. Aiza stares at Kito in disbelief while Alma grins in amusement. The room remains silent waiting for Aiza's response, but Rona grabs Kito's collar and pulls him towards her with a raised hand.

"What part of, keep your mouth shut, didn't you understand!?" Aiza interrupts Rona before her hand connects with Kito's face.

"Rona—leave him be." Rona lowers her hand, but glares at Kito as if warning him that she's still contemplating the disciplinary action.

"Your disrespect concerns me, Kito. You obviously don't realize how grave a situation you are in. My ruling today will be final and nonnegotiable. So, I suggest you know your place in this matter. You are, but a guest here at Esperanza and we owe you nothing. Your abrasive speech and your insulting behavior are tempting me to throw you out of here. In fact, if your friends had not stood in your defense, I would have already done so. I would show a bit more gratitude and respect towards them and myself if I were you."

Kito was sure his companions had cast him aside. He didn't expect them to speak on his behalf and now knowing they have makes him feel a little ashamed. Just as he doesn't want to be thought of as weak, he also doesn't want to disappoint those who put their trust and faith into him.

"Right now, the evidence is against you. One more outburst from you or a comment I don't like, and I will rule you under Alma's influence," Aiza concludes. Kito keeps his eyes low and remains silent.

"Kito's morals don't need to be questioned," Alma says. She's growing weary of being allied with Lazul and yearns for something that feels more like a friendship rather than obedience. "Creating disturbances is my talent, it's what I'm good at. For I confess the truth that I often allow myself to be distracted. For very often I am not where I am, but wherever my thoughts carry me. And my thoughts are most frequently what I love. Whatever pleases me most, by nature or by habit, is where I will always be. It is true that my objective was sabotage, and my desire was Kito. Think what you like, but the reason for my obsession was because I saw a kindred spirit. I will accept my fate. I only ask for Kito to be spared from punishment."

The courtroom remains quiet as everyone interprets Alma's words. She has shown a vulnerability and Kito proves to have shown sensitivity. How ironic the two people to be labeled troublemakers are the ones to teach compassion.

"You are in no position to be making requests; however, your confession is appreciated," Aiza finally announces.

Ardian stands up and walks over to Kito.

"Amiku once said that we were a team of four and just before leaving Lio's fort we all promised each other to stay a team of four. I'm not about to give up on that." Nydia and Amiku stand up and join Ardian behind Kito. Their actions shatter Kito's defensive walls, and overcome with emotion, he explains his motives.

"During my captivity with Alma I saw someone who lived in an invisible cage her entire life. I was called a delinquent so many times that I adopted it as a compliment—just like she was called evil. We act the way we were treated—we are all victims of circumstances. We become loyal to those who take us in and feel we must adopt some of their ideals. If I didn't meet Amiku, Ardian, and Nydia when I did, I could have gone down Alma's path. I could have joined deception for I would have nothing to compare it too.

For this reason, I saw a commonality between myself and her.

I can live with a choice that ends up being wrong. I can't live with doing nothing if I was right all along. I saved Alma to save myself. So, question my morality if you must, but when you chase your demons and finally have them cornered, lay your eyes on them. You may realize that there is a little bit of yourself in that which you hunt. Can you kill a reflection of yourself?"

Aiza relaxes in her chair and thinks for a moment.

"It is true that circumstance and the surrounding environment can affect how a person develops. But we also have free will and the knowledge of right from wrong. We do have control over our own actions and someday we must pay for the aftermath of these actions. You can have our sympathy, but our forgiveness is a different matter."

Each council member makes their notes and verdicts on a piece of paper before folding it in half and passing it down to Aiza. After she has collected everyone's decision, she begins tallying them up and then lastly adds her opinion to the final docket. Aiza finally stands up to address the room.

"Concerning Kito's actions. It has been decided that Kito has proven himself and no disciplinary action will be sentenced for the events that transpired."

Ardian pats Kito on the back as Lio and Thyst smile to themselves, but Kaz steps out of the room seemly upset of the ruling.

"As for Alma," Aiza continues. "Her past attacks on others that may have led to, or near to, their deaths are too much to ignore. For this reason, we still consider her a threat. Alma is hereby banished from Esperanza and the nearby countryside. Her fate will be decided by her future choices outside of Esperanza's walls. This concludes the case of Kito and Alma verses Esperanza. This courtroom is now dismissed."

Esperanza's guards escort Alma out into the fields with Thyst watching from the entryway.

"Alma, you have been spared from death just as long as you never return to Esperanza," one of the guards says as another removes the handcuffs from her wrists. When the guards begin to head back towards the fort it's revealed that Amiku was standing behind them. Alma stands her ground as Amiku advances with an unpleasant expression. Thyst notices the two and becomes alert but decides not to get involved yet.

"You only get this one time. I do not forgive you," Amiku says sternly.

"My fight is no longer with any of you. I have much I need to atone for. My war is now with Lazul. Someday, maybe I can find my redemption." Alma closes her eyes and bows. "Please thank Kito for me. Arigato and sayonara."

Alma then teleports away leaving Amiku by herself. She turns around and starts to walk back towards the fort but stops after a few steps. She sighs and looks over her shoulder while softly and sincerely mumbling her blessing.

"Good luck."

In one of the living quarters of Esperanza, Kito is sitting on the side of his bed when Nydia walks in and sits beside him.

"I see many things in you, Kito, but a delinquent isn't one of them, just a hero trying to break through."

"That's where my demons hide; there's no room for a hero."

"We all have demons, but it's our will to overpower them that brings out our heroes." Kito looks at Nydia with a heartfelt stare.

"Do you always see the best in others?"

"I can only see what is truly there. Despite how well it may be hidden." She stands up and gives him a smile before leaving him alone with his thoughts.

Outside of Lazul's fort, goblins and demonoids are constructing a rocket-sized cannon. The cannon's metal shell is nearly formed, but the wooden base, it will sit on, is still being hammered together. A nearby crane suspends the cannon upright with ropes as the laborers work underneath it. The cannon's enormous size begs to ask for what purpose it will serve. It's too large to be moved without wheels and there's no indication those are in the plans. Whatever Lazul is planning to use this weapon for, it will be executed here. The goblins act as the gatherers and carry wood, stone, and metal to the demonoids who are tasked with building the contraption. Larger demonoids act as overseers and relish carrying out brutal physical abuse on their peons with whips and clubs.

Lazul watches the production taking place from the second highest level. The room itself appears to have been a dining hall. A long rectangle table with chairs occupy the center of the room, but besides that there aren't any other furniture pieces or decor. Alma enters the room and advances behind Lazul with determination. He knows she's behind him but doesn't care enough to acknowledge her. He also knows her true intention for returning. She has always been and will always be a pawn to him—and he's about to make his next move. Anyo steps out from an enclave in the wall and follows behind her. His presence isn't a surprise to Alma. He almost never leaves Lazul's side unless ordered somewhere else.

"I know you didn't dare return to report your failure again," Lazul growls without turning around.

"I have many failures. This is not one of them." Lazul turns around and glares at her.

"So, you wish to offer your resignation, is that it?"

"Something like that," she replies.

"This little slut was never useful to us. Let me kill her," Anyo says, but Alma's temper flares up before Lazul can give his answer. She hurls an energy ball from her palm towards Anyo, but he dodges the orb, and it explodes into the wall. Anyo swipes his claws at Alma in retaliation, but she teleports behind him. Lazul grabs her around the waist with his tentacle and pulls her away from Anyo before slamming her to the floor.

"You dare fight against us!" Lazul flings Alma against the wall before she falls to the floor. "You will never be accepted by anyone. You are a wild, uncontrollable animal to those humans. Thy will never trust you," Lazul adds. Alma picks herself off the floor as Lazul continues. "I think it's time to let your demon out. Shed yourself of this human form, this weakness called humanity. Become what you were born to be."

"Don't pretend to know me."

"But I do know you. Your plan to claim Kito is derived from your insatiable succubae desire to seduce and dominate. I allowed you to play your game of titillation because if he became yours, he then would also be mine. His boiling blood will make him a great asset. Even if he refuses to join us his blood will enhance my current serum to craft a stronger demon. You are a huntress, your nature is to destroy, not to love. Bring me Kito and I will give him to you. I will tie him to the floor so you may place your cunt where you please."

"You know nothing about me. Your demonic interpretation about my feelings of admiration and affection just proved it."

"You know nothing about affection. You've never had it. And

you never will. That's why I chose you," Lazul says.

Anyo punches Alma in the gut to send her to her knees hunching over.

"Kito, like you, have suppressed their demon blood, but haven't won over it. With Kito it is rage that will unleash it. With you—it's pain," Lazul concludes.

Anyo grabs Alma by the hair and pulls her back. He then punches her in the face and follows up with a swift kick to her ribs. Alma rolls over onto her hands and knees but is too slow to stand back up. Anyo kicks her hard in the belly to send her on her back. He soars up with one flap of his wings and then lands almost on top of her. Anyo picks her up by the legs and swings her with ease across the room into the stone wall. Alma's weak from the abuse and is having difficulty lifting herself up; however, she forcefully grunts her defiance with blood streaming from her head and mouth.

Lazul joins in now and whips his tentacles across her face and body. Alma never found her opening to counter and now feels her strength fading. Alma's screams of distress soon become growls and then roars.

She tries to fight the transformation, but it's too late; she is too weak to fight against it. Alma's eyes turn yellow and long brownish-orange fur grows around her body. Her body structure also becomes larger and rips her dress to shreds as it takes its new shape. Her white hair grows down to her ankles and her fingernails grow into claws followed by the formation of two fangs. Lastly, a long tail swats the air behind her as she stands and roars. Some areas of her human skin are still visible on her legs, arms, torso, and face; however, the rest of her is covered with fur. Lazul was right, Alma has turned into a half human, half lioness demon, she has become the huntress. Alma's will is no longer hers, in her demon form she only knows to obey Lazul's orders; and he hastily gives her three.

"Return to Esperanza. Bring me Kito. Kill everyone else."

The next morning, thirty of Kaz's well-armed soldiers reach Esperanza. Thyst and Kaz welcome them warmly and then escort them inside to meet Nichi and Lako. Kito, Nydia, and Amiku observe the newcomers and the introductions taking place at the nearby table, while Ardian seems to be deeply involved reading from the O.D.E. journal. He has found an excerpt about an artifact called the Architect's Box. From the text it sounds like this may have been responsible for bringing demons into the world.

Ardian gets his team's attention and then shares the following with them—

> *According to ancient religious beliefs, the Architect created the world and the universe and then stepped aside to let time and nature take over without any further involvement. The Architect's Box was said to reverse his work, unleashing destruction and evil into the world.*
>
> *It is unknown how many ancient civilizations came in contact with this artifact, but none were able to resist the potential power it could bestow, except for one civilization, the Mayans. Texts show they were far more advanced than they should have been for their time with knowledge of the cosmos and construction capabilities. They guarded this box for centuries without a single incident; however, the Mayans, as well as this box, mysteriously disappeared without a trace.*
>
> *Theories indicated that they may have fled to another world and took the box with them. Such power in the hands of men was no doubt dangerous; however, it is more likely that the Mayans were vanquished in conquest and the box became a spoil of war. The Mayans referred to this artifact as, The Star of Eluvium, but in Celtic lore it was referred to as Abria's Stone, and the Greeks called it Pandora's Box.*

The four wonder if Lazul somehow managed to come into possession of this ancient artifact, but how, is something they can't even begin to guess on. History is full of impossible tasks and overwhelming battles. But somehow people bested the odds and won their freedom from the clutches of tyranny. If there is a way to accomplish that now, this group will find it.

Thyst, Anthulios, Rona and Brax join the four at their table moments later. Kito gets a glimpse of Kaz leaving the area with his men and his intense glare and scowl has caught the attention of Thyst.

"You don't trust him, do you?" Thyst asks.

"Can you blame me? He tried to give me the death sentence."

"I will admit his argument even caught me off guard. I don't want to make excuses for him, but his mind never left the war. He's haunted by the demons that got away and the ones that didn't. He keeps all of them inside him now.

During The Demon Wars, I started out driving trucks, and then became trained to fly helicopters. That's when I met Kaz. It was a rescue mission in the dead of night; twelve soldiers surrounded by demons."

Thyst recalls his past to the group. He's piloting a Black Hawk helicopter and begins to land it at his given coordinates. He gently touches bottom and strains his eyes to peer outside. Finally, the bouncing light from a flashlight indicates men are hurrying his way. Six soldiers climb inside with Kaz following them.

"Where are the others! My intel mentioned twelve."

"There's just us now. The others turned!" Kaz replies over the roar of the rotating blades.

"They're coming!" one of the soldiers hollers.

The missing soldiers rush towards the helicopter as demonized men. Kaz fires upon them from the open door while shouting. "Get this bird in the air!"

Thyst lifts the chopper off the ground and ascends to the safety of the sky. The men finally feel relaxed enough to fall asleep as Thyst flies them back to their base. Kaz was so gracious to Thyst and impressed with his swift action that he personally requested him to be his pilot or driver on every mission he was assigned to.

Unfortunately, less than a year later, the war was lost. Demons invaded the nation's capital and ambushed the president inside the oval office. He collapses to the floor as more demons pour in and attack the helpless man. A pool of blood soaks the carpet; the president has been killed.

After the president's death everyone begins governing themselves and orders from superiors were being ignored. The result is a world where actions came without any consequences. Separation from the fabrication, it was called. This is when Apocalypsia was actualized, and the collapse of civilization was complete.

Kaz returns home to Silver Rock City where he's welcomed with cold stares and harsh words from the neighbors. Kaz was blamed for losing the war due to his failure as a Sargent and his men faced the same prejudice. Even Kaz's wife closed the door on him. He, along with other outcast men, set up a new home in the maintenance and operation room of the sewers. Over the next few weeks, the city tears itself apart with fear and greed and demons hunt the disoriented citizens.

Thyst claims an abandoned fort and names it, Esperanza, a Spanish word meaning hope. That's what this place will be to him and all who come to its gates.

10

Internal Demons

She can feel the soft, wet earth underneath her paws as she sprints through the grass. She can feel the wind rushing over her back and the smell of her prey riding on the currents. She can see trees whizzing past her and hears her breath sync up to her stride. She knows where she's going and what she's planning to do when she arrives. She's fueled by a maddening hunger and an unquenchable thirst to which there is no cure or satisfaction. Every need and desire must be fulfilled immediately. She can't stop herself; nothing will stop her.

Two Esperanza guards keep their keen eyes on the surrounding field, but neither has the urge to look behind them. If they had they might see the huntress stalking closer. Every step she takes is silent, every breath, slow and steady. She stays close to the wall and in the shadows not even the guards on the roof can see her. She is nearly upon the unsuspecting guards at the front gates. How would they have known that today would have been their last. Without a signal of her presence, she finally pounces on the guards. With her claws she slashes their stomachs and with her sharp fangs puncture their necks.

The attack has caught the attention of the nearby citizens and other soldiers. Screaming fills the entrance of the fort as people make a hasty retreat while, the soldiers rush forward to defend. With blinding speed, the huntress somehow manages to dodge the bullets being fired at her as she increasingly closes the gap between her and her attackers. She darts forward on her hands and feet while using her tail as balance. She yanks the rifle out of the first man she encounters and tosses it behind her. She utilizes a combination of kicks and claw swipes to take him down before leaping towards another man. Her whole body is a weapon, and her acrobatic moves are lethal and quick. Her combinations of kicks, spins, jumps, and dives soon eliminate the resistance blocking her from entering. She continues into the fort with a bipedal stroll while sniffing around to locate her targets.

Kito, Brax and Nydia are first to arrive.

"What is that?" Brax asks when he lays eyes on the huntress.

"It can't be—" Kito utters as a whisper.

"It is," Nydia confirms.

Thyst, Lio, Nichi, Lako and Rona are next to reach the chaotic scene. People are still trying to push their way through the crowd or remain huddled against the walls.

"You need to get the rest of these people out of here!" Rona says to Thyst.

"Okay, I will try to hurry back," he promises. He creates a loud whistle with his fingers to get everyone's attention. "Follow me below to the storm shelter!" The citizens scramble down the hallway after him and then down a staircase into a large open area where the vehicles are stored. Aifina intercepts him here.

"I will take it from here. They will need you up there." Thyst smiles and nods, but she grabs his arm just as he turns around. "Be careful. That's an order."

"Yes, my love."

Amiku and Ardian join the others in the now cleared out area as the entire group face Alma alone. Alma lays her eyes on Kito and forms an energy ball before hurling it toward him. Nydia quickly steps in front of him and waves her hand to the side. The orb is redirected and explodes into the stone wall. She then counters with her own energy blast, but Alma dives away from it.

Alma paces back and forth while keeping her eyes on the group. Knowing that she's able to dodge bullets the group depend on their swords, but even that seems to be a risky plan of attack. Thyst rejoins the group and draws his sword that's strapped to his belt. Alma crouches down and places her hands on the floor before leaping into the air with a snarl. She claps her hands together and then pulls them apart creating and tossing six yellow energy blasts toward each person. Nydia is immediately dumbfounded at this ability. *How can she do that,* she thinks to herself.

Everyone scatters in different directions as the energy blasts explode where they were standing. In the confusion and rising smoke Alma attacks her targets with a flurry of kicks, spins, and claw swipes. She overpowers Nichi and Lako before kicking Thyst in the chest and then sweeps Rona's legs to send her to the floor. She then scurries toward Brax and slashes his arm when he tries to defend himself. The smoke clears to reveal that Anthulios and Kito are facing Alma while Amiku, Ardian and Nydia are behind her. Being surrounded doesn't necessarily concern Alma; she's fast enough to turn the tables back in her favor, but someone else has entered the fray. She picks up on a new scent that takes her attention away from the group standing around her. Kaz steps out from around the corner and aims his pistol at Alma. With just enough time to be seen he pulls the trigger. The gunshot echoes in the room as a wisp of gun smoke rises from the tip of the barrel. To everyone's amazement Alma remains standing and unfazed. It's only a short moment of stillness before Ardian collapses to the floor with a wound in his ribs. Kaz must have turned the gun slightly before firing.

"Ardian!" Nydia kneels beside him and lifts his head onto her lap while applying pressure to his wound. The others begin picking themselves up from Alma's sneak attack, but Thyst is fuming.

"Kaz? Why Kaz!? You're meant to help us, not betray us!"

"Betray!? Who betrayed who, Thyst?! I risked my Goddamn life for almost three years trying to fight these demons; only to come home and be treated like a common criminal. I thought if anyone would understand it would be you. But you had to start your own little community here." Kaz barks as he waves the gun in the air. "We saw you visit our city, but not to see how we were. No, you came well-armed and took whatever you wished and left us to live like rats on a sinking ship."

Kito takes off his coat and tosses it to Amiku, who drapes it over Ardian as she and Nydia stay beside him as he fades in and out.

"I offered you a place here. You refused," Thyst argues back.

"I don't need your charity or your sympathy. I was a Goddamn sergeant! I give the orders; I don't take them!"

"That's it then, isn't it? You refused my offer because you didn't want to answer to me. You still needed be in charge. It is that need for control that put you where you are, not me."

"You don't deserve to be a leader. You can't even tell when you've been played," Kaz chuckles. "I didn't send you to the airport to use the radio, I didn't even think any of them would work. I sent you there hoping you would not survive the raptors. I have been planning your demise for a long time."

Thyst suddenly becomes concerned for his wife and citizens. Kaz's men were among the crowd that was being led to safety.

"Aifina," Thyst says in a worried whisper. Kaz cocks his pistol and points it to Thyst.

"It's too late for them; it's too late for you. What was yours is now mine." Two of Kaz's men run into the room with machine guns and stand beside him. They were the ones who made sure the door closed behind the people of Esperanza. "Didn't you ever wonder why Alma would just happen to show up in a control tower of a dilapidated airport?" Kaz continues. "Long before you finally came to visit, I made a deal with Lazul to disrupt neighboring forts, of course we shared a mutual goal to see Esperanza fall. In turn I would get one castle of my choosing, anywhere in the world, filled with slaves. As for Alma, her part to play was psychological warfare." Kaz gives Kito a taunting smile. "You were a pawn in Alma's game right from the start."

Alma focuses on Kito before tilting her head to the side; she has a memory of him and is trying to regain her self-control. Amiku stands up and points her katana at Kaz.

"You're a disgrace! The only reward you will receive is my katana across your throat."

"Well, aren't we brave. Hasn't your mother ever told you that a woman is supposed to be seen and not heard?" Kaz motions his men to grab her. "Bring her here." Amiku attempts to swing her blade at one of the men, but his gun blocks it. The other restrains her arm while the first man pries the sword from her grasp and then tosses it away.

"Let go of me!" Amiku yells.

The men drag her towards Kaz.

"Don't do it, Kaz! Let her go," Thyst orders.

"I will destroy you and all who stands with you." Kito chimes in with an aggression that is far beyond what he had shown in the past. Kaz holds the barrel of the gun toward Kito.

"I should have killed you when I had the chance." Thyst steps in front of Kito.

"You don't want their blood on your hands, Kaz."

"I'm used to having blood on my hands. I didn't hide in a truck or a chopper waiting for the few minutes that I needed to venture into hostile territory."

"That's not fair and you know it." Kaz takes Amiku from his men and gazes at her.

"So much fire in those eyes. My men and I will tame you." Amiku spits directly in his eye; Kaz responds by slapping her across the face and then holds her arms behind her as he throws her into the wall. "Fuckin' bitch! I will teach you how a woman should behave!" Kaz stands behind her and pulls her coat off her shoulders, but an energy ball soon explodes into his back. Kaz loses his hold on Amiku, and she wastes little time to deliver a swift high kick and double punch combo to the men standing next to Kaz.

Nydia has let Rona take Ardian so she could stand up to make her attack.

"I hope you take one more step so I can spread that which you adore all over the wall behind you," she says. Alma prowls toward Nydia and then pounces to force her to the floor.

"Animals are so unpredictable," Kaz laughs. Amiku attempts another high kick at Kaz, but he catches her leg and holds it. "You like to have your legs up, well get ready for a long night because soon they will be." Kito feels a heat rush into his face and a fire burning in his skull, his fingernails grow into long, sharp points and he begins to lose his sense of reality. "My men haven't been with a woman for a long time, and I doubt they will be gentle," Kaz continues. He wraps his arm around Amiku and throws her into the wall again. Kito's eyes turn red, and his skin becomes pale with a blackness forming around his eyes. No one notices what is happening to him since they are fixated on Kaz's actions with Amiku. "You will be our whore!" Kaz shouts into her ear. Just then Kito lets out a deep, low-pitched growl originating from the very depths of his throat. Fangs sprout from his upper gums and his hair extends up into rigid spikes. Everyone looks surprised at his transformation, but his colleagues become disheartened and worried.

"Don't give in, Kito. Fight it," Nydia yells. Kaz looks at his men while pointing at Kito.

"Shoot him!"

Amiku lands a forceful palm into Kaz's chest and then breaks free to send her shoulder into one of the men to make him lose his sights on Kito. She then punches the second in his neck just before Kaz grabs hold of her again and slaps her across the face.

Kito dashes toward the men and smashes both their heads into the wall with such force that their skulls are crushed instantly. He then darts for Kaz, but Alma tackles him from the side and the two become tangled while rolling as they fight for dominance. Her roars and his growls continue as they stay deadlocked in this heated battle. As soon as they break free from each other, Alma lunges at Kito to scratch him, but he dodges and then grabs her neck and slams her back against the floor. She propels her feet upward to connect with his torso that sends him sailing backwards. She regains her footing quickly and then pounces on Kito's back. He tries to shake her off, but her grip is tight with her legs around his waist and her arms around his neck.

There's nothing anyone can do but watch them fight. Kito may not recognize his own team, and no one wants to make that choice to harm him. At least for right now, Alma has him distracted.

Kito spins his body around to deliberately fall forcefully on his back. Alma is slammed hard against the floor and lessens her grip around his waist and neck. He grabs her leg with one hand and her arm with the other. He then picks her up in a swinging motion before letting go. She is thrown across the room and slides across the floor before coming to rest in the fetal position.

Kito advances toward her slowly as she lies motionless and possibly unconscious, but when he gets close it turns out to be a bluff. Alma kicks his knees to throw him off balance and then leaps toward him. She pins him to the floor with her entire body and roars before placing her claws over his heart. She's building up to push her claws into his chest to finish him off, but something stops her. She stares into his eyes with curiosity as he looks back into hers. She sniffs around him and then lowers her head to his to take in his smell. She nuzzles him and then licks his cheek. She remembers his scent and identifies him as a member of her kind. She retracts her claws and backs off him just as his eyes return to normal. Kito begins to lose his demon form and gradually returns to himself. Alma hovers over him until he passes out. She now has an instinct to protect him. She hunches over and turns to glare at Kaz while snarling.

"Fuck this shit," Kaz says. He holds Amiku in front of him and lifts his pistol over her shoulder. Alma sprints toward them to force Kaz to fire, but her zigzagging motions make him waste the rest of his ammo without landing a hit. She then leaps up just as Amiku ducks to give Alma an opening to Kaz's chest. He's thrown to the floor with Alma's teeth sinking into his neck. She keeps her mouth on his neck while slowly tightening her jaws as Kaz thrashers underneath her. The sound of cracking skin and popping veins, and muscles are heard until Alma's teeth meet and Kaz's body goes limp. Alma lifts her bloody mouth and looks down at her kill.

"You said something about animals being unpredictable?" Amiku gets the last say.

Alma steps away from Kaz's corpse and then makes eye contact with Amiku. Alma takes a step towards her as she takes one back. Amiku glances at her sword that's too far to reach and then back at Alma. She takes another step closer towards Amiku before dropping to her knees in front of her. Alma shifts back to her human form in an extremely exhausted state. Amiku takes her coat off and covers Alma's naked body when she hits the floor unconscious.

It is at this time Aifina enters the room holding an AK47 followed by a dozen citizens, and soldiers all equipped with guns. Thyst runs to her relieved and hugs and kisses her.

"Are you okay?"

"Yes, dear. Kaz thought he had us trapped, but he didn't know the room we sought refuge in was also our secret stash for weapons. We have the rest of his men at gunpoint." Aifina notices Ardian, Kito and then Alma lying on the floor in an unpleasant state. She gives Thyst a confused and worried look. "What happened here?"

"They were injured during our fight with Kaz. They will all need medical treatment." Aifina gets the hint that Thyst means to include Alma into their care and gives her order to those near her.

"Someone alert Mika that she's needed. The rest, help these three to the infirmary."

Small groups of citizens and soldiers gather to carry the three wounded allies to Mika, who already has three beds ready to receive them. Ardian is still conscious and holding his hand over his wound with Nydia beside him. Mika checks him out first and knows he will need pain killers before she can retrieve the bullet and then stitch him up.

As for Kito and Alma, both their vitals show signs of intense stress on the heart and strain to their muscles; however, there is little Mika can do for them except make them comfortable until they awake. Only time can help them, so she focuses her attention on Ardian. Without anesthetics Mika will have to search for and take out the bullet with Ardian fully awake. The best she can do is provide him a double shot of absinthe. Perhaps the burning sensation in his throat and chest will divert his attention away from Mika poking around in his side. Nydia keeps his hand in hers and tries her best to keep him calm and still. Mika finally finds the bullet using a flashlight and pulls it out with pliers. She then proceeds to sew his wound, but not before Ardian requests another shot of absinthe.

Aifina, Nichi, Lako and Thyst walk the remaining twenty-eight of Kaz's men to the front gate by gunpoint as soldiers line up on either side of them while holding guns. Two soldiers open the gate to the nightly world outside of Esperanza's walls.

"Wait, you can't just throw us out there without any weapons. It's already dark," one of the men cries out.

"Oh, I'm sorry. You mistook us for allies," Lako replies.

"We were just following orders, but Kaz is dead now. We will join you," another man desperately suggests.

"I have no need for men with flip-flop allegiances," Thyst answers.

"Esperanza does not want you," Aifina adds.

Several guards force the men outside and several paces from the front gates. The guards return, but Kaz's men look back hoping this is only to scare them. Their assumption proves to be incorrect when the metal gate is closed and locked followed by the shutting of the double wooden doors.

Meanwhile, Anthulios, Brax and Rona are standing on the rooftop watching the exiled group begin to navigate the meadow just beyond the light of Esperanza's torches. The parting blades of grass in the field ahead of them means something has picked up their scent. The movement rapidly draws closer to the unsuspecting men before a pack of gnolls ambush them. Their bloodcurdling screams do not save them as the dead or dying men are pulled out into the field to be devoured at another location. The blood-stained grass will be washed clean with the next rain and the demons finally have claimed the last of Kaz's army.

"Is there fairness in our choices?" Brax asks.

"Maybe not all of them, but this one is divine justice," Rona replies.

"What she said," Lio agrees.

Later that night, Ardian, Kito and Alma are sleeping when Thyst peeks into the room to assess the situation. Mika gives him a positive report concerning Ardian but knows a large amount of energy was consumed by both Kito and Alma that made their bodies shut down to regulate itself. Another mystery is why Alma was nude, but Thyst can't answer either of those questions in a way that would help Mika understand what had happened to them any clearer. He also doesn't want to raise alarm about either of them if anyone else found out. He trusts those who were there to witness it and that's as far as it will go.

"They helped us with great sacrifice to themselves. That's all I can say," Thyst explains. Mika nods and doesn't pry for more information. He has earned her trust and fears no reason to doubt it now.

Thyst steps out of the infirmary and turns the corner to almost collide into Amiku, who was leaning with her back against the wall and her arms folded.

"Why didn't you tell her."

"About what happened to Kito or what Alma did?"

"Both."

"Everyone is on edge and bloodthirsty right now. I don't need anyone asking questions to get answers they won't understand. As far as I'm concerned if everyone thinks Kito and Alma helped fight a traitor and chase away a demon cat, the general public will be at ease and allow them to rest. In order to help Kito, I also had to help Alma. I hope you understand." After a pause Amiku responds.

"Thank you," she says emotionally. She walks around Thyst and makes her way to Kito's bedside and sits down.

The next morning, Amiku is still at Kito's bedside when he begins to wake up. Kito reaches for her hand and slides his fingers through hers.

"Are you alright," he asks concerned.

"You ask me if I'm okay after all you've been through? I guess there is some chivalry in you after all."

"It doesn't fit me, does it?" Amiku runs her fingers through his hair while smiling.

"Well, I didn't say that." Kito notices Alma asleep in the bed next to him.

"She's here?" Amiku glances over at Alma and then back at Kito.

"Maybe she is just a tormented soul. I don't know what she's going through emotionally, but you may have taught us to hesitate on our judgment. Kito, keeper of the lost."

Amiku sets a cup of water on his side table and then leaves so he can get some rest. Kito remains sitting up as Ardian sleeps on one side of him and Alma is just beginning to awake on his other side. Her movements make Kito turn in her direction and it's him she first sees when her eyes open.

"I wish you were under these covers with me," she says while smiling. Kito only smirks but doesn't respond. Alma brings herself to an upright position and realizes she's in a night gown. She rests for a moment before looking back over at Kito. "How do you feel?"

"Drained, hollow, and my legs feel like lead."

"Once you get a taste of that power it's hard to go back to being human. You and I were only exposed to it for a little while and the thought of standing sounds impossible. It's like trying to walk after swimming all day. Your body feels heavy. The longer you are exposed to this power the harder it is to overcome it. Anyo and Lazul are no longer human; they have been in their demon skin for too long. If they reverted back now, it might kill them. They have become their demons."

"Do you remember anything?"

"Yes, I know what I was doing. I just couldn't stop myself. We're mostly driven by instinct and impulse and not much of anything else."

"Does everyone's demon look different?"

"Yes, your demon form is unique to you. How cruel you are as a person, the more hideous your demon will appear. It symbolizes your essence. I'm the huntress, one who must hunt to survive; fueled by a wild instinct with no concept of moderation."

"I don't know what mine means."

"You are the vampire, Kito. The pariah of society; the desire to take your rampant longings rather than earn or compete for them. I told you we were a lot alike. We both desire to indulge beyond our fill. Our demons indicate who we would be if we didn't have our souls. Power can be very tempting; the cost, however, is your mind. Power, it seems, is a double-edged sword. Don't be led to believe you need it, Kito. It will always eat you alive."

Mika arrives to check Kito's vitals and nods at the favorably results after reading his monitors.

"You'll be back to your old self in no time," she says. "I'll give everyone the bad news." Kito smirks.

"I didn't know you made jokes." Mika remains smiling as she makes her way to Alma to check her monitor.

"I want both of you to stretch your legs soon, but otherwise, I don't see anything to be concerned about."

Alma self-motivated herself to get out of bed and take a walk, but Kito needed a little more nudging from Amiku. She helps him up, but his first step causes his knee to buckle. Amiku catches him and holds him up while instructing him to stand in place and bend each knee back and then down several times. Kito leans heavily on Amiku while taking his first few steps, but her persistence pays off and Kito's fatigue soon vanishes.

Kito and Amiku are finishing their last lap down the hallway, but his silence gives her a clue that something is bothering him.

"Whatever you're thinking about, knock it off," she says.

"I will never lose my demon blood, Amiku."

"Kaz was closer to a demon with regular blood. Your demon

blood doesn't mean a damn thing to me."

"What if it comes out again?" Amiku stops Kito and makes him face her.

"We all were born with demons, so stop giving yours more weight."

Kito ponders her words. He knows she's trying to make him feel better, but the truth is he doesn't know what he's capable of. He doubts his abilities and his worth to the rest of the team, but he keeps these feelings to himself. What he fails to understand is that these thoughts might become obvious to those who know him best, and they may be responsible for irrational actions. Ninety percent of every battle begins with a clear and resolved mind, and he just lost that.

Alma was given access to unclaimed and salvaged clothing in one of Esperanza's storage rooms. Her new wardrobe now consists of a blue long-sleeved, button-down blouse with a wide black buckle belt and a simple, yet stylish hijab around her head. She bides her time on Esperanza's roof while staring into the distance until Anthulios meets up with her.

"Do you know anything about, the Star of Eluvium?"

"The Star of Eluvium is a myth."

"So, it doesn't exist?" he asks. Alma sighs.

"I take you for a man of science and there are just some things that science cannot explain. Some mysteries are better left unsolved."

"This is for the sake of the human race, Alma. If you know something, please help us. Kito risked a lot to help you. Maybe you can repay some of that back."

Anthulios leaves her to contemplate her past choices, and those yet to be made.

11

Before They Were Demons

Ten years ago, it was a period of normalcy with the usual day-to-day operations and routines. Downtown sidewalks are crowded with pedestrians going to and from their jobs or looking for a good spot to get lunch. Highways are busy and parking lots are packed with cars.

Lazul never had much purpose, he's an aging man who lives alone in a low-income apartment with a dead-end job that barely pays for his weekly food and the cheap rent. Most people will admit they don't know him, but those that do have a strong dislike for him. Lack of ambition and a severe case of self-pity has made him a bitter old fool with little hope of success.

The Metaphysical Realm is a small magic shop that attracts inquisitive teenagers and fascinated adults alike. It is such a place for Lazul to look for an unconventional way to gain luck and fortune. He picks up a book from the bookshelf and flips through the pages before fitting it back into place. He then grabs another one but seems to have little interest with every selection. The store stocks plenty of books about herbs, crystals, tarot cards, runes, and charms, but Lazul wants a book on spells. The elderly man who runs the shop walks out from behind the counter and approaches Lazul.

"You have a very heavy aura around you." Lazul looks up from his current book and answers in a voice that has yet to become deep and raspy.

"What do you mean by aura?"

"Your aura is the essence of who you are. It tells me you are troubled or angry, maybe both. But I sense a power inside of you struggling to break free. Perhaps, I may offer you some assistance." The man heads back towards the counter as Lazul follows him. The shopkeeper reaches down below the countertop and then brings up a thick hardcover book and places it in front of Lazul. The book's cover is faded, worn and lacks any traces of art or even a title.

"If you want power—if you desire strength—and if you have a strong will. Then maybe all which you seek can be found in here." The yellowed pages secrete a woody, musty, and vanilla scent when Lazul flips the cover open.

"What book is this?"

"It's simply referred to as, *Liber Daemonum*. It's very old and its author is unknown." Lazul turns to a random page and instantly feels a surge of energy rushing through his body and deep growls echoing inside his mind.

"How much is it?

"It was given to me a long time ago as a gift, I shall do the same. Consider it as me passing the torch."

"Sounds too generous."

"Generosity has nothing to do with it. I cannot care for it much longer and it always needs to have a home." Lazul agrees to take the book and walks out with it resting under his arm. The store clerk grins sinfully as he shrinks back from the front window. As he retreats from the sunlight his face becomes gray with boils that only show in the shadows.

Lazul returns to his rundown apartment with peeling paint and rotted wood frames around the cracked windows. Countless holes litter the walls and interior doors while evidence of water damage stains the ceiling. Dishes are piled up in the sink and on top of the kitchen counter and the floorboards are scuffed, scratched and in disarray. Several roof shingles are lying on the grass and have been ignored while the rest of the yard is overgrown with untrimmed shrubs and a lawn that looks as if it had never been mowed.

At midnight, Lazul takes a seat in front of an open window with the full moon in sight. He opens the book and reads one of the passages out loud.

"Release the chains that separate and bind. Allow my body to be the vessel for any to pass through. I call forth those who wish to have their names unknown. Confront me and I will have a brand-new name. Guide me into your dimension. Promise me my desires fulfilled and you shall have my allegiance!" Lazul waits in silence, but nothing happens. He turns to the next page and continues reading. "I offer my mind for your knowledge. I offer my body for your strength. I offer my soul for your power."

Suddenly a violent wind rushes through the window to send books flying off the shelves from this mysterious force. Lazul looks around startled as strange shadows dart back and forth on the walls and growling of some unseen vicious dog surrounds him. Chairs slide across the room and light bulbs explode inside their lamps.

"Obey me! And I shall give you the world of man," he says after witnessing the disturbance. The commotion halts and Lazul is once again alone in an eerie stillness.

Black fog slowly creeps closer to him while growing in width and height. He stands up a little apprehensive of the smoke that's slowly starting to engulf him. He begins yelling when completely overtaken by this mysterious fog. His terrifying screams gradually become deep growls and roars. Several tentacles finally burst out of the black smoke before it begins to fade into nothingness. His voice is now deep and raspy.

"When the fates give you nothing—take everything." He has been consumed by his hatred and desire for power. He becomes a demon by choice; however, if his strength weakens this entity will betray him. It is the risk he has taken and unknowingly has signed away his freedom if he should fail.

It's just before dawn when six police cars pull up in front of the closed bank. The policemen get out and duck down behind their vehicles with shotguns drawn. The bank's rear service door forcefully swings open with Anyo hurrying through carrying a backpack. As a small-time safe cracker, he had planned a heist to target the safe of the investments office. His every move was meticulous, from his entry to the opening of the safe, and even his planned getaway. His mistake was tripping the motion detector on the office door. He didn't think there would be an interior security system; nonetheless, the cops arrived in eight minutes on a planned ten-minute job. With the breaking of the safe successful and the money in his pack—all he has to do now, is not get caught.

He jogs down the vacant alley hoping if he gets far enough away, he will be in the clear. As soon as he turns the corner four policemen quickly surround him. Some of them are holding shotguns while others keep their Glocks firmly grasped and pointing in his direction.

"Hold it right there! Turn around and put your hands on top of your head," one of them shouts. Anyo begins to obey the command, but when the cop gets close behind him, he swiftly spins a kick around and knocks the gun out of the cop's hands. The other men rush him to try to pin him down, but he grabs one of their arms and twists it back until it cracks. He pushes the screaming man aside and then trips another to the ground. He delivers a fast jab to the side of his jaw that knocks him out cold. The third policeman pins Anyo's arms against his sides from behind him. Anyo jerks his head back into his nose to break it. He then turns around and karate chops the side of his neck. The last cop lifts a shotgun, but Anyo sends his foot into his gut. The man is forced back and loses the grip on his gun. Anyo gains control of the weapon and presses the barrel against his forehead. The terrified policeman stands motionless.

"Bang," he teases before smacking him in the head with the butt of the gun. Anyo smiles at his accomplishment and continues down the alley leaving the four defeated policemen behind him. Anyo backs into a dead-end section of the alley while looking around to make sure no one has noticed him entering. He plans on staying here for a bit until the heat dies down. He turns around abruptly when he hears footsteps behind him.

"You fight very well, not many can pull off such a bold and daring escape," Lazul says in his deep and raspy tone.

"What do you want old man," Anyo asks.

"I'm starting a war that will change the world. Join me and I will give you unimaginable power and strength."

"Your offer sounds really tempting, but you look like you are at the end of your life span."

"How many banks do you think you can rob and escape from unscathed? Don't waste all that potential power as a mere human. There's more for you out there. Take it all and know nothing can stop you. Rape society, and then rule over it."

"You're delusional." Anyo turns and begins to walk away, but Lazul extends his tentacles around his arms and waist.

"The world will soon change. Do you want to die with it or reign over it?" Lazul retracts his tentacles as they disappear into his back.

"How did you do that?" Anyo asks in shock.

"I will show you. But just out of curiosity, how well did you do in science?" It's almost as if he foresaw people's response to resolve a new problem. Then again, it's easy to predict the future when you are on the committee that invents all the solutions. To his satisfaction Anyo responds,

"Aced it, why?" Lazul grins and lets out a deep rolling chuckle.

Alma is in her late twenties when she joins an American dojo. She is well-adept in her abilities by now, but still tries to keep to herself without attracting unwanted attention; however, her unchecked, and often out-of-control, temper is rarely held back after she's been pushed. She picks out a vacant table in a break room and sets down with her sandwich, chips, and a carton of milk. She's wearing the same white karate-gi as everyone else in her class, which signifies her as a novice—even though she had already passed this level in Japan. It also doesn't take long for her to gain a reputation.

As she attempts to enjoy her lunch, she is disturbed by three white-belt karatekas who approach her from behind. Any person who is practicing karate is known as a karateka, and these three have a score to settle. Earlier that day, their fourth member, Yama-san, told her to wash her cunt after losing to her in a match. The laughter from his friends and the embarrassment she felt made her lash out by sending him sailing across the room with nothing but the flick of her wrist.

One of the men cracks his knuckles but Alma doesn't turn around. "Only three?" she says.

"You cocky bitch; I'm not waiting for a match to kick the shit out of you," one of them replies. Alma pushes her chair back and stands up before slowly turning to face them.

"Go ahead, make the first move—then I won't feel bad when I break your arm." Enraged, the man swings a punch at Alma's face, but she easily dodges it. She quickly grabs his arm and twists it behind his back while forcing him to the ground. In an instant, she pulls it up to his shoulders resulting in a compound fracture. The man screams in agony as everyone in the room falls silent while looking at Alma with surprise. Her action will cause him to forfeit the rest of his training and future tournaments.

The sensei scurries over and kneels beside him to inspect his injury. "Take him to the clinic," he says. The man's buddies help him up carefully as he groans while holding his arm. The sensei then stands to look at Alma. "Once again you have overreacted."

"I have the right to defend myself."

"I know you are beyond the white-belt rank that you hold here. With all your skills, and the knowledge you have acquired your options included many that could have been less severe. You do not just want to defeat your opponents; you want to destroy them. Your first moves are always the ones that should be saved as a last resort. Your advancement is hindered by your pride, and I cannot teach you discipline. You are no longer welcomed here. I pray someday you will gain control over this harshness which you wield so freely." The sensei bows before Alma, but she doesn't return the bow. Instead, she remains looking at him with a scowl.

"One day I will destroy all of you. Fuck you, sensei."

The other students gasp at her last act of disrespect, but the sensei only shakes his head as she walks away.

In the evening hours, after a rainstorm, Alma is sprinting through the puddles as a group of people chase her. She climbs a chain-link fence and leaps over the top to land on the wet grass. She continues across the empty street but can hear her pursuers catching up.

"She's over here!"

"Kill the witch!" they shout as seven men cross the street diagonally to cut her off. She didn't think they would be fast enough to find her, but now it seems a confrontation is unavoidable. They surround her and smile or laugh as they hit their open palms lightly with their bats or metal poles as they close around her. Alma takes her stance and waits for her moment to strike.

Just then, Anyo and Lazul jump out from the shadows and attack the men around Alma with superhuman strength. Every one of their punches or kicks throws them quite a distance away. No one is allowed an opportunity to counter, and within moments they retreat.

"Why did you help me?" she asks as she relaxes her arms down.

"We need to watch out for our own," Lazul answers.

"Your own? You don't know me."

"I know your aura. It is burdened, but also powerful," Lazul continues.

"Aura? I do not believe in such things."

"Neither did I, but it's there whether you believe in it or not," Anyo replies.

"If you guys are bible pushers, I'm not interested." A deep, rumbling sinister laugh comes from Lazul's throat without him parting his lips.

The wind begins to howl just as a strong gust hits Alma. She holds her arms against her chest while rubbing them.

"Thanks for your help," Alma says before starting to walk away.

"Where are you going when there's nothing to go to?" Lazul says. Alma stops and turns around. "Perhaps we can offer you some assistance."

"You obviously have me mistaken for some little girl you can fool into your grasp. Some entertainment for long nights, but I can kill both of you right here with little effort," Alma replies forcefully. Lazul laughs again.

"I like your spirit. I do not doubt your fighting skills. I also believe you may have defeated those men without our aid. The truth is I'm declaring war on all who are not like us. I offer you an opportunity to enact your revenge. How would you like to make everyone who has ever wronged you suffer, and be the one who personally makes it so?" The recent events at the dojo and with these last men remind Alma of her desire to destroy those who were unkind to her.

"With us you will gain even more power. Your abilities will become stronger and new ones will make you a force to reckon with," Lazul tempts.

"It's true, I too was doubtful, but I have seen what lies ahead. Frequently home can appear very far away, but sometimes—it's right in front of you," Anyo adds.

"We have a warm place you can stay and plenty of food. You will be free to leave as you wish, but at least for one night you don't need to wonder lost in a big city," Lazul concludes. Alma is by no means gullible, but their words spark a hidden need inside her heart. The desire to feel she belongs. No one else has offered her anything close to a home. The streetlights turn on as dusk approaches and she stares down the desolate street without a destination in mind. Lazul and Anyo smile when Alma begins to advance toward them and the three begin their walk.

"Exactly what are you planning to do?" Alma asks.

"I'm going to make the world end and then reshape it in my image," Lazul replies.

"And how are you going to accomplish this incredible feat?"

"With energy—"

For a year Lazul bides his time until the moment when his move will deliver the largest impact. This moment arrives on the day a new president is declared. What better time to send the world into chaos than just after an election.

The front-page headline of the local newspaper reads:
Philanthropist Elected President!

The successful politician waves to the cheering crowd from the stage in the middle of a residential park. While many view this is a reason to celebrate there are always those who feel disappointed and wronged in some way. A reporter covers the story live with the stage and crowd in the background.

"The election of our new president has everyone here excited and hopeful. A man who has donated time and capital to schools, churches, as well as, to events and special projects, and all the while never asking for anything in return. It comes to us as no surprise that he has won this election by an enormous landslide. Everyone is sure that this is the start of a better and brighter future. His plans are sure to improve life as we know it. With the unemployment rate so high many of us are relieved to hear that the first thing on his list are new and better paying jobs—"

Without warning several gun shots are heard and the newly elected president collapses on the stage. The reporter turns around shocked as people scream and run in all directions. The anarchy only worsens as the day unfolds.

The ending of the day doesn't end the unrest as riots rampage through the streets at this late nightly hour. Another reporter is yelling over the noise of a rioting crowd and the destruction occurring around him, including a store that's engulfed in flames behind him.

"It is pandemonium out here! Everyone is consumed by anger and hatred now that sorrow has subsided! The question, who shot our president, is being answered by rumors and accusations! Some people are saying it's a government conspiracy, others are saying it was a hit hired by the opposing party. Some are so bold to point their fingers at their own neighbors! Rioting has escalated beyond the control of the local police! Behind me is a corner store which was just ransacked and set on fire! The owner of this store was unfortunately killed while attempting to escape! Vandalism, arson, murder, rape, and robbery are plaguing our country! It seems that almost nowhere is safe! We need to ask, just what is going on here?! Did having our hopes crushed so suddenly make us forget our humanity?!" The reporter pauses and puts his finger to his earpiece to better hear the updated feed. "Reports are now coming in from other countries about similar rioting and looting taking place! One must ask, where is all this hatred and anger coming from—"

Suddenly a mob of people attack the reporter and cameraman with bats while yelling. TVs that were tuned into this broadcast switch to static.

Like a vulture on its stoop, looking for prey, so is Lazul with his tentacles outstretched while laughing insanely on his penthouse balcony. He gazes at the disorder taking place below him with utter delight. At his feet sits the Architect's Box with a glowing sphere hovering above it; this is the Star of Eluvium. A shimmering disturbance in the air gradually opens into a portal. A demonic arm followed by its head crawls halfway out while growling.

"The world is weak, take it—kill them—burn it all down." Lazul has started his war; Apocalypsia is born.

Alma is glaring at her reflection in the mirror of her guest bedroom. She spent the entire night reminiscing on everything that had happened to her and how she reacted to it. Justifiable or not she now feels some form of remorse. Not so much for those who had it coming but for those she never gave a chance. *Every time I see my own reflection, I never know who's looking back at me,* she thinks to herself.

She gently touches the glass with her fingertips and a vision of her huntress form flashes in the mirror. She becomes startled at first, but then becomes furious. She shatters the mirror with a single blow with her fist and then claws at her face while screaming.

"I am not her!"

She tosses a lantern across the room and then tips the nightstand over. She pulls the sheets off the bed and then kicks the pillows that had fallen to the floor. After she has exerted her energy, she falls to her knees and sobs. She wants to put her anger to rest and stop feeling an endless flow of hate. Kito and his group showed her more compassion as enemies than her own allies. If the world should end again, she at least wants to be on the right side. The one she chooses, next to the one she loves.

Alma removes her hijab and then cuts her long hair down to shoulder-length with a pair of scissors. She then submerges her head in a bucket of water to wash out her platinum blond dye. Now with her hair shorter and being returned to its natural black color, she feels renewed and ready to start over. A return to innocence, before the world proved how cruel it really was, before her heart hardened, and before her hope died. A strange feeling overcomes her, a feeling not felt for a good long time—she feels human.

In the main hall, Aifina pours Kito, Amiku, Rona, Brax and

Anthulios a cup of green tea to help calm their nerves. She believes green and herbal teas have healing capabilities and can put the mind at ease. She pours two more cups for herself and Thyst who has just arrived. He drops a thick hardcover book in the middle of the table with a thump.

"Of all the books in our library; this is the only one that talks about, the Star of Eluvium." Thyst sits down and picks up his cup of tea to sip it.

"You have a library?" Brax asks surprised. Thyst sets his cup back down and nods.

"Yes, our past is just as important as our future. So, I have salvaged some books throughout the years."

The book Thyst brought is entitled:

Symbols and Mysteries of the Old World

The ribbon bookmark suggests the chapter of interest is on page forty-seven and titled:

The Disappearance of Atlantis

There are many theories of what may have happened to Atlantis. It is widely believed that Atlantis was an advanced society with improved living conditions, knowledge in medicine and science; and may also had flight capabilities and electricity long before the rest of the world. Then, within one day and night, Atlantis disappeared. How does a society so advanced disappear so suddenly? Some scholars and scientists alike believe Atlantis was in possession of an energy source that was unknown to the rest of the world. That energy source may have also aided in Atlantis' final end. This energy source has been translated from ancient texts as, The Heart of the Earth, also known as, The Star of Eluvium.

"I thought Atlantis was destroyed by a tsunami," Brax recalls.

"Many believed Atlantis had a powerful navy and military and that they also had the knowledge to make apocalyptic weapons. Some say they accidentally used one on themselves. Maybe this star thingamajig is it." Rona points out.

"I remember hearing that Atlantis wasn't even in the Atlantic Ocean, but in the Mediterranean Sea, on the island of Crete to be more specific; and that a massive volcano eruption or tsunami was responsible for their destruction," Lio adds.

"Easter Island's stone heads are believed to be Atlantian also," Thyst says.

"And the Azores have been said to be the mountain tops of Atlantis," Kito joins in.

"Then there are all the strange things that happen around the Bermuda triangle too," Amiku concludes.

It seems everyone has heard some hypothesis on what may have happened to Atlantis, but Aifina is less convinced it was ever a place to begin with.

"If no one ever saw Atlantis then how does anyone know their lifestyles, or if they really were advanced; or if they ever existed in the first place? How many ancient peoples have laid claim to something that is eventually debunked centuries later? Atlantis could have been any group of unknown people for that time."

"Plato wrote that it was beyond the pillars of Hercules, but look at how many people have searched for it since? No one would have put so much time, money, and resources into something unless they believed there was some truth behind it," Kito argues.

"Human beings are by nature curious, Kito," Aifina continues. "We have an unquenchable desire for knowledge and the hows and whys of everything around us. Ever since the beginning of time we wanted to know how we came to exist? How the universe formed? Why is there day and night? And over the years science did answer these questions, but what science could not answer we became obsessed with trying to prove, especially the men of our species. If there was an Atlantis maybe their quest for ultimate knowledge destroyed them, maybe we aren't meant to know everything. Maybe there is a lesson here somewhere."

Alma makes her presence known when she invites herself into the group's discussion. Everyone sets their eyes on her new hairstyle with a keen observance, but only Kito comments.

"You changed your hair." Alma smiles at him.

"Sometimes one feels the need to change how they are perceived." Amiku interrupts Alma batting her eyelashes at Kito.

"Since I know you've been eavesdropping, what's your take

on the Star of Eluvium?"

"The Star of Eluvium isn't a star at all; it's a sphere of pure energy. Much like what myself and Nydia can form from our inner essence; only this is much more powerful." Alma sits down and helps herself to a cup of tea from the pot. She smells it and then takes a sip. She gives it an approving nod and then continues her story. "Lazul attained the Star of Eluvium from the mafia operating out of the Balkans. I don't know how they acquired it, but their reach was widespread. He plans to put the orb into a cannon and shoot it into the atmosphere. The change in altitude will make it unstable and cause it to explode. This will dissolve the force field that prohibits Hell from interacting with Earth.

All of Hell will pour into this world and no amount of fighting will ever lessen their numbers. These goblins and demonoids you run into now are just minions. What lies in waiting are far more menacing and Lazul is foolish enough to think he will remain in power. We need to stop him, and we don't have much time to do it." Amiku was going to comment on her involvement with Lazul's maniacal plan, but reconsiders. Alma seems to be trying to make amends for her actions, and for now, will be given the opportunity to prove it.

This discussion and strategy planning is abruptly interrupted when Nydia hurries past the archway of the room. Everyone turns to get a glimpse of her before she disappears down the corridor. They exchange puzzled glances at one another before getting up and running after her.

Nydia hurries into Ardian's room and becomes horrified to notice a ghostly figure of a woman floating over Ardian. The ghostly image is tightening her hands around his neck as Ardian begins choking in his sleep. The woman's face transforms into a gruesome demon and roars at Nydia who immediately flicks an energy ball at it. The rest of the group enters the room to see the ghostly foam bursting into flames while screeching and howling before finally fading away. Nydia hurries to Ardian's side and shakes him awake.

"What the hell was that thing, and how did it get in here?" Rona asks.

"Spirit assassins," Alma answers with a sigh. "They're restless souls unable to move on for one reason or another. Lazul recruits them to work for him." Ardian opens his eyes and then sits up while coughing.

"I was having a nightmare," he exclaims. Nydia gently rubs the back of his head.

"Me too, but you're safe now."

A deep horn sounds throughout the fort followed by soldiers running down the hallways and the shuffling of weapons being prepared or gathered.

"What's going on?" Brax asks.

"The battle horn," Thyst answers after a moment for it to sink in. "We're being attacked." Thyst and the others swiftly run out of the room to investigate.

"Stay here, Ardian," Nydia says, but he attempts to get out of bed.

"I can help," he insists, but Nydia pushes him back down.

"No Ardian, you were just shot."

"I feel fine."

"I said no!" Mika bolts into the room and aids Nydia in restraining him.

"Go Nydia, I got him," she exclaims.

"I'll come back, Ardie," she says before leaving the room. Ardian reaches for her while Mika struggles to keep him in bed.

"Nydia!"

The soldiers gather on top of Esperanza's rooftop in the fading sunlight astonished to observe a dragon circling their fort. The dragon swoops downward and the soldiers open fire with their machine guns and mounted turrets. The dragon flies into the barrage while letting out a loud high-pitched yelp. It collides and pries up one of the mounted turrets with its talons and then drops it over the side of the fort onto an ATV that was driving into the field. The dragon flies back around and spits a fire ball toward Thyst.

"Everyone, get down!" Nichi yells. Thyst dives out of the way just as the fireball explodes into the ground where he was standing.

Inside the fort, this last attack shakes the main room as rubble rains to the floor.

Outside, another fireball is hurled toward the fort. This one explodes into the side making a large chuck of the outer wall crash to the ground.

"How are we going to fight this thing? Our bullets are doing nothing," Lako hollers at Nichi. Before he can come up with a game plan the dragon swoops back down and flies low over the top of the fort. Soldiers hold their positions while firing at the beast, but its wing collides into the standing men to throw them across the roof or over the edge. Nichi is one who is unable to avoid the dragon's wing and is knocked over the edge of the fort.

"No!" Thyst screams out in dismay. He can do nothing to save his captain from his fatal fall. Alma teleports from her place beside him and then reappears in midair to catch Nichi. She then teleports back to where she was and sets him down. She responds to Thyst's gratitude with a small smile and nod.

The dragon spews another fire ball at the side of the fort. This explosion dislodges even larger chucks of rock toward the ground.

"It's going to tear this place apart unless we can stop it!" Lio points out.

The dragon grabs a nearby soldier with its talons and flies out over the trees. Within moments the man's body parts rain over the trees when he's squeezed and torn apart. Thyst closes his eyes and looks away from the horrid scene.

"Thyst, where's that tank of yours?" Brax asks.

"It's coming, but it will be a tricky shot for it. We don't have a lot of ammunition and the way this dragon is flying we'll never get a fix on it."

"What if we can lure it in a certain spot?" Nydia suggests.

"That's not a bad idea, but how?" Rona questions.

Nydia watches the dragon's movements intensely before shooting an energy ball ahead of its intended path. The blast explodes in its chest causing it to let out a hiss.

"We need to combine our powers," Alma tells Nydia.

"Okay, and how do we do that?" she inquires.

"Take my hand. Our powers will combine as we form our energy blasts; it should be a massive attack. If we can aim for one of its wings; it may cause the dragon to lose altitude long enough for the tank to get a fix on it. However, we only have one chance to get this right. This attack will drain us almost completely."

The tank begins to make its way into the field, but the dragon notices it and shoots a fire ball down at it. The fire ball explodes on the ground as a near miss. The tank keeps moving while the cannon starts rotating.

"We need to tell those men to hold off," Thyst commands.

Lako receives his order and agrees to make the trek to tell the armored calvary regiment their plans concerning the dragon.

Thyst and the others peer over the edge until Lako is seen running out the front gates and towards the tank. He opens a small door at the rear of the tank and picks up the phone. Several moments later he hangs up and makes eye contact up at Thyst with a thumbs up.

"I guess that's our cue," Nydia observes.

"Now only if the dragon's movement wasn't so radical," Alma says with some concern.

"It needs to be distracted on something," Amiku thinks out loud.

Kito notices a gun turret with a charred soldier still in the seat. He rushes to it and pushes the soldier off. "Sorry, sir," Kito says. He then turns the turret and starts firing a spray of bullets into and around the dragon. Kito has successfully gotten its attention and it flies toward him with incredible speed.

"Alright, Nydia, let's do this," Alma says. She and Nydia hold hands while stretching their other arm forward. They begin to form an energy ball in their palms that slowly grow in diameter. The enraged dragon closes the gap between it and Kito while the girls wait for their energy to reach full power.

"Now!" Alma orders. The two energy blasts travel side by side before combining into one massive swirling sphere. The dragon is so focused on Kito that it soars into the energized attack without time to change course. The energy sphere explodes into its body just under one of its wings. The dragon lets out a bloodcurdling screech while frantically flapping its opposite wing to keep it afloat, but it slowly starts to descend from the dead-weight of its injured wing. The tank fires its round at this moment. The warhead explodes into the dragon's belly and sends it lifelessly spinning to the ground. The thunderous impact it creates sends shockwaves radiating outwards. Nydia and Alma collapse while taking several deep breaths. Alma's prediction was correct about them feeling completely drained and exhausted. Amiku squats down and lightly touches Nydia's arm.

"Are you okay?" Nydia gives her a weak smile before falling into her chest.

Kito advances toward them while rubbing his ears.

"You're supposed to wear ear protection when operating that,

Kito." Thyst explains a little late.

"What?" Kito replies; only this time he's not trying to be funny.

Later that night, the dragon's burning carcass casts dancing shadows on Esperanza's walls in the stillness of night. Thyst, Rona and Anthulios watch from inside Esperanza's gates as the fire crackles.

"Fifteen injured and sixteen dead because of that thing," Thyst reports.

"We were caught completely off guard," Lio says.

"How could we have prepared ourselves against a dragon of all things?" Rona adds.

"Good point, Rona," Lio agrees.

A long pause passes between them until Alma invites herself into their huddle.

"I thought you were sleeping," Lio questions.

"I couldn't."

"What do you know of this dragon, Alma? Did Lazul send it?" Thyst pries.

"Dragons are not a new species; our history is littered with them and not all the stories are made up. If I remember correctly dragons are byproducts of a mixture between magic and nature, or science and witchcraft, the natural with the unnatural. The Star of Eluvium is responsible for this creation." Alma pauses to think for a moment. "It begins with an actual host. This dragon could have been anything, or anyone prior to this transformation."

"Lazul is using guerrilla warfare to run us down little by little. He'll keep this up until our supplies are depleted and our defenses are beyond repair. I'm afraid we can't wait for our reinforcements to arrive," Thyst explains.

"If we don't do anything Lazul is eventually going to attack when we can't defend. Then he will win," Lio explains further.

"That's right; it's the most efficient way to destroy a stronger foe. Force them to take defense with many smaller battles and avoid a direct confrontation. We need to counter, and we need to do it now." Thyst concludes.

"If you will allow it, I would like to join you in defeating Lazul," Alma says with a lowered head.

The group briefly exchange looks. "Get some sleep, Alma," Thyst replies. "We march against Lazul tomorrow."

12

The City of Zombies

Kito is submerged under clear water with his legs ensnared by the Anaconda root. His lifeless body sways in the currents, yet all is calm and quiet. A splash from above sends a stream of bubbles around him until they rise to the surface. A figure of light appears in his sights before taking the shape of Amiku. She takes him in her embrace and then parts her lips over his to breathe into his mouth.

Fear and danger are absent, as well as the need to struggle for air. He is in a relaxed surrender and allows this moment to be everlasting. Life returns to him, and he opens his eyes to the sunlight pouring in through the window. He lies in bed while thinking, *why do you live in my dreams, Amiku?*

After Kito prepares himself for the day he visits the spot behind Esperanza where he had once seen Amiku in a sword dance among the dandelions. She isn't here this morning, and neither are any of the dandelions. He remains lost in his memory while also recalling his dream when Lio advances behind him.

"I never saw you daydream before," he says when he reaches Kito's side. Kito glances at him and smirks.

"What makes you think I'm daydreaming?"

"Unless you see something out there that I do not, you are daydreaming." Kito chuckles.

"Trying to decipher a dream I had, that's all."

"If a dream has you this preoccupied it must have involved a woman." Kito looks at him but doesn't respond. Lio laughs knowing his guess was correct.

"There is only one thing on Earth that can make a strong man, weak, an intelligent man, foolish, the greatest of wordsmiths, lost for words, and the most balanced, clumsy—and that is a woman."

"I didn't know you were a poet," Kito admirably jokes.

"Well, I did study mythology, philosophy and poetry in Lamia."

"Lamia, what's that?"

"It's not a what, but a where. Lamia is the capital of Central Greece. That's where I'm from."

"Greece seems nice. Why did you leave?" Lio gives him a sly smile.

"A woman."

"She must have been some woman."

"She was a Boston girl on vacation, and I loved her accent. But sometimes when you move across the world for someone, they don't always stick around. It wasn't all bad, though. I tutored philosophy at Harvard and sold ice skates in winter."

"And this whole time I thought you were boring," Kito says. Lio laughs and slaps Kito on the back.

"Come on, I think Thyst wanted everyone to meet at the front gates."

Kito and his companions stand at the front of the assembly as Thyst and Alma prepare the crowd for their attack against Lazul.

"We have fought and survived in a world we learned to get used to," Thyst begins. "But change doesn't come to those who wait. We never lost the war because the war never ended. It remains ongoing, every day, and it's time for our Hail Mary pass. It's time to attack our enemies before they come to us!" The soldiers and citizens cheer from his energized conclusion. "I will now turn the floor over to Alma who has more information on what we are going up against." Alma nods and takes a step forward.

"Lazul and his demon horde are located around a fort just past the city of Goldthorn. However, getting there will be a challenge in itself. This city has the highest concentration of zombies than any other place that I know of. After we get past Goldthorn there is nothing but wide-open countryside, which means Lazul will see us coming long before we get close. Expect large waves of his demonic army to attack as we advance."

Brax glances at Lio after Alma's explanation. "Looks like today we all become legends."

"Too bad legends are never true," Rona chimes in. Anthulios responds to his captains unaware that the surrounding congregation is listening to him.

"Whether a legend is true or not doesn't matter. What does matter is how that legend motivates us. How it shapes our beliefs and our goals. How it guides us to become who we are meant to be or who we want to be. Legends are there to remind us that sometimes good can prevail, against all odds, against formidable foes and against certain doom. It is the sacrifices that are made and the choices we make. And inside our beating hearts, hope survives, love blooms, and humanity shines through."

Several people applaud his reflection as he glances around in bewilderment. Thyst grins and lays a hand on his shoulder.

"I want to show you something, friend." Thyst leads the group to a nearby table where a wide variety of guns and ammunition are spread out. He picks up a rocket launcher with an excited and eager grin. "Say hello to the Swedish anti-tank AT dash 4, Rocket Launcher. Range, 400 yards, projectile, 84 millimeters, missile travel time, 820 feet—a second. This weapon is recoilless but does have a nasty back blast. And it's all under fifteen pounds too. Shoot this baby into a crowd of smelly zaaambies and watch it rain blood and guts."

"Ewww," Nydia exclaims with disgust. Thyst laughs as he rests the weapon on his shoulder.

"I do what I do best—and that's killing zaaambies."

"Can I have one?" Kito asks with an envious expression. Thyst places the rocket launcher carefully back on the table.

"No offence Kito, but I wouldn't give this to you if my life depended on it." Amiku bursts out laughing, but Kito just lets out a retired sigh.

The soldiers of Esperanza follow the orders of Nichi and Lako as they prepare to depart. Some drive and lineup the vehicles in the field, while others fuel them with gas cans containing salvaged fuel from forgotten gas stations. Among the ATVs is Kaz's Humvee with a machine gun protruding from its roof. Thyst's Abrams tank and chopper cycle are also fueled and stocked with weapons, ammo, and other supplies. The soldiers also take careful note to ensure that they themselves are also fully stocked with ammo, machine guns, pistols, and a sword—just in case. Everyone buttons or zips up their vests and secure their body armor and then affectionately say goodbye to their loved ones.

Lako holds his son in his arms and Nichi squats down to hug his daughter. The children of Esperanza understand the world at a young age and must sacrifice some of their innocence and imagination to gain survival skills. Anthulios is kissing a blond-haired girl he had met, while Aifina and Thyst share a passionate kiss.

"You come back to me; you hear?" Aifina orders.

"I will always come back to you," Thyst smiles.

The citizens gather outside to send the army off with heartfelt goodbyes and best wishes. Thyst shouts one final word of encouragement to his men.

"Alright men! Pray for strength and luck and leave the rest to your trigger finger!" The men cheer as they wave back to the crowd. The tank and Humvee lead the convoy of ATVs and the chopper, as Thyst and Lio lead the foot soldiers behind the convoy.

Kito advances up the formations to walk beside Lio. No one is a stranger to fighting and survival but going to war is a different feeling entirely.

"Are you nervous?" Lio asks with a smile.

"I've been walking into uncertainty my whole life. The only difference here is I'm not doing it alone."

"No, you're not," Lio says. Kito waits a moment before glancing back at him.

"Who was that girl at Esperanza?" Lio chuckles realizing he was caught in a public display of affection.

"Her name is Shara; we met a few nights ago. Every man

needs a good woman, Kito. To feel your bodies against one another and to be wrapped up in each other's arms. As passion and desire unite under the moon to create curious hands and traveling lips." Kito intensely stares at Anthulios eager to hear the details he's offering so freely, but he ends it there.

"You need to stop reading your Greek poetry," Kito replies. Lio laughs, but the joking subsides when the tank and Humvee stop the convoy and the following battalion.

"Legion approaching!" Nichi yells after exiting from the passenger side of the Humvee. The men raise their guns while others lie down on their stomachs after setting up their guns on tripods or stabilizers. Thyst and Lio jog up to meet Nichi with his eyes firmly pressed against his binoculars.

"Who—or what are they?" Thyst asks. Nichi hands the binoculars to Thyst after spying through them.

"It looks like another army, sir." One of the men at the head of this opposing army lifts and waves a white flag.

"White flag," Thyst says while lowering the binoculars. He then looks back at his men and shouts, "At ease!" He returns his gaze back to Nichi, "Take us to meet them."

Thyst and Lio step into the rear of the Humvee as Nichi reclaims his front passenger seat before Lako accelerates slowly toward the waiting army. When the vehicle stops, Thyst and Lio exit to confront the leading men.

"Who leads this army?" Thyst asks. Dixon steps forward and advances alone.

"My name is Dixon. We are looking for a man by the name of Anthulios." Thyst glances at Anthulios standing beside him.

"I am Anthulios," Lio replies.

"We spoke briefly via radio. We heard your broadcast and wish to lend our aid."

Thyst and Anthulios exchange smiles at this fortunate turn of events.

"Your timing is perfect then. We are moving against Lazul at this very moment," Thyst replies.

"Thank you for coming," Lio adds.

"We contemplated if your signal was legit or perhaps a trap. But we are familiar with the locations you mentioned and decided to make the journey. I'm sorry for the delay, but it took some time to organize and supply our expedition."

"No need for apologies. We welcome any help when it's offered," Lio continues.

Now with Dixon's and Thyst's army joining forces over a thousand men march toward Lazul.

"It appears some good came out of our voyage to Silver Rock City after all," Thyst reminisces.

"Kaz's intentions may have been grim, but we prevailed because our hope to unite was stronger than his plans to separate," Lio explains.

"I'm promoting you to brigadier," Thyst says warmly. Anthulios glances at him with a wide grin.

"That sounds prestigious."

"It is," Thyst smiles.

The assembly has made it to the ill-fated city of Goldthorn. The city looks abandoned at first glance, and the streets are littered with rubble and trash. This first appearance suggests an uncontrollable fire had blazed through this entire sector. Charred and dilapidated structures and the blacked stone exteriors of buildings, with no windows, are all that remains of a city once known for its prosperity and well-to-do citizens. The green welcome sign is cracked with some of the corners missing and the weathered letters of the *G, D,* and *H* are no longer visible.

WELCOME TO
OL T ORN

"Welcome to all torn. What a fitting name," Ardian observes.

"I suggest we all stick together here; unless anyone else knows how to teleport?" Alma jokes in a serious tone.

"It looks completely deserted," Brax says while studying the surroundings.

"Don't be fooled by first appearances, this city is a walking cemetery," Alma warns.

The armies advance slowly while everyone carefully checks around them. The tank and Humvee lead and the ATVs travel on the sides of the marching soldiers to shield them in case of an attack. It's not long before they come upon a decaying pavilion in the center of a grand plaza. It may have been a popular location to entertain and gather, but the disembodied corpses littering the area make that hard to believe now. Dried blood and intestines, organs, limbs, and decapitated heads inhabit the grounds proving this was an assembly gone horribly wrong. Passing this grotesque scene is accompanied by gaging or vomiting while others try their best to hold their breath. It's not the best place to linger, but an anomaly appears in the form of a silver glowing orb floating in the distance. It becomes larger as it speeds closer towards the curious onlookers. Alma focuses on the mysterious orb before gasping and grabbing Anthulios' arm.

"Everyone, grab someone!" She yells. With no time to explain her reasoning but trusting in her judgment Anthulios takes hold of Thyst's elbow while Brax wastes little time to grab Rona's hand. Alma reaches for Kito's fingertips but fails to make the connection before the orb swiftly expands over the entire mass. The blinding light is void of sound and nothing can be seen except for an intense whiteout. All senses are numbed inside the light as it spreads over the entire army and engulfs them before finally dissipating.

Nichi and Lako take their faces out of their shoulders and look around them. Nothing seems to be different until Nichi glances into his side view mirror. His jaw drops and he remains frozen in disbelief.

"What is it?" Lako asks noticing his expression, but Nichi cannot form words to answer him. Nichi pulls the door handle and pushes the door open with a little hesitation. He then steps out of the Humvee and looks behind the vehicle at the two lines of ATVs and nothing more. The entire army of foot soldiers are missing.

Kito opens his eyes to find himself alone in another part of the city. Elsewhere, Brax looks around anxiously while still holding Rona's hand.

"What happened?"

"I don't know, but you can let go of my hand now," Rona responds somewhat annoyed. Brax gives her an innocent look before she forcefully pulls her hand out of his grip.

Meanwhile, in yet another area of Goldthorn, Alma, Thyst and Anthulios notice they've been separated from the others as well.

"Where is everyone?" Thyst asks.

"This is Lazul's doing. That coward," Alma replies.

"How did Lazul do this, Alma?" Lio asks before Thyst has a

chance.

"It's his spell, Divide and Conquer. It creates an aura around every individual it encounters and then displaces them. However, if one person is holding onto another the spell will read the connection as one person. The unpredictable part of it is its randomness. It can move everyone inches from each other or miles away. There's a strong possibility that others could be nearby; however, it's also possible that the opposite may be true too."

"Then let's start looking for the rest of our men. We can't afford to waste time," Thyst orders.

Only the tank, Humvee and ATVs and the men operating them, were unaffected by this unexplainable occurrence. They can advance together through the city on their intended route, but for everyone else, they will need to find their own way through the city of zombies.

Amiku is also alone and discovers she's on the roof of a one-story ranch with an attached garage. She cautiously navigates around the edge while glancing down to see if there's an area to jump off that won't result in breaking her legs. She makes it to the opposite side of the house and looks down at the roof of the garage directly below her. The garage's roof also slants downward to make a shorter drop off point to the ground. With her parkour skills, she's sure she will be able to make both these jumps with ease. Amiku takes a few deep breaths and then makes the first jump onto the roof of the garage, but the weathered roof caves in immediately. She falls through the roof and then on top of a car, which is concealed under a white cover, before sliding down the windshield and rolling off the hood to the floor.

"Ow," she audibly expresses. "That did not go as planned." She stands up and then brushes herself off before admiring the mystery vehicle underneath the cover. "I wonder what you are." She lifts a section up to reveal the red paint of an aggressive fender. Excited, she pulls the entire cover off to reveal a stunning masterpiece of a vehicle that spreads a grin of pure satisfaction from ear to ear.

Elsewhere, a collection of dead leaves tumble across a small neighborhood playground as squeaking swings sway to and fro. Ardian strolls up to a decrepit playset while also trying to make sense of what had just happened. He too found himself alone in a new area and takes a moment to get his bearings. The last thing he wants is to walk in the wrong direction. The overcast day makes the sun's location unreliable, but he does have another trick up his sleeve. He begins searching for a leaf that's not too curled or brittle. He finally finds one that's nearly flat and collects it. He places the leaf in the tiny pool of rainwater, that's located at the bottom of a curved plastic slide, to ensure it floats. He then takes the M4 off his shoulder and slides out a pin. He rubs the pin on his sleeve for several moments to charge it and then sets it on top of the leaf. The leaf slowly rotates in the puddle and then stops when the pin is pointing north—he has his heading.

Unnerving squeaking and groaning of the many rusted springs, chains, and metal parts of the long deserted toys bring a chill to Ardian as they begin to operate. Seesaws slowly rise and fall, merry-go-rounds spin, and swings jet back and forth as if unseen children are playing around him. The stillness suddenly becomes a wailing wind as it whips the leaves around Ardian's legs, but it soon dies back down to leave a distant moaning in its place. Ardian listens to what may be the sound of children singing. He steps under and around the play set to the opposite side to investigate. Ahead of him are five children holding hands in a circle while swaying from side to side. He cannot recall seeing them when he first arrived and can't imagine how they gathered without him noticing. He tries to justify it by thinking he was preoccupied and may not have been observant to anything else.

"Rosies, rosies pocket full of posies. Ashes, ashes, and we all fall down," the children sing.

Ardian observes them inquisitively. He ponders why these children are in the city of the dead, and how they would survive—how could they survive?

"Rosies, rosies pocket full of posies. Ashes, ashes, and we all fall—" the children suddenly stop singing and swaying while remaining silent and motionless.

Ardian suddenly receives an uncomfortable feeling and takes a step back. The children turn to face him simultaneously and finish their rhyme in a deep growling tone.

"—DOWN!"

It's clear that the children are demonized with elongated jaws and sunken in foreheads. Ardian holds his gun in front of him. "This is starting to make me hate kids," he says to himself. The children release their hands and arch their fingers while creeping closer towards him with low growls.

Suddenly, an energy blast collides into each one of the kids in a fast secession. Each kid is thrown back on impact to land motionless and smoldering on the ground. Ardian whirls around to see Nydia with her arms still held out in front of her. Convinced the children are not getting back up she relaxes and gives Ardian a smile. "Are you tired of being saved by a girl yet?" He recovers from his expression of awe and chuckles.

Meanwhile, Kito is trying to find his way through a commercial block inhabited by office buildings and small businesses. While Ardian's approach, to find his direction of travel, was logical, Kito's approach is more spontaneous. He thinks he may be heading towards where Alma had previously explained their path must be, but there is no way for him to confirm his choice is correct.

So far, his solitary journey has progressed without incident and with no signs to raise concern, but that is about to change drastically. A rough dragging sound leads Kito to believe something is following him. He draws his gun and then turns around to a desolate street with no person or creature in sight. Kito inspects his surroundings quickly before continuing in the direction he was heading. The dragging sound begins again. It feels as if someone is dragging their shoe behind them or a large canvas tarp. Kito whirls around, but again sees nothing. *What is it, where is it? Is my mind playing tricks on me?* Kito thinks to himself while listening.

The dragging is louder now, Kito turns to his left to finally see the cause of the sound. A lone zombie lady is sluggishly dragging her nearly severed foot behind her as she steps off the sidewalk. The bottom portion of her tibia is all that's left to step down on since her foot is broken above the ankle and the fibula is protruding outwards. Rotted flesh and muscles leave a bloody streak in her wake as she advances toward Kito. "There you are," Kito says, feeling confident he has plenty of time to take his aim before she can pose a threat to him.

Just then, a low growl comes directly behind Kito as a pale hand falls on his shoulder. He sidesteps and then turns around in a panic to see another zombie woman with dried blood around her mouth. She snarls and lunges toward him before he can fire a shot. His gun now becomes his only barrier against this zombified woman. He keeps the AK47 under her chin as she chomps her black teeth while growling. He pushes her back with his gun and then takes aim while she's recovering, but the pulling of the trigger fails to fire a bullet. "Goddamn safeties!" he shouts realizing the issue, but he's lost his opportunity. To make matters worse the second zombie is now almost right behind him too. He can fend off the zombie in front of him, but doesn't have a defense for the one closing in.

The sound of a powerful engine roars in the street just ahead. The muffler kicks out a deep, angry groan as its driver accelerates toward Kito. It takes the muscle car three seconds to approach and collide into the zombie that was behind Kito. The impact liquefies the entire body to leave an explosion of guts in the street. The car speeds past and then drifts around and heads back with a wailing crackle. Kito pushes the zombie away from him and then retreats just before the car smashes into the second woman. The zombie rolls up over the top of the car and then down the back before falling in the road severed at the waist.

Kito admires the car as soon as it screeches to a halt after completing its mission—a red 1969 Pontiac GTO with a black hood and spoiler to accent the body. The tinted window slowly descends to reveal Amiku looking out.

"Hey baby, need a lift?"

Kito stares back with a dropped jaw and lost for words. Amiku has somehow developed a knack for stealing Kito's ability to speak or respond and this time is no different.

"I never saw you speechless before. Are you a zombie?" she continues.

"Uuummm—" is all Kito manages to utter.

"Well come on already, hurry up," Amiku replies while tapping her hand on the outside of the door. Kito sighs and slightly shakes his head before walking around the GTO to get inside. After he shuts the door, he begins admiring the black interior and the multitude of gauges on the dash.

"How did you get this?"

"Oh, good, you found your voice," Amiku jokes. "It was just sitting in someone's garage."

"So, you stole it?"

"No, I rescued it. Most likely her previous owners are dead and it's a shame to keep something so beautiful locked up. I bet this baby is running close to 500 ponies under the hood. Just listen to this engine." Amiku revs up the motor as it makes a deep aggressive roar while gently rocking the body with every acceleration.

"There are feelings inside of me that I cannot yet explain," Kito admits.

"I know what you mean." Kito wasn't just talking about the car like Amiku may have assumed. He's no doubt fascinated with the car, but he's completely enthralled with Amiku. Somehow her and the car together have turned Kito into a love-sick puppy. Amiku puts the car into gear and squeals off with a burnout.

Amiku drives the GTO with precision steering as she speeds through the ruined city and around fallen debris without losing speed or control. It's obvious Amiku knows how to handle the car and her response time is nearly perfect. Kito gazes at her as she drives; he must admit that she's able to put him to shame behind the wheel. Amiku keeps her focus on the road but can tell he's watching her.

"What is it, Kito?"

"Nothing," he answers abruptly and returns his view to the windshield, but it's not long before his head turns back to Amiku. She looks back puzzled by his odd behavior.

"What?!"

"Do you have black eyes?"

"No—they're dark brown. People—I should say normal people, can't have black eyes; it's unnatural."

"I know what brown looks like and that's too dark to be brown."

"There are different shades of brown, like hazel is lighter."

"All I'm saying is it's kinda creepy that you have demon eyes." Amiku stops the car and pulls Kito's collar towards her.

"Look. Can you see the brown tint now?"

Kito remains gazing into her eyes unable to say a word. Without intent he begins to inch his head closer to hers. She doesn't push him away or back away from his advancement and soon finds herself leaning forward to meet him. They close their eyes and wait for their lips to touch. Amiku's hand slides around Kito's shoulders and up the back of his head to guide him towards her. However, the clinging of a metal pipe being kicked across the pavement interrupts their anticipated moment. Their eyes open and look forward at a large horde of zombies advancing toward the GTO.

"Damn zombies—" Amiku whispers. Kito sits back and reaches for his seatbelt while giving Amiku a sly look.

"Let's go bowling." Amiku returns his smile and accepts the implied challenge.

She spins the tires, steps on the clutch, and then puts the car into gear before speeding towards the mob of undead. She drifts left to take out the zombies with the side of the car and then continues the drift around in a wide circle that gets gradually smaller. The zombies roll over the car, bounce off, or are torn apart on impact. She accelerates and rotates into a right drift for one final pass before running out of momentum and coming to a stop. Only one zombie is left standing.

"Almost, Amiku," Kito jokes. Amiku frowns and rolls down her window, and then pulls out her pistol and fires a bullet into the zombie's forehead to drop it to the ground.

"I like the way you think, but that's still considered a spare."

"I challenge you to do better."

"Well, I actually never learned how to drift," Kito admits in a somber tone.

"Really? I guess that's something I'll have to teach you then, isn't it?" Amiku grins.

Meanwhile, Ardian and Nydia have taken cover behind a dumpster while watching four zombies stumbling around in the street ahead of them. Nydia concentrates on the zombies for a long moment before lifting her bow. She assumes if Ardian fires his gun, it may attract more to their location, but her silent approach could keep their presence here to a minimum.

Her first shot soars directly into one of the zombie's temple. She then fires another arrow rapidly at the zombie that was behind it. Lastly, she loads two arrows and shoots them consecutively. The arrows fly side by side and gradually veer away perfectly to strike the last two zombies that were walking together. Ardian never doubted Nydia or her skills, but she continually impresses him.

"Where did you learn to use a bow?" he asks. Nydia explains as they step out of hiding and continue their walk.

"It was part of gym when I was a freshman in high school; I liked it so much that I joined the archery club afterwards. Towards the end we had a championship against all the other schools. I won first place in three categories, accuracy, distance, and most points accumulated. I always know the exact path my arrows will take. I see it as a neon streak in the air. All I have to do is point my bow."

"You are like a cross between a mage and an Amazon—Amagezon."

"You just made that up," Nydia giggles.

"Yes, I did."

As they continue onward, Nydia gradually sides up to Ardian, but he's unaware of her close proximity or the intent behind her nonchalant advancements. After several moments she decides to speak up.

"It's a shame we lost contact with each other for so long. How ironic that it took the world to end to bring us back together. I still remember that night, Ardian; that night when you saved me from those wolves." Ardian gives her a shy smile.

"I had always thought it was you who saved me. I don't think I would have survived this long without you. Your grace brought me sanity, your compassion brought me hope. I don't know what I would do without you." Nydia stops walking and takes his hands into hers. They face each other admirably for several moments before Ardian gently strokes her cheek with his fingertips. "The light in your eyes cannot be dimmed."

Nydia cannot conceal her emotions any longer. She slides her arms around him and draws him inward. Their eyes close as Ardian lines his lips up with hers and steadily moves in. He feels her breath on the tip of his nose before screeching tires and a thump force their eyes open. They look in the direction of the distraction too startled to complete their long overdue moment.

A GTO has stopped in the middle of the street with a zombie flailing on the ground just in front of it. Amiku sticks her head out the window to check her fender.

"My paint job!" She exclaims.

"Hey, there's Ardian and Nydia." Kito observes from the passenger window.

Ardian and Nydia exchange heartfelt looks. Kito and Amiku somehow keep finding ways to interrupt them, but this time they share in a common feeling of surprise and amazement towards the muscle car in their possession.

"Come on you two. Flight 1969 is departing—destination, anywhere, but fuckin' here," Amiku yells.

"This is why we don't fly standby," Ardian says as Nydia chuckles. They advance toward the open door that Kito is standing beside and crawl into the backseats.

Not too much farther are Anthulios, Thyst and Alma, who have just reached Goldthorn's boundary. Alma points ahead at a small dark structure in the distant countryside.

"That's Lazul's stronghold."

"Well, since Lazul already knows we're coming, we might as well let our own know where we are." Thyst takes out a flare gun from his belt and aims it into the sky before pulling the trigger.

Kito and Amiku notice the flare exploding in the horizon ahead.

"That must be our finish line," Kito points.

"Hold on," Amiku warns.

She drifts through a wide intersection while avoiding large stones and deep potholes before speeding down a straight road heading towards where the flare was seen. The speedometer needle slowly creeps past 110 miles per hour as Amiku continues to push the car to its limits. She lifts the emergency brake and drifts around a pile of debris from a collapsed section of a skyscraper. Once cleared, she encounters another obstacle too great to traverse. The car slides sideways and leaves long, curving trademarks in its wake before finally screeching to a halt. Blocking the street ahead is a collapsed railroad bridge with no way around it.

"Shit!" Amiku utters in frustration.

"Detour ahead," Ardian jokes from the backseat.

Amiku notices the on-ramp to a suspended highway that had collapsed some time ago, but directly in front of this ramp is a mall with an ornate and intricate window pattern that makes up the entire side of the building. She smirks and puts the car in reverse.

"When you can't go around—go through." Kito follows Amiku's stare and knows what she's planning.

"That's never going to work."

"Oh, it'll work. This is just a simple math equation. Forty-five-degree angle with, let's just say twenty-five-foot gap, divided by the Earth's velocity of thirty-two feet per second, times the weight of our car, approximately three-thousand five hundred pounds, gives us our momentum. Which, if my math is correct should be one-hundred and twenty miles per hour." Kito gives her an intense puzzled stare.

"You just made all those numbers up."

"She's not going to do what I think she's going to do. Is she?" Nydia asks worried. Amiku's smile indicates utter joy in completing her stunt. Kito immediately reaches for his seatbelt and warns the others to do the same.

"Your juxtaposed math problem forgot the variable of seatbelts."

The car's rear tires spin up a cloud of dense smoke before screeching into motion. Kito keeps his eyes on the needle slowly passing ninety-five and then looks ahead at the ramp fast approaching. He glances back at the needle now at one-hundred-twelve. He doubts Amiku will be able to get the car up to the speed she had hypothesized. The world almost slows down as she speeds past the ruined cityscape. She hits the ramp at one-eighteen with the engine revving and muffler roaring. She finally hits her estimate of one-twenty just as the front tires leave the pavement.

The GTO becomes airborne and soars up before straightening just before smashing through the wall of windows. It falls hard in the hallway of the mall as Amiku howls with excitement and celebration. She continues speeding down the aisle while crashing into benches, flowerpots and through kiosks and display stands. The end of the hallway is indicated by a metal fence but offers little resistance when the car bursts through and falls with a jolt on the lower level. Amiku drifts around the large empty water fountain and continues down another aisle.

A massive herd of zombies suddenly rush out to surround them and collide into the sides of the car while others are run over, and others begin chasing after the speeding vehicle.

"Looks like you woke the dead," Kito jokes. Amiku hands him her pistol.

"Then put them back to sleep." Amiku continues driving as Kito rolls the window down just enough to make the barrel stick out. These zombies are faster and capable of sprinting as opposed to the slow, stumbling ones outside. They could have been infused with demon DNA or just adapted differently.

Amiku veers right and bursts through the glass display window of a department store. She drives into the clothing display stands as the zombies continue to pursue them.

Dresses and gowns become snagged on the side view mirrors as Amiku takes out manikins and display stands as she tries to navigate to the opposite end of the store. She smacks into a lingerie rack just before bursting through the glass doors and metal detectors of the entrance. A pair of red frilly panties slaps into the middle of the windshield as the car skids around a seating area. Amiku and Kito exchange intrigued looks before she activates the windshield wipers to push them off.

The entry lobby finally can be seen at the end of the hallway, but more zombies join the chase and crowd their exit.

"I hate malls, I really do," Kito admits.

Amiku floors it down the home stretch while bombarding the zombies out of the way with little resistance. One zombie grabs a hold of the passenger door handle and holds on while sucking the outside of Kito's window. He makes a disgusted look and pokes the pistol out the slit. The zombie's grip ultimately fails, and it falls just as Kito prepares to take his shot. The timing is perfect when the car drives over the fallen creature and creates a bump that throws off his aim as soon as he fires. By another coincidence, the last store before they make their escape, happens to be a grilling outlet with a display of propane tanks. Kito's bullet finds one of them and sets off a chain reaction and massive explosion that consumes all the nearby zombies.

The GTO crashes through the exit doors, and soars over the stone steps as the fire expands behind and over the top of the car. The car hits the pavement and roars forward nearly unscathed.

"Damn, Kito," Ardian exclaims stunned and excited at the same time.

"Some like it hot—I like mine burnt," Kito replies with a grin.

"Not bad," Amiku laughs. He looks at her smugly.

"Not bad? Perfection is hard to improve."

At this time, the rest of the army has made it to the edge of

Goldthorn and have been accounted for.

"We're just waiting for them now," Rona says while giving Thyst a worried look.

"I hope they're okay," Thyst replies. The distant sound of the GTO's motor turns Anthulios' head behind him. Within moments he spots it drifting around a bend and then speeding towards him. Lio and Thyst exchange smiles and laughter knowing no one else could possibly make an entry like Kito and Amiku.

The GTO arrives with dented fenders and the front bumper hanging on by a single bolt. Amiku and Kito get out of the car with broad smiles.

"You're late," Thyst jokes as the final members of their team exit the vehicle. Alma carefully pulls a black bra out from the grille and then holds it up.

"Honestly, I'm not all that surprised, but I would have picked a better time." The group exchange looks, but no one explains the actual incident to rest Alma's curiosities.

The time has come to advance on Lazul and his demon army. The soldiers stand in their formations as Dixon gives his motivational speech.

"Make every breath you take count, for today we fight to exist! Not to survive, but to live. Not to hide and scavenge, but to thrive and build. Let history remember this day when we refused oppression! Your immortality is here and now. Be proud you were part of this day! No fear; no hesitation!" The army cheers and begins their determined march.

Lazul's army stands in unfathomable numbers consisting of four rows on each side of his fort—from little goblins to flying watchers to massive demonoids. They all wait for their orders while snarling with anticipation. On top of the highest balcony are Lazul and Anyo concentrating on the black mass heading towards them.

"They have no chance of winning this war, yet they walk with their heads high and proud," Lazul continues. "Send them a welcoming party. Let's see how long it takes for them to retreat." Anyo eagerly flies over the ranks and lets out a demanding roar followed by several rows of demons sprinting across the field. "Let destruction rain," Lazul growls with delight. Everything has led to this epic moment between heroes and demons. The final war has been declared and this outcome decides who inherits the Earth.

13

Two Worlds Collide

In these last few moments before battle there is a calm reflectiveness throughout the marching ranks. The clatter of gear and shuffling of feet are joined only by the silent cues from nearby friends. Seasoned soldiers and armed civilians know survival demands a degree of organized chaos. This world always required offerings of blood and tears, but never promised victory to anyone who shed them. Hope is a fool's gold that lives in the hearts of all who feared to dream, but a glimmer of it now whispers a chance to begin anew. If death is the fate of all who dared to love, then let us die unburdened.

Ardian, Nydia, Kito, and Amiku all exchange supporting grins. Everything before this moment feels like a lifetime ago. Who could have guessed how far they would travel and where they would be needed?

The demoralizing stampede of demons is felt thundering in the chests of the men until they are seen cascading over the hills ahead.

"To arms! To arms!" Thyst cries out.

The time for action has come and the full gravity of the situation has only just begun to sink in. This army of demons consists of agile goblins, armored demonoids, and flying watchers.

The men open fire at the oncoming mass, but the quick demons crawl over their slain with ease until the opposing armies finally collide. Some are still able to rely on their machine guns, while others are forced to trust their swords.

Several watchers fly overhead as each lift someone into the sky. A watcher bites a man's head off and then lets the body plummet to the ground. Two others join in pulling another unfortunate soldier in two with their talons.

"Shoot those watchers!" Lio commands.

The mounted guns, on the ATVs and Humvee, send a flurry of bullets into the circling watchers. A raining of guts, and severed body parts from the dead watchers fall over the warring parties. A goblin is about to leap at Kito when a watcher crashes on top of it, with a thump, and crushes the tiny body. Kito shrugs his shoulders and then returns with his scatted shots at the foes running through the fighting men.

The armored demonoids fight with swords or flails, but their fast attacks make it difficult for anyone to melee them. Ardian and several civilians join side by side to shoot them before they can get close enough to strike. Unfortunately, they cannot target all of them in time. The flails smash in skulls and crush ribcages or amputates limps with each blow, while their swords decapitate and skew their victims.

Thyst and Lio team up to fire upon several advancing demonoids when two goblins rush up behind them. Kito switches to his sword and races to slice one of them across the stomach and then stabs the other through its neck. The two men give him a smile and a nod in thanks.

"Now I know how Custer must have felt," Kito says.

"Let's hope we have a better day than he did," Thyst replies.

Nydia forms and hurls her energy orbs hastily and with pinpoint precision as they explode into the scampering goblins. Her attacks are lethal to the tiny creatures that are tossed across the battlefield as smoldering corpses. The watchers and armored demonoids; however, are only injured and take the cooperation of the nearby soldiers to deliver a barrage into the dazed behemoths.

Ardian utilizes every weapon he has when he finds the moment to do so. He stabs goblins with his sword or smashes them with his mace and then rotates his M4 off his shoulder and fires into a group of goblins or the larger beasts stampeding through the fray.

Amiku still prefers her katana but carries her simi-automatic and a pistol just in case she needs the extra firepower. After killing a demonoid she leaps on top of its shoulders as soon as its knees hit the ground. She pushes herself off and uses the momentum to shove her sword through another demonoid's eye socket as it bursts out the back of its skull. She then wastes little time to draw her pistol to shoot a goblin that has leapt onto someone's back.

A rather large demonoid bursts through a gathering of goblins and clobbers them with its large maul before setting its sights on Kito. Their eyes meet from across the field that initiates a silent taunt. The monster roars and kicks the ground before sprinting forward. Kito fires his AK47, but it does little to slow it down, he has no choice but to melee it now.

The demon lands an immensely powerful first contact hit that sends shockwaves through Kito's blade. He's knocked backwards, but the speed of this heavyweight leaves him little time to counterattack or prepare for the incoming ones. Kito is forced into a permanent defense as the monstrosity continues its onslaught. What's worse is the fact that Kito's ability to slow down his foe's movements doesn't appear to be triggering. He has been shaken out of his resolve and without his calm and focused mind he is unable to concentrate. Fear grips him and doubt robs him of his confidence. His actions become desperate and lacking in skill. His wild swing fails to strike the beast and leaves him open to the next attack. The demonoid lifts the maul above Kito's head and holds it with both hands as Kito's eyes scroll up to see it being brought down upon him.

Alma and Nydia blast their energy orbs into the head of the hulking creature as Ardian and Rona act as a firing squad. With the monster distracted, Amiku gets close enough to thrust her sword into its belly. It hunches over and roars at her, but the final blow comes from Brax who severs the monster's head with his mighty axe. The group try to give Kito an encouraging grin, but the ordeal has left him in a paralyzing free fall. He cannot attack, he cannot defend, he swings at nothing, thinking that something might just stumble in his way.

"Another wave is approaching!" Dixon cries out.

"Let them come. Today my axe is thirsty," Brax laughs.

Dixon, Nichi, Lako, and Thyst, fire their machine guns into the swarm of demons.

"Kill as many of them as you can before they arrive!" Thyst advises.

The ATV machine guns, and those on the tank and Humvee, support the men by mowing down large numbers of the approaching threat, but close combat becomes unavoidable for this wave of reinforcements as well.

Anthulios fires his AK47 until it runs out of ammunition. With no time to search for another clip, he tosses the gun aside and draws his sword to slice through the goblins foolish enough to think he had just become defenseless.

Ardian is quickly becoming overrun by imp-like goblins. He stabs one of them and then glances at Kito who's standing nearby frozen in place. To Ardian it looks like he has cleared his threats and may just be observing where he is needed next. The idea that Kito has lost his will never occurred to him when he enlists his aid.

"Kito, I need your help over here!"

Kito hears his call but struggles to overcome his paralyzed daze. Greater than his fear of death is his obsession with being thought of as weak. He takes a moment to compose himself by closing his eyes. Ardian calling his name becomes distant, the gunfire fades away, and the snarling and roaring demons become muffled. An explosion nearby by someone's grenade snaps Kito out of his trance and brings all the sounds of war back at once.

"Kito!" Ardian calls out again.

I'm not weak, Kito thinks to himself. Feeling returns to his legs and he grips his sword tight. He bolts into the mob surrounding Ardian while swinging his sword wildly and unpredictably. He body slams the goblins and tackles them to the ground before he lifts his sword to pierce their chests. He also sweeps his weapon around his body to easily slice through those surrounding him. While others may see him as a madman on the loose and cheer his voracity, those who have come to know him know this is not his fighting style. No one is judging him with more prejudice than Amiku. While eliminating her own attackers she observes Kito at a distance. His technique has become barbaric and differs greatly from his once calculated and planned executions. For as long as Amiku has known Kito he has always been more of a defender. This rampaging lunatic, who's attacking everything in his path, is not Kito.

Against his better judgment he has developed a habit of swinging his sword in a direction before he's looking where it will be. He has ignored his own advice and is now fighting by assumption and making best guesses. *I'm not weak. I'm not weak.*

"I'm not weak!" Kito thinks out loud. He brings his sword down without looking, but it collides with another blade. Kito looks up at Anthulios, whose imposing glare causes Kito to retract his sword in embarrassment.

The sounds of battle lessen as people begin to rejoice or finish off straggling demons with sparse gunfire. This battle ends with a victory for humanity, but it does not come without heavy losses and the war is still far from over.

Lio lowers his sword and glares at Kito with a dominate composure.

"To be truly strong is not to be without weakness but knowing when to recognize it. You are not alone, Kito, so quit fighting like you are. Success without sweat is meaningless."

"Sorry, Lio." Kito lowers his head and walks away.

Thyst approaches Lio knowing some occurrence just took place between him and Kito.

"What happened?"

"Nothing, he was remembering his past, but had forgotten he already moved forward from it."

Soldiers and citizens are restocking their supplies and ammo while others triage the wounded. Amiku finds Kito standing away from everyone else hoping to be alone. If she doesn't get through to him now, he will continue to spiral out of control or even succumb to his inner demon.

"Have you learned nothing?" She says assertively.

"What are you talking about," Kito somberly replies without turning around.

"You can't fake your way through this one. You're either prepared or you're waiting to die."

"I'm not in the mood for this right now." Kito takes a few

steps away, but Amiku grabs his arm and pulls him around. She could try to explain how sometimes it takes a joint effort to overcome tough obstacles or foes; or how he doesn't need to be the strongest one on the battlefield to be valuable. From experience she knows he fears being afraid and this makes him rush into things without his wits. She also knows talking rarely had a strong enough impact with Kito. She will need to utilize another technique.

"You aren't going to listen, and I'm not done talking—" Amiku sweeps her foot toward Kito's ribs, but he pushes her leg out of the way before it makes contact. "—That means I'll have to knock some sense into you another way."

"Stop it, Amiku," Kito demands. Amiku ignores his request and sends a flurry of punches and slaps at his shoulders, chest, and arms. He's forced on the defense, but only blocks a few of her attacks when he should have been able to stop all of them.

"Why are you not blocking these? I know you can."

"I can't anymore!" Kito finally admits.

"You lack concentration. An innate ability just doesn't disappear overnight."

"Mine has." She narrows her eyes and lands a direct kick to the middle of his stomach. Kito is sent hurling to the ground with only a grunt exiting his lips. Amiku towers over him with her arms folded across her chest.

"Who is this man I'm looking at right now? This is not the Kito I know. If you were my enemy, I would have killed you by now." Kito slowly comes to a stand with a determined look.

"Is that so? Then prove it."

"You have always been sensitive when someone attacks your integrity. Sometimes it's better to ignore stuff like that or others will always be able to choose your path for you. I'm not letting up this time. If you fall you will have to find your own way back up."

Amiku makes combinations of hand and foot strikes as Kito attempts to protect himself from her fast jabs. Kito misses a block and endures the sting as the onslaught continues. Amiku's hands and feet bounce off his forearms or palms until a well-placed kick sends him back to his knees. As promised, Amiku refuses to let up and sends her foot into his chest that knocks him on his back.

Neither have noticed that their hand-to-hand combat has attracted a crowd of onlookers who relish the entertainment.

They voice their sound effects that signify the pain Kito must be feeling along with some laughter. Among those in the crowd are Nydia and Lio who are watching them carefully. Nydia develops sensitivity towards Kito and feels it's time to end his abuse. She glances up at Lio with concern.

"Maybe you should help him." Lio keeps his focus on the sparring duo with his chin in his hand.

"I am, Nydia."

Amiku remains in her stance and allows Kito to regain his footing.

"Don't get mad. Stay calm," she advises.

Amiku throws her fist, but Kito dodges as it rushes just past his ear. She tosses another punch at him, but this one he catches in his hand. Amiku grins before sending a flurry of swift jabs and perfectly timed kicks. Amiku's jabs are swift, and her kicks are perfectly timed, but Kito has stopped missing them. The audience continues watching in amazement while responding with their *ooos* and *ahhs*. To them, Amiku's attacks seem too fast to avoid, but Kito's ability to see his opponent in slow motion has once again kicked in. Now that he's able to block or catch Amiku's attacks he can begin his offence.

Amiku blocks his palm with hers and then puts him back on the defense with a kick. Kito pushes her calf away and then counters with an elbow towards her chin. She slaps his elbow downwards and then follows up with an aimed kick to his face, but he deflects her leg with his arm. Amiku spins around and attacks with her other foot, but Kito dodges it easily.

Their spar is now taking up more surface area and forces the crowd to backup to give them a larger circle to move around in. Both Kito's and Amiku's usage of defensive and offensive techniques appear to be evenly matched as they exchange punches or deflections. Neither looks to be at a disadvantage or at the mercy of the other as they trade-off between defending and attacking methods with neither able to gain the upper hand. Finally, Amiku and Kito reach for the other's neck and wrap their fingers around the exposed skin at the same time. Their intense focus lightens as they exchange smiles. The audience claps thinking this performance was merely a show of force and nothing more.

Alma had observed Kito and Amiku far behind the dispersing

audience. She still secretly desires his affection, but also knows she cannot compete with Amiku. *In another life, Alma.* His words echo in her head as she replays the moment over and over. Why must she wait or why must he choose? *Give me an hour, a night, or a day. That's all I ask, love. Amiku can have you after,* she silently wishes.

The army relishes the short few moments they are given to rest, repair or gather their gear before resuming the march toward Lazul's fort. Kito is sitting on the slope of a hill when Anthulios joins his side. He lies his sword on the grass between them and sits down. The two allow a long moment of silence to pass before Lio breaks it.

"When I first recruited you, I saw someone who never had a purpose or a calling. Not until you picked up that sword. That's when you gained a responsibility to protect. What I'm trying to say is sometimes we don't become who we are until we are pushed. Occasionally, we are pushed to our breaking point or held down and beaten, but in the end, we are stronger because of it."

"It took the world to end for me to find my place in it."

"The world went through a change and so did we. No one cares where the oceans were during the last ice age. You can only navigate them where they are now. Who we were doesn't seem to matter all that much anymore either. We who adapt will always survive." Anthulios seems to have words of wisdom for every circumstance and Kito admires his outlook. Kito lowers his eyes and notices the engraving on Anthulios' blade just under the guard:

Το χέρι του Θεού

"Why do you have Elvish written on your blade?" Anthulios laughs at his interpretation.

"It's not Elvish; it's Greek. To chéri tou Theoú. It translates as, the hand of God."

"You named your sword, The hand of God?"

"Yes, I did," he answers grinning wide. Kito pauses to think about it more in depth.

"That's pretty bad ass actually," he finally replies.

The soldiers begin lining up in the field and picking up their things as Thyst and Dixon wave everyone up and into formation.

"It looks like we're moving again," Anthulios says while

standing up and sheathing his sword. He pats Kito on the back and the two advance toward the rest of the group.

The remaining progression forges on without incident until their voyage is nearly complete. Lazul is standing on the balcony with his tentacles flailing around him while glaring at the gathering mass halting a short distance away. He's in a permanent scowl while growling with a deep hatred toward all in this force.

Nichi observes the demon army through his binoculars as Thyst joins his side.

"How does it look, Nichi?"

"Not good. We are outnumbered five to one and that bastard Lazul is watching us."

"Yeah, I'm sure he's not going to want to miss a damn thing," Rona says. Thyst turns his attention to Alma.

"Can you get to the Star while the rest of us deal with Lazul's army?

"Yes, but it's being guarded. I may need some help."

There's an uneasy silence that falls over the group until Kito nominates himself. "I'll go." Ardian glances at Kito and then back at Alma.

"I will too," he replies.

"Really? I get two handsome guys in my group. I'm such a lucky girl," Alma teases.

"Good Luck," Lio says. Alma takes Kito's and Ardian's hands and the three vanish in a blink of the eye.

"I still don't trust that woman, Amiku calmly admits." Anthulios smiles and puts a hand on her shoulder.

"Well, there are plenty of demons out there for you to unleash on."

Alma, Kito and Ardian appear inside Alma's bedroom. The dark stone walls and light gray flooring give a sense of elegance with a desire to be concealed—a perfect duality that is either welcoming or overbearing if denied a change. A king-sized canopy bed occupies the center of the room, and a large oval mirror hangs on the adjacent wall. Lastly, an elegant standing harp sits in the nearest corner next to the lone window.

"I didn't know you played an instrument," Kito says when he notices the harp. Alma smiles and lightly strokes the glossy finish neck.

"This is my talent—my spell. The music is meant to calm

all who hear it." Alma starts playing the soothing music while looking deeply into the harp. She doesn't realize Ardian and Kito have fallen into a trance as she continues playing. "It's a hypnotic melody known as, The Siren's Song. It's meant to rob people of their self-awareness. It eliminates pain, worry, fear, and sorrow, but also strips away their free will. The person succumbs to the will of the harpist." Alma glances back at Kito in his relaxed state, and then between him and the bed. She has another chance to carry out her desires and it wasn't too long ago that she would have without hesitation or regret. She lowers her gaze and lets out a disappointing sigh. "If only I had the ability to stop time," she says softly. She plucks a low cord and Kito and Ardian snap out of their passive states. "Sorry, old habits die hard," she says carefreely. It is common for power, and the knowledge of how to use it, to thieve those of their morality.

Meanwhile, on the battlefield, Lio steps out from the front line to make sure Lazul can see him.

"Lazul! You have evaded us for the last time! Your deeds demand your fate shall be death and damnation!" Lazul snarls into a grin that shows his blackened teeth.

"You never had the courage to fight me; but now, you don't even have the power!" Lazul leans forward and roars with all his tentacles extending forward. He stands above all like a Caesar waiting to be entertained by his gladiators.

The demon legion snarl as they stampede eagerly into combat. The Humvee, ATVs, and tank open fire into the demon masses before machine guns and swords begin slicing through demon flesh and bone.

Anthulios transitions between his rifle and sword flawlessly as does Amiku and Rona between their pistols and melee weapons. Thyst and Brax rely heavily on their machine guns but have their melee weapons readily available if they find a need for them. Nydia prefers her bow to fire multiple, yellow, glowing, energy infused arrows that burn through her targets and sometimes those behind her victims. She will also lower her bow to push foes back with her telekinetic open palms or shoot energy orbs by slightly curling her fingers.

The return of the grizzly boar makes its second appearance by mauling several soldiers in a ferocious and gruesome display of carnage. The unlucky prey to this beast are unfortunate enough to witness their own bodies torn to pieces or see their internal organs splatter to the ground before they expire.

"You may now look upon my pet before you are devoured, Lio!" Lazul yells while laughing manically. Thyst hands the AT-4 rocket launcher to Anthulios while smiling.

"Let's teach this bitch how to play catch." Lazul's pet grunts and growls as it charges toward Thyst and Lio with heavy footsteps to carry its large mass. Anthulios takes a knee with the launcher on his shoulder and carefully takes aim at the beast. "Fire in the hole!" Thyst warns the nearby men. A burst of flame explodes from the rear of the rocket launcher as the warhead travels toward the beast before exploding. The expanding flames and blast radius consume more than fifty demons, while painting the surrounding area with their innards. Nothing but charred earth and smoldering corpse particles remain where Lazul's pet once was. Thyst and Anthulios rejoice with high-fives as Lazul scowls at the sight of his pet's demise.

In the meantime, Alma, Kito and Ardian are walking up a flight of stairs as they advance towards the top level.

"The Star of Eluvium is on the next floor," Alma explains. Ardian cautiously looks around the corner of the landing and then proceeds up the last flight of stairs. Alma waits for him to disappear around the wall and then throws herself against Kito. She pins him between her body and the wall and kisses him several times before he's able to gently push her back.

"Alma," he whispers in a tone that's part surprise, but more upset.

"Just give me one night. One night to have you completely," she whispers back. Before Kito can respond Ardian returns after observing no one was following him. Alma smiles and tries to hide what she was doing or contemplating. "Come on then—and try to be quiet." She says nonchalantly while playfully tugging on Kito's collar. "We don't want to draw any attention to ourselves."

While the ongoing battle outside has mostly everyone distracted, Anyo has noticed their ascent from the landing below. He gazes upwards and grins sinfully just as they disappear to the next floor.

Alma motions the boys to stay out of sight as she enters the last room of the corridor. Two armored demonoids hold their large swords in front of them with the points resting on the floor.

Just behind them is the pulsating Star of Eluvium levitating above the Architect's Box.

"You wouldn't happen to know where the ladies' room is?" Alma calmly asks as she strolls toward the demon guards. They sneer at her presence and lift their swords to prepare for their attack. Alma tosses an energy orb from alternating hands that explode into each of her opponent's chests. Kito and Ardian hurry into the room, with their weapons drawn, to strike the stunned demonoids.

Kito pushes his sword through one of the demon's necks while Ardian smashes his mace into the other's skull and then stabs his sword through its eye. Without a chance to fight back the two beasts collapse to the floor, with a thud, as their blood pools around them. Enthralled at the sight of the floating glowing orb, the three slowly advance toward it with admiration.

"That's the Star of Eluvium?" Kito asks.

"How can it be suspended like that?" Ardian adds.

"It's the oldest and purest form of energy in our solar system," Alma explains. "Gravity has no power over it. Don't touch it either or you will be dematerialized. There's a reason why it was kept inside of a box." Alma observes the star as it gently spins like a miniature planet, while emitting a soft pulse. "Amazing the power of such a small thing," Alma continues. "This Star has enough energy to supply the whole world with electricity for generations. It could very well advance us into a future only alive in science fiction. But we cannot trust the greed that rests in the hearts of man. We cannot risk these dark days repeating in the future. We must return it back to Atlantis."

"We could try to harness it. A new energy source to fuel everything invented and yet to be invented. Light for our homes and power to run new machines; maybe this is the answer science needed to build a better future," Kito theorizes.

"The road to Hell is paved with many good intentions, Kito. Just look outside," Alma reminds him.

"Yes, welcome to Hell," Anyo says before appearing through the doorway.

"I didn't know Lazul gave you permission to leave his side," Alma teases.

"I wanted to kill you for a long time," he barks.

"Keep waiting," Alma fires back.

Anyo growls and rushes toward her, but she teleports behind him and squeezes her arms around his neck. Anyo reacts by flying up and smashing her against the ceiling. She's unfazed by the attack and drops to the floor on her hands and feet. Anyo dashes toward her but is forced to dodge the energy orb that she shoots up. The blast leaves a crater in the wall and a pile of dust and pebbles just below.

Kito and Ardian slowly lift the Architect's Box upside down and over the Star of Eluvium. They close the lid and snap the buckles in place before turning it right side up.

Alma pushes her hands forward to create a burst of wind that knocks Anyo back. She immediately forms a large energy ball with both hands and then hurls it into his chest. He's sent soaring into the wall as stone chunks and support beams crash on top of him and pin him down. Alma then turns to face Kito and Ardian.

"Come on! The two of you need to get out of here."

Anyo is starting to claw his way out of the rubble. Though he's struggling, he's also slowly making some progress.

Alma looks down from the only window in the room. "It's clear right here for you to jump."

"Are you mad!" Ardian says surprised at her suggestion.

"Don't worry. I can guide both of you down gently."

"What about you?" Kito asks. Alma gives him a small grin.

"Thank you for thinking about me, Kito, but I have a score to settle. Now go."

Kito and Ardian run toward the window while holding each side of the box.

"I'm very uneasy about this," Ardian admits. Alma makes good on her promise by guiding them out the opening, with both hands, and then slows their descent as she keeps her open palms hovering over them until their feet rest softly on the ground.

Anyo tosses the last hunk of debris off him and rises to his feet.

"You think your plan will succeed? You have just sent them to their deaths."

"Life and death are so closely related that they are willing to die to make sure others can live. They are not fighting out of fear, but out of hope. They are stronger than you."

Meanwhile, the numbers of the human soldiers are starting to dwindle giving the demons a commanding lead. Amiku becomes preoccupied when two goblins jump on her back and begin scratching her face. A nearby demonoid notices her in distress and charges to make an easy kill. Kito intercepts the monster just in time to make the block and then hastily stabs the beast through the heart. The excess weight from the goblins makes Amiku collapse. Kito delivers a powerful kick to both imps as Nydia sends an energy bolt into each of their skulls. Kito helps Amiku up before she lays her head on his chest as they embrace each other. "Take a break. I'll defend you," he says softly.

In the meantime, Anyo delivers an elbow into Alma's jaw and then lifts her into the air to throw her into the hallway like a pitcher would a fastball. She slides across the floor for several feet before she's able to stop herself. She wipes a drop of blood from her bleeding lip with her thumb before standing back up.

"You can't defeat me!" Anyo taunts as he proudly advances proudly. "You are an insect, beneath my foot, begging for mercy."

"I won't be the one who's begging," she replies.

"All living creatures have fear. It exists to ensure survival by avoiding things that can kill. I have no fear because nothing can kill me."

"You aren't immortal, and I'll prove this to you before the day is done."

Anyo swoops toward Alma but misses his chance to attack when she teleports before his arrival. Anyo quickly turns around, undeterred by this minor setback, just as Alma reappears. He delivers a swift punch to her gut before she realizes he has predicted her move. Anyo grabs her around the neck and strikes with an uppercut.

"I know all your moves, witch!"

Alma recovers from the blow and remains focused on Anyo without showing an expression or responding. She clenches her fist until a glowing orb encircles it and keeps it closed as the orb slowly engulfs her hand while radiating outwards.

"Your magic is useless against me," Anyo continues. "The only thing you were ever good for was a piece of ass to rape." Suddenly, the orb shifts from a yellow glow into a deep red hue.

"Thank you," Alma says calmly, "For pissing me off!" She extends her arm forward and sends the red energy ball rocketing toward Anyo. The blast explodes into his shoulder, chest, and face to melt away skin and muscle tissue instantly. Anyo hollers out in agony as his wound continues to expand around the initial point of impact. His flesh liquefies into goo as it drips to the floor to reveal bone and teeth. He roars and growls before attempting to swipe his claws at Alma. She fires a smaller red orb at his hand. Horrified, he watches his scaly hand recede, like the tide, to show his skeleton.

Alma forms another orb, but Anyo puts his good hand in front of him.

"Wait—please," he pleads.

"See, I told you. It won't be me who begs," she smirks. "At least you could try to die like a man," she adds.

"Fuckin' bitch!" Anyo shouts.

"Sayonara, baka." Alma says before bringing both hands together and then pulling them apart to stretch the red orb into a huge sphere.

The massive blast consumes Anyo's body as it roars down the hallway with him inside. The orb explodes through the stronghold's solid stone structure to send an avalanche of blocks, crumbled stone, and dust to the ground. Among the rubble lies the skeletal remains of a winged beast stuck in an eternal scream. Here lies one who was formerly known as Anyo.

The outcome is looking very bleak on the battlefield. The remaining soldiers are slowly becoming overwhelmed due to the superiority of the demonic army's population and their own exhaustion. Several demonoids and watchers attack and kill the men who are operating the machine guns on top of the tank and Humvee. More soldiers rally to try and retake the position, but the idea that this is a major asset has not escaped the demons. They now stand guard near the vehicles to slay any who approach. The demonic army has gained the upper hand and their success is now evident. Several ATVs drive through or encircle the demons while firing into their masses. Many of the exposed drivers are easily swooped up by watchers or knocked off their seats. The last few remaining ATVs are overturned, and their drivers are slaughtered and devoured. Anthulios observes the grim scene with dismay, is this our end, he wonders.

Thyst struggles to eliminate a congregation of imps fast enough and soon becomes surrounded without anyone to lend him aid. They jab their crafted spears, made from rigid twigs, at him, but his body is tougher than their makeshift weapons.

He steals their weapons and then snaps them when he whips them over the head with them. A mob of demonoids are rushing toward him while he's preoccupied. He glances up to see them coming and knows he won't be able to fight all of them at once. He tries to prepare himself for his inevitable end, but before he resigns himself to the fate an explosion blows the nearing demons apart. He looks around to discover where this blast could have originated.

On the uppermost section of a nearby hill peeks the front line of a huge human army. They begin to scream and shout as they stampede down the slope toward the battlefield. Two tanks roll alongside them while firing their warheads into Lazul's fort. Large sections of the construction are blown off and fall on top of the demons unfortunate enough to be underneath. Lazul scowls at the sight of this new battalion and growls at the destruction of his fort.

Heavy gunfire, projectiles and rockets are shot around Lazul and into his forces. Flamethrowers engulf the nearby demons and grenade launchers clear large densely concentrated areas in the distance. In one single moment Lazul's victory is denied. Lazul struggles to keep his balance when part of his balcony collapses followed by an entire side of the fort. With a final roar he retreats inside. Now that his fort is in ruins the tanks turn their cannons to the demon army. Large area explosions hurl body parts in all directions while machine gunfire, flamethrowers and grenade launchers finally force the demons to scatter and break formation. With Lazul absent from the battlefield the demons are free from orders and scurry across the plains.

Lazul exits the back of the fort and follows it until he reaches the end where he discovers Anyo's remains. "You gave up too soon you weak bastard." This is how he pays his respects to his trusted companion before finally abandoning his current location. The armies are so preoccupied with chasing the retreating goblins that they don't notice a decrepit old man walking away with a cane.

Thyst fires his AT-4 rocket towards Lazul's cannon to spoil Lazul's plans once and for all. The base explodes into pieces followed by the cannon crashing to the ground. The fields are filled with elated cheering from the relieved army and sparse gunfire from those who are still bloodthirsty.

"Let them run," Nichi announces. "Take care of our injured; remember our dead."

In the shadow of the demolished fort the wounded men are triaged with the help of Amiku's plasma rejuvenation and Nydia's medical background. Brax, Lio, Ardian, Kito, and other men inspect their fallen comrades to make sure no one is mistaken for dead and moved to where the burning pyre is being constructed. The reddish-purple horizon reminds the army that the sun is setting and precautions for camping out at night must be taken. The recent reinforcements are the most able-bodied and are ordered to begin with setting up guard posts and building fires throughout the area.

Thyst and Rona are resting on top of the downed cannon when Dixon, Nichi, and Lako arrive with news from their surveillance.

"Lazul escaped," Dixon reports.

"The men did report seeing a sickly old man hobbling away," Nichi continues.

"But they were looking for some beast with tentacles and paid him no mind," adds Lako. Thyst shakes his head with a sigh.

"Illusions and tricks. That clever bastard. Where was he heading?" Dixon points toward the mountain ridge that borders the vast meadow in the far-off distance.

"Toward the mountains. Some of my men claim to know of a cave over there and believe Lazul may be hiding in it," Dixon answers.

"Should I rally the others?" Nichi asks.

"We are wounded and exhausted while Lazul is still at full strength. The last thing we need is to explore his home turf this close to night," Rona points out. Thyst nods in agreement.

"We will go after him, but on our terms not his," Thyst confirms.

"Loud and clear. Lako and I will then see where our help is needed." Dixon takes a seat next to Thyst as Nichi and Lako leave the vicinity.

"How did so many arrive?" Thyst asks while admiring the staggering number of soldiers that have just joined their ranks.

"I recorded your message and then put it on a loop. Others must have heard it," Dixon replies. Countless of individual groups have collected and traveled far to reach this location. Anthulios' hope that people will one day come together has arrived.

Alma is sitting alone with her thoughts as she observes the sunset over the mountains. *I can only pretend what life would be like past all of this. The questions of life are the answers of death. Why someone dies is why they lived. They say love can save someone, but love is like a boat. It sails effortlessly on a calm, sunny day, but when the wind and rain come the boat is tossed from side to side and smashed into pieces. Love can only survive in a world without storms.* Her thoughts become burdened with regret. *The actions of a few shaped a beast out of me, but it was my aggression that hurt me most.*

Nichi is collecting rifles from the battlefield, which may still be loaded with the invaluable ammunition their stocks so desperately need. Alms stands up and takes a few paces into the field. He observes her focused contemplation with a gaze that's clearly directed on the mountains.

"What are you up too, Alma?"

"Redemption." Her tone is direct with her eyes never shifting from her intended destination. Alma vanishes before an exchange of words can take place.

Clarification isn't needed. Nichi knows Alma is going after Lazul alone.

14

Heroes and Demons

Sometimes someone doesn't know who they really are until they spend a time being someone else. A person can spend forty years thinking one thing and then mysteriously wake up one morning and feel very strongly towards an idea they never considered. Some call this maturing, but that's an outdated term that refers to someone more concerned with paying the bills than their own satisfaction. This change in perception is due to, situational displacement, or in other words, where you are isn't where you belong.

When Lazul and Anyo first crossed paths with Alma she took the only offer that was available, and over time identified with their personas and motives. When she met Kito, he was just another captive who would submit to her will when beckoned, but when the two really looked at each other; they saw themselves. She saw a life she had only dreamt about with the only one who could truly understand her. She wanted that life so bad that she tried anything to make it real, but cruel is the hand of fate when it arrives too late. Both Kito and Alma saw themselves too weak to achieve greatness, but too proud to settle for mediocrity. Blinded by hate and envy of lovers, they chose to live outside the norms of society. When the world called for heroes, they stayed at the back of the line. But by some unknown circumstance and unseen force they now find themselves at the forefront of it all.

Never has she felt the need to protect or feel a responsibility to act. With a change of heart and mind, Alma is determined to risk everything to go after the man who mislead her for so many years. Beyond the rolling hills and the proceeding flatlands Alma finds Lazul. Proving his escape did not go unnoticed, she appears in his path. He shows her a discomforting grin while uttering a low growl.

"So, my little renegade returns."

"I'm not that lost little angry girl you found all those years ago."

"Oh, but you are lost; you will never escape that. You were born lost and lost is how you will die."

"I've always said that I will never use any weapon I wasn't born attached to," she announces while drawing a short sword that was hidden in the small of her back. "But if this is what it takes to defeat you, then I will break my rule just this once."

"Really, a little dagger?" Lazul jokes.

A yellow aura forms around Alma's hand and then expands around the entire sword. She teleports out of view and then reappears near Lazul to slash his side with the energy infused blade. She then quickly teleports away before Lazul counters.

Lazul reveals his tentacles by forcing them through and shredding his disguise. He pulls the tattered cloth away from him and discards it at his feet. Alma appears near him again to slice one of his tentacles. The energy she's slowly releasing heats the blade to make it both slice and scorch with every attack. Lazul growls while flailing his tentacles around him as Alma reemerges several feet away.

"You are too weak to kill me. My wounds are already healing themselves," he says. While his wounds are capable of being fully healed in a matter of hours, he's not immune to feeling pain. Alma takes great satisfaction in knowing this fact and wishes to exploit it for however long she can.

"The last thing you will see is your ass when I behead you," she replies.

"Still talking tough, are you? I suppose it's finally time to shoot down this spitfire."

Lazul's eyes glow red as new horns start to sprout from the top of his head with smaller spikes sprouting around his chin. His torso bulks up and barbs extend out from his shoulders and arms. His feet become clawed and more animal like as all signs that Lazul was once human finally vanishes. He raises his arms over his head while roaring.

"Excito scelus evictis animos patibilis intemporaliter!" The Latin phrase translates as, *I summon all wickedness to conquer every soul and to endure for an eternity.* A large sword begins to materialize in his hands. It's four and a half feet in length with the metal guard meeting the serrated blade and the pommel is crafted to look like a dragon's head in mid-roar. "Look upon your death—The Dragon King's Sword!"

This weapon was said to have been crafted by a powerful summoner in the mid-1100s. The entire piece was created solely from the fire of a dragon, and he honored the beast in his pommel. Inscribed in the blade is an ancient incantation, which simply translates as, *No one can escape it once it has been drawn, no one can resist it,* a spell that ensures victory to all who wields it. Alma bends her knees while holding her sword over her head with the point towards Lazul.

Back at camp, Nichi had just informed the group his assumption that Alma is pursuing Lazul. The news is disturbing to most, but to Kito it's unacceptable. When he thinks no one is looking he sneaks away to a secluded area where an ATV was left behind. He sits down and starts the vehicle up without any issues, but Amiku suddenly steps in front of him and grabs the handle.

"What are you doing?"

"I'm going to bring her back, Amiku. I'm not letting her fight alone." Amiku takes a quick glance around to notice no one is nearby or looking in their direction.

"I'm going with you," she says before hoping on board behind him. Kito accelerates toward the mountains without informing anyone of his plan.

In the meantime, Alma's infused sword sears Lazul's skin with every slash as she teleports close and then away after making her attack. Her constant appearing and disappearing act makes it hard for Lazul to get a fix on her and he has yet to swing his sword. Alma reappears out of his reach again.

"Is that sword just for show?"

"This sword is meant for only one thing—to kill. Not to wound or deflect."

"I won't let you hurt anymore people."

"So, your motive is repentance then, is it? But it's too late for you. I know your destiny. It's to die and spend an eternity as a concubine for all the legions of Hell."

"You do know what they say about a woman scorned, don't you—" Alma's glowing energy around her sword turns from yellow to red. She rushes toward Lazul and jumps up into a barrel roll before bringing her sword down his chest and stomach. The deep smoldering gash spreads out into a gaping canyon of dead flesh and tissue that hardens into walled deformations.

"—Hell hath no fury." She answers her own question as Lazul howls and roars in agony.

Alma is ready to end her game of cat and mouse and go in for the kill. She appears close enough to slit Lazul's throat, but his flailing tentacles block her intention. She dodges his swatting attempts before finally retreating to recalculate. Lazul's tentacle is ready when she makes herself visible again for a second opportunity.

"You have misjudged your distance, witch," Lazul laughs. A tentacle coils around her neck as another one wraps around her waist. He keeps her suspended high in the air as she desperately tries to free herself. "You have always been a disappointment to me." Lazul swiftly brings Alma towards him with the point of his sword held in front. The entire blade skewers through Alma's torso and explodes out her back.

Sound and color dissipate for a moment as her world becomes silent and void of elements. Her body becomes weightless, and time has all but stopped. The shock subsides to make her brain register pain and a long gasp exits her lips. Alma's glowing sword slowly fades back into a dull metal weapon before falling from her grasp.

"I know iron locks your powers. That's why I coated this blade with iron dust. It is now in your bloodstream. I doubt your rejuvenation ability will be of any use to you now." Lazul pulls his bloody blade from her and then lets her drop to the ground. She gasps and wheezes, while frozen in the position she had fallen. "Now do the only thing you can't fail at—die."

Lazul leaves her in the field without another thought to even a desire to look back as he continues towards the cave in the distance.

Alma gazes at the streaks of vivid hues above her and wonders why she never noticed how beautiful the sky can be sometimes. A sound of a motor draws nearer and she hears her name being called. She maintains her gaze as the rumbling motor stops nearby and her name is spoken again.

"Alma," Kito cries out and kneels beside her. He slides his arm under her shoulders and cradles her in his arms. Amiku takes out a bottle of plasma rejuvenation and pours it on Alma's stomach wound, but the severity of it is more than one potion can repair.

"We are going to take care of you," Kito says in a broken voice.

"No," she responds in a hushed tone. She lightly squeezes his hand and rests it on top of hers. "It's too late."

"Why did you go after Lazul alone?" Kito asks.

"It was always meant to be my fight. I got Anyo—I thought maybe I could finish this—"

"Amiku gave you something to help you heal. You just need to rest," Tears pool in his eyes before escaping down his cheeks, this is the second time he's tasked with holding a dying girl in his embrace. Alma too breaks down as fear sets in.

"Please don't leave me. I don't want to die alone," she cries.

"You aren't going to die. I'm going to save you," he replies. He brings her shivering body closer to his chest in hopes to keep her warm.

"I never told you this, but I had a dream about you," Alma says softly.

"What was it about?"

"I was lying in a warm field, and you were looking down over me. I felt you pick me up and carry me. What does it mean?"

"It means I will carry you," he replies. Alma lets her emotions and thoughts pour out of her without fear of holding them back.

"Now you can see my heart—

I've only shown it to you.

You saved me—you saved me.
You're the one,
I would have loved.
Where were you—
when I was not yet broken?
I was just a girl when the world branded me a monster,
but when I was a demon—
you saw me as a girl.
Ironic, isn't it?
How fate and time always must fight." Alma gives Kito a weak grin as tears stream down his cheeks.

"Why do you cry for me?
I'm just a memory.
I will miss our talks—
our walks,
all the times,
I wished—
I had you.
Not as a monster,
but a woman.
One chance to feel human.
Everything hurts—
now numb—
but still—
the only time I ever felt warmth.
Here, in your arms—
Is the only place I want to be." She then turns to look at Amiku.

"I'm sorry, Amiku." Amiku lightly places her hand on Alma's shoulder and looks into her eyes. "I've caused you many vexations," Alma continues.

"I feel none of them now," Amiku answers while shaking her head. Alma continues while keeping her focus in Kito's somber eyes.

"I will wait for you—
if your promise you will keep—
In another life—"
Alma's grip becomes weaker and her breathing more labored. "I promise to save you," she whispers. Kito kisses her cheek. She smiles and her eyes close. With one final exhale her breathing

stops. Alma dies feeling loved.

The array of colors fades to black as the sky turns to night. Moonless and still, as if the environment itself is giving Alma a silent and mournful send off.

People respectfully gather around near a circle of lit torches including Nydia sobbing in Ardian's embrace. Nichi, Lako, Lio and Thyst carefully carry Alma to the center and lies her down. Thyst folds her arms across her stomach as Anthulios rests his hand on her forehead with shut eyes.

"Rest now child, for you are home and with far better company."

Kito departs from the crowd with quickened steps as Amiku scurries after him.

"Stop Kito." Her voice cracks as she reaches for him. He pulls away and tries to keep walking, but she brings him towards her. "Kito, I'm sorry," she continues. He doesn't want to break down, but he can't fight against it any longer. He falls to his knees and sinks into her arms as the two share their tears.

When morning arrives, everyone gathers with their heads bowed as a man and woman sing a duet to remember the fallen. The remaining deceased have been brought to the funeral pyre in the center of the lit torches where Alma was laid the night before. Dixon steps forward after the song ends to give his eulogy to all.

"Today we have mixed emotions. We have had a great victory against an evil that reigned supreme over us for so long, but we have also lost many friends and loved ones in the process. We remember and honor these fallen heroes together, both those that were known to us and those we never met. We are sad to say goodbye to so many brave warriors and those we still have a desire to hold. But they will live inside our hearts and minds. We were lucky to have known them and to be known by them. From this day forward this spot will be known as, Hero Hill. We now lay them to rest."

Several men step forward to lift the torches and then light the thatch and branches. Flames rise as fire consumes the bodies of the fallen. Among them is Alma still smiling.

"Earth to earth, ashes to ashes, dust to dust; in sure and certain hope of the resurrection into eternal life," Dixon concludes.

"Goodbye, Alma." Nydia whispers her farewell.

The time has come to march onward and engage Lazul inside his last stronghold. The final battle is only hours away but before the army advances there is still one important task that needs to be addressed. Thyst hand-picks a group of four men to be couriers of the Architect's Box and to ensure its safe arrival to Esperanza. Most of the army marches silently towards the mountains as a Humvee of four return home, but neither is less important than the other.

As the journey progresses, Kito can't help but look at the blood-stained grass where he and Amiku had found Alma the day before. Her scent still lingers on his clothes and his hand still feels her grasp. He forces himself to keep up with the rhythm of the others and continues past the place where she drew her last breath.

The ranks reach and gather outside the black abyss that marks their intended path. The vibe here is shared collectively as a place to avoid and no one is eager to venture forward. Nydia steps out of the halted company and stands at the mouth of the cave. She extends her hand in front of her and shuts her eyes. She sees herself soaring through the twists and turns of the passageways until she advances behind Lazul. He turns around and glares at her while growling as if sensing her presence. She picks up on his aura and follows his path. She now knows how to navigate through the cave.

More images and visions reveal themselves as she remains connected to this spot. Shadow people dart across the floor and up the walls, while sounds of people screaming fill the air. Bloody corpses hang upside down from the ceiling as blood pools below them. Demonic roars and heavy breathing resonate throughout the entire area as the shadowy figures dart and jitter sporadically across the chamber. Suddenly a pair of bloodshot eyes open directly in front of Nydia's view.

Nydia lets out a scream before collapsing to her knees with her face buried in her palms. Ardian squats down beside her and places his hand on her shoulder. After a moment Nydia looks up.

"There's so much suffering and agony here. Both long ago and still to this day."

"What did you see, Nydia?" Lio asks. Nydia looks at him and whispers loudly.

"There is great and powerful evil here."

Thyst, Dixon and Anthulios take the lead through the narrow, gloomy corridors while Nydia directs them in the right direction when they are met with multiple options. Their tactical flashlights illuminate the ground ahead and acts as a beacon for the men behind to follow. There's an uneasy feeling of watchful eyes belonging to an unseen thing or creature peering out of every darkened spot.

The troops continue until they come to a vast open area. The expanse consists of several steep plateaus rising from a depth that cannot be measured. These formations are connected by suspended rope bridges that snake around to the opposite side where the passageway continues. On the far end of the room is a steady stream of water trickling down the cave wall. Anthulios glances over the edge of the first plateau to observe the rock side continuing into blackness.

"Nobody fall, it's a long way down," he warns.

Kito curiously takes a step towards the edge to look down, but the rock cracks and slides loose. Amiku quickly grabs his arm and pulls him back just before the section falls.

"Thanks for the heart attack, Kito," Rona says after breathing a sigh of relief.

"I think we should tread carefully here. We will advance to the next plateaus in small groups," Thyst suggests.

"That's a good plan. I can lead the first group if you don't mind," Dixon volunteers. Thyst nods and steps aside to allow Dixon and six men to test the first bridge. Everyone watches their crossing intensely until they arrive safely on the next plateau. Confident that the bridges are well constructed, Thyst picks out his group and then begins to lead them forward.

Scratching, tapping, and clawing followed by cascading pebbles begin below. The sounds become more frequent and closer as if something is crawling up the plateau ledges. Lio moves his hand to grasp his sword hanging at his side. He has a good idea that whatever is coming won't be friendly.

A clawed hand, with three long fingers and an opposable thumb, slaps on top of the surface of the plateau. A slender gray arm rises followed by the head of a creature. They are known to be cavern goblins and only reside in dark and damp locations. Unlike their relatives, that roam above ground, these have longer arms, and legs and a smaller face with recessed large black eyes.

They also have teeth like a barracuda and communicate by screeching.

A multitude of screeching echoes throughout the area as countless cavern goblins emerge from their climb to the tops of all the plateaus.

"It's an ambush!" Nichi cries out. Dixon is on the third platform while Thyst has just reached the second when they are attacked. The party begin firing or slicing at the goblins while others are bitten, clawed, and tackled over the edge, leaving nothing but their fading screams behind.

"Know your targets! We don't want to start shooting each other!" Lio advises.

Ardian takes his single shots carefully and with perfect aim that sends his kills back to the depth from whence they came. A goblin leaps onto a soldier's back and sinks its teeth into his neck. It lifts its head to swallow the chunk of flesh it tore off before the goblin and its falling victim disappear over the edge.

"I'm out," Ardian says while releasing and pulling out his magazine. Anthulios tosses a spare clip into his waiting hand.

"That's my last one; make it count," he explains.

Amiku fires her pistols from each hand and manages to maintain a perfect record of landing strictly headshots. When Kito's clip becomes empty he tosses the gun to the ground and then draws his sword. Amiku's next shot is the clicking of an empty chamber. She chucks the pistol in the middle of an advancing goblin's forehead and succeeds in knocking it over the side of the plateau.

"Fuck you," she says, proving she doesn't need bullets to keep her streak going.

Nydia flicks her energy blasts into mobs of goblins to successfully hit multiple targets with a single attack. Her next blast explodes into several goblins and tosses the gang into an unrecoverable plummet.

Rona helicopters her staff to swiftly trip or smack the goblins around her. She will also leap over her staff while spinning it to make both her feet and stick lethal weapons in a wide arc area.

A goblin leaps onto Amiku's back, but she stabs it through the mouth with her katana. The weight of the falling creature drags her back to a point where she's unable to regain her balance. Her footing slips from the platform just as Kito dives to grab her hand.

She vaults off the rock side as Kito pulls her safely back to the surface. They exchange smiles and nothing more.

The gunfire lessens as everyone's ammunition slowly runs out and they're forced to rely on their swords. The threat of the cavern goblins is easily manageable as their population have been greatly reduced. Most of the surviving ones conclude that this walking buffet may be more trouble than it's worth and retreat to settle for those who had already fallen to their death.

As the cavern goblins scatter back down the vertical ledges a new danger arises. Dark streaks jet up from below and swirl above everyone's heads. These black shadows dart across the cave walls and then transform into spirit assassins. They dart into bodies and then exit with their victim's hearts in their hands.

A female spirit assassin flies toward Ardian as he attempts to swing his sword at her, but his blade goes through her smoky form and leaves her unharmed. She smiles and then thrusts her hand into his chest. Ardian lets out a gasp but can neither speak nor scream. The assassin squeezes her grip on his heart as Nydia watches horrified.

"Ardian!" Her energy blast collides into the spirit assassin and dissolves her instantly.

Ardian looks down at his chest while rubbing it, but no wound can be seen. Nydia hurries to his side with concern for his health as he regains the ability to breathe again.

"I'm alright," he smiles after taking several deep breaths.

Spirit assassins' uncanny talents for removing hearts while remaining immune to swords make them lethal adversaries. Fortunately, they are not immune to Nydia's magical energy attacks. After she has dissolved several of them the remaining fly out through the corridor yet to be taken.

Thyst and Dixon exchange smiles and nods from across the gap of their plateaus after the enemy threat diminishes; however, their celebration may have come too soon.

The loud crunch of something powerful being forced into and against rock continues until a monster, that has never been seen prior, lifts itself onto the last plateau blocking everyone's intended path.

This demonoid has rather large quills running the length of its arms and smaller spines down its ribs. It also sports large, curved claws on each of its knees and elbows. A large, raised sail runs the length of its spine and a tail lay curled on the ground. These clues, along with its long snout and reptilian eyes, make it clear this was not a person, but some lizard that transformed and learned to stand on its hind legs. Its jaw opens wide to reveal several rows of tiny, serrated teeth when it lets out a long hiss. It then releases several of its quills from its arm after flicking it forward. The large sharp spikes soar through the air in tight clusters toward its closest target. Dixon hasn't the time to dodge and is pierced in his torso, arms, and legs. His body becomes numb as the irritation spreads rapidly across his skin cells and poison rushes into his bloodstream.

Kito and Amiku sprint across the bridges and plateaus toward the beast just as Thyst hurries to shield Dixon from the charging sailfin demon. The lizard redirects its focus away from them when Kito and Amiku arrive.

Kito lowers his body and then thrusts his sword into the lizard's stomach while Amiku propels herself off Kito's back to slash the lizard's neck. Blood gushes out of its severe neck wound, like a fountain, as it hisses. The monster steps back onto nothingness and tumbles off the plateau in an unrecoverable spin. It may have once been a hunter of the goblins that share its habitat, but now it will be a meal for them.

"Did you guys plan that attack?" Ardian asks when he and Nydia reach them.

"No, we always just improvise," Amiku admits.

"You guys are excellent together," Nydia says awestruck.

Thyst is kneeling over Dixon as he coughs up blood and struggles to breathe.

"Medic!" Thyst yells out. Dixon forcibly grabs Thyst's hand and holds it tight.

"No, don't waste nothing on me." He coughs again and then continues. "I did what I was meant to do. My men are under your orders now." He utters his last request with the last of his strength. "Give—that bastard—hell!"

"I will. I promise." Thyst bows respectably. Dixon's grip lessens and his head falls. His chest becomes still and his eyes close for the final time.

The remaining soldiers advance in small groups across the bridges. Dixon's men do not walk past him without saluting to their dead officer. "Heroes are never forgotten—" they say before continuing across the final bridge that connects to the passageway. "—But your song will have to wait."

Those who've already crossed wait in the corridor for the others to join their position. Nydia observes Thyst looking at Dixon lying in the middle of the plateau.

"It doesn't seem right to leave him there." Thyst glances at her with a sorrowful stare.

"Nothing seems right anymore. Assume the worst, hope for the best, but don't expect anything. Dixon will understand."

"If it wasn't for Dixon, we would have never made it to this point. He will be honored after all this is over." Lio says.

Thyst addresses the reunited army moments later. "Where do we stand on weapons?" Nichi holds his gun up before letting it drop to the ground.

"I'm afraid we'll have to Braveheart it from here. The damn goblins took the last of our ammunition."

"Leave the guns behind then. No need in carrying obsolete supplies." The men throw their guns to the ground and make their swords readily accessible.

"We're moving out men! It's time to smoke Lazul out of his fox hole," Thyst orders as he and Lio take the lead. Nydia quietly talks to Ardian as they advance with the army.

"I thought I lost you back there with that spirit assassin. How many times do I have to watch you almost die?" Ardian smiles and squeezes her hand.

"Every time I see you, I'm brought back to life."

The passageway opens into a spacious room with no egress and great stalactite and stalagmite formations. Large rocky ledges pop out of the cavern walls like the balconies of grand forts and a long shaft leads up to a past cave in that allows natural light to pour in.

Nydia closes her eyes and feels the air in front of her.

"The air is heavy in here," she says as she continues to pick up on the energy of her environment. She opens her eyes and then looks at Ardian and Amiku beside her. "Very old and powerful evil reside in this space. We are in great danger."

Everyone's presence is known by that which should not be disturbed. An evil as old as creation itself gathers behind the veil of understanding and beyond natural sight. The slight hint that something is near draws Nydia to swiftly turn to her side with an open palm in preparation to blast what has appeared. What stands before her numbs her judgment and lowers her guard. In the company of disbelief and confusion, lies become stronger than gained knowledge. Before her is none other than Sonya. Overtaken by the desire to embrace her dearly departed sister, she lets this smiling image advance closer. Even Kito is stunned at first, but what his eyes see doesn't convince his mind. Her essence is off; this Sonya is false.

"That's not Sonya," Kito whispers. Rona hears him and trusts him enough to act. She slams her staff on the floor in between Nydia and this representation of Sonya.

"I'm sorry, hon, but I don't think that's who you hope it is." With its cover blown, Sonya transforms into a black smoke demon with two tiny red glowing dots for eyes and an open mouth that shares the same dark emptiness as a black mamba. These shadow demons can read minds and take the form of someone an individual is familiar with. This ruse causes their victims to unknowingly trust them and advance with a lowered guard.

Nydia tosses an energy blast at the demonic form to make it bust into a yellow fire. It lets out a high-pitched scream before dissolving with the dying embers.

"How dare you corrupt the image of my sister!" Nydia shouts.

Deep laughter echoes throughout the room as Lazul steps to the edge of one of the ledges. Everyone looks up to see him in his new form for the first time.

"And here I thought he couldn't get any uglier," Brax says to those in earshot.

"Lazul! Come down from the safety of your distance and fight us!" Thyst taunts.

"Why should I step on ants when they are already in the spider's web?" Lazul lets out his usual drawn out rumbling laughter while raising his arms over his head. A large horde of shadow demons emerge out from the cavern walls and spirals or swoops down toward the army below.

The demons transform into women, children or other men and then advance toward their targets with smiles and open arms. Once the person is soothed by their appearance and brought close the demons drop their guise. Their eyes become empty sockets and their pale lips curl back into wide grins with thin, silk-like threads that connect the upper and lower gums. Hidden teeth viciously rip through necks or other areas that have exposed skin.

Thyst thrusts his sword into one of these creepy girls and causes her to fizzle into black smoke before fading. Unfortunately, it's too late to save the man she was attacking. It's clear that when the demons are in physical form they can be killed by physical means; however, unless seen in the process of changing or attacking, second guessing and uncertainty prohibits eliminating them easily.

Nydia's advantage is that her energy blasts can harm the demons in both forms and from a distance, but confusion and panic spread throughout the ranks. The most vigilant must wait for an ally to come under attack before acting and the speed these things go from beautiful to hideous is so quick that the number of human casualties and demons slain are almost one for one.

Many cannot bear the thought of harming those they hold dear, but to someone else they are only strangers. The soldiers finally decide the best strategy to fight this battle is to create small groups of people they know and defend the ones near them.

Rona spots a woman in a white dress and knows she's not dressed for war. She attempts to deliver a few fast jabs with her batons, but her target immediately returns to its shadow demon form. Rona's strikes pass through the creature that has now flown behind her. The demon reveals its frightening grin and then darts forward to chomp down with no preference of what it gets. Brax steps in front of Rona and lifts his arm to accept the demon's sinking teeth. It suddenly fades into thin air after Nydia finishes it off with an energy ball.

Rona gently inspects Brax's bleeding arm before looking up to meet his eyes.

"You risked yourself to save my life," she says. His answer finally impresses Rona.

"If this noble scar is the price I pay to ensure you are spared from an ounce of pain, then I will gladly sacrifice my other arm."

"Have you been reading my books?" she says with a smile.

A hand softly rests on Amiku's shoulder. When she turns around to see who's trying to get her attention, she sees her father.

"I know it's not you," she says while shaking her head. Charles smiles and gently takes her by the hand and pulls her closer to him. Amiku knows this is not real, but the desire to have another moment with her father pushes reason to the side. She doesn't see his face change or realize a mouth of fangs is creeping closer to her neck. She is caught in a daydream where she is once again in her father's loving embrace and nothing else matters.

Kito slices his sword down the demon's back to impale it on his blade. It wails while dissolving into black smoke and spiraling around Amiku before disappearing for good.

"I'm sorry, Amiku," Kito says tenderly.

"Thank you, Kito," she replies while forcing a smile through her tears.

Vigilance and strategy have turned the tide in the troops' favor. Many of the demons are being vanquished due to appearing out of place in the crowd or when they are trying to manipulate someone. It isn't long before the last shadow demon is triumphantly defeated and fades from view, this is further reinforced by Lazul's scowl and frustrated roar. Lio looks up and hollers at his adversary.

"We have the Star of Eluvium, Lazul. You lost!"

"The Star of Eluvium was only one piece of a much larger network. You see, some lands contain hidden energy that attract old powerful beings and no amount of cleansing will ever close a gate that has been open for eons. This cave is such a place, and it is here that I will call upon those with the blackest of hearts to aid me in my conquest. For this mountain is the direct link to Hell, and as long as it stands, I will have its power.

The Gods are too fat and lazy, gorging themselves on fruit and wine, to care about the troubles of this earthly world. They think of you as an ant farm. So fascinating at first, but then it becomes more fun to destroy. Like a favorite toy of a child who has outgrown it. Once cherished and never far from their grasp now lies abandoned and forgotten under the bed. So is this human race.

You will all now be ruled by demons. Today your world ends, tomorrow mine will be born."

"The only thing coming to an end is your delusions," Thyst shouts while pointing the tip of his sword up toward Lazul.

"Your little rebellion was somewhat entertaining at best. But now I grow weary of your kind and so it's time to start over," Lazul replies with a sinful grin.

Lazul levitates off the ledge and descends to hover just above the troops. His tentacles coil around some of the people and then toss them against the walls or let them fall from great heights—his victims' skulls break open and their necks break on impact.

"It's time we separate him from those appendages," Brax says as he lifts his axe to his chest. While Lazul maintains a safe distance from the battalion's weapons, Brax has a plan that may bring Lazul right to him.

"Don't be hasty. We need to think about this," Rona warns him.

"I was never good at thinking. I'm sure you have plenty of comebacks to that, but what I lack in brains I make up in strength. We use the abilities which we are given, and when the time comes to use that ability, there's nothing to think about." Rona isn't given a chance to respond. With a final smile and a wink Brax sprints toward Lazul while shouting his battle cry. Rona jolts forward to chase after him, but Lio holds her back. Brax may not have a lot of stamina, but across a short distance his speed and power are unstoppable. Brax holds his axe up with both hands and raised to his side. The commotion redirects Lazul's attention toward him and proves his plan is working. Fearing Brax is planning to throw his axe toward him, Lazul draws his tentacles back and then extends all of them toward Brax.

Brax rotates his body around the flailing appendages while leading with his axe. He's able to change directions swiftly and manages to avoid being grabbed while also chopping each tentacle off one by one. His maneuvers allow his targets to always stay in front of him as his axe is swung down, up or to the side. Victory is within reach, but his risk comes with a price. The last tentacle Lazul has avoids the axe and speeds past to explode into Brax's chest. The impact stops him in his tracks as a fleeting breath is pulled out of his parted lips. He notes the object embedded in his lung and only takes a moment to gather his air reserves. Defiant and strong-willed, Brax lifts the axe one last time and severs the final tentacle from Lazul.

The axe slips out of his grasp and lands at his feet. Overhead, Lazul retracts his bleeding stubs while growling in agony. Rona and Anthulios rush toward Brax who collapses to his knees with the tip of Lazul's tentacle still in him.

"Don't remove it or he will bleed to death," Rona advises.

Amiku also arrives with a bottle of plasma rejuvenation in her hand.

"Drink this; it will help you heal," she says as she guides the vial to his mouth. Rona inspects his wound with light touches.

"You need to remain still. Just take slow and steady breaths," she tells him. She then turns to Lio. "He has a collapsed lung."

"Hang in there, buddy," Lio says. Rona remains at his side as Lio rises into a dominate pose and advances toward Lazul. He is soon accompanied by Kito, Amiku, Ardian and Nydia and Thyst, Lako, and Nichi advance behind them.

"You consider us as ants, do you? Perhaps you are unaware that a large colony of ants can overtake enemies several hundred times larger than them," Lio says.

"You can't defeat me. I will destroy your race!" Lazul roars. He then extends his arms out and growls his next words. "Excito scelus evictis animos patibilis intemporaliter!"

The Dragon King's Sword materializes in his hand just as it had before. Lazul swiftly dives to the cavern floor and sends shockwaves throughout the area when his clawed feet crash to the ground. A small shard falls next to Nydia and shatters. She glances up to see a huge cluster of various sized stalactites above her. Lazul swings his arm in a wide arc to decapitate four people close to him and then lets out a long and deafening roar that leaves everyone stricken with immovability. The Phantom's Breath is another one of his spells and has the power to paralyze all who hear it. The effects only last for about twenty seconds, but that is more than enough time for Lazul to kill his greatest threats without any opposition.

Lazul rests his eyes on Amiku and sneers. "I will kill you first." She cannot defend herself and no one near her can help as Lazul's sword is brought down upon her. No one, except for one. Kito's blade shields Amiku from Lazul's attack. Lazul is at first surprised since no human can resist his spells, but then he remembers Kito has demon blood in his veins. It is this blood that has made him immune to the spell's effects. Lazul draws back his sword with a scowl.

"You've been an annoying little pest for a long time."

"I didn't know you were so easy to upset," Kito taunts.

"I killed Alma with this sword and now I will kill you. Give her my regards when you find her in Hell!"

Lazul swings his blade with great speed and precision, but Kito successfully blocks the attack. Lazul's claim that this sword always kills on the first swing has been disproven twice now.

"You aren't that fast," Kito says.

Lazul becomes more agitated with every failed attempt to land a fatal wound. His swift attacks are almost nothing but streaks in the air for those watching, but Kito's ability can see Lazul's movements in slow motion. He deflects or dodges the incoming attacks with ease. Lazul is so focused with his intent to kill Kito that he has forgotten the remaining duration of his spell. Kito just has to stall him long enough until it wears off.

Their wild duel has forced Kito slightly away from his frozen allies while Lazul's frustration grows with every mad and powerful swing that explodes through the stalagmites surrounding them. Lazul's recklessness also causes some of the stalactites to break off and plummet to the cavern floor.

Another wild swing sends his sword into a thick stalagmite where it becomes stuck. Kito takes this opening to slice Lazul's lower stomach. He then rushes behind him to slash his mid-back. Lazul growls and pounds his fist against the stalagmite, above his sword, to make the top portion break off. Kito returns to Lazul's front to swipe his blade across his chest. Kito blocks Lazul's next enraged attack and then counters with a deep gouge in his thigh.

Nydia can move her fingers slowly as the Phantom's Breath spell begins to wear off.

Lazul looks to prepare for a sideways slash and Kito readies his sword to block, but Lazul doesn't complete the swing. He has noticed that Kito is only focused on his sword and finally tricks him with misdirection. Kito is taken by surprise when Lazul's fingers close around his neck, and he's slammed against the wall. Lazul pulls his sword back and forces the blade into Kito's lower stomach before he can react. His body goes numb, and he's sent into instant shock. He sees the room closing in around him and then rushing back out. For a moment the only sound he hears is a hollow wind flowing through his ears and his own heartbeat. He loses feeling in his fingers and never felt his sword slip out of his grasp.

"That's the same look Alma had," Lazul laughs. Amiku screams out in horror from witnessing Kito's injury. Lazul withdraws his sword and then tosses him towards Amiku. "Now you can have him," he says relishing his victory.

Kito holds his hands over his wound as the blood seeps through his fingertips. He gasps and shivers as his body warmth slowly escapes from him. Amiku takes him in her arms and holds him close to her as tears swell up in her eyes.

Just then, an energy blast hits Lazul in the neck, but it fails to leave any indication that it caused him harm.

"So, the witch is awake," Lazul says while turning to face Nydia.

"I'm not a witch—" A yellow glow forms around her hand and then quickly expands to outline her entire body. She becomes completely encased in it before it suddenly bursts into a red aura, and her hair extends outward from her scalp. Her arms remain fully outstretched downward at her sides with her palms facing upwards as she levitates slightly off the ground. "—I'm a mage, bitch!" she yells as a continuous barrage of red energy balls rapidly fire from her palms toward the ceiling.

Lazul looks up just as the large cluster of stalactites descend on top of him. His arms are torn out of their sockets and his head, neck, shoulders, torso, and legs become pierced by the great many falling sharp projectiles.

Nydia's aura fades and her hair falls back around her shoulders. Lazul is still standing, but his body is a shredded mass of blood, broken bones, and torn skin.

The final blow comes from Amiku when she tosses her katana with all her might. The sword rotates hilt over blade until it pierces guard deep into Lazul's chest.

"Fucking bastard!" she yells.

Lazul collapses to his knees in a pool of blood. Anthulios notices Lazul's sword lying with its inscription facing up. He advances toward him with his blade held up so Lazul can clearly see it.

"Your sword isn't the only one that has a message, but mine is more commanding. You shall know its meaning soon enough." Anthulios slices his blade across Lazul's throat with one quick strike before resting it back at his side. Blood gushes from his wound and he finally drops to the floor.

Meanwhile, Amiku is applying more pressure to Kito's wound as deep red blood oozes out. She digs through her pockets frantically before taking out an empty bottle of plasma rejuvenation. She looks at it disappointingly before yelling and throwing it across the room. Tears run down her cheeks as Kito softly touches her arm.

"It's okay, Amiku," he whispers.

"No, it's not okay. It's not!" She rests her head on his forehead with her arms around him while crying. "I don't know what to do."

Rona and Nydia hurry over to inspect his wound.

"I think his intestines have been perforated," Rona says.

"I don't like how dark red this blood is. It might be his kidney," Nydia adds.

Their assessment is halted when the mountain starts shaking violently. The rocky ledges begin to crumble, and the remaining stalactites come loose and crash around the area. Amiku leans over Kito to protect him from the falling debris. A swirling black and crimson vortex takes shape near Lazul and grows larger until it begins dragging him closer to its center.

A pair of glowing red eyes appear from the middle section followed by the formation of a horned beast. A solid dark black arm darts out of the vortex and grabs Lazul's ankle. He glances behind him horrified and frantically tries to escape its pull.

"Let go of me, fiend! I control you! You can't do this to me! I control you!" The vortex demon speaks in a loud booming deep tone.

"You have no control over me! It is I who lent you my power. It is I who now will claim you." With one final forceful tug the demon drags Lazul entirely into the portal. The vortex slowly begins to close, but just before it completely disappears a burst of energy sends a powerful shock wave throughout the vicinity.

Amiku's katana lies on the floor where Lazul and the portal had been. Thyst picks up the sword and admires the clean blade. Not even a drop of Lazul's blood was left behind. He was completely claimed, both body and soul, to be a living denizen in Hell.

"Looks like Lazul discovered he wasn't the most powerful being after all," Thyst says.

The mountain begins to quake violently again, but this time it shows no signs of stopping. The last few stalactites plunge downward, and the walls begin to crumble.

"The mountain is collapsing!" Lako yells.

"Help the wounded up and follow me!" Nichi orders. The soldiers dash out the only exit of the room with Nichi and Lako leading.

Anthulios and Thyst help Brax to his feet and then put his arms around their necks.

"Come on buddy. We need to get out of here," Lio says.

"What about Kito?" Brax asks as he groans in pain with every step. Anthulios glances behind him concerned about Kito as well.

"We'll help Kito. You just get Brax to safety," Ardian assures him.

Amiku, Rona and Ardian help Kito to his feet. He leans against the cave wall with his hand over his wound while taking in deep breaths. Amiku takes off her coat and ties the sleeves tightly over Kito's injury as he grunts in pain.

"You need to get out of here, Amiku," Kito says weakly. Amiku looks at him sternly.

"Do not say that to me. I'm not leaving you." She brings her arm around his back and allows him to lean on her while Rona supports him on his other side.

"Lead the way for us, Ardian," Rona says. Nydia stays in between Ardian and Kito's group so she can help either side in case they run into danger.

"This is going to be slow, but in his condition, we shouldn't be moving him at all," Nydia points out.

"I know how the body works, but I'm choosing to ignore knowledge for now," Amiku replies.

Kito, and his rescuers are the last ones to leave the stalactite area just as most of the ceiling breaks apart and crashes down. They pass through the narrow corridor again and soon make it to the plateaus. Large slabs of rock fall from the ceiling into the abyss or smash on top of the plateaus. The waterfall, that was once just a trickle, is now gushing into the room and new waterfalls have burst through the failing cave walls.

The team hurries onward while glancing up to ensure their next step is free from falling rocks. They clear one plateau and begin to cross the first bridge, but Kito's legs give out. Amiku and Rona bend their knees to withstand his body weight and slowly lift him back up.

"Come on Kito, just a little bit farther," Amiku coaches.

They proceed across the next bridge and then to the following plateau. Finally, with just one more bridge to cross and the last raised area connecting to their exit the group feels a spark of hope.

A colossal chunk smashes just behind them to make the platform crack down the side and across the top. Large pieces slide off as the entire structure threatens to fall apart.

"We need to move!" Nydia warns.

The cracking follows them to the bridge and another large section comes loose that descends into darkness. The swaying bridge proves to make the crossing a treacherous one as Rona and Amiku hold on to Kito and the rope to maintain their balance. Ardian and Nydia make it to the last plateau just as the bridge jolts when the last supports on the collapsing plateau snap. Nydia raises her hands to keep the bridge remaining levitated despite the absence of the other side. As soon as Rona and Amiku step off the bridge she releases it, and it swings down. The two sides are now separated forever.

"I hate bridges," Kito manages to joke.

Anthulios appears in the archway to the passageway they first traveled.

"Come on! We found a way out," he shouts while signaling them to advance with his hand.

Nydia and Ardian make it to the passageway with the others only several feet behind them. A large portion of the rock face breaks loose from the wall above the opening and smashes the last spot yet to be crossed.

A deep crack creeps down the side of the platform and across the surface while spidering out in all directions. As soon as Rona steps on the unstable area it crumbles. She quickly pushes Kito and Amiku back from the edge and then makes a desperate jump to the other side. She falls short, but Anthulios and Ardian are there to catch her arms and pull her up as she pushes off the side of the wall with her feet. The once fully connected area is now separated with a wide gap and Kito and Amiku are stranded on the unfortunate side.

"I won't make the jump," Kito observes. Amiku gently embraces him while caressing his cheek.

"Yes, you will. Listen to me. You can make this. Lio and Ardian is right on the other side. They will catch you."

Anthulios and Ardian have their arms outstretched while

Rona and Nydia stand next to them ready to help. Slabs of rock continue to fall around Kito and Amiku while their plateau sways as its base begins to shift and crumble.

"It's too far, Amiku," Kito says while shaking his head.

"I'll throw you over," Amiku replies.

"You can't pick me up," he points out.

"Yes, I can. Just shut up and let me."

"You can't," he calmly replies.

"Stop it!"

"Shh, it's okay," he whispers.

"No!" Amiku cries as she debates with Kito.

"I promised myself a long time ago to protect you. And once you've made up your mind to protect someone, nothing else matters," Kito softly says. They embrace tightly as Amiku cries. She doesn't want him to be right; deep down she knows he is, but she doesn't want to be right about that either.

The plateau leans sideways at a sharp angle that puts too much stress on its base. The top of the plateau cracks and begins to slide off.

"Hurry up guys! You're running out of time," Nydia yells. Kito puts his hands on Amiku's cheeks and smiles.

"I love you. I've always loved you."

Kito holds Amiku by the waist and spins his body with the last of his strength to send her soaring into Lio's and Ardian's waiting arms. She's caught and lifted to solid ground.

Her eyes remain locked with Kito's, but she can't find the words to respond. She wants to yell, but her voice cannot escape the boundaries of her mind. She can't even fully process his confession yet. She doesn't want to accept his sacrifice or that their silent farewells will be made solely with their eyes. She needs to tell him so much, but time will not allow it.

The avalanching rockside takes away the much-needed support that held up the surface of the plateau. With a thunderous crack the base snaps and the entire platform plunges down. Kito and Amiku keep their eyes on each other until the moment that Kito falls and disappears into darkness. In just a short moment, but unmeasurable to Amiku, Kito is gone.

Amiku finally finds her voice in the form of a sorrowful scream. She collapses to her knees and extends her hand down into the blackness while crying loudly.

"Kito! No! Kito!" She tries to struggle to free herself from Lio's arms as he desperately tries to hold on to her. "No. Let go of me! We need to find him!" Anthulios pulls her back and hugs her as tears swell up in his eyes too.

"I'm sorry, Amiku. I'm so sorry."

Kito finally understood Sonya's message to save a life, but it wasn't a sacrifice. He realized there was something greater than himself. Greater than life or death, he discovered love, and that's what he chose to save.

15

Forgotten Beauty

The rumbling ceases and the mountain is once again quiet. The link to the demonic gateway has been concealed by the cave-in and its access is permanently cut off. Though the doorway to the realm of demons was shut when Lazul was dragged through the hellish portal; the world will never be the same. The line between natural and unnatural have been blurred and the fabric between living and dead is torn. A scar has been left on the land that will forever grant some creatures a way into our existence. Some may only be a fleeting glimpse while others will be more brazen. As much as we try to tame nature, most of it will remain wild. We must share it with imps, goblins, demons, and cryptids.

The mouth of the cave leads to a gravel hill that leads down to a lush valley of gentle flowing streams with smooth stone and pebbled banks and patches of smooth sumac litter the landscape. This area between the mountain ridges becomes a sound resting place and makeshift triage camp.

Busy hands begin constructing stretchers and crutches from the sumac to aid the wounded back to Esperanza. The trek will be slow moving down the grass-covered rocky hills before eventually reaching the flat grasslands.

Thyst maintains a focused gaze towards the cave until Lio and Amiku emerge followed by Nydia, Ardian, and Rona. Thyst advances to welcome them with a smile, but as he draws nearer his smile begins to fade. The absence of Kito, and the watery eyes from his friends, hint towards a tragic outcome. Thyst fears the answer to his question when they rejoin where the gravel earth meets the grassy field.

"Where's Kito?" Amiku falls to her knees and sobs as Nydia hurries to embrace her. Sympathetic eyes watch from the field as joyous cheering and laughter is replaced with a respective silence.

"Ever since our paths crossed, I thought of Kito as a son," Lio begins. "I taught him and watched him grow, praised him, and scolded him. Today, I bury him." Thyst lightly puts his hand on Lio's shoulder, but what words could possibly be said at a time such as this? The world has always been unfair to the brave, unforgiving to the lost and forsaking the lonely.

All who are able help in the gathering of materials or craft the needed tools and gear to return to Esperanza. Amiku is the sole exception and sits in solitude with dried tears on her cheeks while staring at the next mountain ridge in the distance. Ardian and Nydia notice her state but are lost on how to console her.

"I couldn't help him," Nydia admits as her tears begins to show. "I tried to reach for him, but I didn't have the energy to lift him." Ardian brings her into his chest and hugs her.

"Kito chose to save Amiku. He knew what that meant. And he did it anyway. He's nothing less than a hero."

Amiku closes her eyes and remembers Kito in her mind. From the day they first met to their drive through Goldthorn and the moment when they almost kissed. Amiku opens her eyes again and pictures Kito's silhouette standing ahead with the bright sun at his back. In her trance-like state she recognizes the flapping coat still wrapped around his waist as he slowly advances toward her.

Her focus intensifies until it registers that her view is not a hallucination. Neither a dream nor imaginary, but real. She stands up and takes a slow step forward refusing to lift her eyes from the image in front of her.

"Kito," she whispers to herself. "Kito?" She takes another step and then pauses. The silhouette ahead of her continues to advance but struggles with a limp that prohibits a full sprint. "Kito," she says louder and louder. "Kito!" She takes off running with all her might as others hear her call and look where she's heading. "Kito! Kito!" His features come into view as they hurry toward each other. The sudden release of euphoria causes Amiku to throw her arms around him. She pulls away slightly and becomes lost in his eyes.

"Forgive me," Kito says. He brings his lips to hers and unleashes his hiding passion into a long, powerful kiss. She's only stunned for moment before closing her eyes and then surrendering herself to his lips. Neither pulls away from each other; they let the moment last for as long as they desire.

"I love you, Kito," Amiku finally admits. She feels his soaked hair and wet clothes. "You're drenched. What happened? How did you make it out?"

"You—you led me out," he replies.

The bottom of the cavern has become a deep pool from the many waterfalls pouring into it. Kito's plateau splashes into the water and continues down to wherever the bottom may be. Unresponsive and helpless Kito too sinks deeper as rocks continue to fall above him and descend around him.

Kito resigns himself to his fate. He lets his body be carried down and allows the water to pour into his lungs. There's no fear or struggle to live, but a peaceful calm that surrounds him. He keeps Amiku in his heart and remembers Sonya and Alma, the three women who saved him. Kito is not defined by his parents' abandonment or his adolescent rebellion, but by the experiences that shaped him into a hero. Not because he was free of vices, but because he knew them all too well. He survived in a world dictated by need and greed by giving himself to it.

The next splash that breaks the surface of the water resembles the form of a woman. She dives toward Kito and wraps an arm around his waist before swimming back up with him.

Kito regains consciousness while lying on a stony incline beside the water's edge. He rolls onto his side while coughing and spitting out water. The mystery of how he got here is unknown to him as he can't recall coming out of the water. He looks ahead and notices the narrow slope leads to a faint light at the top. He rests for a moment before putting his hands on the cave wall to help him up. He slowly climbs up the rocky passage but twists his ankle on a wet stone and falls. He hollers out and tries to find his footing again. The stinging sensation by applying pressure to his injured foot and the lack of anything to grab onto make his recovery troublesome.

"Come on Kito, just a little bit farther." Kito looks up to see Amiku standing in the middle of the light shining in from the cave's exit.

He loses sight of her after he blinks, "Amiku," he says. *Where did she go*, he wonders. He forces himself back up and proceeds the rest of the way towards the intensifying light.

He steps out of the cave into a tranquil stream that flows from a lake that's nestled in between the mountains. Kito wades across the nearly knee-deep stream until he reaches the meadow on the other side. He looks up into the sky and closes his eyes to bask in the warmth of the sun. A dainty hand gently falls on his shoulder. He turns around to see Sonya smiling at him.

"Sonya? Did I die?" She laughs and shakes her head.

"No, but you were willing to in order to save another."

"You said I would die. How did I survive?"

"That would be me, love," Alma says as she walks into view and stands next to Sonya.

"Alma. How can this be?" He says unable to believe his eyes.

"I promised to save you. Don't you remember?"

"All of your choices brought you to this moment, Kito. One can save a life if tasked to do so, but when love is involved everything changes," Sonya answers. She unties Amiku's coat sleeves around his waist and then places her hand on his stomach wound. Thick, black, coagulated blood seep out of his laceration and then plops to the ground.

"You are cured of your ailment," Sonya says.

"You took the demon blood from me? That means I lose my ability too."

"Honey, that demon gave you nothing. Slowing movements down came from me," she says smirking. Alma reties the coat sleeves around his wound and then kisses his forehead.

"Go to her. She's waiting," she whispers.

"I will miss our talks," Kito repeats. Alma giggles.

"We will see each other again. Of that, I'm sure." Alma returns to Sonya's side as they both smile.

"Tell Nydia that I'm very proud of her," Sonya says. She and Alma become encased in a light, but once it has faded neither are standing where they were. A quick glance around proves to Kito that he's by himself.

Amiku brings Kito to where Ardian and Nydia are waiting.

"Must you always procrastinate?" Ardian says with a grin.

"It is my way," Kito answers.

When the four return to camp they are welcomed with cheering and clapping. Lio, Thyst and Rona take turns embracing Kito before he visits Brax on his stretcher.

"You look worse than me," Brax laughs, but it hurts too much for him to continue. Kito smiles.

"I didn't know you lost your eyesight too." Brax chuckles and lifts his arm up onto his elbow. Kito takes it and they squeeze each other's hands.

The victorious army marches back to Esperanza with careful attention given to the wounded. Kito's wound has been cleaned and lightly cared for with a wrap, but he will need further care from Mika. He insisted on a crutch, thinking that would be ample, but Rona and Nydia overruled him and forced him on a stretcher. Amiku stays by his side the entire journey while offering endearing glances and smiles.

Hope survived, love endured, and in the end, tenacity won out. We are on the cusp of a new age.

Esperanza is aflutter with the return of their missing soldiers and citizens as they celebrate the news about Lazul's defeat. Mika and her staff keep their focus on the injured coming in as they rush to get them to the care they need. The fort becomes a whirlpool of emotions as people either gather joyfully or hurry through the crowd worried about the state of their loved ones.

Rona and Lio clear a path to allow the stretchers an unhindered way towards the infirmary. Brax and Kito are carried in and quickly taken by several nurses who begin to assess their wounds. Mika stays busy throughout the night to ensure all her patients are stable and showing signs of improvement. Her time for celebrating will come when all her beds are empty.

Days later Kito is awake, but still resting in the infirmary with

Amiku sitting beside him. He glances over to the neatly made bed where he remembered Alma was last time. His silent reveries don't go unnoticed by Amiku as she ponders a question that was never asked—until now.

"Did you love her?" She asks softly. Kito turns to face her while taking a moment to think about his response.

"I identified with her. In some way I saw her as a piece of myself. The piece no one else wanted to find."

"That's not true. I want the whole puzzle that makes up Kito." She runs her fingers through his hair as they exchange smiles.

"Are you sure? I can be—complicated." Amiku giggles.

"I think I know what I'm getting myself into."

Mika pulls back the curtain and advances to Kito's bedside with a clipboard in hand.

"I've seen many sword wounds in my life, but this one is an anomaly."

"Why is that?" Kito questions.

"Because this one should have killed you; yet miraculously it appeared your body healed itself before arriving in my care." Mika turns to Amiku. "You said you didn't give him any plasma rejuvenation, right?

"I was out," Amiku confirms with a shake of her head.

"It defies explanation then."

"It doesn't need explanation," Amiku smiles.

Kito and Brax are released three days later and receive warm welcomes by their comrades as they join the month-long festivities taking place in the main hall. Within a week Mika's beds are once again vacant and she's honored and toasted for saving so many lives in such a short time. Among the praised heroes are also Dixon and Alma who are talked about in high regard with glasses raised in their names.

"Dixon would never ask for a fanfare," begins one of his men. "He was sworn to duty and the care of all who stood beside him. He didn't ask his men to follow him or to love him, but we all did.

He believed in honor, virtue and remembering all who fell in battle. He was a man who saluted deceased strangers and always said the difference between a man and a demon was seeing a man in every demon, not the other way around. The angels will have a hard time convincing him to rest." The man raises his glass as others do the same. "To Dixon."

"To Dixon!" The congregation repeats. Kito is next to stand up. He was never one for public speaking and never wanted everyone's attention to be focused on him. He waits for the hall to fall silent before beginning his speech.

"Some of you have had the same allies for some time. Others may have joined along the way, some may have left, and some proved to be untrustworthy. For me—my allies began as a questionable acquaintanceship—at its best." Those who know Kito can't help but smile or utter a small laugh.

"Many saw Alma exactly how she wanted to be seen," he continues. "As an enemy, someone to fear, to avoid, to hate. But all she desired was acceptance and compassion. She found both here, but she still felt she had so much to make up for. I believe we would not have been victorious if it wasn't for Alma's help. From Kaz to Anyo to retrieving the Star of Eluvium. She had nothing else to prove—she was already one of us. I don't remember Alma as a villain. I remember how ferociously she fought—how courageously she sought hope—and how bravely she loved."

Kito looks down at Amiku. She smiles and raises her glass while giving him a private stare and whispering, "To Alma." Kito returns the smile and raises his glass.

"To Alma!"

"To Alma!" everyone repeats.

Everyone has someone to remember as they stand up to mention their names. When finished, another stands up after the room rejoices with clinging glasses or pounding on the table. This isn't a time for grieving but celebrating. This is not a sorrowful event, but a proud one. This lavish party is to honor the lives of the fallen, not mourn how they perished.

The people of Esperanza, and the rest of humanity, return to a time of peace with a mindset on rebuilding. The celebrations have ended, and many have left to begin their lives anew.

Ardian's room contains a twin bed, a nightstand, with a lantern, and a writing desk in front of his window. He's sitting at the desk with the cap of his pen to his chin as he gazes outside. He then looks down at the last few blank pages of his leather-bound journal. With his thoughts gathered, he puts the pen to the paper and begins writing.

It has been five weeks since Lazul was dragged into Hell. He was the essence of unrefined and pure hatred, the definition of evil, I do not know of any fate more fitting than his. After all, there's no deal that can be made with the devil that will ever end with him being bested.

Thyst talks about expanding Esperanza and building a town in the surrounding field. He has ample land to do so and the deconstruction of abandoned buildings for material has already started. These forsaken cities that were once home to so many are now taboo; haunted by spirits no one wants to live with. People would rather start over in new towns than go back to a place they have finally moved away from. I do not blame them as I feel the same way. We are desperate to start living new lives, building our own homes, starting families and for once feel a sense of security. We all suffer from a form of cabin fever caused by this eight-year winter. We return to simplicity; farming, hunting, gathering and trade, but it's far better than scavenging, evading goblins and avoiding outside after dark.

I still remember the first time I met Kito and Amiku. Who would have thought one day we would be standing side by side at the end of one age and the beginning of another? However, I do have one concern. What will happen to us now? Will we stay together, or will we go our separate ways? I hope Nydia at least stays. All this time with her and sometimes I'm still lost for words when I look into her big brown eyes.

Nydia enters Ardian's room and strolls toward him without him knowing.

"What are you writing, Ardie?" She asks while trying to look over his shoulder. He gently closes the journal before answering.

"I'm telling our story and documenting all our experiences. This will be our history and it should be remembered."

"So, it's a diary."

"It's not a diary. It's a journal."

"Can I read it?"

"Well, it's not finished yet."

"Just let me read the first page."

"It's not ready."

"Let me hear your first sentence then." Ardian hesitates, but eventually feels sharing one sentence should be harmless. He opens the cover to the first page, but before he can begin reading Nydia snatches the journal and runs away giggling.

"Hey!" Ardian yells while chasing her out of the room and around the corner. He's immediately grabbed and pushed against the wall with a gentle shove. Nydia is tired of waiting for the perfect moment and decides to make one herself. She presses her lips against his and the two finally engage in a long overdue kiss. Neither wants the moment to end as they remain kissing until Nydia stops to look at him.

"I love you."

"I love you too." Ardian takes the journal from her and smiles. "But you're still not reading my book." Nydia giggles.

Sonya's message has yet to be delivered and at the ending of another day comes an opportunity for Kito to make good on his promise. He peeks into Nydia's room through her open doorway and finds her looking at the sunset. She glances back and smiles when he walks in.

"Hello, Kito."

He advances to her side without a word. Nydia senses he has something to say and looks at him until he begins.

"I saw Sonya."

"You saw her?"

"Yes, she appeared to me in the valley."

"I wish I could have seen her one last time."

"She's been watching you. She's proud of you." Nydia smiles.

"Did she say that?"

"She did. She had an ability too."

"I didn't know that. What was it?"

"Slowing down movements." Nydia thinks for a moment before responding.

"You mean what you can do?" Kito slowly shakes his head.

"That only started after her blood entered my body." Nydia smiles and turns back towards the sunset.

"Somehow, I've always known that. I don't know how, but I knew you and her had a deeper connection than just a coincidental meeting." She gives him an emotional look and a grin. "Thank you, Kito. Thank you for telling me."

Another month has now passed, and several towns have already been established. Today we will be leaving Esperanza to venture on a journey of our own and hopefully meet a few old friends along the way. One final mission still awaits us, but what happens afterwards, I cannot say, Ardian writes.

The beginning of a new road replaces the field in front of Esperanza and leading to its main gates. Stone slabs will eventually be laid down, but for now it's just gravel. Ardian, Kito, Nydia and Amiku meet Thyst, Aifina, Nichi and Lako beside two ATVs stocked with food and supplies.

"May you succeed in everything you attempt," Thyst says with a firm handshake.

"Thank you. I'm sure we will hear much about Esperanza in the near future," Ardian replies. Aifina hugs Nydia and then Amiku.

"You are all welcomed back here anytime."

"Yes, we will always have a room ready for you," Nichi adds.

"When we do, we expect to see a magnificent city," Nydia says.

Several buildings are in their early wooden frame stages and markings for future roads are being staked. Everyone is busy building or wheeling carts of wood and stones back and forth. Another group studies an illustration of the projected layout of the town while pointing in the distance.

"Our plans look promising," Thyst says proudly.

An expanding city needs to have order if it is to thrive. Just as the fort of Esperanza has departments and those who oversee that sector, so will Esperanza as a full-scale city. Which is why Thyst promoted Lako to head of the building unit. This means he's responsible for assigning tasks and setting building priorities, as well as, having a good idea when each project should be completed.

Ardian and Nydia hop on their ATV and Amiku takes the driver's seat of the other as Kito says his farewells.

"It's not often that I say this, but I might actually miss some of you," Kito says while smiling.

"Come here you rebel." Thyst laughs and pulls Kito in for a hug. Aifina is next to hug him followed by the handshakes from

Nichi and Lako.

"Keep him out of trouble, Amiku," Thyst says with a smirk.

"Oh, I intend to," she replies.

"Be careful out there. I heard reports of a few straggling demons still roaming around," Nichi warns.

"We will. Thank you again for everything," Nydia replies.

Aiza, Mika and the citizens and soldiers stop working to cheer and wave to them as they drive through their city in progress. After leaving the gravel turf, the two ATVs accelerate across the meadow toward their next destination.

A small town is nestled in a cozy clearing near the edge of a small forest. The homes here are constructed of stone bases with wood siding above and a small generator on the side of each home suggests they also have electricity. The name of the town is chiseled into a wooden sign staked at the town's entrance, Anthulios. It is here that Lio meets everyone with open arms and a huge grin.

"Welcome, friends." Kito looks at him and then at the sign. Lio makes the connection and laughs. "Ah, yes, you see, Shara founded this town and decided to name it after me. It's quite an honor really."

The steady sound of horseshoes on cobblestone redirects everyone's view towards a single steed pulling a cart. Brax halts the horse and then jumps off the cart seat as Nydia pets the horse's head excitedly.

"Awww, where did you find the little horsey? You are so cute, yes you are," she exclaims.

"They're herds of them running around in the wild. I lured this one out with an apple."

"What are you going to use him for?" Ardian asks curiously."

"I'm going to be a traveling merchant and tradesman. I figured there will be a high demand now for materials and supplies and not everyone will have access to them. So, I decided to travel from town to town to make that possible."

"That's actually not a bad idea," Lio replies a little impressed. "Did Rona arrive yet?" Brax asks eager to see her again.

"Yes, she's inside with Shara, but I have something to show you all first," Lio answers. Anthulios leads everyone into town and then towards a blacksmith shop with the sign, *Lio's Metal Works*, above the doorway. "I bet none of you knew this, but I'm quite the metallurgist. Opening my own shop was always a dream of mine." He advances toward a table that has two weapons concealed under a cloth and a katana. He picks up the katana first and hands it to Amiku. "Your katana, ma'am, sharpened, polished and with a new wrapping on the hilt." Amiku takes the sword while smiling. If she didn't know any better, she might assume it was a brand new sword.

"Wow, thank you, Lio."

Anthulios turns back to the table and gently removes the cloth from the first weapon to reveal a double-bladed axe.

"For Brax I have a double-bladed war axe with a unique twist." Anthulios holds the axe near the blade and then opens an ornate fastening. He pulls the two blades apart and holds a single bladed axe in each hand. "Now you have a choice to use one powerful axe or dual wield two smaller ones; also good for chopping wood." Anthulios says while chopping the air in front of him. He attaches both blades again and then hands it to Brax.

"This will come in handy. Thank you, Lio," Brax says in awe while admiring the spectacular craftsmanship. Anthulios reveals the last weapon and holds up a glistening sword. The top of the blade is serrated with four holes drilled out just under the guard, while the blade itself widens out before coming to a thin point. He takes a few steps away from the group to swing the sword through the air. The sword makes whistling sounds as it slices through the air. After the short demonstration Lio hands the blade to Kito.

"This is for you. The sound you hear is the wind being forced through the holes of the blade; it also results in a lighter weapon."

"Are you kidding me, right now?" He says in disbelief as he inspects the magnificent weapon in its entirety. "Thank you, Lio."

"This sword is designed specifically to tear flesh from bone. If your target is still moving after a few quick slices or jabs with this then the only explanation is you must have missed," Lio further explains.

"Is it strange that I want to kill something right now?" Kito asks.

"For you, no." Ardian's swift response triggers the others to chuckle.

Lio's house is quaint and cozy with just enough room for him and Shara to live comfortably. Behind his house is a plot of land where he has a modest garden of vegetables, a firepit, that provides warmth and a place to cook, and a lantern beside the back door that's powered by the generator when needed. With the forest nearly on his doorstep his yard is perfectly shaded by the canopy all day. Everyone gathers around the picnic table already set with a pork dinner and fresh vegetables from his garden.

"What are your plans, Rona?" Amiku asks.

"I've always wanted to live in the Australian outback; some place that's private and won't get crowded. Maybe I can teach people self-defense or something."

"You're gonna be one of those people who everyone needs to find to reach spiritual enlightenment and personal growth, aren't you?" Kito jokes.

"Yeah, maybe," she laughs.

"I guess this will be the last time we are all together," Nydia says somberly.

"Who knows what the future will hold. Fate may find a way for our paths to cross once again," Lio says optimistically.

After dinner, Lio helps Brax load some food and supplies in the back of his cart before he sets out.

"Good luck, buddy, and if you come across any metal I will most differently be interested."

"I will keep that in mind. I can even carry some of your crafted goods on consignment."

"Sounds good to me."

Brax leans his axe against the back of his seat to make the handle easy to grab and then prepares to say his final goodbyes. He hugs Lio first as they exchange pats on the back and then moves on to everyone else until lastly, coming to Rona. He looks at her with a grin and his arms wide open; finally, after a sigh, she allows him the hug.

Brax steps up onto the cart and takes the reins in his hands. With one final wave he snaps them and rolls away while singing a self-praising song.

> "Brax is a man—
> who carries an axe.
> He fights to the max—
> and trades a lot of sacks."

Lio can't help but shake his head and laugh.

Rona is next to hug everyone as she says her farewells.

"How are you going to get to Australia?" Nydia asks.

"I'll figure it out," Rona says with a smile.

"Thank you for sticking by my side all these years," Lio says.

"I've never trusted anyone more. You are a rarity in these times, and I will gladly stand with you again," she responds with a smile. She gets on Thyst's chopper before shooting a glance at Amiku while pointing at Kito. "Keep an eye on him," she says.

"Why does everyone always say that?" Kito replies softly. His response manages to get a laugh out of everyone. Rona revs the chopper and then lastly looks at Shara.

"Watch over Lio for me. He's in good hands with you." Shara smiles and nods.

"I will, dear." Rona revs her cycle and then speeds off toward the horizon.

Shara turns her attention to the last remaining group.

"How about the rest of you? Do you have any plans?"

"We have one more journey still ahead of us," Ardian answers.

"A promise we made to someone," Kito adds.

"Ah, yes, I remember. I may have something that can help you with that," Lio says.

A short walk through the trees leads to a white sandy beach and the surf of the Atlantic Ocean. Lio leads his friends down a wooden plank pier to a roped-up sloop-style sailboat. The name on the stern reads, *Shara*.

"I found her washed up here one day and decided to repair her. I'm confident she's seaworthy—in calm weather at least."

"So, you have a town and a boat," Kito says with envy.

"Come on. You know me. What's mine is yours," Lio chuckles. "I was planning on using her for fishing, but she should get your task done."

"Thank you, Lio. This is most generous," Nydia admits.

The waves gently rock the sloop to and fro as it rests with its sails down. Across the sea are the hazy peaks and outlines of the Azores islands on a calm morning. Nydia checks the coordinates on her map and then looks at the nearby compass. After two long weeks they have finally reached their destination.

"This is the general area where people believed Atlantis used to be."

Kito picks up The Architect's Box with a metal chain coiled around it and a large padlock to ensure it stays sealed. He carries it to the starboard side and holds it over the side.

"I return you now to the place of your origin." He lets the box splash into the ocean as the team watches it sink beneath the waves and out of sight for good. "I think I understand now what Alma was talking about. This energy solves flaws the world needs to keep," Kito concludes.

"Well, at over seven-thousand feet, I think it's safe to say it's not being recovered anytime soon," Amiku points out.

The sun setting in the horizon marks the end of the first day of their two-week voyage back to the mainland. Kito and Ardian stand at the bow gazing at the colors reflecting off the waves as Amiku and Nydia sail into it.

"I almost forgot how beautiful the world really is," Ardian observes.

"Somehow I never noticed it before either," Kito begins. "It's almost like we discovered a new planet. I look back now and can't imagine how the hell we survived everything we've been through."

"Not to mention how we avoided killing each other," Ardian adds. Kito smirks and takes out a bottle of rum he had hidden in his coat pocket. "Where did you get that?" Ardian asks with surprise.

"Let's just say I know a guy in the trading business."

"Son of a—" Ardian begins.

"Well, we're in the middle of the ocean with rum and women. Let's get drunk and see what happens," Kito jokes. Ardian looks behind Kito and then back at sea without saying a word. Kito gets an unsettling feeling and regrettably asks, "Amiku is behind me, isn't she?"

"They both are."

Amiku and Nydia stand looking at Kito while frowning with their arms folded across their chests. Kito turns his head around to glance at them.

"Just what were you hoping might happen, Kito?" Amiku asks sternly.

"Beautiful and meaningful conversation is all that I was implying."

"Somehow, I doubt that," Amiku replies.

The boat drifts into the clear night littered with stars and a full moon. The consumption of the rum has taken its toll on the sailors, but it's Kito and Ardian who are most affected by it.

Kito stares up at the surreal sky while lying on the deck near the stern. The gentle rocking and the ocean breeze let him fall into a restful sleep until Amiku finds him.

"It's warmer below deck." Kito opens his eyes and gives her a smile.

"Maybe, but I've never experienced the ocean before. Something about it is enthralling." Amiku lays down beside him and curls up into his arms.

"I suppose we can stay out for a little while."

Meanwhile, at the bow, Ardian raises his sword in front of him as he pretends to be in the golden age of pirates.

"A calm sea and a gentle breeze. Onward to eternity where my destiny awaits me. I am Ardian, the most infamous pirate of this new world. Take whatever isn't nailed down, maties and then come back with a crowbar. "Nydia is standing behind him in bewilderment.

"Ardie? You haven't been drinking the sea water, have you?" Ardian looks at her and then smiles.

"Would you like to be my first mate?" Nydia smiles and puts her arm around him as she lays her head on his shoulder.

"Oh, my fearless captain. What be our heading on this fine night?"

"Wherever your heart desires, my lady. That is where I shall sail."

The warm, sunny days of summer turn into the overcast and cool weeks of late autumn. The townsfolk are getting ready for winter and the local traveling merchants, like Brax, are happy to supply warmer clothing, quilts and stockpiles of smoked food and wooden logs.

Nydia has accepted the role of educator and mentor to those who develop abilities such as hers. She instructs young men and women to control and hone their skills in an outside arena dedicated for their practice. Groups of teens take turns tossing their energy balls at stationary targets. Once they have finished Nydia demonstrates her magic abilities before turning back to her pupils. Her goal is to ensure no one feels ostracized like Alma did or confused like she was. There's been a recent surge of people who are born with these unique abilities and Nydia aims to eliminate fear and hostility toward it. Science calls it, survival evolution. Living in an environment inhabited by demons triggers a part of our mind, that was once dormant, to develop.

One of the great significances centered around this idea is the founding of the Science and Library Society; popularly known as, SLS. Unlike O.D.E. this organization is a bit more prestigious. The society researches, discusses, and educates about advances and studies in everything natural, biological, medical, and experimental. It is a place for everyone to discover and catalog knowledge about everything that was, is and will be.

Several goblins are seen running across the countryside and into the cover of the nearby forests. With demons still roaming around, and people still needing protection from these creatures, a new group is also formed to combat the demonoids and imps plaguing trade routes, townsfolk or halting work and projects.

On the outskirts of a small town is a bluff overlooking the coastline below. Amiku advances behind Kito as he gazes philosophically at the grand landscape.

"We have reports of goblin activity nearby," she says while standing with her arms folded. "Come on. We have work to do." Kito turns around and spreads a smile that hints a feeling of pure enjoyment.

"Finally, a job that I was born for." He picks up his coat, which was draped over a rock, and then puts it on while walking alongside Amiku. Within moments, Ardian and Nydia meet up with them and the four walk together toward a finished stone slab road.

"What do we know?" Kito asks.

"A group of six goblins are stealing food from the town's smokehouse for several night's now," Nydia confirms.

"The town is about five miles from here," Ardian adds.

"I'm driving this time," Kito demands.

"I don't think so," Amiku says.

Ahead of them is the repaired and modified GTO. *Demon Hunters* appears below an image of a goblin with a sword through its torso in the middle of both doors. *Demon Inspection and Eradication,* and its acronym, *DIE,* appears on the fenders. Amiku sprints toward the driver's seat with Kito following close behind. She gets to the door first and smiles while glancing back at him.

"I'm still faster than you," She teases. Nydia and Ardian crawl in the backseat as Kito waits beside the passenger door.

"That's because you pushed me," he attempts to defend why he lost.

"I did not push you," Amiku laughs. Once everyone is inside Amiku puts the car into gear. The GTO lets out a deep roaring growl as it speeds off road and across the grassy countryside.

Back at Esperanza, Thyst and Aifina sit at a table, in the main hall, as a trader displays his rugs and linens that are for sale. Esperanza succeeds in becoming a well-developed city consisting of a central market, clinic, courthouse, residential homes, and the fort is positioned at the rear to act as a base of operations and meeting area. It becomes a central hub for traders, artisans, and commerce.

"A team of four call themselves, The Demon Hunters. People say they have superhuman powers and fight with weapons given to them by the Gods and—that they drive a GTO," The trader says spreading the gossip he's heard.

Thyst laughs hysterically while slapping his hand on the table. Aifina also smiles knowing full well the party that's attached to this rumor.

"It seems they are doing what they do best," Thyst tells his wife.

Elsewhere, two men are standing outside a wooden barricade, surrounding a small town, while peering into the distance.

"Are they supposed to be any good?" the first man asks.

"They come highly recommended," the other replies.

"How will we know it's them when they get here?"

Before an answer becomes necessary, a powerful engine of a muscle car is slightly heard. The silhouette of the GTO appears over a hill as it swiftly advances towards the two men. Amiku drifts the car to make deep tread marks in the soft grass before stopping in front of the barricade. The two men exchange stunned looks as the doors open. The four get out and stand facing the men who hired them.

Kito swings his sword up to make the whistling sound before he rests it gently on his right shoulder. Amiku folds her arms across her chest and leans against Kito's left arm and part of his chest. Ardian steps up and stands beside Amiku and then cocks his machine gun with an upward jerking motion of his arm. Nydia stops at his side and forms an energy ball and holds it slightly suspended in the palm of her hand—she has finally mastered her abilities completely.

"Does someone have a problem?" Ardian asks.

A lone goblin gurgles nearby while watching them. Nydia flicks her wrist and releases her energy blast to send the charred remains of the creature several yards away.

This is no longer the age of Apocalypsia.

Welcome to the age of demon hunters.

"The world is small. Books make it bigger."

SPOILERS BEYOND THIS POINT

The following appendices contain a collection of information, descriptions, key points and expanded explanations from the entire story that will reveal character arcs.

READ LAST!

Appendix A
The Characters

Ardian: *(First introduced in Chapter 1)*
He's a patient and cautious individual who tries to protect those close to him.
His first weapons are a mace and short sword.
He wears a pair of torn jeans and a button-down shirt.
His zodiac sign is Capricorn.

- **In Chapter 3:**
  Ardian gets new clothes which consist of brown cargo pants and a deep forest green vest with a black shirt under it.

- **In Chapter 8:**
  Ardian receives a M4 assault rifle.

Nydia: *(First introduced in Chapter 1)*
A kind, sweet girl who desires to learn how to fight to protect herself as well as others.

Earned a degree in emergency medical technician (EMT) a year before The Demon Wars.

Nydia has the ability to sense when danger is near and can dream about events yet to unfold. She also develops telekinesis and an ever-evolving magical power.

While she rotates through several weapons, her main form of attack eventually becomes her energy blasts.

She and Ardian knew each other before the war when they worked at the airport together as ramp agents.

Her zodiac sign is Taurus.

- **In Chapter 2:**
  Nydia's first weapon is made from the blades of hunting knifes which are attached to both ends of her broken walking stick, giving her two double bladed sticks as weapons.

- **In Chapter 3:**
  Nydia gets new clothes which consist of black pants and a gray long-sleeved shirt with a dark blue mesh shawl.

- **In Chapter 4:**
  Nydia finds a compound bow and arrows in an old military camp. This bow becomes her main weapon of choice.

- **In Chapter 4:**
  Nydia, through her grief, tapped into a hidden telekinetic ability. With practice, she's able to move or stop objects and people or knockback foes with her hand motions.

- **In Chapter 6:**
  While fighting Alma, Nydia shoots an arrow that becomes a yellow energy bolt as soon as it leaves the bow. It is the beginning of a new power Nydia will soon possess.

- **In Chapter 8:**
  Nydia receives a M4 assault rifle.

- **In Chapter 8:**
  Nydia is now able to shoot energy bolts out of her bare hands without the assistance of her arrows.

- **In Chapter 14:**
  Nydia becomes encased in a red aura that causes her hair to extend outwards from her scalp. This is the visual appearance of her power at its maximum.

- **In Chapter 15:**
  Nydia can now suspend her energy ball above her palm, indicating that she has mastered her abilities completely.

Kito: *(First introduced in Chapter 1)*

He's impatient, impulsive, stubborn, and easily angered. He considers himself an outcast and feels that's how he should be treated. His attitude derives from a poor upbringing and guilt from a previous incident.

He fights with a large wide-bladed sword and has an ability that allows him see movements slowed down in battle, which speeds up his reaction times; however, this ability works better if he remains defensive; if he tries to return any attacks, he loses his concentration.

He wears a black trench coat with a red trim.

His zodiac sign is Pisces.

- **In Chapter 2:**
  Kito takes the demonoid's gatekeeper sword after his is broken in battle. It has a long blade and metal tentacles curving out and downward from the guard that attach to both sides of the blade.

- **In Chapter 8:**
  Kito receives an AK47 assault rifle.

- **In Chapter 10:**
  Kito's demon form takes over and resembles a vampire-like creature. His fingernails become longer and into sharp points. His eyes turn red and his skin becomes pale with blackness forming around the eyes, fangs sprout from his upper gums and his hair extends up into rigid spikes. His only vocals are deep, low-pitched growls made from the very depths of his throat.

- **In Chapter 15:**
  Sonya cures him of the demon blood that entered his bloodstream, she also reveals that his ability to slow down movements came from her.

- **In Chapter 15:**
  Lio makes a new sword for Kito. The top of the blade is serrated with four holes drilled out just under the guard, while the blade itself widens out before coming to a thin point. Swinging the sword will create whistling sounds as the air is forced through the holes.

Amiku: *(First introduced in Chapter 1)*

She's a strong-willed woman with a tough; take no crap attitude, yet she remains feminine.

She fights with a katana and advanced hand to hand combat. Her fighting style is very acrobatic from her experience in gymnastics. She is also skilled in parkour* and potion making.

She wears a medium purple trench coat with a gold trim.

Her zodiac sign is Scorpio.

- **In Chapter 8:**

  Amiku receives an AK47 assault rifle. She also has a pistol.

Parkour is the physical discipline of training to overcome any obstacle within one's path by adapting one's movements to the environment; as if moving from an emergency situation and using skills such as running, jumping, climbing, and vaulting. The object of parkour is to get from one place to another using only the human body and the objects in the environment.

Anyo: *(First introduced in Chapter 3)*

He was once an O.D.E. scientist and knew Amiku's father. He worked in the Weapons and Warfare division, then in Shelters, and lastly, in Chemicals and Chemistry.

He betrays Amiku and admits he was responsible in her father's death.

Amiku kills him, but that isn't the end of him—

- **In Chapter 5:**

  Anyo is discovered to still be alive and working with Lazul. He took the O.D.E. demon serum which gave him a rejuvenation ability. He can transform from human to demon at will but prefers to stay as a demon. In his demon form Anyo has two large wings giving him the ability to fly.

- **In Chapter 13:**

  Anyo is killed by Alma.

Charles: *(First mentioned in Chapter 3)*

Amiku's father.

Started working at O.D.E in Technology and Programming, and then moved to Chemicals and Chemistry.

Murdered by O.D.E.

Ania: *(First mentioned in Chapter 4)*

Amiku's mother.

Died in a car accident when she was 12.

Amiku's AI Eye is named in remembrance of her along with her vocals.

Lazul: *(First introduced in Chapter 4)*

A tall, skinny man who talks in a deep, raspy tone.

He only cares about riling up others in his favor or increasing his status and power over them. He is the quintessential vile mastermind who knows how to use the emotions of others against them or to his benefit. He's a plotter, a conspirator, and a saboteur who's hell-bent on usurping Lio's fort. He's not trusted by many but is popular enough not to be banished.

Eventually it's clear that his plans are to turn people into demons and then control them. He's the leader of the demon army and has made his own version of a demon serum from O.D.E.'s notes.

- **In Chapter 5:**
  Lazul reveals that he has hidden tentacles that sprout from his back and can be used as weapons. He's also a master of dark magic with the ability to move objects with his hand or summon demons and even storms.

- **In Chapter 12:**
  Lazul casts his spell, Divide and Conquer. The spell creates an aura around each individual and then displaces them. However, if one person is holding onto another the spell will read the connection as one person. The teleportation can be a few feet from the original location or miles away; however, he lacks the strength and power to affect heavy objects, such as vehicles. Anyone inside or attached to those would remain unaffected.

- **In Chapter 14:**
  Lazul's eyes turn red and new horns sprout from the top of his head with smaller spikes around his chin. His torso bulks up and barbs extend out from his shoulders and arms. His feet

become clawed and animal like as all signs that Lazul was once human finally vanishes.

- **In Chapter 14:**
Lazul summons the Dragon King's sword. The Latin phrase he utters is, *Excito scelus evictis animos patibilis intemporaliter*, which translates as, I summon all wickedness to conquer every soul and to endure for an eternity. The Dragon King's Sword was crafted by a powerful summoner in the mid-1100s. The entire piece was said to be created solely from the fire of a dragon and he honored the beast in his pommel. Inscribed in the blade is an ancient incantation, which simply translates as—*No one can escape it once it has been drawn, no one can resist it*—a spell that ensures victory to all who wields it.

- **In Chapter 14:**
His Phantom's Breath screech is a deafening roar that paralyzes and lasts for about twenty seconds.

- **In Chapter 14:**
After being weakened in battle, he's dragged into Hell alive.

Anthulios *(Lio for short, pronounced like Leo)*:
(First introduced in Chapter 4)

He's the commander of his fort and is mentally and physically strong. The people hold him in high regard and consider him to be a fair and just leader. Anthulios will offer aid and support to where and who needs it, but he demands respect and his rules obeyed in exchange. Order and laws must be upheld, and deviants must be prosecuted accordantly, yet he's not without compassion.

His weapon is a long sword.

He met Kito during The Demon Wars and taught him how to fight.

- **In Chapter 8:**
Lio receives a M4 assault rifle.

- **In Chapter 12:**
His origin is reviled. He's from Lamia, the capital city of Central Greece and studied mythology, philosophy, and poetry. He moved to Boston for a girl, but when it didn't work out, he tutored philosophy at Harvard and crafted and sold ice skates.

> *In Greek, Lamia means large shark, but that's not
> where the name of the city comes from. According to Greek
> mythology Lamia was a beautiful woman with a strange
> hunger for children and sexually predatory towards men.
> She is considered, by many, to be the first Succubus. In
> Christian religion she is known as Lilith. In both references
> they are depicted as either wearing snakeskin or holding
> a snake, and sometimes even part serpent herself. In the
> poem, Beowulf, Grendel's mother was said to be Lamia and
> forced him to conceive a child with her.*
> —Anthulios, on the topic of his home.

- **In Chapter 13:**

  His sword has a Greek engraving:

  Το χέρι του Θεού

  To chéri tou Theoú, which means, **The Hand of God.**

- **In Chapter 15:**

  Anthulios opens a metal shop called, *Lio's Metal Works*, where he crafts weapons and other metal objects. He lives in a town named after him because Shara founded it. He returns the favor by naming a boat he had repaired after her.

Sonya: *(First introduced in Chapter 4)*

She has red hair and is Nydia's older sister.

She helped Kito fight a demonized man; however, she was fatally wounded in the process and left Kito guilt stricken.

She appears to Kito on occasion as a messenger.

Rona: *(First introduced in Chapter 5)*

She's one of Anthulios' captains with a short fuse and boasts an Eastern European accent.

She values physical fitness and hard work. Laziness and slacking off among her ranks are simply not allowed and are dealt with harshly. She's in charge of assigning duties to the fort guards, organizing training exercises and checking the fort's defenses.

She fights with two batons that can extend and even be combined into one long stick, then unhooked and stored on either side of her waist.

She has medical knowledge and knows CPR.

- **In Chapter 8:**
  Rona receives an AK47 assault rifle.

- **In Chapter 15:**
  Decides to teach self-defense in the Australian outback after Lazul's defeat.

Brax: *(First introduced in Chapter 5)*

Another of Anthulios' captains who keeps track of all food and supplies stores and their distribution to everyone daily or if requested.

He's a heavy-set man, but his excess weight doesn't slow him down or shorten his stamina. He's strong, muscular and can outlast men half his size on the battlefield. He's also known to be easy going and laid back, but if provoked can hold his own in a fight and wields a battle axe with ferocity.

He's completely smitten by Rona and makes his feelings towards her very obvious, even though he may not always notice it.

- **In Chapter 8:**
  Brax receives a M4 assault rifle.

- **In Chapter 15:**
  Lio makes a double-bladed war axe for Brax. Opening an ornate fastening creates the ability to separate the two blades that gives him the choice of wielding one large axe or two single-bladed axes.

- **In Chapter 15:**
  After Lazul's defeat, Brax becomes a traveling merchant and trader.

Brax's Song

Brax is a man—
who carries an axe.
He fights to the max—
and trades a lot of sacks.

Reginald: *(First introduced in Chapter 5)*

A citizen in Lio's fort that Lazul *trained*. He was actually injected with Lazul's version of O.D.E.'s demon serum that turned him into a demonoid. His demon form consists of fangs, horns on his head and above his eyes, a reddish complexion, and black eyes. His fingernails also become claws and his feet morph into hooves.

Alma: *(First introduced in Chapter 6)*
Japanese heritage.

She has long platinum-blond dyed hair and dressed in a black Chinese cheongsam with a red floral pattern that runs diagonally from the top left of her shoulder to the bottom right end of the dress.

She likes to laugh and talk often while also being highly sexualized towards both men and women.

She has an ability similar to that of Nydia's only hers has been mastered. She's able to move objects, create wind, and shoot energy blasts with her hands.

She has a fast demon regeneration ability; however, when around iron she cannot use any of her abilities.

At sixteen, while practicing late in a dojo, she was sexually assaulted. After using her magic on the three boys who defiled her, she was branded a witch. She's been exiled ever since.

• **In Chapter 7:**
Alma tells Kito she was born in Kyoto, Japan and have been fighting since she was five. She's very well advanced in karate and judo and, since from Japan, she has a habit of bowing during some conversations as well as speaking Japanese*.

• **In Chapter 9:**
Alma's demon form takes over, she turns into a half human, half lioness, known as a huntress. Her eyes turn yellow and long brownish-orange fur grows around her body. Her body structure also becomes larger. Her white hair grows down to her ankles and her fingernails grow into claws followed by the formation of two fangs and a tail. Some areas of her human skin are still visible on her legs, arms, torso, and face; however, the rest of her is covered with fur.

• **In Chapter 10:**
Alma's attire now consists of a blue long-sleeved, button-down blouse with a wide black buckle belt and a simple, yet stylish hijab around her head.

- **In Chapter 11:**
  Alma cuts her hair shorter and returns it back to her natural black color.

- **In Chapter 13:**
  Plays the harp. *The Sirens Song* is a hypnotic melody that robs people of their self-awareness. It eliminates pain, worry, fear and sorrow, but also strips away their free will. The person succumbs to the will of the harpist.

- **In Chapter 13:**
  Her energy blasts turn red** when angered, otherwise they remain yellow.

- **In Chapter 14:**
  She can release yellow glowing energy slowly to surround her sword. The energy infused blade heats up so it not only cuts, but also sears, making her attacks much more deadly.

- **In Chapter 14:**
  Alma is fatally wounded by Lazul's *Dragon King's Sword*, which was coated with iron dust to prevent her from healing.

  *Alma's translation of her spoken Japanese words:
  Sayonara- Goodbye.
  (Domo) Arigato - Thank you (very much).
  Baka- Fool, Idiot.

  **Both Nydia's and Alma's energy blasts can be yellow or red. Yellow blasts are normal and are about 1400°F. Red blasts are formed emotionally through anger or fear and heats up to about 2200°F.

Nichi: *(First introduced in Chapter 7)*
  Captain of Esperanza's army.
  Reports to Thyst when necessary.
  Responsible for strategies and orders on the battlefield.
  Has a daughter.

Thyst: *(First introduced in Chapter 7)*
  A bald muscular man.
  Leader of Esperanza.
  Married to Aifina.

At times, acts as General in his army.
Fight with either an AK47 or a M4 but favors the AK47.

- **In Chapter 9:**
  Thyst tells everyone that he used to drive trucks and fly helicopters during The Demon Wars. That's where he met Kaz.

Lako: *(First introduced in Chapter 7)*
First lieutenant and second in command of Esperanza's army
Reports to Nichi and carries out or enforces his orders.
Has a son.

- **In Chapter 15:**
  Lako is promoted from lieutenant of Esperanza's army to head of the building unit. His new role allows him to assign tasks to the workers and set building priorities. He also has a good idea of knowing when each project should be completed. This means he's now spearheading the expansion of Esperanza from just a fort, in a field, into an attractive city.

Aiza: *(First introduced in Chapter 7)*
Head council member and acts as judge for the council—she relays their decision to the people. She has final say for rewards and or punishments for all crimes or deeds carried out by the citizens, army members, or strangers in Esperanza's territory.
Usually doesn't fight and remains in or nearby the council chamber.

Mika: *(First introduced in Chapter 7)*
Head of the medical department with final say on all treatments and medical department issues.

Aifina: *(First introduced in Chapter 7)*
Equally ranked with Thyst and married to him.
Usually doesn't fight but commands the fort when Thyst is away.

Kaz: *(First introduced in Chapter 8)*
Short for Kazminski.
His first name is not known.
Used to be a sergeant in platoon 352 during The Demon

Wars, which is where the code comes from to get into his sewer hideout in Silver Rock City, which is also his home city.

He only fights with guns.

- **In Chapter 10:**
Kaz betrays Thyst. He is eventually killed by Alma.

Dixon: *(First introduced in Chapter 8)*
The leader of his army.

He meets Thyst and Lio on their way to Lazul after hearing Lio's call and agreed to fight alongside them.

Dixon is his last name; his first name is never known.

- **In Chapter 14:**
He is killed by a Sailfin Demonoid.

Shara: *(First introduced in Chapter 12)*
A citizen of Esperanza that Lio settles down with.

Appendix B
The O.D.E. Journal

Operation Demon Eradication (O.D.E):
Named after an old military code name.

An organization that was set up purely to invent new weapons, shelters, and techniques to protect people and fight against demons.

Monsters & Demons

Mutant Wolves: *(First seen Chapter 1)*
Starving wild wolves that roam freely scavenging for food. They have come in contact with demon DNA and have been mutated into larger, highly aggressive, and slightly deformed versions of their former selves.

Goblins: *(First seen in Chapter 1)*

Small demons that are sometimes in groups but pose little danger to well-seasoned fighters.

They attack with their claws and teeth but are also known to fight with daggers.

They have little intelligence and almost no cognitive abilities.

Raptors: *(First seen Chapter 2)*

Red and orange raptors.

One of the many experiments that went wrong for O.D.E. They were bred to hunt demons but could not be controlled and turned on people as well. They eventually escaped into the wild and reproduced.

They are very intelligent with an advanced cognitive process and live, hunt, and communicate in packs. They will hunt both people and demons without any preference for one or the other.

Demonized Raptors: *(First seen Chapter 8)*

Their skin is rotting away to reveal muscle tissue and bone. Their teeth are exposed due to the missing skin that make up their lips and snout, and their eyes can be white or yellow. The cause is likely due to the ingestion of demon flesh.

Demonoid: *(First seen Chapter 2)*

Someone who has become a demon.

Demonfication

The process in which a person turns into a demon.

Transformation occurs when demon DNA enters the bloodstream of an individual. The person then goes through two main stages of transformation.

Demonized

The first stage.

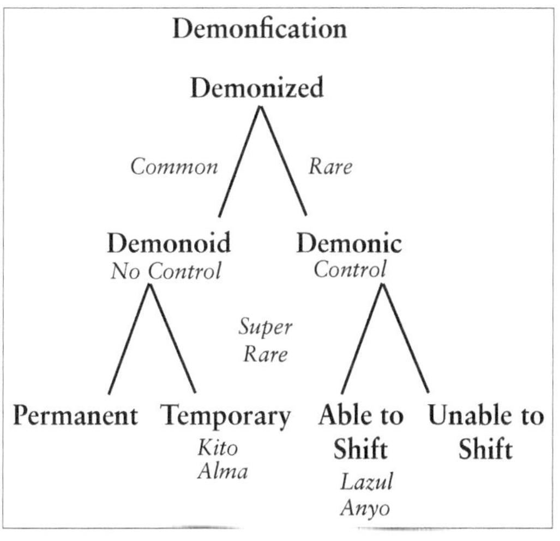

This will affect appearance, adoption of abilities and change aggression level, but they still know who they are and recognize others around them.

Demonoid

The final stage.

At this stage all memory of their former selves has been taken over by a mindless instinct to kill and feed.

The time between stages and their final appearance, ability, or power, varies greatly from person to person, with no possible way to predict the outcome.

This is usually a permanent and irreversible change, but it also can be temporarily triggered and then suppressed; however, this makes up such a small percentage it hardly seems worth noting.

Demonic

When a person fully merges with the demon DNA.

They keep all their memories and can still act on their will, while this is rare. Rarer still is the ability to shift between human and demon form when desired.

Armored Demonoids

These wear armor and fight with weapons, although they are more so just utilizing what they have or find without planning their advantage.

Note: Just as no two people are identical, the same also applies to demonoids, since they transform uniquely from each infected individual; however, the transformation always adds height, weight and muscle mass to the original body type.

Giant Bat: *(First seen in Chapter 3)*

A bat that somehow grew to an enormous size of 10 feet.

Watchers: *(First seen in Chapter 3)*

These winged demons are covered with black and gray randomly shaped markings and contain two spiral horns on top of its head. Their mouth is made up of four rows of fang-like teeth and despite their large size they are fast and agile fliers.

Large Snake: *(First seen in Chapter 4)*

A monstrous pit viper.

Both animals and people are affected by demon DNA in
different ways. The body deformation is common, but sometimes
the DNA also acts as a growth additive during the evolution
process.

It's impossible to predict how demon DNA will affect all
forms of wildlife, but it can be assumed that this planet will be a
very hostile place to live if this remains ongoing.

Grizzly Boar: *(First seen in Chapter 5)*
The body of a bear and the head of a boar.

It's an aggressive mutation that, unlike the other wildlife,
happened unnaturally. This beast was made by Lazul's
intervention, and he considers it his pet.

Zombies: *(First seen in Chapter 6)*
Contaminated corpses that rise after death and become mobile
to attack others.

In *Forlorn Swamp* these zombies are dressed as soldiers or
citizens. Their death was most likely due to being attacked by the
zombies already present or being victims of the *Anaconda Root*.

Note: These are not demonized humans as they are dead
before reanimation, while a demonized person turns into a
demon before death.

Gnolls: *(First seen in Chapter 7)*
Resembles a hyena walking upright with cackling vocals.
Always in packs.

Destructors: *(First seen in Chapter 8)*
These manufactured monsters were the creation of O.D.E.
and vary in appearance greatly.

One of them is described as having two saber-tooth-like fangs
and several rows of sharp teeth lining both the upper and lower
portions of its mouth. Its head is riddled with large warts, and it
includes large red bulging eyes. Its feet have three clawed toes, and
they have the strength to break cables with even the highest tensile
strength ratings.

Though these have not been formally named we refer to

them by their lab nickname as Destructors, for they will destroy everything in their path.

Spirit Assassins: *(First seen in Chapter 11)*
Restless souls of those who have died with unfinished business.

They kill under orders in hopes to gain what they seek as a reward.

They lack a physical form and cannot be harmed by physical means.

Dragons: *(First seen in Chapter 11)*
Dragons are byproducts of a mixture between the natural with the unnatural, such as, magic and nature, or science and witchcraft.

The Star of Eluvium's energy can infuse living cells with an advance adaptation and cloning gene.

This allows a host, be it human, animal, or other organic living substance, to evolve randomly, or merge with supplied elements and/or tissues. With a knowledgeable hand this could create a dragon.

Imps: *(First seen in Chapter 13)*
Smaller goblins.

Some carry crafted spears made from rigid trigs, but these weapons are not very efficient in battle.

They are poor builders, but great scavengers.

Scorpion Cats: *(Never appeared)*
Feral cats with claws instead of paws and their tails resemble that of a scorpion.

They are scavengers that feed off other kills.

Solo or in small groups they will avoid confrontations and run away or hide.

Cavern Goblins: *(First seen in Chapter 14)*
These goblins are grayish in color and have long arms and legs, which better suit them for climbing and jumping. Each hand has three long fingers and an opposable thumb, all with clawed tips in place of fingernails.

Unlike their surface-dwelling counterparts, these have a smaller face with recessed large black eyes and teeth like a barracuda.

They communicate by screeching and only live in dark and damp places such as caves and underground.

Sailfin Demonoid (a.ka. Quill Monster): *(First seen in Chapter 14)*
This demonoid has rather large quills running the length of its arms and smaller spines down its ribs. It also sports large, curved claws on each of its knees and elbows.

Features, such as a large sail on its back, a tail, a long snout, and reptilian eyes, suggest it was a lizard that mutated and evolved to stand on its hind legs.

Its mouth contains several rows of tiny, serrated teeth and its vocals consist of a hiss.

It also has the ability to shoot the spikes on its arm by flicking it forward.

This demon lizard is estimated to be about eight feet long, or tall if rearing up.

Scavenging off the leftovers from the cavern goblins and then hunting the goblins themselves could explain its current state.

Shadow Demons: *(First seen in Chapter 14)*
Shapeshifters that lack a physical form and can take the image of someone who is familiar to an individual.

They are capable of reading minds and using the emotions of their victims against them.

The most common appearance, when not in a human form, is a black smoke demon with two tiny red glowing dots for eyes and an open mouth that resembles that of a black mamba.

When in physical form they can be harmed by physical means; however, when in spirit form only magic attacks will harm them.

Spirit Assassins vs. Shadow Demons

Both are spirit entities, but *Spirit Assassins* are deceased humans, while *Shadow Demons* are demons, originating from the dawn of creation, and were never alive. Shadow Demons can also shapeshift whilst Spirit Assassins only have one form.

Vortex Demon (A true demon): *(First seen in Chapter 14)*

A horned beast demon with red eyes.

This is a truly powerful and evil demonic being from Hell.

It announces that it was the one who allowed Lazul to gain its abilities, and now in his weakened state, claims him.

It's believed that this demon is a high-ranking prince of Hell, but its identity is not disclosed.

Plants

Adonia:

A plant created in O.D.E. labs by combing elements from existing plants and creating a new species.

Which plants were used to make this man-made hybrid is still unknown.

Adonia is a vine type plant with flowers that are yellow at the top and orange on the bottom while the vine itself is blue. This is the main ingredient used to make the potion, *Plasma Rejuvenation.*

Blood Fire Mushroom:

These fungi are small in size, only about 1 inch in height, and grows in clusters.

It's easily identified by its bright red top and contains green spores that are extremely poisonous.

This is the main ingredient used in the potion, *Green Death.*

Anaconda Root:

A carnivorous plant that holds its victim underwater until they drown before consuming them.

O.D.E Departments
and their Inventions

Technology and Programming:

Motto: Using technology and computer programming to make the world a safer place.

- *AI Eye (Artificial Intelligence Eye):*
     An advanced security system that projects the outside perimeter to an inside computer of a shelter.
     It's capable to showing 360° in a 50-yard radius of the shelter and comes with night vision.

- *O.D.E. Shield:*
     A metal shield that can go around any above ground shelter.
     The shield is folded into sections underground when not in use and is activated by remote control—it is indestructible.
     The process of melting and then layering Platinum, Tungsten and Titanium creates this metal nicknamed, Tintuntanium (ten-ton-tanium).

Weapons and Warfare:
Motto: Teaching demons fear, then showing them no fear.

- *Exploding Bullets:*
     A bullet that is a timed bomb as soon as it leaves the barrel of the gun.
     It will detonate moments after entering the victim's body.

Shelters:
Motto: All the comforts of home, only fortified.

- *O.D.E. Hatch Shelter:*
     An underground shelter no bigger than 450 sq. ft.
     Provides running water, from a water pump that passes through a water purifying process.
     Electricity is made possible due to several hydro fuel cells built inside the walls. These cells are connected to a generator that forces the water to move through the fuel cells. The separation of the hydrogen and oxygen from the water creates energy and generates an unlimited supply of power, since the fuel cells also charge the generator.
     Contains appliances, facilities, furniture, and technology capabilities.

Chemicals and Chemistry:
Motto: Using science, to reinvent science.

- *Plasma Rejuvenation:*

Potion that speeds up the body's natural healing capability. Red in color.

- *Green Death:*
Highly toxic liquid that melts flesh and entrails.
Applied to weapons to add a devastating, and usually fatal attack.
Green in color.

- *Human Demon DNA Manipulation and Transfer (HDDNAMT):*
O.D.E.'s first attempt to inject people with demon DNA in hopes that superhuman abilities would develop.
Unfortunately, the infected became demons themselves.

- *F6VI (For those 6 Volunteers Injected):*
O.D.E.'s second serum to try to give people superhuman qualities after the first serum failed.
This one used the DNA of demons as well as orangutans and was advertised to also act as a vaccine against demonic infections.
This too eventually had the same end result as the first.

Note: With F being the sixth letter and VI being the roman numeral six. This serum was discovered to equal 666.

Lesser Known O.D.E. Departments

Guard Dog:
Motto: Man has a new best friend.

Bred and trained raptors to cull the demon population.
Ultimately failed as people also became its prey.

Demon Captivity and Control:
Motto: Harvest, Harness, Create, Deploy.

Control or sedate and transport non-human, or no longer human expendable soldiers into the battlefield.
Fear will destroy enemy moral and their territories will become infested with a force difficult to completely annihilate.
Future goals will be to amplify aggressiveness and overall efficiency to seek out and dispatch targets.

We understand the likelihood that wounded enemy soldiers will turn on their own and with the absence to recover our deployments a residual effect may occur. This; however, will be ruled as an interior issue that doesn't warrant our involvement.

Bio Weapons Development:
Motto: It's easy to kill a group when you just have to target one.

The development of biological weapons to be used on both demon and possible human threats, including bacterial and virus experimentation and evolution.

Animal Research:
Motto: Mistakes lead to discoveries.

A department used only for testing demon DNA on animals and recording behavior and appearance changes.

Townships & Housing Development:
Motto: Taking care of our own, so we can save others.

Supplies O.D.E. employees, freelancers and their families exclusive access to necessities, amenities and accessories from direct trading outlets and closed to the general public.

O.D.E offers an I.D. card that also doubles as a credit card for purchases to be made. With many of the banks out of order, payments are deducted directly from their payroll.

That was how they described it, but what they actually did was clear out local stores to hoard all remaining goods.

Anyone who did not work for or had a family member who was employed with O.D.E., wasn't allowed to make purchases. This led some citizens to join O.D.E.'s workforce solely to be granted access to these highly sought after goods.

Without knowing how much O.D.E. had marked up their goods many employees soon discovered they were in debt to O.D.E.

Science and Library Society (SLS):
Unrelated to O.D.E. Founded after the fall of Lazul.

A prestigious organization dedicated to research, discuss, and educate advances and studies in everything natural, biological, medical, literary, inventive, and experimental.

It's a place for everyone to discover and catalog knowledge about everything that was, is, and will be.

Artifacts

The Architect's Box:

Much mystery surrounds this little-known artifact, but what follows are based on facts and testimonies from well-respected individuals.

The Architect's Box has been speculated to exist since the dawn of time. It was known to be of great importance and well-guarded by ancient civilizations, including the Egyptians, Mayans and even the fabled Atlantis. It is thought that this may have been the cause of Atlantis' mysterious disappearance.

The Mayans kept this box in a large underground temple. The temple itself was said to have more than forty-seven different passageways and a fair amount of hidden staircases and moving walls; many of which lead to fatal traps. Only one passageway led to The Architect's Box and only the high priest or priestess knew the safe passage, which was strictly passed on by spoken word from their predecessor. The Architect's Chamber is where the box was believed to sit for thousands of years, until its abrupt removal, either intentionally or unintentionally.

The contents of the box were never known until the early 1920's when cross-referencing and research uncovered new information. Ancient philosophies and religious beliefs dictated that the Architect created the world and the universe and then stepped aside to let time and nature take over without involvement. Much like an Architect would build a building and then turn it over to others who will run it. Therefore, the Architect is similar to God in Christian faith and this box was said to contain the power of his creation, but also the way to undo his work. Many prayed to it to convince the Architect not to open the box or use the device inside to destroy their world.

The Architect's Box is merely a container that holds the true item of power and different cultures knew it by different names. Abria's Stone from Celtic lore, The Star of Eluvium, or

The Earth Star, from the Mayans, and one we may all be familiar with, Pandora's Box from Greek mythology. It is said that this box will someday be responsible for opening a direct portal to Hell and unleash the demonic forces to destroy all of humanity, as prophesied in the End Times; once activated the effects can never be undone or reversed.

The Star of Eluvium:
A sphere of pure energy held within, *The Architect's Box.*

It's capable of giving society an everlasting clean energy source; however, it's also capable of dissolving the force field that prohibits Hell from interacting with Earth; which, in turn, will allow a constant flow of demons to enter our world.

The Dragon King's Sword:
A heavy sword that is 4.5 feet in length with the metal guard meeting the serrated blade and the pommel is crafted to look like a dragon's head in mid-roar.

It was crafted by a powerful summoner in the mid-1100's. It's said that he crafted the entire piece only from the fire of a dragon, and he honored the beast in his pommel.

Inscribed in the blade is a Hebrew phrase:

ברגע ממנו להימלט יכול לא אחד אף

לא אחד אף, נמשך כבר שהוא

Translated it means:
No one can escape it once it has been drawn, no one can resist it.
A spell that ensures victory to any who wield it.

Locations

Copper Bay:
Once held a population of 33,000.
The prior home for Ardian, Nydia, Kito and Amiku.

Industrial Block:
Positioned just outside of Copper Bay, mostly to keep real

estate prices high, this area is where all the manufactured goods were created packaged, and then shipped.

During The Demon Wars, O.D.E. claimed many of these buildings, warehouses, and factories to set up labs and testing facilities.

Rundown warehouses and factories as well as abandoned or disabled trucks are all that remains of this once busy hub.

Raptor Island:

Location of an O.D.E. lab named, *Guard Dog*, where breeding of raptors took place.

Army Camp:

This army camp consists of several barracks, an armory with a leftover supply of weapons, a cafeteria with boxes of MREs (Meals Ready to Eat) and medical supplies inside the clinic.

With many cities being overrun by demons, the need for rally points and army bases increased exponentially. They needed to be close to red zones to increase response time, but also somewhat away from constant attacks.

Many of the surrounding wildness and forests were seized by the army and O.D.E. to be zoned for camps, forts, and small boomtowns in hopes to rebuild, resupply and repopulate.

Forlorn Swamp *aka Swamp of Death:*

This area fell victim to deforestation and the extraction of the rocks and stone, from the nearby cliffs, were used to build, not just Anthulios' fort, but were also hauled away to build other fortifications.

The changed landscape could no longer absorb the rainfall and the overflowing lakes never receded.

Due to some mysterious unnatural force those who perished in this area return as zombies to claim more victims. Many were citizens from the nearby fort or guards on patrol.

The Tale of Forlorn Swamp
Author unknown

A great battle fought here claimed many who will never leave the bog. Some skeleton remains of these victims still occupy the marsh while other corpses rest more preserved under the muddy goo and still water; corpses with rotting flesh, empty eye sockets, teeth, but no lips, and long twisting fingers reaching out of the swamp grass and ooze. It is a most unpleasant and cursed area expanding far beyond the lush forest that boarders it. The foul stench of decomposition taints the air and patches of ground fog floats above the peat. It is home to giant insects and bugs, reptiles, and amphibians; all of which will deliver an infectious bite or make one feel uneasy at their appearance alone.

Visitors to Forlorn Swamp are uncommon; however, every once in a while, an unwary traveler will venture through it, or in this case, a man on the run. His simple attire, torn and grimy, indicates a profession that of a farmer. He frantically sprints through the wild weeds and hops over dead tree logs with coiled millipedes the size of an adult's foot. He glances behind his shoulder periodically as he continues his frenzied run. The cause of his anxiety reveals itself in the form of two men on horseback. They have just cleared the forest but stop their beasts almost immediately as they watch the man, they were pursuing run farther into the mire. Their refusal to advance may be their willingness to allow the poor farmer to escape or perhaps their belief in the tales of the swamp.

The farmer is more concerned with the two men watching him from a distance than the wiggling fingers of a decayed hand protruding out of the muddy water. The man unknowingly steps too close and is quickly grabbed. He lets out a blood curdling scream as the body, belonging to the hand, rises out of its grave. The cadaver's scalp has long unruly hair with leeches nestled on top. Its skin is wrinkled and pale from decades of being submerged. The unsettling gaze from its partially decomposed eyes sends the helpless farmer into a fit as he desperately tries to free himself by prying the cold, clammy digits from his leg. Giant mosquitoes fly out of the corpse's mouth before it chops down on the man's arm. The farmer begins to sink into the wet ground as the undead soldier pulls him downward. When the man has sunk chest deep the cadaver places its hand on the unfortunate's head and pushes him under the muck. The farmer's screams disappear with both his body and the corpse's, leaving only tiny bubbles popping to the surface, before all becomes still and silent once more.

The horsemen turn their steeds back around towards the forest and retreat from the scene without a word. Their business with the farmer is finished. Whether they desired justice or were fueled by wicked intentions does not matter; for the swamp cannot tell the difference between citizen and drifter or the respected verses pariah. It claims all who are foolish enough to trespass. What lives infects with poison and disease. What dies awakes to become death. That is the tale of Forlorn Swamp.

Silver Rock City:

Contains an O.D.E. lab and a large airport with demonized raptors.

Goldthorn:

Once known for its prosperity and well-to-do citizens, it's now sits in devastation and ruin from previous rampaging fires.

Contains a large shopping mall and home to a plethora of zombies, and a GTO*.

*The Pontiac GTO is a 1969 Judge with 500 horsepower. It has a red body with a black hood and spoiler.

- **In Chapter 15:**
  The GTO now contains **Demon Hunters** below an image of a goblin with a sword through its torso, positioned in the middle of both doors.
  Demon Inspection and Eradication and its acronym, **DIE**, appears on the fenders.

  Kito, Amiku, Ardian, and Nydia remain a team who protects towns from lingering demons.
  DIE is their program, but the term, *demon hunter* is a profession, which anyone can take up.

Hero Hill:

Named by Dixon.

It's the plot of land in the rolling hills butting up to the mountain ridge.

Dubbed for the massive loss of life in the battle with Lazul's demon army.

Anthulios:

Named after Lio and home to him and Shara.

The homes built in this town are constructed with stone bases and wooden siding on top, and the sign of small generators beside every home, suggest they have electricity.

The citizens who live here are farmers, who grow vegetables, fruits, care for livestock and fish.

Lio opens his blacksmith shop called, *Lio's Metal Works,* where he forges weapons and other metal related crafts.

Lio's house is quaint and cozy with just enough room for him and Shara to live comfortably. Behind his house is a plot of land where he has a modest garden of vegetables, a firepit, that provides warmth and a place to cook, along with a lantern beside the back door that's powered by a generator when needed.

With the forest nearly on his doorstep his yard is perfectly shaded by the canopy all day long.

As a joke, Kito, Ardian, Amiku and Nydia plan a town named after themselves.
Kito: *Kitoville*
Ardian: *Ardianton*
Amiku: *Amikuopolis*
Nydia: *Aidyn (Nydia spelled backwards).*

Esperanza:

Once just a fort in the middle of a dandelion field, it's now a well-developed city consisting of a central market, clinic, courthouse, residential homes, and the fort is positioned at the rear to act as a base of operations and meeting area. It becomes a central hub for traders, artisans, and commerce.

THE AGES

The Demon Wars

The 3–4 year span of the army and society fighting the demons before the fall of O.D.E.

Apocalypsia

4–5 years following *The Demon Wars* and during Lazul's war.

The Demon Hunter Era

Presently active.

While society is slowly progressing forward following the fall of Lazul, demons and goblins are still active, giving the rise of demon hunters, who are tasked with their elimination.

Also present are more people being born with abilities similar to Nydia's. She accepts any opportunity to help them train and control their powers.

Demon Hunters:

Individuals or groups that combat demonoids and imps that plague trade routes, townsfolk or halting work and projects.

Demon Inspection and Eradication (DIE):

Kito, Amiku, Ardian and Nydia's program as hired demon hunters.

About the Author

Jerry J.C. Veit was born in the spring of 1983 to a German and Portuguese family. He developed a love for writing at a young age and a fondness for classic literary works by Charles Dickens, Mark Twain, Edgar Allen Poe, and others.

His introduction into writing began with screenwriting in 2008. After making it to many of the finals in several screenplay contests and writing countless query letters to literary agencies, he ultimately decided to abandon this form of writing. In 2016 he explored self-publishing and transformed all six of his screenplays into novelized scripts that resembled a play. It wasn't until 2021 that he decided to rewrite, reformat, and extend all his titles once again—this time into traditional novels starting with his debut novel, Apocalypsia, and a two-volume anthology of his novellas containing five stories total.

He currently resides in southeastern Wisconsin working by day as a graphic designer at an ad agency, but by night he's a builder of worlds who enjoys writing character-driven stories that inspire, entertain, and hopefully leave an everlasting impression on his audience. He's passionate about writing in the genres of fantasy, dystopias and paranormal, but also penned an inspirational story as well.